THE BURNING HOUR

EAGLE BROTHERHOOD SERIES

KAT LE VEQUE

OLIVERHEBERBOOKS

AUTHOR'S NOTE

They call themselves the Eagle Brotherhood.

We've all got 'that' group of friends. People we've bonded with that just 'get' you and you get them. Whether you bond over common interests, or a job, of even just mutual friends, we've all found that connection at one time or another.

Same with the Eagle Brotherhood.

It started with five Americans. They were young, brilliant, idealistic, and met during a semester abroad. When I first wrote this series, many years ago, it was originally called the American Heroes series. It was supposed to be about guys who knew each other as young men, but who went on to live their own lives and have their own adventures. Ordinary guys in extraordinary circumstances was how I described it. There were only five in the beginning, but somewhere along the line, we added two Brits as 'honorary' members. There are actually more books slated to be written, but I just haven't gotten around to it yet. One of the Eagle Brotherhood — Nash Aury — even has a sequel mostly written to his book, so this is really a series that has a lot of growth potential. And why not? It centers around men who are honorable, chivalric, and end up facing some really stressful and, in a few cases, dangerous situations. Some explainable, some not. That's the fun of it.

But it all had to start somewhere.

Each Eagle Brotherhood book starts out with the same *"How it began"* preface so you, as the reader, knows where these guys connect because they don't appear in each other's stories. It's a rather interesting connection, but one that opens up the hero of each tale — and eventually the heroine — to one heck of a story. These guys are connected to me as much as to each other.

They really are a true brotherhood.

I hope you enjoy the stories in this series because they were a labor of love to write. You don't have to read them in any particular order:

The Burning Hour
The Sunset Hour
The Secret Hour
The Unholy Hour
The Devil's Hour
The Killing Hour
The Ancient Hour

Happy reading,

AQUILA FRATRUM

Seven men.
Each with a story to tell.
Welcome to the world of the Eagle Brotherhood.

Years ago, five Americans on a semester abroad met at the home of their sponsor in Yorkshire, England. They were taking the same course at the University of York, including the son of their host. But it wasn't the course in International Law that bonded them. It was an incident from that time, something that happened on a dark and stormy night in an alley behind a bar in York called *The Calcaria.*

It is something that changed their perspectives forever.

These days, the men who once called themselves the *Aquila Fratrum* or the Eagle Brotherhood — a name based on the Americans who were military-based at that time — have gone forth in their lives. They are men in normal, everyday professions who succeed in extraordinary things. Their paths aren't smooth, and they aren't perfect, but they understand more than most that life is never about the smooth or the perfect. It is about the imperfect and the difficult. It's even about the unexplainable.

And, above all else, light overcomes the darkness.

Aquila Fratrum.

Ordinary men who have lived extraordinary circumstances.

And the women who love them.

HOW IT BEGAN

MORE THEN TWENTY YEARS AGO, THE CALCARIA, YORK

MICK MCCONNELL, PROPRIETOR

"Beck." A big man with a crown of auburn hair spoke with a drunken slur to his words. "Beck. *Seavington!*"

The blond Californian on the other side of the table, who had been half-lidded as he watched a group of women across the darkened room of the pub, jerked at the sound of his name as if he'd just been slapped.

"What?" he said, looking at the man with the auburn hair. "Christ, Phipps. Can't you just leave me alone for a minute?"

Archer Phipps struggled not to laugh. "Why?"

"Because you're breaking my powers of concentration, you ass."

That broke the table out in snorts of laughter. The man seated next to Beck, big and blond and with a mega-watt smile, put a hand on Beck's shoulder.

"What in the hell are you concentrating on?" he said, leaning over to see what Beck might be seeing. When he spied it, he gestured. "Over there?"

Beck full-on pointed to the women across the pub. "There."

"Those?"

"*Those.*"

"Well... what are you trying to do by staring at them? Just go talk to them."

Beck scowled at the man. "Because I'm trying to lure them with the power of suggestion, Trevor," he said. Then, he looked around the table and pointed. "It works. Colt over there has a laser stare. He doesn't even have to say anything — women know what he's thinking just by the expression on his face. Isn't that right, Sheridan?"

Colt Sheridan, clean-cut and square-jawed, waved an annoyed hand at the man he'd spent nearly every day with for the past six months. "Some of us don't have to be obvious," he said. "Look at Nash. All he has to do is give them one of those sexy, down-home expressions and they're falling all over themselves. I don't have anything on him."

Across the table, Nash Aury, the quiet and diplomatic sort with a Louisiana drawl, laughed softly. "It's all in the face," he said, gesturing to the big dimples in each cheek. "I don't have anything y'all don't have, but we don't have anything that Serreaux has, so maybe we should just give it up and let him take the lead."

The group looked over at Ethan Serreaux, a man with a French parents even though he was born in America. Dark-eyed and dark-haired, he looked like he'd just come off the pages of a men's magazine. When he saw that the entire table of semi-drunks was looking at him, he smiled lasciviously.

"*Belle fille,*" he said in his best Maurice Chevalier impression. "*Asseyez-vous sur mes genoux et dites-moi à quel point vous me voulez.*"

Everyone burst out laughing except for Beck, who slowly banged his forehead on the table. "You sound like Pepe Le Pew," he said. "Shut *up!*"

More laughter, most especially from Archer and the last man of their group, a giant of a figure who wasn't part of their academic group. Fox Henredon was in the process of obtaining his Ph.D. in Archaeology with an emphasis in Egyptology from Oxford. In fact, he'd come back a few months ago from a dig near Aswan and when he visited his best friend from grade school, Archer, he'd come across the Americans temporarily housed in Archer's pad. He'd gotten on so well with them that they'd made him an honorary member of their group. But not just the group — of their secret society, as well.

Aquila Fratrum.

The Eagle Brotherhood.

The whole secret group was really meant as a joke, but the basis of it — the honor, the patriotism — they took seriously. Three out of the five Americans had come from Annapolis and all five of them were majoring in International Law, hence the purpose of the semester abroad course. Archer was taking the same course, and he'd been the host house, and given that they were all within a few years of each other age-wise, they'd all bonded over common likes, common dislikes, and a passion for adventure.

It was a guy gang like no other.

But tonight, they were drinking to the group that would soon be separating. The course at the University of York was finished and the Americans would soon be heading back to their native lands, but promises of reciprocal visits had abound all evening. Nash, in particular, had invited everyone to New Orleans for the holidays because his family, having made their money in sugar, had a massive house that could accommodate everyone. Beck, Cord, and Colt had already committed to it, but Ethan had family obligations he needed to get out of. Archer was trying to figure out how to break the news to his parents, who were possessive of his time, while Fox was on the verge of committing. He'd never been to New Orleans and a street named after liquor intrigued him. As the Brotherhood planned their next gathering, Beck stood up from the table.

"I need to find the loo," he said, looking around. "Where is it? Back behind the bar?"

The problem was that he was drunker than the rest of them and probably not in great shape to find anything, so Cord stood up next to him.

"Back in the corner," he said. "Come on, little brother."

He had Beck by the neck, pulling him back behind the bar where there was a dark corridor that led to bathrooms and the kitchen. The term 'little brother' was essentially referring to Beck's age because he happened to be the youngest out of their group. But he was also the toughest. Beck Seavington could out-fight anybody, Fox included, and Fox had participated in underground fight clubs during his earlier college days. He'd won money at it, too.

But Beck's fists were quite lethal.

The Navy wanted him that way.

Cord went with Beck so he wouldn't get into any trouble. Cord was an enormous man, having played football, and the rumor was that he was being scouted by the NFL. He wasn't a fighter by nature, but no one was going to test of man of that size. He'd just push the scrapper, Beck, in front of him, anyway, and let the career Navy man do the damage.

Every group had a scrapper.

It smelled like stale booze and bleach back here and the door to the men's room was locked. Beck rattled it but it remained fixed. With a heavy sigh, he looked at Cord.

"I can't wait," he muttered.

Cord tipped his head in the direction of the door to the alley out back, which was next to the kitchen door.

"Outside?" he said.

Beck nodded, which nearly threw him off balance, and charged through the back door. Cord followed him and they ended up in the dirty, damp alley behind the bar. It smelled worse out here, like garbage and animals. There were crates against the wall, broken down cardboard boxes, and little else. There were two ends to the alley, but they were standing closer to the end that dumped out onto the street where *The Calcaria* was located. Beck was looking for a discreet place to relieve himself when the back door smacked back on its hinges again, spilling forth the rest of their group.

"I think we're done with this place," Archer said, rubbing his eyes because the alcohol was messing with his vision. "There's another pub down the way called Valhalla. Let's go there."

Beck had found a spot behind some crates. "Are the women more proactive there?" he asked. "I mean, will they actually come up and talk to you? I don't think my mind control is working."

Archer grinned. "Do you seriously want a woman that approaches you?" he said. "The wooing of a woman is an art, Beck. You don't want some nervy woman up in your grill, do you?"

The others snorted in agreement. Ethan and Nash were by the back door, leaning back against the wall, as Colt went to stand next to Beck. Fox went to stand with Cord, maybe as a lookout since they really shouldn't be pissing in an alley, when three men suddenly appeared from what was a small walkway between buildings. It was dark, so no one really noticed, until one of the men walked up behind Colt and put a knife to the man's back.

Then, everything changed.

The drunken, happy mood was gone.

"Easy, big man," the man said. He was short, with a dirty

jacket, but the knife he'd produced was quite large. "If you want to keep your kidney, you'll relax, mate."

Everyone froze — Ethan, Nash, Archer, Fox, Cord, Beck, and most of all, Colt. But his features never changed expression, even as he felt the prick of cold steel against his right kidney.

"If you're looking for money, you're too late," he said steadily. "We're coming out of the bar, not going into it. We've spent our money."

The man in the dirty jacket grunted as his friends also produced big knives. "Somehow, I doubt it," he said. "We were watching you inside. I think you're from money, so you've got more where that came from, Yank. I think all of you have more."

With that, his friends began to move. One of them was heading for Ethan while the other one was heading for Archer. The group, as a whole, instinctively started to back away from the men approaching, but Fox refused to budge. At seven inches over six feet, he had that luxury of being stubborn.

"You blokes really think you're going to rob guys who are twice your size?" he said incredulously. "You're either incredibly stupid or way too overconfident."

"I'll go with stupid," Cord muttered.

Fox quickly agreed with him. "Stupid, for sure," he said. "There are seven of us and three of you. You may be able to take out a couple of us, but there are five of us left who will break your fucking necks. Are you ready for that?"

That brought some pause to the man's companions, but the man in the dirty jacket poked Colt enough to draw blood.

"Give me your fucking money!" he hissed. "Another word and I'll cut a hole in this man big enough to stick my hand through!"

Colt didn't even flinch when the man jabbed him. He kept his right hand up while his left once reached into his pocket for his wallet. But as he was doing that, and the other two men with knives were advancing on Ethan and Archer, no one happened to be watching Cord.

And that would be their fatal mistake.

"*Quaere ferro scopum tuum,*" Cord suddenly mumbled. "*Oboedite mihi!*"

Inexplicably, the man holding the knife to Colt's back jerked. He jolted. His hand flew up and the big blade he'd been forcing on Colt flew up and into his own throat, straight back through so that the tip came out of the back of his neck. It went through him like a bullet. As he staggered back and fell to the ground, his friends were momentarily startled and that gave Cord the opportunity to turn against them.

"*In molles venter it ferrum,*" he growled, lifting a big fist as if to punch the men straight in the face. "*Utrumque vestrum!*"

The men screamed as the hands holding the knives came up and plunged the blades into their bellies as if they had a mind of their own. They went down as Ethan, Nash, Archer, Fox, Beck and Colt made haste to back up, away from what was evidently going on. No one knew what was happening and it was best to get clear considering knives were slashing all over the place.

At least, everyone but Cord backed up. He pointed a finger at the men who had just stabbed themselves in the belly.

"*Ferro ad carnem, ferrum ad os,*" he said in a low tone. "*Collum secari debet.*"

The men with knives in their bellies suddenly withdrew those knives and stabbed themselves in the neck, three or four times, until they could stab no more. They simply lay there and bled as Cord turned to his stunned group of friends.

"We need to get out of here," he said quietly. "Before the cops come. *Quickly.*"

No one moved. They stood there, eyes wide at what they'd just seen. Colt, who was the closest to Cord, grabbed him by the arm.

"What in the hell just happened?" he asked in awe. "What did you do?"

Cord looked back at the men bleeding out on the alley floor. "I protected us," he said simply. "We really need to go."

"Protected us *how*?" Fox was at Cord's side, his handsome face seriously. "What did we just see, Cord? Hypnosis of some kind?"

Cord scratched his head. "No," he said reluctantly, looking at the curious group. "Can we just get out of here, please?"

"Not until you explain," Fox said.

He was serious. No one was moving, not really. Exasperated, Cord sighed heavily. "Fine," he said. "I did it to save Colt's life. That guy was going to kill him."

Colt, who had blood running down the right side of his torso, stepped forward. "He probably was," he said. "Nobody is disputing that. But *what* did you do?"

Cord looked at his friend. "It's not something I really talk about," he said hesitantly. "I haven't... I haven't done that stuff since I was younger, but you all know I'm descended from Abigail Williams. When we all talked about our families and stuff, I told you guys that I was descended from one of the chief accusers of the Salem Witch Trials."

"You did," Colt said as his gaze moved to the men on the ground. "But what does that have to do with it? And done *what* stuff?"

Cord was clearly reluctant. "My dad likes to call us Casters," he said. "Abigail Williams was an accomplished witch and that trait is passed down in my family, like red hair or freckles. Only it's some kind of power we can summon. What you saw was a spell. I turned their knives against them."

"You're a witch?" Colt repeated in shock. "Seriously, Cord? Like — magic?"

Cord didn't answer. He just started walking, very quickly,

and the others instinctively followed. They came to a walkway that led out onto the street and, nearly running, they headed up towards the main road.

"Yeah, like magic," Cord finally said as they came to the main avenue. "You saw it. I can't explain it more than that, but I wouldn't have done it if I thought we could have gotten out of that without Sheridan missing a kidney. Just... do yourself a favor. Forget you ever saw it."

"Wait," Ethan said as they began to walk, very quickly, towards the area with the car park. "We can't just leave. No matter what happened, or how it happened, we have to call the police."

"And tell them what?" Cord said. "That we got attacked and that I used a spell to turn the weapons against the guys who attacked us? They would think we were nuts."

As Ethan shook his head in disagreement, Archer grabbed him by the arm and pulled him along. "They would want to know who stabbed those guys," he said. "They'd take our finger-prints and find out that none of our fingerprints were on the weapons. How in the hell are we going to explain that?"

Ethan wasn't sure, but he didn't like running from a crime scene. "Guys, we can't leave," he said, trying to drag his feet. "We were witnesses to what happened. We have to..."

Cord suddenly came to a halt and grabbed Ethan by the shirt. "What do you think is going to happen?" he hissed. "Ethan, I don't want to run any more than you do, but I'm the one who killed those guys. That's the bottom line. And I'm not doing time for it and I'm not going to show the York Police how I turned those weapons against them, so forget it. We're not calling anyone. We're getting out of here and you are giving me your word that you'll never repeat what you saw. I need you to swear that to me."

Ethan could see how upset Cord was and he put up his

hands in a gesture of surrender. "I swear that I'll never repeat it," he said. "Don't worry about that. But if anyone else saw us..."

"Who is going to see us?" Cord said, letting go of his shirt. "No one saw us. We're going to fly home tomorrow, anyway, and we'll be out of here. Done."

Ethan nodded, but he wasn't happy about it. Even if he wasn't happy, at least he understood. The entire group began walking again, very quickly, with the car park in sight. Beyond that, freedom.

Freedom from something they hoped wouldn't come back to haunt them.

Cord most of all.

"You... you really *did* that?" Beck finally said. He was still astonished by what he'd witnessed. "How in the hell did you learn how to cast spells?"

Cord school his head. "I told you," he said. "It's in my blood. But I don't like talking about it, so let's just drop it... okay?"

"But we saw it."

They had reached the car park by now and Cord came to an abrupt halt, facing the group. He was normally a congenial guy, but the event had him spooked.

"I know you guys saw it," he said. "But you need to swear that you will never repeat it. You will never tell anyone. Because if you do, I'm going to be in a shitload of trouble. How in the hell am I going to explain to anyone that I used witchcraft to kill some criminals?"

"But it was in self-defense," Ethan stressed. "No one is going to convict you, or any of us for that matter."

Cord's frustration bled through. "But we would have to explain *how* it happened," he said. "Don't you get it? One question would lead to another, questions you don't want to answer. Trust me."

Nash, who had been silent for the most part, put a hand on

Cord's shoulder. "Cord, where I'm from, voodoo and witchcraft are part of the culture," he said quietly. "I've seen things I can't explain, so I believe what you're saying. I know what I saw. You have a gift, but it's a gift people don't understand. We've all witnessed something tonight that was... well, pretty damn amazing."

Cord registered some relief as he realized he had the support of Nash. The guy wasn't going to hound him. After a moment, he looked at the rest of the group. "You know, we've joked about calling ourselves the Eagle Brotherhood, but I think we really *are* a brotherhood now," he said. "We've experienced something that could have cost us our lives. It was small, but it happened. You saw something you shouldn't have seen because I did something I shouldn't have done. But to protect you guys... I'd do it again. I hope you know that."

"I feel like I owe my life to you," Colt said, reaching out to shake Cord's hand. "You were brave to do what you did, Cord, knowing... well, knowing that it wasn't something for all to see. But you did it and I'm grateful. I'll take an oath of silence on the Eagle Brotherhood if that's what it'll take. To protect you because you saved my life, I'll do anything. And if you ever need me, no matter where I am, I'll come. That's a promise."

More hands began shooting out, covering Colt and Cord's hands. It was a vow, a promise, not to discuss the event that bonded them more than a school or allied nations could. It was a bond that went deeper now because they harbored a secret. More than that, they had crossed into the realm of a brotherhood that would protect or kill for one another.

The true test of a brotherhood.

It was an oath that would take to their graves.

Wherever life would take them.

PROLOGUE
SALEM, MASSACHUSETTS, 1702 A.D.

"A breath of wind,
a mark of sin,
evil doer drink of blood.
Beneath the earth,
feel my curse,
with my hand to 'ever crush you.
Malum infans, putrescet Satanae ut canis. Te et
    matrem tuam aeternum ardebit."

A WOMAN WAS HUNCHED over a desk, scribing beneath the
weak light of a single tallow taper. On the small oak desk sat a
small pewter bowl, filled with a thimbleful of her blood from a
cut she had made on her ankle. She dipped her quill into the
bowl as she finished writing the last of the bitter words.

In the attic of the home she shared with her husband and
children was the only place she could inscribe such words of
hatred and terror. The children must not know. Her husband
must not know. This curse, this hatred, was hers alone to bear.

Outside, in the dark and stormy night, she could hear the
bay of distant hounds. She knew the men were drawing nearer

and she was forced to hurry her task. Hastily, she finished the words she had been bound to write and she sanded the bloody script, hoping it would dry sufficiently. It had to be effective.

As the sounds of barking dogs grew nearer, she quickly rose from her desk and shuffled across the attic floor to a spot near the southeast corner. There, an already-loose board had been pried up. She pulled it further and stuffed several pieces of vellum beneath it. Taking her shoe, she pounded it back down again, hiding her written curses from the world. Or, at least she hoped so. There were many who had to pay for their sins against her and she did not wish her curses interrupted. In the darkness of the attic, the fates of her enemies had been sealed.

Outside, the rain pounded and the wind howled, filling the hollow beneath the woman's home with an unearthly terror. Men on horseback dragged their captured quarry across the dark and barren woods towards the house on a rise in the distance. One might have thought it was an animal being dragged for all of the inhuman noises it was making. But upon closer inspection, the wet and muddy details formed a small and terrified woman.

But the men on horseback didn't seem to care that they were mistreating her. She screamed and grunted, trying to get to her feet as the horse moved swiftly. But she was unable to keep the pace. She ended up falling and being dragged, pulled across stone and grass and mud, tearing her meager clothes, as well as her skin, to shreds. By the time they reached the house, a massive two-story structure with a wide planked porch, the woman was nearly unconscious from the beating she had taken. One of the men dismounted his animal and made his way up onto the porch, pounding on the heavily-fortified door.

The only light was the paltry glow emitting from the down-stairs windows, barely illuminating the porch. The man had to knock twice more before the door was unbolted and slowly opened. A young woman with dark hair, dark eyes, and a long face stood there, gazing back with some apprehension. The man, his clothes soaked from the storm, spoke.

"We found her, Goody Holcombe," he said. "What does thou wish to do with her?"

Goody Holcombe emerged from the house, looking nervously at the group of men on horseback at the base of her porch. She pointed inside the house.

"My husband is in the basement," she said. "He wishes her brought to him."

A couple of the men dismounted, hauling the injured woman up onto the porch. By this time, Goody Holcombe was no longer appearing nervous. Now, she appeared steely and cold as she gazed at the semi-conscious woman. When the men paused, she snatched the woman by the chin.

"Did thee think to get away with what thou hast done?" she snarled. "Thee are a wicked and evil girl, Dorothy Good. Thou deserves to be punished."

Dorothy struggled to open her eyes, fixing on the very angry face of Goody Holcombe. She knew she was facing a horrible fate but that did not tame her pride. She was as bold and fearless as always.

"The poison between us is old," she muttered, missing teeth where the men who had captured her had beaten her. "Thou cursed my mother and killed my sister. Thou deserve a measure of the same. Vengeance is a swift and tasteless order."

Goody Holcombe slapped her, hard. Dorothy's head snapped sideways from the blow. "Thou took my child's life," she cried. "Vengeance will come to thee now and thee will suffer as thee has never suffered before!"

Goody slapped her once more for good measure as the men dragged Dorothy inside the home. Goody Holcombe followed, wringing her hands, weeping, and thinking of the daughter she had lost to the woman. A little girl, an infant, who had been abducted by Dorothy Good and tossed into the well beneath their home, as witnessed by Goody Holcombe's other children.

Dorothy, a girl that neighbors had hired to work in their kitchen, had been able to get close enough to the Holcombe house, known as Evenshade, to enter it. The dead infant had been the result and Dorothy had screamed of vengeance, too, at the time, just as she was screaming of it now.

But here, it would end. Goody Holcombe would get the last swipe of revenge. As she stood in the kitchen of Evenshade, she could hear the men dragging Dorothy down to the basement where her husband, Ezra, awaited. There, he had something particularly gruesome planned for Dorothy, and Goody Holcombe wasn't the least bit sorry. It was small justice for her daughter's life.

As Goody Holcombe stood at the basement door, she could hear muffled speaking. It was her husband's voice mingled with Dorothy's higher pitched tones. There was arguing going on and finally what she hoped to be pleading. She heard panic and weeping. The last she heard was of mournful wailing and the scraping sounds of brick and mortar as Dorothy Good was bricked up in the wall of Evenshade's basement as punishment for murdering young Martha Holcombe.

Buried alive.

ONE

"FOR THE LOVE OF GOD, MONTRESOR!"

"Yes," I said, "for the love of God!"

But to these words I hearkened in vain for a reply. I grew impatient. I called aloud—

"Fortunato!"

No answer. I called again—

"Fortunato!"

No answer still. I thrust a torch through the remaining aperture and let it fall within. There came forth in return only a jingling of the bells. My heart grew sick; it was the dampness of the catacombs that made it so. I hastened to make an end of my labour. I forced the last stone into its position; I plastered it up. Against the new masonry I re-erected the old rampart of bones. For the half of a century no mortal has disturbed them.

In pace requiescat!

———

He had woken himself up to dreams of that shady novel, the words of the dead rolling around in his head. He had no idea why Poe's *The Cask of Amontillado* was filling his dreams, but he didn't like it. He hadn't even liked the story when he had been forced to read it in an English Lit class years ago and thought that he had properly erased it from his brain once he had passed the class. But it was back, whispering strains of people being bricked up alive in his sleep-hazed mind. Weird how the brain worked sometimes.

It was just before dawn. He could see the sky turning shades of gray and yellow, signaling the onslaught of a new day. He rolled over in bed and ended up rolling on one of the dogs, who grunted but didn't move. So he rolled over to the other side and sat up, wearily rubbing his eyes, accidentally kicking the other dog that was sleeping on the floor. Full-grown and over one hundred pounds each, Manitou and Aram were pure-blooded German Shepherds, brothers, because when he and his boys had gone to pick out a puppy they couldn't decide on which one. Chris picked Manitou and Kyle picked Aram, so they ended up bringing them both home. He had two big, slob-bery babies.

The little puppies had grown into enormous dogs that followed Dad around like shadows. They'd spend time with the boys, of course, but they slept with Dad because his bed was big and empty after the boys' mother left. This morning, as he pulled on his jeans and a long sleeved t-shirt, he couldn't even remember the last time a woman had slept beside him. Only dogs. God, he was pathetic.

The house was dark and quiet at this early hour as he made his way down the stairs and into the kitchen. He'd lived in this house since before the boys were born and it always had the same smell in the morning, like cold earth. It wasn't surprising, considering the old Colonial had been built in the mid-seven-teen hundreds and was one of the earliest homes in the area.

Still, it was his house and he loved it. Full of men and dogs, he thought it was cozy and homey nonetheless.

The kitchen was a big mess because his youngest, Cole, had ignored directives to clean the dishes. So he rifled around the dishwasher for a spoon and proceeded to make coffee. As the sun began to rise through the tree line to the east, he poured his coffee into a travel mug and unlocked the back door. The dogs, knowing it was time for a walk, waited excitedly next to him as he opened up the door.

The animals bolted out into the dewy lawn, happy, peeing all over the place or rolling around on the damp grass. He stood there a moment on his wide porch, one that wrapped around the entire house, and watched the dogs play. He loved mornings like this, so peaceful and serene as the world around him awakened, but he always felt like there was something missing. More than once, he had wished for someone to share these mornings with. It was an old dream, but one he still dreamt.

After a few sips of coffee and watching his neighbor across the street open up his garage, he whistled to the dogs and they came running. Taking the stairs off the porch, he began to walk around the side of the house. His house was situated in a some-what rural area of Danvers, most houses sitting on an acre or more, and several of them very old. Back in the day when the Pilgrims arrived, this area was settled by some of them and people around here still carried those old bloodlines, including him.

In fact, there was a very old home up the road that had just been sold after having sat vacant for several months. He had heard a new family had moved in so he was curious to take a look at the house and, perhaps, meet his new neighbor. He could see the house from the west side of his house, sitting on a rise over-looking the land. Evenshade, the name the locals knew it by, had been built back before the Salem witch trials. About a half mile from his house, he walked up the road with the dogs racing ahead of him, avoiding the cars that were passing by as people headed off to work. As he neared the house, which still looked cold and dark, he began to hear what he thought was a distressed voice.

Drawing nearer, he was at the edge of the long driveway when he suddenly heard a thump and a yelp. Concerned, he turned into the driveway and saw a woman, half-in and half-out of the side door, with a very large piece of furniture in her hands. As he watched, the furniture shifted and she went down on her behind.

He broke into a run, sprinting up the driveway until he came to her. A very big man with very big arms, he easily lifted up the dresser and righted it. Then he reached down to extend a hand to the fallen woman.

It was a moment he would remember for the rest of his life.

———

She shouldn't have been trying to haul all of that old furniture out herself but she just couldn't help it. *Seriously!* She thought to herself angrily. *Who just abandons a house and leaves a bunch of crap for the people who come after them?* It was that irritation that drove her into action. She had always been the hasty decision making type, anyway, which sometimes worked against her. This time, it had.

She started working at dawn. The little tables had been easy enough to take out to the big shed that looked more like a barn. A couple of chairs had followed. And then she got the bright idea of dragging out a dresser that was about three times heavier than she was. She didn't think it would be a huge issue to drag it across the yard, so rather than wake up her sixteen-year-old son and ask for help, she was certain she could do it herself. He would have just griped at her, anyway.

It had been a mistake. As soon as she pushed and pulled the thing to the back door, it had gotten wedged against the door jamb. Frustrated, she had pushed and shoved again until it came free. Then, she was determined to drag it out onto the driveway, whereupon the thing shifted and lurched forward, knocking her onto her behind. She yelped in pain and shock because a corner had pinched her thigh, but before she could yell to her son to get his butt out of bed and save her, the piece was suddenly removed and a big hand was stuck in her face. Startled, she found herself looking up into stunning blue eyes.

"Are you okay?" he asked. "Let me help you up."

She took his hand, grunting as he pulled her to her feet. Sheepishly, she laughed. "Where in the world did you come from?" She had a hard time looking him in the eye, feeling like an idiot. "Did you hear me screaming in the next county?"

He grinned. "I saw the Bat-Signal up in the sky above your house and came running."

She laughed again, brushing off her backside before extending her hand. "Thanks, Batman," she said. "You saved the day."

"Glad I could help," he shook her hand warmly. "Are you sure you're okay?"

"I'm fine."

"Good. In that case, I'm Cord Trevor."

"Alix Hendry."

His smile grew. "Nice to meet you," he replied. "Actually, I was out for a walk and heard you yell. I live about a half mile that way."

He was throwing a thumb over his shoulder to the east. "Good thing you keep an eye out for the Bat-Signal," she said.

"It's a talent."

They snorted as the moment turned rather warm and flirty. Alix was eyeing the man but trying to make it look like she wasn't. He was enormous, five or six inches over six feet, with a blond crew cut, superhero granite, square jaw, and a megawatt smile. When he grinned, all she could see was teeth, which made her want to grin right along with him. The man wore rimless glasses, which only seemed to enhance his excruciatingly handsome face, and the hand that had shaken hers was the size of a frying pan.

He was a big, muscular, well-built guy and she'd known him all of thirty seconds and he was already making her feel rather giddy. Tearing her eyes away from him, she gestured at the dresser.

"I didn't think that thing was as heavy as it was until I started moving it." She didn't want him to see that her cheeks were flushed. "I guess I'll have to wait for my son to get out of bed before I try to move it again."

Cord nodded, his gaze drifting over the big, old-style, saltbox Colonial home that was badly in need of restoration. The rotting eaves, peeling paint and rotting boards had stood for untold decades, waiting, watching. The house was rather creepy.

"I'd say you'd better wait for your son *and* husband to get out of bed before moving this thing," he told her. "That's way too heavy for you. Batman says so."

She grinned again before shaking her head, not even realizing that he was trying to find out if she was married without being obvious about it.

"My son's the man of the house, so it'll be him and his mom dragging this thing across the yard," she said, making humorous gestures to go along with the statement. "But thank you for saving me from being crushed to death. I really appreciate it."

Cord thought himself rather clever to have found out her

marital status within the first couple minutes of knowing her. Increasingly thrilled to realize she was single, or at least didn't have a husband, he realized he didn't want to end the conversation. At the risk of making a nuisance of himself, he pointed at the dresser.

"Tell you what," he said. "Since I'd hate to see my new neighbors get into trouble with this thing, why don't you let me move it into the shed."

Alix put up her hands. "Oh, heavens, no," she said. "I couldn't let you do that. It can wait until my son gets up."

"I'm trying to be neighborly, ma'am. It would help if you'd just go along with it."

He was smiling as he said it, which set Alix off to grinning again and her pink cheeks grew even pinker. She could feel them. Like an idiot, she put her palms to her cheeks to feel how flaming they were, noticing that he was smiling quite openly at her. She just laughed for lack of a better reaction.

"Really," she insisted, "you can be just as neighborly by simply introducing yourself. You don't need to schlep around this old junk to demonstrate it."

He backed off, the gentlemanly thing to do, rather than argue with her. He didn't want to come across like a pushy creep, even if she was the most beautiful woman he had ever seen. Petite, with long reddish-gold hair that had some curl to it and a sweetly oval face with big gray eyes, she looked like a porcelain doll. He guessed she was somewhere in her thirties and from what he could tell under the jeans and jacket, she had a sexy little figure. Match her spectacular looks up with the bubbly personality and he had to admit, he was enamored right off the bat.

"I was only trying to help," he held his hands up in surrender.

"I appreciate it, really."

He opened his mouth to speak but the dogs, which had been inspecting Alix's front yard, suddenly ran up and happily greeted her. They were big, wet dogs. But rather than recoil, she was very friendly with them and they loved it. All the while, Cord just watched her, trying to think of a way to continue the conversation so he wouldn't have to continue on his walk. He really had no interest in doing anything other than standing there and talking to her.

"So you just moved in," he stated the obvious.

She looked up from Manitou as the dog licked at her chin. "Yes."

"Where are you from?"

"California. Los Angeles." She stood up and wiped her dog-wet hands on her jeans. "We actually took possession yesterday, came here, and went right to bed. I haven't even really seen the house in the daylight. This is the first time I've gotten an up close and personal look."

"You didn't see it before you bought it?"

She shook her head. "Not in person," she said, looking at the amused, yet curious, expression on his face. "I've just always wanted one of these old Colonials. Out where I come from, everything is so new. No charm to anything, so homes like this have always been kind of fascinating to me. I just happened to see this one come up for sale when I was surfing the web one day, so I called the agent. Next thing I know, I own a historical home and I'm thrilled to death."

He could see that just by the look on her face and he smiled at her a moment before his gaze drifted up over the eaves of the home. "You picked a good one, that's for sure," he said. "This home is the oldest one around here."

"Have you lived here a long time?

"All my life."

She was very interested. "Really? Then maybe you can tell

me what you know about this house. I've done a little research into it, but there are always stories that only the locals know."

He was very happy to tell her what he knew. He was confident he could drag it out into a half-hour conversation or, at least, come back another time to talk to her. Either way, he was eager to do it.

"Sure," he said, pulling Manitou down from jumping up on her. "Maybe some time when you're not busy getting smashed by dressers?"

She laughed softly. "I just made a pot of coffee," she said. "Would... would you like some? I really want to hear what you know about the house, if it wouldn't be interrupting your walk."

"No interruption at all."

"Are you sure? The dogs might have something to say about it."

"As long as they're not at *my* house, they're happy. They like to visit."

Her gray eyes twinkled at him a moment before giving him a somewhat alluring glance as she turned for the house. "If you say so," she said. "Do you want to see inside? Being a local, I'll bet you can tell me all kinds of things about these houses. I don't have a clue."

He probably couldn't tell her a whole lot more, but he was more than happy to take her up on her offer, anyway.

TWO

"SO THE REAL estate agent didn't give you the lowdown on the house?"

The question came from Cord, leaning against the kitchen counter with a steaming cup of coffee in his hand. Alix shook her head in reply.

"Other than the fact that it was a historical house, she really didn't tell me much," she replied as she poured herself a cup of coffee. "She told me that it used to be called 'Evenshade', so I looked up what I could on the internet. An article I found said that the husband of Abigail Williams built the house in 1690, right before the Salem witch trials. His name was Ezra Hyde Holcombe and he married Abigail right after the witch trials, when she was fourteen and he was thirty-eight. Other than that, the articles I read said Ezra was a slave trader and a farmer, but not much else."

Cord sipped at the strong coffee. He glanced around the kitchen, which was stuck in the nineteen fifties with its ugly, gray laminate countertops and ancient stove. Wallpaper was peeling from the walls and the old linoleum flooring with its black and green dots was starting to pull up in places. It smelled like mold.

"I've lived on the east coast all of my life," he said. "I'm not sure how it is in California, but in this part of the country, there are some really old families and their lineage means a good deal to them. I'm part of the family that was the original owners of this house, the Holcombes. The house remained in the family up until ten or fifteen years ago, but then it was sold."

Alix's eyebrows lifted. "Really?" she was very interested. "So you're descended from the original owners?"

He nodded, somewhat modestly. "I've got history coming out of my ears."

She grinned. "What do you mean?"

He sipped at his coffee. "Ezra and Abigail, who was one of the chief accusers at the Salem Witch Trials, had four children," he began his story. "Elizabeth, Mary, Matilda and John. My mother's father is a direct descendant of John Holcombe, which makes me a direct descendent also. Plus, on my father's side, I'm a direct descendent of the Mayflower shipwright, John Trevor. My full name is Cord Van Wyck Holcombe Trevor."

"Van Wyck?"

"Mother's mother was a Van Wyck, one of the original settling families in upstate New York. So I guess that makes me a blue-blooded American more than most."

Alix was impressed. "That's *so* cool," she said. Then she eyed him. "So all of that old furniture left behind belongs to you, then."

He shook his head, a smile playing on his lips. "Not me," he said. "My great-aunt, the last person from the family who lived here, moved out thirty years ago and let her children handle it. Then they sold it about fifteen years ago and there have been renters in the house until you bought it."

"Oh," she said. Then she shrugged. "Why did your family sell it, then? This house is like part of the family."

He lifted his big shoulders. "I don't even know. I guess it was a cash cow for a while but with the age come repairs. Maybe they just didn't want to sink that kind of money into it and thought they'd sell it and get their money out of it. You know it needs a lot of repairs, right?"

She nodded, looking around the kitchen as she thought of all of the money she was about to spend. "I do," she said softly. "This house was a steal at three hundred and fifty thousand, but I'm guessing I'm going to be putting at least another one hundred and fifty thousand into it. But I don't mind; I like the challenge."

He grinned at her as he sipped his coffee. "You must," he said. "So what do you do for a living that is going to enable you to pay for this white elephant?"

"Emergency Medicine," she replied. "I have a new position with North Shore Medical Center in Salem in their Emergency Department. I start next week."

"Nurse?"

"Physician. Trauma surgery."

He lifted his eyebrows; now it was his turn to be impressed. "*Dr.* Hendry," he said as if correcting his bad manners. "North Shore is a good place. We may see each other once in a while."

"Why is that?"

"Because I'm with the fire department. That's my district's hospital for medical runs."

"Oh," she wasn't displeased at the thought of seeing him again. "Paramedic?"

"I was, once. Now I'm a captain."

She grinned. "How long have you been in that line of work?"

"Twenty-three years," he sighed. "A long time."

Alix watched him as he leaned against her counter, feeling more and more drawn to the man the more she got to know him. He'd come inside to tell her about the house but they'd hardly talked about it. They were talking about each other, as if they were getting to know one another for personal reasons. He was a hunk, no doubt, but other than the fact he was her neighbor, had two dogs, and was a firefighter, she really didn't know that much about him. She didn't even know if he was married. If he was, then he was being a bit of a flirt and she wasn't sure she liked that at all. But if he wasn't....

"Do you have any kids, Cord?" she asked as she sipped her coffee.

He nodded. "Three boys," he told her. "Chris will be a senior in high school in the fall, Kyle will be a junior, and Cole is entering the ninth grade."

"My son will be a junior in high school, also," she said. "He'll be going to Danvers High School. I also have a four-year-old daughter who will be entering preschool."

He lifted his eyebrows at her. "You don't look old enough to have a sixteen-year-old."

She grinned, flattered. "I was a baby when I had him."

"You must have been."

"Actually, I had him while I was in Medical school. I was lucky enough to have him in July and was able to start my second year right up again in September."

"Good planning. What about your daughter?"

"By the time she was born, I was already established. I took four months off but I wish it could have been more. I loved staying at home."

He was halfway done with his coffee. "The boys' mother was able to stay at home with them when they were very small. I think it's important to have the mom around full time when the kids are young."

"Does your wife still stay home with them?"

He shook his head. "*Ex*-wife," he clarified, and very glad the conversation had allowed him to make the point clear. "We divorced years ago and the boys live with me. She lives in New York."

So, he wasn't married. Alix was back to liking him a great deal, probably more now. "Well," she said casually, "they must keep you very busy. I've got enough to do with two."

"Where's Dad?"

It was a direct question, one she hoped meant that he was as interested in her as she was becoming in him. She had no problem answering.

"Back in Los Angeles," she said. "He's kind of got his own thing going on, but he'll see the kids when he can."

Cord simply nodded, not wanting to probe her too deeply on that subject. At least not until he got to know her a little better, but already, they had exchanged a good deal of important information and he was thrilled. He looked around the kitchen as he finished the last of his coffee.

"What else can I tell you about the place?" he asked. "Oh, and by the way – is there any more furniture to move out?"

She nodded. "A few bigger pieces in the dining room. Why?"

"Because I'll do it before I leave. I don't want to take the chance that the Bat-Signal will go up again today and I miss it. You'd better let me do it for my own peace of mind."

Alix laughed softly. "Seriously, you don't have to," she assured him. "Sean and I will get to it once he gets out of bed. *If* he ever gets out of bed."

Cord snorted into his coffee cup. "I've got three of those," he said. "They'd sleep until noon if I let them."

Alix giggled, shrugged, and went back over to the coffee pot, which he was standing next to. She could feel the heat from his body as she picked up the pot, distracting her.

"Do you want another cup?" she asked.

He shifted slightly to hold up his mug but he didn't move, even though she was brushed right up against him. It was a little weird, maybe even creepy if he was to admit it, but he couldn't explain his reaction to her. He'd known the woman all of ten minutes and had never felt such a strong reaction to anyone in his life. He could smell her from where he was standing and she smelled like something cool and crisp and sweet. He found himself inhaling deeply and hoping she wouldn't notice.

"Thanks," he said as he watched her fill the cup half-full. "You make good coffee."

She grinned. "I don't have many vices, but coffee is one of them," she admitted. "You'll always find very good coffee in my house."

He was gazing down at her, noticing she hadn't moved very far away from him. "There's a gourmet coffee shop in town about a mile up the road," he told her. "I always stop there on my way to work."

She nodded her gratitude. "Thanks," she said. "I'll have to try it."

She was still standing there, no more than a few inches separating them, and Cord was seriously having a difficult time focusing on anything other than her lush lips when they both heard noise in the doorway that led from the kitchen out into the dining room. The adults looked over to see a tall, skinny, young man with a head of messy blond hair rubbing his eyes. Sean Patrick Hendry gazed at his mother with some irritation.

"What did you want, Mom?" he asked sleepily.

Alix put her cup down on the counter and went to her son. "Nothing," she said, reaching out to stroke his blond head. "What do you mean?"

"You knocked on my door, didn't you?" Sean sounded annoyed.

Alix shook her head, glancing over at Cord as if to reaffirm she hadn't left the kitchen. "No," she said. "Are you sure? Maybe you just dreamed it."

Sean yawned, finally catching sight of Cord standing over by the sink. He eyed the very big man. "I don't think I did," he muttered, lifting his hand because he and Cord had made eye contact. "Hi."

Cord smiled faintly, raising his hand in response. "Hi."

Alix did the introductions. "Sean, this is our neighbor, Mr. Trevor," she said. "He's got three boys your age."

Sean yawned again but didn't seem particularly impressed. "Cool," he stumbled over to the myriad of cardboard boxes that were stuffed in, and blocking, the utility room, and began ripping open the tops. "Where's the cereal?"

Alix watched him as she went back over to the counter and collected her cup. "No cereal," she told him. "I wasn't shipping cereal across country in a box. I'll go to the store this morning and get some bread and stuff for breakfast. Meanwhile, I think there are some crackers in there."

Sean turned his nose up at crackers for breakfast. But before he could argue, a piercing scream came from the second floor. Startled, Alix slammed the cup down on the counter and bolted and, instinctively, Cord did the same. In his profession, one usually ran towards danger rather than away from it, so he was acting on his training. He followed Alix up the narrow back stairs to the second floor where the distinct sounds of a child crying were evident. Alix ran into one of the doors and Cord followed.

A little girl was sitting up in her messy bed, rubbing her eyes and sobbing. Alix sat down on the bed and pulled the child into her arms.

"Shhhh," she whispered soothingly. "You're okay. What happened?"

Cord was looking around the room, dingy and full of boxes, for anything that would have caused a hysterical child as the little girl answered.

"A bad girl," she said rather angrily. "She wanted my kitty and I told her no. But she took it anyway."

Alix looked around to see the stuffed cat on the ground a few feet away. Cord was following her focus and saw the cat, also, picking it up and handing it to Alix when she tried to get off the bed and hold her daughter at the same time. Alix took it from him, smiling gratefully.

"Here's your kitty." She gave it back to the child, who cuddled it. "No one took it. It just fell off the bed."

The child hugged it, getting her snot and tears on it. She was growing more lucid; enough so that she noticed Cord standing in the doorway. She immediately shrank against her mother, her big eyes wide at the strange man. Alix hugged her daughter, stroking her little blond head gently.

"That's Mr. Trevor, our neighbor," she said. "He's our neighbor. Can you say hi?"

The little girl lifted a hand much like her brother had. "Hi," she hiccupped.

Cord smiled gently. "Hi," he said, then spoke softly to Alix. "If everything's okay, I'll just go back downstairs."

Alix waved a hand at him, collecting her daughter from the bed and standing up. "We'll go with you," she said, wrapping a little blanket around the girl. "This is my daughter, Rose Elizabeth Hendry. Rosie turned four years old last week."

Cord continued to smile at the child, who was genuinely adorable with her honey-colored hair and big eyes. When she looked up at Cord, he could see that they were the color of her mother's, that steely blue that appeared gray in certain light. He followed the pair back down the stairs.

Both kids were crowded around the table and Alix began digging through boxes looking for something to feed them. Cord began to edge his way towards the back door.

"Well," he said, not particularly wanting to leave but feeling rather awkward now that the entire family was up. "Good luck with the house. If you need anything, please don't hesitate to let me know."

Alix's head came out of a box, her hands full of animal crackers and granola bars. "Hold on," she said as she set them down on the table in front of the kids. "I'll walk you out."

Cord stood at the back door, politely opening it for her and then following her out onto the driveway where his dogs were waiting. Before Cord could say anything to her, he noticed the dresser still on the badly paved driveway where he had left it when he pulled it off of Alix. He went over to it and getting a good grip on it, he looked at Alix.

"Where do you want it?" he asked. "In that shed back there?"

Alix sighed heavily. "Really, you don't have to...."

He cut her off by lifting the thing and began walking with it. "In the shed?"

Alix winced as he walked past her; the piece of furniture was very big and very heavy, but he handled it easily. "Oh... brother," she said apprehensively. "You're going to give yourself a hernia."

"Then I know which doctor to go to."

She giggled and followed him across the yard and into the dark shed. He took the dresser over to the corner and set it down with a grunt.

"There." He brushed off his hands. "What more is there in the house?"

Alix shook her head firmly and blocked the door. "No way, dude," she said. "You leave that furniture alone. I'm not going to have you go out on an injury because you were moving my old junk around."

"It's not yours."

"Yes, it is. I bought it when I bought the house."

He made a face at her. "Don't think you can out-stubborn me, Dr. Hendry. I'm going to move the rest of that furniture in here if I have to break into the house to do it."

She gave him a quirky grin. "I have a teenage son who is not nearly as strong as you are, but he's capable. Plus, it will give him something to do."

"The same teenage son that's sitting in the kitchen, waiting for his breakfast? I can do it a lot faster than he can."

Alix gazed at him, her smile fading. She appreciated the offer, his sense of humor, and everything about the man, so far. But she couldn't, in good conscience, let him move all of the old furniture out of the house as if he were somehow responsible for it. He seemed far too eager to help and, to be truthful, that freaked her out a little bit. He was coming on strongly but not in an obvious sort of way; it was gentle, firm and insistent, like she couldn't say no to him no matter what. She had just met the man and was undeniably attracted to him, so she wasn't sure what was holding her back, only that something was. Maybe she didn't want him to think she had taken advantage of him. Maybe she just didn't want to become dependent on him, because it would be so easy to....

"Absolutely not," she said firmly, moving through the door and out into the yard with Cord on her heels. "Thank you for saving me from being crushed to death by the dresser, but that's the one and only piece of furniture you get to move. Sean and I can do the rest."

Cord could see she wasn't going to let him help, but there

was more to it now. She wasn't as warm and open as she had been only minutes before, like an invisible wall had been raised. He sensed that he'd overstayed his welcome and sought to make amends. He wanted to see her again and he didn't want her to be cautious about it because he'd come on like a bulldozer the first time.

"Okay," he backed off considerably, realizing she wasn't being receptive. Then he crooked his finger. "Come here; I want to show you something."

Alix followed, somewhat hesitantly, as he motioned her over to the edge of the driveway. He pointed to the east, down into the vale where the road carved a path. There were a few houses down there amongst the trees and fences, all Colonials set on big lots, but he was pointing to one in particular.

"See that blue house down there with the dark blue eaves and the big white porch?" he asked.

Alix spied the structure. "Yes."

He stopped pointing and looked at her. "That's where I live," he said. "If you need anything, day or night, please don't hesitate to knock on my door. I'm assuming you don't know anyone around here or have any family, so don't feel like you're all alone. I'd be happy to help, whatever you need."

She was still hesitant. "I appreciate that, but...."

"And," he cut her off, pulling his wallet out of his back pocket, digging around, and pulling forth a business card. He handed it to her. "My cell phone is on that. Call me if you need anything. Please."

Alix could feel her resistance breaking down again as she gazed up into his handsome face. She didn't sense any ill-intent; simply a true eagerness to help out. But there was more to it than that. She could see it in his eyes and it both thrilled and scared her. Torn, she nonetheless gave him a genuine smile and held out her hand again.

"You're very sweet," she said quietly, sincerely. "Thank you. I hope I won't ever have to bother you."

He held her hand a moment, shaking it gently. But more than that, he just wanted to hold it. She was spectacular, in every way, and he was succumbing quickly.

"I hope you do."

With that, he let go of her hand and whistled loudly to the dogs, who came running. Alix watched him make his way back down the driveway, waving at him when he turned to look at her. He waved back. She continued to watch him until he faded from sight, realizing there was a big, fat grin on her face when she turned back for the house.

THREE

IT HAD TAKEN all day for Alix and Sean to move the furniture, piece by piece, into the old shed. Alix was something of a neat freak so they just couldn't dump it; it had to be neatly arranged, which set Sean off to no end. As Rose followed them around with a rag because her mother had asked her to clean off the furniture, the entire family got into the furniture moving business.

Alix took the kids to town halfway during their day so they could go to the supermarket, but they passed a Dunkin' Donuts and both kids went crazy. So she ended up stopping at Dunkin' Donuts and buying a bunch of crap just because the kids wanted it. Usually, she was much stricter about what they ate, but considering they had just moved across country and had a fairly stressful few days, she relented and let Sean eat jelly donuts for lunch and let Rose have a soda. The result was that by the time they hit the supermarket, both kids were bouncing off the walls.

When they returned from the market and put away the groceries, Alix put the kids on unloading their boxes upstairs while she finished up in the kitchen. Now that she actually had groceries, she put dinner on in the crockpot and headed upstairs to help Rose unpack. As she neared her daughter's big bedroom at the front of the house, she could hear the little girl talking to someone. It was playful talk, as little girls do when they are pretending, and she smiled as she entered her daughter's bedroom.

"Who's your friend, Rosie?" she asked as she headed over to a half-unpacked box.

Rose shrugged, more interested in the doll in her hand. "I don't know her name."

"Oh?" Alix was already involved pulling out bed linens. "What does she look like?"

"Sad."

Hands full of folded sheets, Alix looked at her daughter. "Sad?" she repeated. "Why is she sad?"

"Because she has to live here and she's scared." Rose turned to her mother. "Mommy, can I have a pony?"

Alix's expression twisted with surprise. "A pony?" she asked. "Where in the world did that come from?"

"My friend had a pony," Rose said. "She wants me to have a pony, too."

Alix's eyebrows lifted. "I see," she was on to her daughter's game. "Well, we'll have to see. I don't think we have any room to keep a pony here."

Rose turned back to her toy, disinterested in what her mother was doing and not particularly distressed by the answer, as if she didn't really care. As she sat on the floor with her toy, she began to hum a soft little tune.

"'*A holiday, a holiday, the first one of the year'*," she whispered in her sweet little voice. "'*Lord Arlen's wife came into church, the gospel for to hear'*."

Alix grinned as she organized the linen, listening to her daughter sing; she didn't want to put anything into the closets or cabinets yet because they were going to paint, so she tried to put the more used linens towards the top. Still, she was distracted by the song.

"Where did you hear that song, baby?" she asked.

Rose shrugged her little shoulders. "My friend singed it to me," she said. "Mommy, can I watch T.V.?"

Alix really had no idea what Rose was talking about, but that wasn't unusual. The little girl had a huge imagination and would often make up songs and playmates, or draw pictures of animals that didn't exist. It was all part of Rosie's sweet charm.

"Sean is getting the television hooked up downstairs," Alix said. "You can watch a video after dinner, okay?"

"Okay."

"I'm going to go back downstairs and see if I can get the washer working, okay?" Alix looked at her daughter's cluttered room, hating the fact that it would be several days at least before they could start packing stuff away, at least until the painters got busy. "Rosie, please unpack your box with the stuffed animals in it and put them in your chest so I can move that box out of here, okay?"

Rose was focused on her doll. "Okay."

"Now, Rose Elizabeth. Please help me get everything straightened out."

Rose simply nodded and Alix left, thinking that her daughter probably wouldn't get around to doing as she was told until she was reminded again. Rose did what Rose wanted to do when she wanted to do it, and that was final. Sticking her head into Sean's room to see that the young man had a lot of his boxes pulled apart and was shoving stuff into his dressers, she continued downstairs.

Just as she hit the bottom step, thunder let loose overhead that sounded like an earthquake and all of the lights cut out.

———

It was raining in a steady downpour and lightning streaked across the sky as Cord pulled his Ford truck into Alix's driveway. From the base of the driveway as it arced up to the house was about 100 feet but even so, he could barely see the house through the sheets of rain that were pounding down. He pulled the truck up as far as he could and then put it in park, turning to the three young men in the car.

"Okay, boys," he said. "Grab the firewood and the flashlights. Cole, grab the box of candles down there at your feet."

"Dad," Kyle, the middle son, whined, "do we really have to do this?"

"Yes, we do."

"But we don't even... I mean, who *is* this lady?"

"I told you." Cord was losing his patience. "A new neighbor. Her house is all torn up and if we don't have any electricity, then she doesn't have any. I'm sure she could use the help. This is part of being a good neighbor."

"Nobody was ever a good neighbor to us like this."

"Shut up and get out of the car."

The boys grunted and made faces at each other, but Cord ignored them. The three young men began grabbing around for supplies as Cord opened the truck door and bailed out. The four of them, arms full, jumped onto the old porch, which was sagging in places and made their way to the front door. It took three rounds of banging at the big, warped front door before it timidly opened. Alix's eyes opened wide at the men on her doorstep.

"Hi," she said, shocked. "What in the world are you doing out in this storm?"

Cord realized he was very glad to see her, like his heart lightened the moment she opened the door. She was dressed in skinny jeans and a long-sleeved shirt that showed every curve. He also realized he been right about one thing; she had an amazing body. It was hard to tear his gaze off the modest cleavage she was showing.

"Do you have power?" he asked.

She shook her head. "No."

"How about firewood?"

Again, she shook her head. "No."

He threw a thumb back at the collection of teenage boys behind him. "We do," he said. "We thought we'd share with our new neighbor."

That brought a big smile from Alix and she stepped back, opening the door wide. "Did you see the Bat-Signal again?"

Cord laughed softly as he and the boys came in the entry. "In fact, I did," he said, indicating the young men next to him. "So I brought Robin, Superman, and Aquaman."

The boys had no idea what he was talking about, but Alix laughed. "Wow," she said. "The whole Justice League. You've got connections."

Cord shared her giggles before turning and pointing to the boys in order. "Actually, these are my boys – Chris, Kyle and Cole," he said. "Boys, this is Dr. Hendry. She just moved in with her two kids."

Alix smiled warmly at the three young men, all very tall and handsome like their father. Chris and Kyle were quite big and muscular, whereas Cole looked like he hadn't quite caught up in the muscle department. He was tall and rather skinny, and he smiled awkwardly when their eyes met.

"Hello, gentlemen," she said, noting all of the stuff they had in their hands. "Well, come on in and set that stuff down. It's like Christmas!"

She said it so gleefully that the four of them grinned. Up until about fifteen seconds ago, Alix wasn't feeling so great.

The electricity was out, she couldn't figure out the heating system, and the only thing working seemed to be the stove as it ran off propane. Her dinner in the crockpot was only half-finished because of the electricity outage, the washer was stopped mid-cycle, and Rose was having a meltdown because she couldn't watch her videos. The unexpected appearance of Cord had her feeling some happiness and relief. Plus, she was just the least bit touched that he would go to the trouble. Even if he was coming on strong, she realized that she was very glad to see him.

"I would have called you, but I realized I didn't have your number," Cord said as he set a couple of flashlights on the kitchen counter.

Alix grinned. "I'll take care of that before you leave. You really didn't have to come all the way over here just to see if we were okay."

He ignored the last part of her statement. "So," Cord put his hands on his hips, surveying the kitchen. "What's first?"

Alix cocked her head. "First?"

"Yes," he nodded, looking over at the boys who were piling up the wood against the kitchen wall. "Kyle, go light the fireplace in the living room. Chris, you can light the fireplace in here."

The boys swung into action as Cord returned his attention to Alix. "I'm assuming the chimneys are clear?"

Alix was a little taken aback as the man took charge. "Yes," she nodded. "They had to be to pass the home inspection. But we wouldn't need the fireplaces if I could just figure out how to use the heater."

He shook his head, snapping his fingers at Cole, who produced a Coleman lantern and fired it up. "It won't work," he said. "The thermostat is probably electrical. Your heater is dead in the water until the power comes back on, but I'll take a look.

Meanwhile, we'll light the fireplaces and that should heat the house up a bit."

Overhead, the thunder rolled as if to punctuate the terrible weather outside. It seemed to rattle the entire house. Sean picked that moment to come down the back stairs, his eyes widening at all of the activity in the old kitchen. Alix caught sight of him.

"Hi, Sean," she said, pointing to Cord. "You remember Mr. Trevor?"

Sean nodded as Cord kicked in. "Please, call me Cord," he told the boy. "Mr. Trevor sounds like I'm the high school principal or the boss you like to hate."

Sean grinned, noticing another boy in the room as he tried to start a fire in the big, old brick fireplace. He was very curious. Cord could see where the boy's attention was.

"That's my son, Chris," he said. "Kyle's in the living room and that tall kid standing next to the stairs is Cole."

Sean came down the stairs, acknowledging the young men who seemed to have infiltrated his house.

"Hey," he said casually.

The boys waved back to varying degrees except for Kyle, who was in the living room. Sean stood somewhat awkwardly at the base of the stairs.

"What's going on?" he asked his mom, or anyone who could answer him.

Alix looked at Cord as she spoke. "Cord came to the rescue with firewood and lights so we won't be in the dark," she said, lifting her shoulders as if giving up on trying to curb the man's determination. He wanted to help and she was apt to let him. "Thank God, because I really have no idea where I packed my candles or flashlight."

That seemed to satisfy Sean as he made his way over to his mother, still looking rather bewildered with all of the activity.

"Are we still having dinner?" he asked.

Alix nodded. "The stove is propane, so I can make us something," she said, looking to Cord. "Did you guys eat? The least I can do is make dinner for all of your trouble."

Cord, who had been peering over Chris' shoulder as the teenager tried to light the fire, turned his attention to her.

"No trouble at all," he assured her. "This storm is supposed to go all night so we just thought you could use the help."

Alix's eyes glimmered at him and the wall of uncertainty she had put up against him earlier in the day was fading fast. The man was handsome, charming, and thoughtful. She certainly couldn't fault him for those qualities.

"And I appreciate it," she said. "But if you don't let me do something for you, I'm going to cry."

He grinned. "I didn't bring wood over so you'd feed us."

"I realize that," she said, turning for her stove, "but I'm going to do it, anyway, and no argument from Batman and the Superhero Legion."

Cord didn't say a word. The truth was, his plan had worked perfectly and, once again, he was speaking to the woman he'd thought about all day, every minute of the day, until the storm broke and he saw another opportunity to make a nuisance of himself. He decided right then and there that he was going to see her every day, with any excuse, until he got up the nerve to ask her out. He wasn't one to work quickly when it came to women, but he was willing to make an exception in her case. He didn't want the opportunity to slip past him.

As he took over from Chris lighting the fire in the old hearth of the kitchen, Alix banged around behind him. She was pulling out flour and cans of stuff, and he saw her pull a roasted chicken out of the refrigerator. As he finally got the fire started, he just stood there, pretending to monitor the growing blaze when what he was really doing was watching Alix work from the corner of his eye. It had been so long since he'd watched a woman cook in the kitchen that he'd forgotten what warm and homey feelings it brought about. He'd missed them.

As Alix began to pull apart the chicken and got some kind of stew cooking in the big pot on the stove, Cord meandered over to the counter to see if there was anything he could do.

"Can I help?" he asked.

She shook her head. "No," she said flatly. "You're a guest."

"I've done my share cooking. I know my way around a stove."

She looked up at him, craning her neck back because the man was so tall. "Do you cook a lot at the firehouse?"

He nodded. "We take turns," he said. "Some of the guys can't cook at all, so they're the ones that usually buy the groceries. Guys like me, who actually like to cook, take the duty so long as we don't have to buy the groceries or clean up."

She smiled at him as she pulled apart the chicken breast. "What do you like to cook?"

He shrugged as he moved to the sink to wash his hands. "I cook a lot of beef," he grinned, drying off his hands on a kitchen towel. "Chili, burgers, steaks, that kind of thing. My boys were raised on an entire herd of cattle, I swear."

Alix laughed softly. "You do the cooking for them, too?"

"I do."

"Don't they see their mom on occasion?"

He moved over to the chicken she was pulling apart and picked up a leg. He began to shred it and put the meat in the simmering pot.

"Not really," he said, his voice rather subdued. "Dianne and I were married when we were both students at Cornell, but she went on to get her Ph.D. when I went in to the NFL, and that's when things started to change. We had Chris and Kyle right off the bat, but by the time Cole came, we had just really grown apart. Cole was two when we divorced and she remarried pretty soon afterwards and had more children. I think she forgets about her first family. She's pretty busy with her work and her younger children."

Alix was watching his face as he spoke, the somber tone. She could see the distress on his face no matter how much he tried to mask it.

"It upsets you," she observed softly.

He looked at her, shaking his head. "Not me personally," he said. "But I do feel bad for the boys sometimes. It's hard to have a mom that treats you like an afterthought."

Alix's brow furrowed with sorrow as she went back to pulling chicken meat off the bone. "That's sad," she agreed quietly. "I feel bad for them, too. Actually, your kids and my kids are kind of in the same boat. My ex-husband is kind of a paradox in that he financially supports his kids completely, provides them with insurance and all that, but it's like pulling teeth to get him to come to a school play or a back-to-school night. He's much more active with Sean, at least as much as he can be, but I think he forgets Rosie exists sometimes. She was our 'oops' baby."

He finished pulling the meat off one chicken leg and was going in for another. "How many years between her and your son?"

"Twelve and a half."

He nodded in agreement. "That must have been a surprise."

Alix laughed softly. "A wonderful surprise," she clarified. "She's my angel."

He grinned as he put chicken meat into the bubbling pot. "She's a cutie, that's for sure."

Alix's smile turned grateful as she finished with the meat and washed her hands. He wasn't finished yet with the legs and wings, but the truth was, he could have been finished minutes ago except for the fact that he just wanted to stand there and talk to her. So, like a dork, he was milking the situation for everything it was worth. As Alix began to measure flour into a bowl, the thunder clapped again and the windows rattled. She jumped and so did the flour.

"Dammit," she hissed, noting the flour on her shirt. "I hate storms."

He grinned. "You'd better get used to them," he told her. "We get a lot of weather around here."

She made a face at him as she began to pour cold water into the flour. Before she could reply, Kyle and Chris came into the kitchen and headed for their dad.

"Dad, the living room chimney is smoking a lot," Kyle said. "Water is coming down into it."

Cord quickly washed his hands before following the boys back into the living room. A good deal of white smoke was rolling out of the fireplace and he got down on his knees, trying to peer up the chimney to see what was going on. Alix had followed them into the living room and now stood in the doorway, wiping her hands off.

"Don't tell me something else is broken in this old house," she said rather fearfully.

Cord was trying to look up the chimney without getting his hair singed. As he did so, his cell phone went off and he pulled it out of his pocket and put it to his ear.

"Trevor," he said shortly.

He was still looking up the chimney as someone on the other end spoke to him. Alix gave up standing there, not really wanting to know if something else was wrong with the house and went back to the dumplings she was making. She could hear vague voices in the living room as she rolled out the dough and began to cut it into long strips, putting the strips into the simmering chicken broth and adding a can of creamy celery soup and a can of green peas. As the dumplings began to cook, Cord came back into the kitchen.

"I'm so sorry to ruin your dinner, but I have to go," he told her. "I've been called in to work."

She looked concerned. "That's too bad," she said. "Is it the storm?"

He nodded. "Apparently, it's wreaking havoc and they've got rigs going out all over the area on calls. The system is overloaded so they're calling in reinforcements."

Alix was disappointed but tried not to show it. "I'm sorry you have to go, too," she said. "You've put in so much work here today that I feel bad that you have to run off before I was able to feed you."

He smiled weakly at her, his blue eyes glimmering behind the rimless glasses. "I hope this won't be the last invitation we ever get."

She smiled in return, allowing herself to feel the warmth of the strong attraction she had towards the man. She was fairly sure he was feeling it, too, judging from the expression on his face.

"Of course not," she said softly. "There will be other dinners, I'm sure."

His eyes held her just a moment longer, the mood between them moving from polite and interested warmth to something a little deeper, a little more probing. Cord eventually opened his mouth as if he wanted to say something more but he stopped himself, snorting nervously when she grinned at him and giggled. He was pretty sure he wanted to kiss her goodnight but there was no way he was going to do that. At least, not tonight. So he backed away, purely to help his self-control.

"I'll get the boys out of your hair," he gestured back towards the living room where they were still gathered.

"Wait," she stopped him. "Why not leave them here? I'll

have more than enough to eat and I can drive them home when they're finished."

His brow furrowed. "I can't let you do that," he shook his head. "This is only your second night here and...."

She cut him off. "That has nothing to do with it," she insisted. "Leave them here, let them help me finish off these chicken and dumplings, and I'll drive them the half mile to your house. I promise I won't speed."

He grinned at her and she could see that he was considering it. "Are you sure?"

She waved him off. "Of course," she said. "If there's enough left over, I'll send you home a care package. Batman has got to eat, too."

He laughed softly. "Okay, you win," he said, glancing over his shoulder to see that young Rose had come downstairs and was standing with her brother as Kyle tried to talk to her. "I'll let them know. They'll be good guests, I promise."

Alix smiled, putting her hand on his arm before she really thought about what she was doing. She was the touchy-feely sort, anyway, always hugging and kissing people, so it was natural for her to touch him. He was warm and firm beneath her fingers.

"If they're half as polite as their father, I'm sure they will be," she said, her gaze lingering on him a moment before they joined the kids. "Thank you... well, thank you for all you've done today. You've come to my rescue twice and I'm very grateful."

He felt her fingers on his arm like a searing brand; bolts of electricity were pouring out of her hand and through his body, enough so that he started sweating. He wanted nothing more than to reciprocate the touch, but there were five kids behind him in the living room and he didn't want to do anything to freak any of them out, mostly because he knew he couldn't stop at a simple touch. He wanted to taste her, too. So he grinned nervously and made a conscious effort to keep his hands off her.

"You're welcome," he said, turning to the boys behind him because he couldn't look at her anymore and not try to do something about it. "Hey, guys, listen up; there's been a change in plans."

The Trevor boys weren't particularly sorry that they had to stay for dinner at their new neighbor's house, mostly because she made the best chicken and dumplings any of them had ever had. Plus, she made a fruit cobbler that was to die for, slathered with ice cream she had just bought that day because the freezer was out and they needed to eat it before it melted.

All in all, Chris, Kyle and Cole ate until they were sick and enjoyed every minute of it, sitting with Alix, Sean and Rose, and coming to know what seemed to be pretty nice neighbors. Kyle and Sean, in particular, seemed to hit it off, which was both a thrill and a relief to Alix. To make friends the first day in their new home was more than she could have hoped for.

When Cord came home early the next morning, it was to a quiet house, leftover chicken and dumplings, and a big slab of peach cobbler. There was also a business card tucked into the bag with Alix's cell phone number on it. Cord ate the dumplings as he inspected the card, over and over again, until he had memorized the cell number. He was just finishing up the last of the cobbler when his phone rang. Seeing the number, he grinned as he answered it.

"Are you even out of bed yet?" he asked.

On the other end of the line, the man snorted. "Of course I'm out of bed," he said. "I didn't even sleep last night. I've been on a plane and you know I can't sleep on a plane."

Cord chuckled. "I remember coming home from Cancun with you a very long time ago and you slept the entire way."

"I'd been drunk for a week, Cord," the man said. "Of course I'm going to sleep. But that's not usual with me."

Cord laughed. "I know," he said. "I'm just giving you crap. So what has you calling me at the break of dawn in California?"

"You on duty?"

"Not anymore," Cord said. "We had a hell of a storm last night and I'm heading home, but I've got a few minutes. What's up, Beck?"

Lt. Commander Beck Seavington was a Navy SEAL. The Teams, they called them, and they didn't come any better or braver than Beck. But the man seemed a little ill at ease on the other end of the line, which peaked Cord's attention. The Beck he knew wasn't the type to be ill at ease.

"I need some advice, I think," Beck finally said. "I met somebody."

There was a pause. "Met somebody?" Cord said. "Who?"

"A woman."

"Oh," Cord said as he realized what Beck meant. He further realized why the man had seemed ill at ease. "Hey, good for you. I'm happy for you. How long has this been going on?"

"Not long," Beck said. "I met her a few days before I was deployed for about a week. That's what I'm coming back from and I need some advice."

"About what?"

On the other end of the line, Beck took a deep breath. "Okay, here it is," he said. "We hadn't even known each other twenty-four hours when we slept together. It was totally spontaneous, but we did. I swear, Cord, I've never been so attracted to a woman in my life. Her name is Blakesley and she's just... she's just everything. She's beautiful and sexy and smart. She's way too good for me. Since I went away right after we slept together, I need to know... how should I handle seeing her again? Should I assume we'll pick up where we left off? What if she's had time to think about it and doesn't want to see me again? What if she thinks the whole thing was a big mistake?"

"Hold it right there," Cord said. "Beck, you need to stop. Don't you say those things to her or she'll think you're an emotionally unstable."

"Christ, I know," Beck said, running a hand over his face. "I'd like to say it's my exhaustion talking, but it's not."

"No, it's not, because your bitchy ex-wife did everything she could to damage your confidence."

"I know," Beck said quietly. "I already had a failure with Blakesley once and she was willing to overlook it. But I don't think she would a second time."

"Then don't," Cord said firmly. "Look, little bro – ask her straight up if she still feels the same way she did a week ago. If she says yes, you're fine. If she says no, then at least you know. That's better than not knowing. But face it with the same bravery you would face a thousand Afghan rebels with. Would you get all needy and uncertain in a combat situation?"

"No."

"Then don't do it with her. She doesn't deserve that and neither do you. Okay?"

"Okay," Beck said, sounding relieved. "Thanks, Cord. I knew I could count on you."

Cord snorted. "Always," he said. "I'll always be here to keep you from making an ass out of yourself."

"God knows, you've done that enough."

"You owe me."

"I do," Beck said. "I'll name a grandkid after you or something."

"Ha!" Cord said. "Why not your firstborn with Blakesley?"

"I'll think about it," Beck said, though he didn't mean it. "Hey, speaking of kids, how are the boys doing?"

"Great," Cord said. "Chris and Kyle have football practice

these days and Cole is getting along. And I've got a new neighbor who might turn out to be my Blakesley."

"Really?" Beck was interested. "Tell me about her."

"Not much to tell right now," Cord said. "I just met her. She's a physician with the emergency department over at North Shore. She just moved in with her two kids."

"Divorced?"

"Divorced and gorgeous."

"Then I wish you all the luck," Beck said. "If I can ever give you some advice, call me."

Cord snorted again. "Relationship advice from you?" he said. "Don't make me laugh. But I appreciate the offer."

Beck couldn't resist. "I know how you are," he said. "You charge in and take control, even in a relationship."

Cord couldn't deny it. "I've been known to, yes."

"Just take this one slow and easy. You've got your kids and they don't need women coming in and out of their lives."

"Don't I know it," Cord said. "They've never reacted well to anyone I'm dating, at least Cole hasn't, but we'll see. At some point, they have to realize their Dad needs to be happy, too.

"Don't we all."

"Sounds like you're about to be."

"Sounds like you are, too."

"Let's hope so."

Beck thanked Cord and hung up, leaving Cord thinking about Beck and his potential lady-love, which inevitably turned to thoughts of Alix. Cord found himself looking at the business card that she'd left him with the breakfast.

Just take this one slow and easy.

Honestly, given the attraction he was feeling towards her, he wasn't sure he could.

He hoped it didn't backfire on him.

FOUR

THE RAINSTORM from the previous night had blown away, leaving a bright blue morning in its wake. As Alix sat on the steps of her front porch, reading the estimate from the painter, she didn't feel much like celebrating the beautiful day. In fact, she felt like turning right around and heading back for California. She'd had two painters come out that morning to give her estimates and both of them had told her the walls and plaster work needed extensive repairing before they could paint. One of them even recommended a contractor. So she sat on the stoop with the cell phone in one hand and the contractor's card in the other for several long minutes, debating, before finally getting up the nerve to call him.

The contractor was more than happy to come out and take a look at the house. He'd restored a few historic homes in the area and apparently knew what he was doing, which made Alix feel better and worse. Better because he seemed very competent and worse because the house was in for a complete overhaul. Although she knew she should have gotten more estimates, she just wanted to get it over with so she engaged the contractor by the time lunch rolled around. He agreed to send a few men over in the morning to get the job started and, with that, she was on her way to spending copious amounts of money on her new home.

Rose, who had been playing contentedly on the porch under her mother's watchful eye all morning, grew crabby by lunchtime so Alix took the girl inside and fed her peanut butter and jelly sandwiches. As she worked in the kitchen, she couldn't help but think about Cord and how he'd been such a fixture in the kitchen yesterday. As Rosie happily finished her grapes and peanut butter, Alix wandered over to the window on the east side of the kitchen that faced out over the grassy, wooded vale. She could just see the roofline of Cord's house.

She found herself thinking of his old-fashioned sense of chivalry, something she found very sweet and refreshing. She hadn't met many men that filled that bill and it endeared her to Cord all the more. He was attentive without going overboard, concerned without being nosy. True, he came on strong at first, but she kind of liked a man who took charge. Initial wariness had faded. She was hoping to see more of him.

Alix leaned against the wall, gazing from the window, thinking of her life to this point. It was just a sense of reflection, in a new house starting a new life far from her home state. She didn't have any huge emotional baggage. She didn't come from an abusive marriage. If anything, she was the one who had outgrown Pat and just needed to get away from him. But the one thing in her life that she had been lacking, since she could recall, was happiness. True, deep and abiding happiness. She'd never been in love with a man who made her toes curl or her heart race and she very much wanted that. But at this point in her life, she'd pretty much given up ever finding that kind of consuming love. At least she had until yesterday.

But she wasn't one to give in to unrealistic expectations, so she moved away from the window to wipe off her daughter's peanut butter hands and take the little girl upstairs for her nap. Once Rose was down, she went back to the porch to lament the ginormous contractor bill she would soon be facing.

With a decorator magazine in hand that she had picked up at the supermarket, she began to walk around the house, comparing it to pictures of painted houses in the magazine. At some point, Sean came outside, bored, and walked around with her, wanting to know if they could build a dirt track for his mountain bike on the side of the house. Alix wasn't thrilled with that idea but Sean seemed to think it was negotiable. As mother and son gently argued, an older model blue Chevy pickup pulled up in the driveway.

Both Alix and Sean turned to see the truck pull up and park. Curious, they watched a man in jeans climb out of the passenger door and realized it was Cord. Alix tried to keep the smile off her face, holding the open magazine against her chest and watching as four men climbed out. Cord immediately caught sight of her and waved. She waved back.

"Hey there," Cord said as he made his way towards her with his boys in tow. "Is the power back on for you?"

Alix was so happy to see him that it was a struggle not to grin like an idiot. "Yes, finally," she said, sounding rather breathless. "But not until about nine o'clock this morning. I'm afraid I lost a lot of the refrigerated food I bought yesterday at the store."

Cord came to stand next to her and he wasn't holding back his smile like she was. He was grinning full-on at her.

"That's too bad," he said. "Speaking of refrigerated stuff, thanks for the care package. That was the best chicken and dumplings I've ever had."

Alix couldn't help the flattered grin now. "You're welcome," she said. "Glad you liked it."

"I did." He couldn't take his eyes off her and just ended up staring at her a moment before realizing he should probably say something. "Hey, we stopped by because the boys are going to town to see a movie and they wanted to know if Sean wanted to go along."

Alix turned to her son, who lit up like a kid at Christmas. "Cool," he exclaimed. "What are we seeing?"

Kyle piped up. "Mechano-Monsters 3D."

Sean was thrilled. "Excellent!"

Alix grinned at her son, so very happy that he'd found someone to hang out with. "Go get your jacket," she told him, watching him bolt off with Kyle behind him. "And get my wallet!"

The last sentence was shouted to him as the boys raced into the house and slammed the door. Then she turned to smile at Cord, who hadn't taken his eyes off her since he had climbed out of that truck. She smiled up at him.

"Was work crazy last night?" she asked.

He nodded with a sigh. "Crazy enough," he said. "We had a lot of medical aide situations for some reason. That always seems to happen during storms; power goes out, the sky opens up, and people freak out."

She nodded in agreement. "I totally get that," she said. "Or a full moon. The emergency rooms fill up."

Cord was glued to her like there was no one else in the world around them, including his other two boys, who were beginning to suspect their dad thought the new neighbor was something pretty special simply by the way he was looking at her. Chris elbowed Cole, who seemed confused by it all.

"I didn't ask you when you start your new job." Cord was oblivious to his boys' expressions. "The hospital was very busy last night."

"On Friday," she told him. "I've got three days to finish unpacking and get things in-hand. Right now, my biggest worry is finding daycare for Rose when school starts. For now, Sean can watch her while I'm at work but when school starts for him, I'll need to find somebody."

"A babysitter?"

"I'd like a live-in if I can find a good one. If you know of anybody, let me know."

"I'll keep that in mind."

They watched the boys come racing back out of the house. Sean ran for his mother, holding out her wallet, which Alix took from him and dug around until she found a twenty dollar bill. She handed it over to him.

"Don't spend it all in one place," she said.

Sean was already heading for the truck. "Thanks, Mom."

"Be careful!"

Sean acknowledged her with a wave as all four boys climbed back into the dark blue truck and Chris very carefully pulled back down the driveway. Cord waved at them as they drove off, turning to Alix to see an oddly wistful expression on her face. She was still watching the truck drive away.

"Chris is a good driver," he assured her, thinking she was worried about a truck full of teenagers. "I wouldn't let the others ride with him if he wasn't."

She tore her eyes away from the fading truck and looked at him. "No worries," she said. "I trust your judgment. Plus, Chris didn't seem like the crazy type."

"You can tell?"

He was joking with her and she gave him a very knowing, very flirtatious expression. "I can tell many things, my friend. Many things."

He cocked an eyebrow. "Is that right? What can you tell about me?"

She broke down into a grin. "I'm not sure yet." She looked away coyly. "But I'm sure it's all good."

He was encouraged. "Really?" he said. "Good enough that you'll let me take you out to lunch?"

She laughed softly. "I'd love to, but Rosie is asleep upstairs. I can't leave her."

He looked up at the house as if he'd completely forgotten about the four year old. "How about if I bring us something back? You said yourself that you lost a lot of food when the power went out. I'll go get us some lunch and bring it back."

Her gray eyes glimmered at him, delighted that he had taken the next step to basically ask her out. It was difficult to keep her excitement at bay.

"I'd love it," she said softly.

His grin returned. "You would?"

"Yes."

"Enough to maybe let me take you out to dinner sometime, too?"

"Sure."

He didn't have much more to say to that. He'd asked the question and she'd answered without hesitation. As they gazed at each other, very sweetly, the moment became warmly awkward and he snorted nervously, watching her giggle. His heart was so light and, at the moment, so unguarded that he couldn't stop himself.

"I've wanted to ask you out since nearly the moment we met," he broke down and admitted it. "I thought I was being pretty clever about the way I pretended I wasn't interested in you."

He was teasing her openly and she succumbed to it. "Clever my foot," she giggled. "You did everything but move in with us."

He laughed, enjoying her sense of humor. "Don't discount that. I still might try."

Alix gazed up at him, thinking she really wouldn't mind if he did but she didn't say anything. All she knew was that she was happier than she had been in ages. In fact, she couldn't ever remember feeling so giddy about someone in her life. The big, blond, handsome fire captain had her heart racing.

"Well," she said, "Let's get to know each other a little first before we decide to get married only two days after meeting."

"We have to wait that long?" he joked.

She laughed again. "I'm old-fashioned that way."

His eyes were twinkling as he looked at her, feeling the resurgence of his desire to kiss her. This time, there were no kids around and nothing to stop him. Stopping short of pulling her into his arms and planting a big one on her mouth, he grasped her hand and brought it gently to his lips. Kissing the flesh softly, he winked at her.

"I'll be back," he said.

Alix watched him walk back down the driveway, her heart racing a mile a minute. She'd never had that reaction to anyone, ever. In fact, she realized that she was having difficulty breathing and it made her feel a little lightheaded. With a grin, she took a deep breath and turned for the house, but not before she turned around at least twice to watch him as he made his way down the road and disappeared in the trees.

As Alix went back in the house, she couldn't help the little victory dance she did just inside the kitchen door. Maybe she *was* destined to have that attraction that most people only dream about.

───────

When Cord returned a short time later with a picnic lunch he'd purchased at the local gourmet grocery, the kitchen door was open. He called out quietly to Alix, knowing the little girl was sleeping, when she suddenly stuck her head into the kitchen from the direction of the front entry. As she raced over to the door, she motioned him inside quickly.

"Hurry up," she hissed as she grabbed his hand. "I need you to come with me."

That was the best offer Cord had had in years, so he quickly set the bags down on the kitchen counter and gladly went with her. They ended up holding hands as she pulled him from the kitchen and into the entry, where it was still relatively dark and dank. In fact, the entire house was dark and dank. It had an odd, eerie feel.

Alix pulled him halfway up the front stairs and then froze. He plowed into the back of her, grabbing on to her so she wouldn't fall over. Once he was sure she wasn't going to topple, he thought it would probably be best if he took his hands off her, but she put an arm around his shoulders, standing a couple of stairs above him, and held him fast. Looking at her, he could see that she was gazing up to the upper floor, staring. His curiosity grew.

"What's going on?" he whispered.

She shushed him, going so far as to put her warm fingers over his lips. Cord was in such a beautifully intimate position with her that it was difficult for him to control himself. He could smell her, that sweet clean smell, and he found himself dipping his head lower so his nose was nearly in her neck. All of that feminine warmth had his heart racing and he wrapped his big arms around her to pull her closer. But she didn't seem to notice.

"There it is again," she hissed. "Did you hear that?"

He looked at her. He hadn't heard a goddamn thing other than his heart beating in his ears. He struggled to pull out of the wild sense of attraction that was overwhelming him.

"Hear what?"

Alix was intently focused on something else. She didn't

seem to realize his face was nearly in her neck. Suddenly, her eyes widened and she pointed to the second floor.

"I hear it again," she whispered. "Did you hear that?"

In fact, he had heard something, so he forced himself to cool, looking to the upper floor when what he really wanted to do was kiss the woman and drown himself doing it. The noise came again and he cocked his head.

"It sounds like whispering," he said. "Is your daughter awake?"

Alix looked at him, a mixture of apprehension and curiosity in her expression. "She's asleep," she murmured. "I've been hearing this whispering for the past fifteen minutes. I thought it was Rose but when I went to check on her, she was asleep. What in the hell *is* that?"

He shook his head, seemingly unconcerned. "I have no idea," he muttered. "Did you check all of the rooms?"

She nodded firmly. "All of them. There's no one upstairs."

"What about the windows? Are they open? It could be a neighbor's television volume turned up too high."

She blinked thoughtfully. "Maybe," she said. "I hadn't thought of that. It just sounds so close, like it's inside the house."

He stood up and pulled her up with him. "I'm sure it's just someone's television up too high," he said. "Come on downstairs. I brought...."

They were interrupted by Rose's voice. She sounded as if she was arguing with someone, telling them to give back her kitty. There was a big thump and then Rose started howling. Alix and Cord bolted up the stairs and into Rose's room.

The little girl was sitting on the floor, weeping angrily. Alix swooped down and picked the child up, comforting her.

"What happened?" she asked. "Did you fall out of bed?"

Rose was angry and afraid. "The sad girl, she took my kitty and I wouldn't let go, so she pulled me on the floor."

As Alix soothed her daughter, Cord inspected the room just to make sure there wasn't some vagrant kid hiding out in the closet. There wasn't anything suspicious, but he noticed that there was a small door at the back of Rose's closet. He stepped inside and opened the door, seeing a narrow stairway leading up to the attic. He peered up into the dusty heights of the attic but not wanting to make his way up there, he closed the door and went back out into the bedroom.

He made his way over to the bed where Alix was sitting with Rose on her lap. When the pair looked up at him, he smiled.

"Nothing in the closet," he said. "The room's clear. Why don't we go downstairs and eat some lunch?"

Alix nodded and stood up with Rose still in her arms. She carried the four-year-old downstairs as Cord followed and the three of them proceeded to sit at the kitchen table and eat the delicious spread that Cord had brought. There were turkey sandwiches, potato salad, pickles, olives, and cookies, which Rose got a hold of and chomped into before her mother could stop her.

Cord sat across the table and grinned at the little girl who found the chocolate chip cookies far more interesting than the sandwiches. She was truly an adorable little thing with silky blond hair and big gray eyes. As lunch progressed and Rose came alive, he came to see a very smart and giggly little girl. He thought she was charming, and her mother... well, charming wasn't the word he had in mind for her. Divine was more like it. He was officially smitten.

Lunch was a sweetly casual setting on a gentle afternoon day as Cord and Alix discussed a variety of subjects. They both liked football and Cord talked about his days as an NFL lineman straight out of college until he severed his ACL and his career was finished. He'd played three years for the New

England Patriots and had been, some sportswriters called him, one of the best linemen in the league. Chris and Kyle were following in his footsteps, which explained why both boys were so big and muscular. Cole seemed to be the more quiet, artsy type, a more cerebral brother to balance out all of the sportsmen. Alix listened to stories about brotherly pranks where Cole's intelligence would win out over brute strength every time. It was touching and hysterical.

Even after lunch was finished, they sat at the table and continued talking as Rose climbed off her chair and wandered away. Alix was listening to a story on Cord's job about a particularly hairy apartment fire and she countered with some of the things she had seen during her career at Harbor/UCLA Medical Center in Los Angeles. At one point, it became a contest of who had seen the most disgusting thing and Cord seemed to have the edge. Picking flattened people off the freeway won out over Alix's tale of a man impaled in the head by a garden implement, so they ended up laughing as the stories turned horror-movie graphic.

At some point during the conversation, Alix got up to see where Rose had gone and found her daughter playing in the living room with the television on. When she returned to Cord, she noticed that he had moved his chair much closer to hers. Fighting off a grin, she resumed her seat. He was bumped right up against her.

"I can't help but notice either this table has gotten smaller or you've moved your chair," she commented.

He looked completely innocent. "It's me," he said. "My size makes everything look smaller. I've been sitting right in this spot the whole time."

She bit her lip to keep from smiling. "I'm surprised I didn't notice before."

"Me, too. How much more obvious can I be?"

Her smile broke through. "Obvious about what?"

With a grin, he reached out and took her hand, bringing it to his lips for a gentle kiss. Alix watched him, smile quickly fading, as a tremor of lust ripped through her. It was the single most sensuous kiss she'd ever had and she watched his mouth as he kissed her fingers again. By this time, her heart was pounding and her smile was completely gone.

"Oh, God," she breathed. "When you do that...."

He didn't even let her finish the sentence before he was leaning over, slanting his lips over hers. He took her comment as an invitation. It was a sweet, very timid kiss at first, as if just testing the waters, but somewhere in the first few moments she gasped and he lost his control, pulling her against him.

The sweet and timid kiss turned hot and lusty in an instant; it wasn't slobbery or gross, but as delicious and tender as either one of them could have possibly imagined. Alix wrapped her arms around his big neck, holding him close as he devoured her mouth.

His hands ended up in her hair and he inadvertently shoved her back against the kitchen wall, positively consumed with her. She was unbelievably sweet and soft, smelling like heaven, and his male senses soaked it up like a sponge. He'd never had a kiss like this in his life, not ever.

But before he could lose his control completely, they could hear Rose in the living room and he abruptly let her go, sitting back in his chair and just staring at her. Her lips were swollen and red, and when she inadvertently licked them, he snapped again and descended on her, kissing her so forcefully that he ended up driving her teeth into her lip. He could taste the blood. But Rose's voice reached their ears yet again and he forced himself away from her again, fearful that a four-year-old would see them in a clutch.

Alix sat plastered back against the wall, breathing as if she had just sprinted a mile. She couldn't catch her breath. She stared at Cord with big eyes, a bit dazed, when he suddenly bolted out of his chair and ended up against the counter over by the sink. As Rose chatted out in the living room, presumably talking to her dolls, Cord stood against the sink with a hand over his mouth.

"Wow," he finally breathed. "That was... was...."

"Really good," Alix finished for him. Then she just grinned.

Cord's hand was over his mouth still, but he ended up grinning in return. "Do you really think so?"

"Uh... yes."

"Want to try it again sometime?"

"Anytime."

His eyes widened. "Really?"

She just nodded. Then she cocked her head, quirky. "You don't greet all the new neighbors this way, do you?"

He broke down laughing. "No, never."

"Be honest," she pushed, teasing. "Women? Young or old? Maybe even men if they're hot enough?"

His laughter grew. "Never in my life, Alix." He held up his hand as if swearing, his eyes warm on her. "Only you. And I'm trying to decide how I feel about it."

Her smile faded, thinking he wasn't so fired up about that kiss like she was. "What do you mean?"

He could see she was bordering on insult. "Nothing bad, honey, I promise," his voice grew softer and he came away from the counter. "I just... I swear, I'm not a hound and I don't make it my goal in life to get into women's pants. My ex-wife and I have been divorced for twelve years and I've had a couple of girlfriends during that time, but nothing too serious. I've just never met the right woman, someone I clicked with on such a deep level. I... well, I'm not very eloquent, but I want you to know that I have nothing but the greatest respect and admiration for you. I'd never do anything to jeopardize and cheapen that. I'm just coming to know you and even if you weren't my neighbor, I'd think you were just about the most amazing woman I've ever met. Being neighbors has nothing to do with it."

She was smiling up at him by the time he finished. "I believe you," she said. "I was just teasing you."

He nodded, sitting down next to her again and putting a hand on her knee. "Look," he said, seriously. "We haven't even known each other two full days yet, but already I can tell you that I am very deeply attracted to you. I knew it from the first. So whatever direction this takes us... wow, that's getting a little ahead of things, isn't it? I don't mean to intimate that we're going anywhere, but...."

Alix reached out and put her fingers over his lips to silence him. "I kind of like you, too," she whispered. "I'm not married, I don't have a boyfriend nor am I particularly looking for one, but I'm willing to explore the possibilities with you. You seem like Mr. Perfect and I'm kind of taken aback by you."

His eyes were riveted to her. "I'm not perfect by any means," he kissed her fingers. "I snore when I sleep, I don't do laundry as much as I should, I work too much, and I tend to overanalyze things. And those are my good qualities."

She laughed as he took her gently by the wrists and pulled her towards him. "I'm looking forward to finding all that out for myself."

"Are you really? You're not just saying that?"

She shook her head. "I don't say anything I don't mean. I realize we haven't known each other all that long, but I think when you're attracted to someone, you don't need days or weeks to figure it out. I think you just know it."

"So you'll let me take you out to dinner sometime?"

"The sooner, the better."

He grinned at her, moving over to kiss her again just as the sound of an engine pulled up the driveway. Rose began hooting that there was a truck in the driveway so Cord kissed her soundly on the cheek and stood up, pulling her to her feet.

"The boys are back," he said, still holding her hand as he peered out the kitchen door and to the driveway.

Alix let him hold her hand, relishing the feel of romantic human contact. She hadn't felt that in a long time.

"Do we keep this on the down-low from them?" she asked quietly.

He turned to look at her. "I'll do whatever you're comfortable with."

She shrugged. "I'm kind of a discreet character."

"Then I am, too."

They smiled at each other and he kissed her hand one last time before letting it go. The boys were climbing out of the truck and lumbering up the driveway, laughing and talking about things. Alix couldn't even hear what they were talking about, but she could hear Sean's voice and he sounded happy. She loved that. All four of the teenagers came in through the kitchen door, the life and energy filling up the house. From her son's excited chatter, Alix gathered that he had loved the movie and was having a good time with his new friends.

She couldn't ask for better, for any of them.

FIVE

FRIDAY CAME AROUND ALL TOO SOON.

Alix started her shift at North Shore Medical Center at two in the afternoon, working a swing shift that would see her off at midnight. She had officially been hired by the group of surgeons who worked for the hospital, a medical group specialty that was its own corporation which was fairly normal in the larger hospitals. There were four men in the group and she was now the fifth surgeon, a junior partner at the moment because she was a new hire. She had met all of the doctors at some point and the day she started, the head of the group, Dr. Levenger, was there to indoctrinate her.

She was anxious to get to work, to get into the swing of things, but she found herself struggling to keep her mind on learning her new routine because her thoughts kept drifting to Cord. Since she'd met the man, the subsequent days could only be described as magical.

Cord was in the middle of a work rotation so he would work twenty-four hours on and twenty-four hours off, so she'd really only seen him one day since that pivotal afternoon in her kitchen. However, he'd spent the entire day with her, following her around while she supervised the construction workers and then taking her and Rose into town to get burgers while the boys went off and did their own thing. Sean was assimilating into the group of Trevor boys without issue and they seemed to all get along.

Rose, however, was another story. She'd never spent an inordinate amount of time with her father and was, therefore, very attached to her mother, which made her very shy around men in general other than her brother. Cord took every opportunity to talk to her, but she was very shy and standoffish, and he didn't push. Still, Rose was intrigued with the big, blond man, Alix could tell. Like mother, like daughter.

He never had the opportunity to take her out to dinner, however. Work schedules gotten in the way. But when she left for work on Friday, there had been a card and a bouquet of supermarket flowers on her windshield to wish her luck. It had been one of the sweetest things Alix had ever experienced. The flowers were still in her car. She had smelled them all the way to work.

So this Friday afternoon was more just getting acquainted with the hospital, the layout, the personnel and the policies, but Alix was a sharp learner and took to it easily. By late afternoon, there were two surgical consults, which Dr. Kelly let her perform, and he was quite impressed with the results. Alix scrubbed up for surgery by dinnertime and performed a laparoscopic procedure on a car accident victim, a flawless procedure that had Dr. Kelly thoroughly awed with her talent.

Alix was feeling pretty good with her first day so far, but it began to grow hairy during the evening. After a twenty minute dinner break, the emergency room seemed to fill up with all kinds of cases and Alix was called in to consult on two appendicitis patients, a ruptured bladder, and a bad car accident that had four victims headed for intensive care. Alix and Dr. Kelly split up to assess the surgical cases and by nine o'clock, Alix was scrubbing up for a lacerated liver. The teenage girl was only fifteen and crying about the scar she would have, but Alix promised she would only have a couple of tiny scars and nothing more. Alix was able to keep her promise.

The emergency room was a wild ride by eleven at night and Alix suspected she wouldn't be getting off work at midnight. She managed to text Sean to let him know, heading back into the emergency room to help the overburdened staff. Nearing midnight, she had her head down suturing up a man who had stripped off most of the flesh of his index finger trying to do some home plumbing when one of the nurses came for her.

"Dr. Hendry," the young woman said, catching her attention. "You're needed in Exam One."

Alix had her bifocals on, looking up from the sutures to acknowledge the nurse, before turning to the Physician's Assistant standing next to her and asking the man to finish up the sutures. Stripping off her gloves and washing her hands, she emerged into the main corridor of the emergency room only to see several firefighters standing around further down the hall, mingling with medical personnel.

She didn't give them much notice as she headed for the examining room at the end of the corridor, but the closer she drew, the more she could see that a couple of the guys had bloody cuts on their heads or bloodied hands. But she reached the exam room before she could give their injuries further thought, entering the room to find a firefighter on a gurney, hooked up to IV drips and monitors. More than that, Cord was standing beside the man, his face registering surprise and pleasure when he realized Alix was making an appearance.

Alix registered surprise and pleasure as well, quickly doused when she saw that Cord had a bloody cut above his right eye and the beginnings of a huge bruise on his right cheek. All but ignoring the man on the gurney, she went straight to Cord.

"Hi," she said with concern. "What happened to you?"

He was so glad to see her that it was all he could do not to take her in his arms and kiss her. He wanted to so badly that his hands started to tremble.

"I'm okay," he assured her gently. "We were rolling on a call and got broadsided by a guy in a pickup truck who just wasn't paying attention."

"That's awful." She peered up at the cut on his forehead. "Sit down so I can take a look at that, okay?"

Cord did as he was told; his eyes riveted to her as she squeezed around him and took a look at the computer monitor on the counter that held the patient's chart information. After a few moments of reading the notes, she turned to the firefighter on the gurney.

"Hi," she smiled at the man as she peeled back his uniform shirt. "I'm Dr. Hendry. How are you feeling right now? Can you breathe okay?"

The firefighter, a young Hispanic man with a painful expression, nodded. "Better now," he said. "I think I cracked some ribs."

A couple of nurses entered the room, one of them helping Alix pull back the man's undershirt which someone had cut right down the middle. Alix put her hands on the man's belly, very gently.

"I think you did more than that," she said. "Tell me where it hurts, please."

He did. As Alix gently prodded, Cord watched from behind, so enamored by the woman that he couldn't focus on anything else. The way she moved, the way she spoke, was mesmerizing. She was sweet, gentle, and knowledgeable. Add that to her gorgeous looks and it was a wonder she didn't have a line of men following her around day and night.

Finally, she finished examining the man and determined that a broken rib had punctured a lung. As he was wheeled out to x-ray, Alix turned back to Cord.

"All right, now," she said as she washed her hands and dried them off, pulling on another pair of surgical gloves. "Let's take a look at you."

He was still sitting on the stool and she got up right next to him, her body against his as she examined the cut above his eye. Cord had to sit on his hands to keep from grabbing her. The last time she was this close, he had kissed her like he had never kissed a woman in his life. Having her so close and not being able to touch her was like torture.

"Will I live, Doctor?" he asked.

She grinned, inspecting the cut. "I think so," she said. "I don't think you need any stitches. Just let me clean it up and you'll be as good as new."

"In your hands, I'm sure I couldn't be anything else."

She stopped in her professional duties, smiling at him. The warmth was there, the flirtatious twinkle in her eye, and he smiled in return.

"You're sweet," she said. "And thank you for the flowers. I love them."

"You're welcome," his voice was quiet. "I just wanted you to know I was thinking about you."

"I do," she nodded, putting a hand to his cheek, just as quickly taking it away. "Are you sure you're okay?"

"Fine."

"No headaches or dizziness?"

He shook his head, slowly and confidently. "If I said I was badly hurt, would you spend all night making me better?"

She grinned broadly. "All night," she whispered.

His grin broadened in response to hers. "I'm off tomorrow morning," he murmured. "I'll probably need to sleep a few hours, but I'd like to take you out to dinner tomorrow night if you're not working."

Her heart sank. "I am."

"Then I'll come to the hospital when it's your dinner break and we can eat together in the cafeteria."

She brightened. "You'd do that?"

His expression turned serious. "For you, I'd do anything. I... I've missed you. I've missed talking to you."

She touched his cheek again, watching him kiss her palm right on the latex glove. It was a sweet, tender moment, but she quickly looked around to see if anyone was watching, moving away from him and pulling out a bandage kit. By the time she returned, he was gazing up at her with a warm and rather amorous expression, and she gave him a demure but flirtatious smile.

"I've missed you, too," she whispered. "But let's keep that stuff out of the workplace, okay? I just got this job and I don't want them to think I'm affectionate with every good-looking firefighter that comes through the door."

He laughed. "Fair enough," he said, watching her face as she drew close to him and began to clean up the cut. "How has your first day been so far?"

She shrugged as she swabbed the wound. "Pretty good," she said. "I've already been in surgery twice, three times when I operate on your buddy in about a half hour. It's been surprisingly busy."

"Feeling good about it?"

"Yes, very good."

"Glad to hear it."

The conversation died, although it wasn't uncomfortable in the least. In the big exam room smelling of alcohol and sterilized equipment, Alix proceeded to put three butterfly bandages across his cut and carefully taped a small bandage over it. Meanwhile, Cord let his hands wander underneath her lab coat to her thighs, drifting up the back of her legs, stroking her discreetly, until she finally snorted.

"If you don't stop that, I'm going to be sitting in your lap doing very naughty things and get myself fired." She looked him in the eye sternly. "Keep your hands to yourself."

He bit his lip to keep from grinning, looking properly contrite. "I'm sorry. I will."

"Good."

A pause. "Do I really have to?"

She was trying not to giggle. "In this building, you do. I'm sorry, but you do, because neither one of us can guarantee our composure when we come into contact with each other. I don't want to put on a display like that, at least... not in public."

"But you don't have a problem with it in private?"

She sighed heavily, giving him an exasperated expression. But it was short-lived; looking around, she made sure there was no one in close proximity before planting a very big, very juicy kiss on his lips. Startled, but in a good way, Cord lifted his hands to grasp her head and kiss her deeply but she pushed him away.

"You're good to go, Captain Trevor," she stood a few feet back, out of his arm range. "I'll take a look at that cut tomorrow and change the bandages, but for tonight, just try not to get it wet. In fact, it's my recommendation that you just go home and go to bed."

Cord was rather breathless at the kiss, smiling at her as he rose from the stool. "Thank you, Dr. Hendry," he said. "I appreciate your professional care, especially for Mike."

"Mike?"

"The firefighter on the gurney."

"Oh, right." She pulled the gloves off and tossed them,

washing her hands again and grabbing paper towels. "So your engine is wrecked?'

He nodded. "They're sending a back-up rig to pick us up right now. I'm going to be doing paperwork the rest of the night."

She threw the paper towels away and headed out of the exam room. "Well, take it easy with that bump. If you start feeling dizzy or nauseous, call me or come back over here right away. Okay?"

He smiled at her, his eyes alight with the magic he was feeling for her. "Okay."

She returned his smile, trying not to be too obvious that it was beyond a normal smile, as Cord's men began gathering around him.

"You okay, Cap'n?" a young firefighter asked.

Cord nodded. "Fine," he told them. "Just a bump. Guys, I want you to meet Dr. Hendry. She's new here, so we'll see her around on occasion."

Four sets of eyes turned to Alix and she smiled at the group, lifting a hand. "Hi."

They responded with friendly interest except for one man, an older guy with a balding head and a radio in his hand. He zeroed in on her right away with intense blue eyes.

"Dr. Hendry," he greeted. "Where did you come from?"

The way he said it was rather seductive and Alix instinctively took a step back from him. She could handle the flirts with the best of them, but her manner turned from warm friendly to cold professional in a flash. She wasn't going to give the guy any response that could be misconstrued.

"California," she said shortly, turning to Cord. "Remember what I told you; any dizziness or headaches and you get yourself back over here in a hurry."

He nodded, a smile playing on his lips. "Yes, ma'am."

With that, Alix turned away from the group and headed back down the hall. The men watched her go, especially Cord and the big bald guy. In fact, the bald guy turned to the group after she had left and lifted his eyebrows in a suggestive manner.

"I think I might have to spend more time at this hospital," he said.

The guys snickered; all except for Cord. His expression was hard as he gazed at the man. He knew Steve Cokes and had for years. The guy was always the one to sleep around with the fire-house groupies and then complain because he couldn't find a good woman. Normally, Cord couldn't have cared less, but Steve wasn't going to set his sights on Alix. No way in hell. Better deter it before it got started.

"Don't bother, Steve," he said, somewhat icily. "She's spoken for."

Steve grinned. "Did you already find that out? You work fast, Cord. That's not like you. I don't blame you, though. She's spectacular."

Cord was having a hard time fighting down a surge of jealousy. "She's also my neighbor," he said, trying not to sound hostile. "She's already got a boyfriend, so leave her alone."

Steve's eyebrows lifted. "Really? Well, that's too bad. Story of my life, though."

Thankfully, he left the subject alone and they ventured off on something else. As the firefighters from Station Four waited around for one of the back-up rigs to pick them up, Cord found his attention drawn to the bowels of the emergency room where he could see Alix moving back and forth between the rooms. A couple of times she caught his eye and gave him a brief smile or a discreet wave. He would do the same, drinking in every second that he was able to do something as simple as look at her.

He was in deep and sinking fast.

———

Alix hadn't gotten home until four in the morning. It had been an eventful night and at around eight in the morning, she could hear Rose screaming about something. Dead tired, she pulled herself up from bed and staggered out of her bedroom and across the hall to Rose's room, where she was, once again, crying about the sad girl who wanted her kitty. Alix wrapped her arms around her daughter and fell over into the little girl's bed, trying to snuggle with her and go back to sleep, but Rose wasn't interested in going back to sleep. She wanted to play.

Sean had heard his little sister and wandered into her bedroom, rubbing his eyes sleepily and seeing that his exhausted mother was trying to get some rest with Rose now jumping on the bed. Sean was a good kid, with a good head on his shoulders, so he rubbed his eyes again and went to pull Rose off the bed.

"Go back to bed, Mom," he told Alix. "I'll get Rose some breakfast and keep her quiet while you sleep."

Alix struggled out of the bed. "Thanks," she said sincerely. "Just give me a few hours. I'll be up by noon or so."

Sean had Rose in his arms. "I saw a park down the road," he told her. "Maybe I'll take her down there for a while."

"That would be lovely, honey, thank you." Alix patted her son on the arm. "Watch the weather, though. I think it's supposed to rain again."

"I will," he said, watching her drag herself back to her bedroom. "Hey? Can I have some money for a new video game?"

Alix grinned sleepily; although Sean was very thoughtful, taking Rose off her hands *and* taking her to the park on top of that was a little too generous, even for him. She should have suspected an ulterior motive. But she was so tired that she was willing to make the bargain.

"Sure," she said. "Do you want to go buy it when I get up?"

"Can I?"

"Keep Rose happy and quiet for the next three hours and I'll take you before I go to work."

Sean grinned happily, already scrambling to get Rose dressed so he could take her to the park. Alix went back to bed but she didn't go back to sleep until the kids stopped by her room to show her that Rose was properly bundled up against the cooler weather outside. Once she heard the door slam down below, she faded off to sleep quickly.

She didn't know what time it was when she heard a car door slam, jolting her from warm and blissful slumber. She almost went back to sleep but something made her roll over, lift her head to listen and, hearing nothing, climb out of bed. She peered out of the front window that overlooked the porch and front yard but didn't see anything, so she went to the window that overlooked the driveway and happened to catch Cord as he was walking back to his truck. Alix unlocked the window and opened it.

"Hey," she called.

Cord came to halt and turned around, already smiling as he looked to the second story window. "Hey," he said. "I wasn't sure if you were awake yet."

Smiling sleepily, Alix leaned against the windowsill. "I am now," she said. "What are you doing here?"

He shoved his hands into his jeans pockets. "I was leaving you something," he gestured towards the kitchen door, which was directly below the window. "I'm sorry if I woke you up."

Alix's grin broadened. "Stay right there."

She wasn't exactly dressed to receive company, but Alix didn't think about that as she took the stairs down to the ground floor. Clad in a snug camisole top that covered her up but clung rather indecently and a pair of yoga pants, she unlocked the kitchen door to find Cord standing there with a bouquet of yellow mums in his hand. She laughed as she unlocked the screen and opened it for him.

"I've never gotten flowers so much in my life," she said as he handed them to her. "Thank you very much; they're beautiful."

He was standing just inside the kitchen door, grinning at her as she went to put them in the same vase as the bouquet he had left her the day before. Cord couldn't help but notice the skin-tight pants and sexy tank top, and all of that exposed flesh. In fact, as he watched her heart-shaped butt as she put the flowers in the vase, his palms began to sweat just a little. The woman had an overwhelming effect on him.

"You're welcome," he said after a moment, as if he just remembered to say something. "What time did you get home last night?"

"About four." She finished with the flowers and turned to him. "And you?"

"Just an hour before you did."

"Did you finish up your paperwork?"

"I did," he nodded. "So how was your first day on the job, overall?"

She smiled. "It was good," she said. "I think I'm going to like it. Everyone seems very nice and very good at their jobs. Speaking of jobs, how's your head?"

He looked around for the nearest chair and planted himself. "I came to let my doctor take a look at it."

Still grinning, she washed her hands in the sink and made her way over to him as she dried them off. Putting the paper towel on the table, she leaned against him as she began to carefully remove the tape holding down the small bandage. With her petite height and his big size, she was only slightly taller than him as he sat in the chair. Cord found himself staring into her neck.

The bandage came off and she very gently inspected the wound. "It looks okay," she said. "Does it hurt?"

He shrugged. "A little," he was quickly becoming overwhelmed with her warmth and closeness. "It just feels like a bruise."

"Hmmm," she grunted, still eyeing it. "Let's leave the bandage off a little while and let some air get to it. I'll put another one on before you leave."

He watched her head over to the trash can and throw the old bandage away. He found himself thinking very dirty thoughts as he watched her shapely backside through those clingy pants.

"Thanks, doc," he replied. Then he peered into the doorway that led to the entry and the living room beyond. "It seems kind of quiet around here. Where are your children?"

Alix yawned, scratching her delightfully mussed hair as she meandered back in his direction. "Sean took Rose to the park so I could sleep in peace," she said. "What about you? What are the Trevor boys doing today?"

He remained in the chair, gazing up at her as she came close. "Chris and Kyle have football practice this morning over at the high school," he said. "I need to get over there in a few minutes."

"Why?"

"Because I'm the defensive line coach for the varsity football team. Looks like my experience in the NFL has paid off big-time."

He was joking as he said it, causing her to smile. He really had a good sense of humor. "So where's Cole?"

"He's hanging out with some friends over at the house," he said. "And as for me, after I finish at the high school, I have a date tonight."

She nodded. "I suppose you do. But what kind of woman

would make you take her to dinner at a hospital? What a weirdo."

He couldn't help himself; he reached out and gently grasped her by the waist, pulling her against him. His big arms went around her, enveloping her.

"I don't think she's weird," he murmured, putting his nose against the flesh of her shoulder and inhaling deeply. He was acquainting himself with her scent and the texture of her skin as he turned his head and laid his cheek against her cleavage. "I kind of like her a whole lot."

Alix wrapped her arms around his neck and head, hugging him tightly and relishing their first real embrace. It was warm and soft and gentle, something that made her heart flutter wildly. The man was as sexy as he could possibly be and she was besotted.

"I think she likes you, too," she whispered.

He didn't reply except to kiss the flesh of her cleavage, very softly and gently as he had his first taste of her. Alix closed her eyes to the sensual bliss of it, concentrating on every kiss and realizing her knees were going weak the more he progressed. Her arms tightened around his head and neck, her hands in his blond hair, as his kisses moved to her shoulders.

Cord pulled her tightly against him as his mouth moved over her collarbone. She was unbelievably sweet, softer than anything he'd ever known, and he could feel his temperature rising. When he got to her neck, she threw her head back and he very nearly lost his control when he realized she was sliding forward, straddling him as he sat on the chair. She ended up on his lap, her head hanging back as he devoured the flesh on her neck. When he reached her little earlobes and suckled delicately, she groaned and lifted her head, slanting her mouth hungrily over his.

The slow, sensual tasting escalated into hot, passionate

kisses. Cord's hands were in her hair, on her shoulders, stroking her back before moving down her thighs. She was hot and delicious, her soft body pressed against him, and he eventually cupped her face as his lips ravaged hers, his tongue invading her mouth and tasting her sweetness. There was no way he could control himself. His hands moved lower.

Alix groaned when a big hand closed over her left breast, wishing with all her heart he would stick his hand under her shirt. She wanted to feel his flesh against hers. When he didn't move fast enough, she yanked her camisole off, tossing it on the tabletop as he got the hint and clamped down on a tender nipple. He suckled hard and she cried out softly, never more aroused in her entire life.

"Upstairs," she gasped.

His mouth was still on her breast but he didn't question her command; he obeyed. Picking her up, her legs wrapped around his waist and his mouth still on her breasts, he somehow managed to make it up the back staircase, heading in the direction she was breathlessly pointing. Once inside her bedroom, stacked up with boxes with a messy bed against the wall, he slammed the door shut with a big foot and laid her down on the bed.

Clothes were coming off. Alix only had her pants to remove and they came off first before she helped Cord yank off his shirt. She fumbled with the fly of his jeans as he unhooked his belt, both of them so wrapped up in their lust that they couldn't see or think of anything else but their ultimate pleasure. He lowered his pants to his knees but Alix didn't wait; her mouth was on his throbbing, engorged manhood before he could get them off completely. Cord nearly lost his mind.

"Oh, my God," he breathed as her mouth worked him. "Honey, let me get these off first."

Alix's reply was to yank his arm, pulling him down on the

bed. As he fell on top of it, she jumped up and pulled off his shoes and eventually his pants, pulling so hard she nearly lost her balance. Then she was on him again, pleasuring him, and Cord was so aroused that he was dizzy with it. His hands were in her gorgeous hair as her mouth plunged down on him again and again.

But he could only take so much. He could feel himself building to a release so he stopped her and lifted her onto the bed, flipping her onto her back and covering her with his big, muscular body. Alix's arms went around his neck, her mouth seeking his, and he kissed her deeply as his hands explored her body, moving into intimate places.

Alix wasn't shy about parting her legs for him and he stroked her thighs, experiencing their silken texture before his fingers moved to the fluff of dark curls between her legs only to discover she was slick and wet. His mouth on hers, he plunged his fingers into her waiting body and she gasped, panting with the sensual intrusion.

Cord didn't make her wait. He mounted her and thrust deep, her hot and wet body closing in around him. It was the most amazing sexual sensation he had ever experienced and he thrust into her, listening to her grunts of pleasure, his hands loving her up as his body did the talking. He'd never known anything like it in his life, an uncontrollable attraction to a woman he felt like he couldn't live without. At the moment, he couldn't even breathe without her. In this brief, passionate and stolen moment, something changed for him. She was consuming him.

Alix's orgasm came with swift pants and a stiffening body, and he fingered a taut nipple, working her through the spasms, prolonging the pleasure as he suckled her breasts. As she struggled to catch her breath, another one washed over her and Cord moved his hands down to her buttocks, holding her pelvis against his as he thrust hard and deep. She began to weep and gasp at the same time, grinding her hips against him, until he felt her release yet again. Unable to hold it back any longer, Cord tried to withdraw but she wouldn't let him. When he finally climaxed, hard, she orgasmed one last time and wept with the pure pleasure of it.

Cord couldn't even think about the fact that he had just ejaculated inside of her, or the fact that they had had the hottest, most passionate, unprotected sex in the history of sex. All he could think about was her soft body beneath him, her hands in his hair and her lips against his neck. It was the most amazing sexual experience he'd ever had.

He shifted so his full body weight wasn't on top of her as their passion cooled, but he made no attempt to move off of her completely or even withdraw. He didn't want to; he wanted to stay like that, forever, feeling her in his arms. Gently, he began to kiss her head, her cheek, her neck and shoulder. There was a good deal of growing emotion in his touch, something he didn't yet have the words to express.

Alix was dozing, recovering from what was inarguably the best sex of her life. As she lay there, she could feel his big body around her, in her, and she savored the sensation. It had been such a long time. But more than that, she was savoring *him*. Cord Trevor had, since the beginning, been attentive to the point of being overbearing. He was smart, wonderful at conversation, and had an air of wisdom about him. He seemed to have a very level head, too, which she appreciated, like he was grounded in reality and was relatively normal. Where she came from, men like that were something of an anomaly. But here she was, having sex with the guy after having only known him a couple of days and wondering, in hindsight, if it hadn't been one big, fat mistake.

Yes, she was attracted to him. Uncontrollably. He had made

it very clear he wanted to go out with her and she wanted to go out with him. She had succumbed to his kisses, his charm, and his muscular body very easily. She'd spent a lot of years fighting off amorous men and in two days, Cord accomplished what a legion of guys in California couldn't have. He'd gotten her into bed. Maybe that had been his goal all along and she had been blinded to it.

Lost to her thoughts and insecurities that had dogged her for years, the squeaking hinges of a door opening jolted her. Alix's eyes flew open and she looked at Cord, who was gazing back at her with equal shock.

"Sean and Rose are back," she hissed.

Cord leapt off the bed and began to hunt down his clothes. "Christ," he muttered. "I'm so sorry, honey. I...."

She cut him off as she jumped onto her feet. "No apologies, please," she whispered, grabbing her yoga pants but realized she'd left her shirt downstairs. She ran for a box half-unpacked of clothing. "Don't ruin it."

He paused to look at her, pants up but unzipped. "Ruin what?"

She shook her head, pulling another camisole over her head. "I don't really know." She yanked on her yoga pants. "The moment, I guess. Don't spoil it with apologies unless you're really sorry about it."

He was rather stricken with her comment as he finished zipping up his pants and threw on his shirt. He opened his mouth to question her but was precluded by the sounds of children coming up the stairs. He grabbed his shoes as Alix gestured frantically to the attached bathroom.

"Hide in there," she hissed.

He bolted into the bathroom but didn't shut the door. Instead, he hid behind it as Alix jumped back into bed and covered up. Just as she was settling in, there was a soft knock on the door.

"Mom?"

It was Sean's voice. Alix tried not to sound breathless as she answered. "Come in," she said.

Sean opened the door with Rose standing next to him. "Hey," he said. "Mr. Trevor's truck is in the driveway. Is he here?"

Alix blinked, quickly thinking of a way out of this one. Sean was sixteen but he was in that limbo between being very astute about the relationships between men and women, and still in that youngster mindset of not really caring. She was praying he didn't smell sex in the air.

"Uh... I don't know," she said. "You... you didn't see him downstairs?"

Sean shook his head. "No."

Alix sat up in bed. "Maybe... you know, that furniture we moved out to the shed," she stumbled over her words. "That belonged to his family, I think. Did you look in the shed?"

Sean shook his head and Rose whined, wanting to take her coat off, so he was distracted as he took her back over to her bedroom. Since the master bedroom had two doors, one that faced the main staircase and a second one that faced the back stairs, Alix hissed at Cord, who slinked out of the bathroom, shoes in hand, and slipped out of the door that faced the kitchen stairs. He blew her a kiss and disappeared down the stairs as Alix climbed out of bed.

Alix watched him go, feelings she couldn't describe bubbling up in her chest. By the time she went to interact with her children, confusion had the better of her.

———

Alix really wasn't sure how she got through her next shift. All she could think about was Cord. He'd started calling her cell phone about three in the afternoon, leaving messages regarding what time he should meet her for dinner, but she didn't call him back. They weren't even that busy but she still didn't call him back. She wasn't sure what to say to him. She wasn't sure what she felt other than excitement, hope, old fears and old anxieties. She was a mess.

So the dinner hour came and went and she didn't call him back and he didn't show up. Grossly depressed, sad and confused, Alix got off shift a little after midnight and headed out to her car in the well-lit parking lot. She had her head down, watching her feet as she walked across the asphalt, approaching her BMW X5 that still had California plates on it. As she hit the unlock button on the key fob, a big figure emerged from the shadows.

Startled, she yelped until she saw that it was Cord. Hand over her pounding heart, she gazed up at him with surprise.

"Oh, God," she gasped. "You scared me to death."

He smiled timidly. "Sorry," he said. "I didn't mean to."

She took a deep breath, recovering her composure. "It's okay," she said, eyeing him with some apprehension. "What are you doing here so late?"

His gaze lingered on her for a moment before sighing heavily. "You didn't return any of my calls." He sounded so hesitant and unsure of himself. "I didn't come for dinner because I figured you were just busy and you would have called me had you wanted me to come."

She was hesitant and unsure, also. "We were fairly busy," she lied just a little. She didn't want to tell him the truth. Then, she broke down and slouched against the car. "Look, Cord, you don't have to keep calling me... you know, you don't have to feel any obligation towards me because we slept together. We shouldn't have done it and I know that, but... well, I guess it was just one of those hormonal things. I don't even know. But you don't have to feel like you need to call me now. I'm a big girl. I can take it."

He looked at her, stunned. "Is *that* what you think?" he said, incredulous. "I'm calling you because we slept together and you think I feel obligated?"

She hung her head. "I'm just saying you don't have to *feel* obligated," she said. "And furthermore, I don't want you to think I'm going to be a convenience. I won't be a bed buddy, so if you're thinking we can just have convenient sex all the time, then don't."

He just stared at her. Then, he shook his head, baffled. "Who in the hell has hurt you so badly that you think there aren't any honorable men left in the world?"

Her head came up, the lower lip trembling. "Look at me," she whispered. "I know what I look like. I know what men think. I get hit on like you can't believe, wooed by millionaires and actors and people who just want a trophy doctor on their arm. My ex-husband cheated his way through our marriage and I've spent the better part of my adult life convinced that every man who comes on to me is only out for himself. I'm sorry if I've insulted you; I really am. But in my experience, that's just the way things are. The way they always have been. I've only known you two days, Cord, and we've already slept together, so you must think I'm pretty easy. I'm not, you know. I've spent a lot of years keeping myself bottled up and protected. But with you... it just happened so easily and that scares me to death. I don't want you to feel like I'm expecting anything from you."

Cord learned a lot in that rambling, sniffling diatribe. He sighed heavily. "Oh... honey, no," he murmured. "I want you to listen to me and listen very closely. I never cheated on my wife and I never played the field. Honor and integrity are important to me. Never in my life have I slept with someone after having known them a couple of days, so what happened between us earlier today was the first time that has ever happened to me. More than that, it was the single most amazing sexual experience of my life because it was with you. The day I met you, it was like the clouds opened up and this angel stepped into my midst. I can't describe it any better than that. I don't care if you're a doctor or a lawyer or a worker at a burger joint. I really don't give a damn. It's you I'm attracted to – your quirky sense of humor, your intelligence, and the way you have of looking at me that makes my knees weak. Don't you get it? I'm not looking for convenient sex or a trophy on my arm. I'm looking for a good woman who fills me like no one else ever has and, so far, you're doing a pretty good job of that."

Alix was gazing up at him with tears streaming down her cheeks. "I just don't know," she whispered. "I'm so scared... I'm scared to open myself up because I can already feel it happening."

"Good," he said, slowly moving towards her. "I feel something for you, too, and I want us to feel it together. I swear I won't hurt you, Alix. Please believe me. I just want to... well, God willing, I just want to love you and treat you right. You're such a special person and I'm sorry if no one has shown you that."

She sobbed softly and wiped at her nose. "I've heard those lines before."

"It's not a line. I swear on the lives of my kids, it's not a line. It's the truth."

She looked up at him, looking so tired and frightened and pathetic. "I want to believe you," she murmured. "I just don't know how."

"Then let me show you. Will you at least give me the

chance? I've always been a big believer that actions speak louder than words. Please... just let me show you."

She wiped at her wet cheeks, having difficulty looking him in the eye. He sounded so desperately sincere and she very much wanted to believe him. After several moments of deliberation, she nodded her head.

"Okay," she whispered. "I'm sorry I didn't call you back for dinner."

He smiled faintly. "Are you hungry?"

"A little."

"Let's go get something to eat."

"But it's the middle of the night."

"I know a few places that are open."

She nodded again, still seemingly sad and depressed, but when she looked at him, he swore he could see warmth. He could see she very much wanted to believe him. Cord put his arms around her and hugged her tightly, gently stoking her hair and kissing her cheek.

"Come on." He kissed her again. "Let's go eat pancakes somewhere."

She managed a smile as she looked up again, thinking that if this man was for real, she could most definitely fall in love with him and have that love, that toe-curling love, she'd never thought she'd ever have.

Maybe she'd been wrong, about a lot of things.

SIX

EVENSHADE BECAME A HOUSE UNDER CONSTRUCTION.
The restoration contractor had found rot in pretty much every part of the house so, bit by bit, floor boards and walls were being pulled up and replaced, and Alix had discovered that she needed to have the approval from the City of Danvers to do any extensive renovations because of the historical significance of the house. So every time a portion of the porch was pulled up, an inspector would show up to give it his blessing. This made for slow work, but the house was starting to come along.

Almost a month after she and the kids had moved in, the restoration was in full swing. The contractor had basically worked from the ground up, so most of the first floor was torn up while the second floor hadn't been touched for the most part. It had been chaotic and expensive, but the ground floor was coming along nicely. New walls, restored floors, replumbed and rewired, Alix was very happy with the work.

Sean started school towards the end of the month. Alix had dropped him off his first day even though he had pleaded to go with Chris, Kyle and Cole in Chris' pickup truck. Alix had to practically beg to take him and he relented, but then she had to promise that he could ride with the Trevor boys from now on. Unhappy but understanding that her son was growing up and didn't need or want mommy driving him around, Alix had agreed.

Additionally, Alix had worked with an agency to hire a live-in housekeeper who would watch Rose when Alix and Sean were unavailable. Her name was Hester and she was a widow who had raised three children of her own, and Rose seemed to like the woman right away. With six bedrooms upstairs, Alix put Hester in the bedroom nearest the kitchen stairs and across the hall from Rose's bedroom. Black, round, and with a lot of energy, Hester blended into their household quickly and easily. Alix loved her.

Most importantly during this time was the relationship developing between Alix and Cord. The boys, all of them, had figured out for themselves that Cord and Alix were sweet on each other and they all approved except for Cole. The youngest Trevor boy wasn't happy in the least, so Cord and Alix were very careful with their behavior when they were around him. Cord tried to speak with his son a few times about what he was feeling, but Cole didn't want to talk about it. On Alix's advice, Cord stopped pressing his son. He figured Cole would talk about it when he was ready.

At the end of the first week of school, there was a football game at Danvers High School and Alix wasn't working so she was able to attend. Sean already seemed to be absorbed into the fraternity of popular boys at the high school thanks to the Trevor brothers and he already had a glut of friends to hang out with. Because Cord was an assistant coach with the football team, it was a given that they'd be attending all of the home games. On this warm Friday evening in late August, Alix packed up Rose and drove over to the high school to watch the game.

Sean had gone on ahead with Cole, Cord, Chris and Kyle, so Alix parked her car in the high school parking lot and collected her blanket before locking up the car and taking Rose by the hand. They got in line with other football fans and parents, paying their seven dollars to be admitted to the stadium.

The mercury vapor lights were blazing a brilliant white light as Alix and Rose made their way to the stands. The football team was in the locker room and the marching band was getting ready to take the field to play the national anthem. The stands were fairly packed because it was the first game and also because they were playing Winthrop High School, a local rival. The energy was high and the crowds were already cheering.

Alix made her way into the stands, grinning when she saw Sean and Cole with a group of boys in lettermen jackets at the very front and center of the stands. They were screaming and yelling, and having a wonderful time. She and Rose found seats further down the stands, right in the front so they could watch all of the action, and next to where the marching band sat. As they settled in, the Danvers Falcons came roaring out onto the field to the strains of the fight song and the crowd went wild.

Alix picked out Cord immediately, dressed in slacks and a royal blue polo shirt with a Falcons logo on it. He was jogging across the field with his linemen, gathering on the sidelines as the two teams settled in for the game. But the moment he reached the sidelines, he began scanning the crowd and spied Alix and Rose almost immediately. He waved at them and Alix waved back.

Rose, however, saw him waving and thought he was waving her over. She had become rather enamored with him over the past few weeks, mostly because he was very sweet with her and would sit and watch cartoons when he wasn't occupied with Alix. He even played Chutes and Ladders with her a few times. Rose really didn't have any friends yet in her new town, so she looked at him as sort of a big playmate. She jumped up from the bench when he waved and ran off before Alix could grab her.

For a little girl, she moved rather well and skittered down the wooden steps of the stands as Alix went in pursuit. Cord saw the little girl coming and was forced to break away from his last-minute huddle with his defensive linemen, including both Chris and Kyle, and intercepted Rose before she got trampled.

He picked the little girl up and greeted Alix with a kiss when she walked up on them. He tried to hand Rose back but she had no interest in returning to her mother. So he took her with him as he returned to the huddle. Alix stood back from the sidelines, near the stands, waiting for Cord to turn her child back over to her, but that didn't happen until almost three minutes into the game. Rose still had no interest in returning to her mother but it was necessary.

Alix liked football so she enjoyed the battle between Danvers and Winthrop. She mostly watched Cord on the sidelines, his powerful figure and handsome features, her heart giddy at the sight of him. She also watched her son as he had a great time with his new friends, cheering on his new school.

Night descended and the game went into the third quarter with a tied score. Rose was growing listless and Alix was thinking about taking her home when there was a big play on the field, a lot of running, and suddenly everything came to a grinding halt. A player was down, and Cord and another coach ran out onto the field.

Alix wasn't paying much attention because Rose was close to pitching a fit, so she was gathering up her blanket and preparing to leave when she began to hear her name. Looking up, she could see several players calling over to her and Kyle, in particular, running in her direction. His young face was stressed.

"Alix, Dad wants you to come," he said breathlessly. "He says hurry."

"What's wrong?"

Kyle shook his head. "I don't know. I guess Bryce is pretty hurt. Dad wants you to come."

Concerned, Alix took Rose by the hand and quickly came out of the stands. Kyle was standing there in his football uniform and she put Rose's little hand in his.

"Watch Rosie, please," she commanded. "Go find Sean and have him take her."

Kyle nodded as Alix made her way through the players on the sideline and out onto the field. The entire game had come to a halt and several Danvers players were down on one knee, several feet away from the downed player. Players from the opposing team were doing the same thing, everyone down on one knee and very quiet. Alix knelt down next to Cord.

"What's the situation?" she asked.

Cord had his hands on either side of the young man's head, holding it still. "Bryce," he said steadily. "Tell Dr. Hendry what you told me."

The young man was bordering on terrified tears. "I got hit," he said, "and I felt this pain in my back and now my legs are all numb. Am I going to be paralyzed?"

Alix put a comforting hand on his arm. "It's okay, sweetheart," she said, then she turned to Cord. "Did you call an ambulance?"

"It's on its way."

She nodded, assessing the situation. "Bring out the backboard and we'll get him strapped down. I'm not going to touch his helmet until we get to the hospital. We'll just strap it all down."

Cord was already in motion. He held the young man's head still as Alix very carefully assessed him, touching his hands, arms, thighs and feet, asking him questions and watching his responses. The kid had feeling, which was a good sign, but he was in a lot of pain. The way he had fallen was kind of odd, so she left him where he was until the paramedics arrived and they were able to use multiple hands to straighten him out and get him on a backboard. As Cord continued to hold the boy's head still, Alix supervised the paramedics as they strapped him down.

The boy's mother and father had come out onto the field and Alix could see the panic-stricken parents standing a few feet away with the head coach. She put in an IV line and as the paramedics taped everything down and got him ready for transport, Alix found out where they were taking him and went over to the parents.

"I'm Dr. Hendry," she greeted them in a calm, reassuring manner. "Bryce has feeling in his extremities, but he also has some numbness, so we've got him stable and we're going to transport him to North Shore for more tests and evaluations. I'll be going with him."

The mother was nearly hysterical. "Is he going to be okay? Did he break his neck?"

Alix held the woman's hands. "At this point, I can't tell you any more than I already have," she said gently. "But he has feeling and he has pain, and that's a good sign. Meet us over at the hospital, okay? I promise I'll take good care of your son."

The parents, shaken, nodded and turned away, rushing out to the parking lot for their car. Alix turned back to her patient to see that the paramedics had him up on a gurney and were moving him towards the ambulance. Quickly, she went to Cord.

"Can you please make sure that Rose and Sean get home?" she asked. "I'm going in with Bryce."

He nodded. "No worries," he assured her. "I'll take care of them."

She smiled. "Thank you," she said sincerely. "It was a good game, by the way. I'll see you later."

His eyes were intense, as if she were the only thing that existed in the midst of the football players, fans, ambulance attendants and paramedics. He only had eyes for her.

"You sure will," he mumbled. "I love you, honey. I'll see you in a bit."

With that, he turned away and began issuing directives to the football players from Danvers who were still down on one knee several feet away. As the kids got up and began to return to the sidelines, Alix watched the man walk away, shocked at what he had just said to her. *I love you, honey.* They'd been seeing each other for about a month and that was the first time he'd told her that he loved her. Out in the middle of a football stadium, of all places. All she could do was smile as she turned for the ambulance.

She was pretty sure she loved him, too.

————

Alix was at the hospital with Bryce all night. An MRI revealed a dislocated vertebra that was putting pressure on his spine, so around four in the morning, she scrubbed for surgery and stabilized the number nine and ten thoracic vertebra. He was out of surgery by eight in the morning and his parents wept when Alix told them that Bryce would be fine. Exhausted, she went to her new office to finish up her paperwork.

Still in the clothes she had worn to the football game the night before, she was just finishing the last of her dictation when her intercom rang. It was the front desk in the emergency room asking her to come to the lobby, so she did, not even bothering to ask why. When she came out into the big common area just inside the emergency room entrance, she caught sight of Cord standing at the desk.

In his blue duty uniform with a radio in his hand, his eyes met hers over the activities of the emergency room and he smiled broadly. Wearily, Alix grinned as she walked up to him. It was then she noticed he had a bag in his hand.

"Hi, honey," he bent over and kissed her. "I came to see how Bryce was doing and brought you some breakfast."

She was deeply touched that he would go to the trouble, not at all concerned with the fact that he'd just kissed her in front of a room full of emergency personnel. In fact, she was quite happy for people to know they were together even though they'd never even discussed a boyfriend/girlfriend relationship. When the man stopped by nearly every day she was working, Alix was pretty sure her new colleagues had suspected there was something going on between them. She took the bag of food from him gratefully.

"Thank you," she said sincerely. "You're so sweet."

He just grinned. "You're welcome," he said, following her as she moved over to some plastic chairs lined up against the wall. "How are you holding up?"

Alix sat down and pulled the Styrofoam container out of the bag. "I'm fine," she said. "Bryce is doing really well, too. Have you seen him?"

He shook his head, watching her flip open the lid and ravenously dig into the scrambled eggs. "No," he replied. "I just asked the duty nurse. She said he was doing fine."

Alix nodded. "The damage really wasn't that bad," she said, her mouth full. "It was just enough to put some pressure on the spinal column, which I relieved when I stabilized the vertebra. He'll be out for the season, though."

Cord sat back in the chair, draping his arm over the back of the chairs so he was fondling her shoulder as she ate.

"Too bad," he said. "He's a senior. He's got some college prospects, football scholarships and all."

She plowed into the hash browns. "If I was him, I wouldn't play football anymore," she said seriously. "I just wouldn't take the chance."

"Did you tell him that?"

"I told his parents."

Cord nodded faintly, thinking about the young man with the ended football career. "Well," he said after a moment. "That's a shame, but I get it."

Alix nodded as she ate. "Did the team win?"

"Thirty-one to seven."

She grinned at him, licking the fork. "Congratulations, Coach," she said. "Good job."

He stroked her shoulder as she put jam on her toast and took a big bite. "Thanks," he said genuinely. "It was a privilege to watch you work last night. You're really amazing."

She smiled modestly. "Thank you," she said. "I guess all those years of medical school paid off."

He just smiled, sat there and stroked her shoulder. She was eating like she was starving, which she was, as he watched her. He really was content when he was just watching her.

"What's your schedule like over the next few days?" he asked.

She finished off the toast. "I'm off for the next four days, starting today," she said. "The contractor is almost finished restoring the floors and he's going to be moving upstairs next weekend to start the renovations up there. I'm suspecting we might have to move into a hotel for a little while because the fumes from the finished floors are pretty overwhelming."

He nodded faintly. "I'm off beginning tomorrow morning,"

he said. "I was thinking of taking you away somewhere for a couple of days."

She looked at him curiously. "Where?"

He shrugged, dragging a gentle finger up her arm. "There's a resort to the west called the Cranwell," he said quietly. "We could spend a couple of days there going to the spa, or golfing, or just doing nothing. It's a gorgeous place set in the woods. How does that sound?"

A twinkle came to her eye. "What about the kids?"

"Yours or mine?"

"Yours."

He shrugged again. "My boys are pretty self-sufficient," he said. "They don't need a babysitter, although I will have my sister check in on them. Do you feel comfortable enough leaving Sean and Rose with Hester for a couple of days?"

She finished with the food and closed the lid. "I think so," she said, looking rather torn. "I'd love to go away with you, but it's such a busy time right now. You've got work and it's football season, and...."

He interrupted her. "And we can go Saturday morning and come back Sunday night. No one will be impacted."

She gazed at him with her beautiful, tired eyes, thinking. A smile began to spread across her lips. "Really?"

"Really."

Her smile brightened. "In that case, I can't say no."

He smiled broadly, cupped her face with one big hand, and kissed her cheek. "That's the answer I was looking for." He stood up, reaching out a hand and pulling her to her feet. "I need to get going. The guys are waiting for me outside in the engine."

Her eyebrows lifted. "You made them wait out there while you came in here to proposition me?"

He laughed. "Honey, I haven't even started propositioning you, trust me. This is only the beginning."

She giggled because he was. Then his radio crackled, which was apparently something meant for him, so he bent over quickly and kissed her on the cheek. "I've got to run," he said, turning to dash away. "Love you."

She stopped him. "Wait," she said, rather loudly. When he came to a stop and turned to her, she looked at him with a rather stunned look on her face. "You... what you said. You said it last night, too."

"What?"

She looked at him as if he were an idiot. "What do you mean 'what'?" she lowered her voice. "Cord, you told me you loved me."

"I do."

She blinked at his reply, no hesitation or embarrassment. He reached out and stroked her cheek. "I've got to go. I'll call you later."

He was running off again and she followed. "Cord," she called after him. "Don't... don't you think we need to talk about this?"

He was nearly to the door. "No." He turned around when she came up behind him, hand on the door knob, and kissed her right on the nose. "There's nothing to discuss. I love you and that's a fact."

He pushed through the door and out into the parking lot, leaving her standing there with her mouth hanging open. She watched him jump into the front of the fire engine and the thing took off, rotators going. She watched until the engine pulled out of the parking lot, out onto the boulevard, and out of sight. Then she blew a kiss at the departing engine and closed the door.

I love you, too.

SEVEN

BY THE TIME Alix got home, the kids were at school and Hester was in the kitchen scrubbing down the newly restored hardwood floor. It stunk from the chemicals they had used and she was trying to get the smell out of it.

Exhausted, Alix dragged herself upstairs to get a few hours of sleep before she had to pick up Rose. She was still thinking about Cord and his declaration, fairly convinced she was madly in love with the man and thrilled to death he felt the same way about her. She suspected she had pretty much smiled from the time he mentioned it earlier, all the way home in the car, and all the way up the stairs because she was smiling now and couldn't remember when she'd started. Sitting heavily on the bed, she pulled off her shoes.

The cell phone in her purse went off and she grabbed for the bag at the end of the bed, pulling out her smartphone. Seeing the caller I.D., she answered.

"Hello?"

A familiar male voice was on the other end. "Hi, Alix." It was her ex-husband, Pat Hendry. "How's the east coast?"

"Fine," she said, not particularly wanting to talk to him but trying to be polite. "It's great and the kids love it. What's on your mind?"

She was straight to the point with him. On the other end, Pat cleared his throat softly. "Did I wake you up?"

"No."

"But you're tired. I can tell. You're always grumpy when you're tired."

Out of patience, Alix struggled not to be short with him. "What do you want, Pat?"

He could tell she wasn't up for pleasantries, which didn't play well into his intentions. "I just wanted to see how you were," he said. "I... I've missed you, Alix. I miss the kids."

"What?" Alix cried with quiet disbelief. "Pat, I don't have time for this. I've been up all night and I need to get to bed. I'd appreciate it if you'd get to the point."

"That *is* the point. Alix, I really need to talk to you."

"What about?"

"Stuff. Us."

A warning bell went off in her head. "You're crazy," she said. "You don't need to talk to me and I have nothing to say to you. We're happy here, the kids have friends, Sean loves his new school, and that's that. Don't start with this begging crap again. It isn't going to work."

Pat didn't rise to spar with her as he usually did. "There's just a lot going on... you know, in my mind, and I know it's beating a dead horse, but I'd be grateful if we could just... you know, talk for a while. I've got a lot I need to say to you."

Alix shook her head. "I don't want to hear it," she said. "Pat, I'm not trying to be mean or disrespectful, but I really, sincerely, don't want to hear anything. You tried this before we moved here and it's not going to work."

"I love you, Alix. I miss you so much."

Alix's jaw ticked with frustration. "Pat, listen to me; I don't love you. I haven't for a long time. I have no interest in getting back together. In fact, I'm with someone now and I'm really crazy about him, so I'm moving on with my life and I'm very happy. I would suggest you do the same thing."

There was a long pause. "I guess I should be happy for you," he finally said. "Who is he?"

"Just someone I met."

"Do you love him?"

"That's none of your business." She was growing agitated. "I really need to sleep, so I'm going to hang up now. I'll have the kids call you later."

She hung up the call before he could say anything more and then she just sat there a moment and stared at the phone in her hand. She and Pat had been separated since just after Rose's birth and she'd lost all feeling for the man long ago. For him to start building bridges again just wasn't going to work. She loved Cord and that's all there was to it. She allowed herself a moment of frustration but nothing more. Pat just wasn't worth it.

So she fell asleep on top of her bed, too tired to actually get underneath the covers, and her alarm went off a couple of hours later. Dragging herself up, she manage to go pick Rose up from school and left her with Hester while she went back to sleep. She awoke later to the smells of dinner cooking, ate fried chicken with the kids before helping Sean with his homework and putting both kids to bed around nine thirty. She went back to bed shortly after them.

Around one in the morning, she woke up to use the restroom. As she was emerging from her bathroom, she heard faint whispers again, or at least what she thought was faint whispers. She might have thought she was just hearing things except that she remembered those same whispers from a few weeks back when Cord thought they might have come from a neighbor's loud television. At one in the morning, there were no loud televisions on, so she slipped from her bedroom to follow the sounds.

It was very dark in the hall except for a nightlight streaming weak light from the bathroom. Alix crept down the hallway, an eerie corridor of creaking floor boards and shadows, as she followed the sounds to Rose's bedroom. The door was cracked open, as it always was so Alix could listen for her daughter, and Alix peered in through the gap between the door and the jamb.

Rose was lying on her bed, soft words coming from her lips. Alix couldn't hear what she was saying, but it sounded as if she were having a conversation. Rose would whisper, then a brief silence would follow, and then she would say something again. Alix could see her daughter, lying there with her kitty in her arms, as she evidently spoke with an imaginary friend.

At least, that's what Alix would have believed before, but she kept hearing whispers that didn't belong to her daughter. It was very strange. Just as she moved to open the door, the panel suddenly slammed in her face, smacking her in the forehead and catching the fingers of her right hand. Alix shrieked as she fell back and ended up falling on her bottom.

That brought Sean thundering from his bedroom. The boy was in the hallway, looking at his mother as the woman gasped and held the fingers on her right hand. As she tried to get up, something unseen and violent slammed her back down again, this time smacking her head against the wall. Alix went out like a light.

———

Alix awoke to distant sounds of a police radio. Her head was killing her and she was half in and half out of consciousness even as she tried to sit up. Gentle hands pushed her back down again.

"Take it easy, honey," Cord said softly. "Everything's okay. We're going to take good care of you."

Alix struggled to open her eyes; everything was rocking around so she just closed them again. "What...?" She put her hand to her head only to realize there was a blood pressure cuff on her arm. Forcing her eyes open, she peered at the cuff. "What's going on? What in the world happened?"

"Mom?" Sean was standing by her feet, his young face full of terror. "Are you okay?"

Alix blinked, looking at her frightened son, who was holding Rose in his arms. She looked at her blood pressure cuff again and, disoriented, yanked the cuff off and struggled to sit up. The more the paramedics tried to push her down, the more she fought them until Cord finally called his guys off and just let her sit up. Dizzy and bewildered, Alix leaned against the wall. Her hands were on her head.

"What happened?" she asked anyone who could answer her. She looked at Cord, crouched a foot or so away from her. He looked frightened and concerned. "What are you doing here?"

Cord was calm, gentle. "Sean called Kyle and Kyle called me," he explained. "He said you hit your head and knocked yourself out, so we came over to take a look and found you unconscious. Do you remember what happened, honey?"

Alix had no idea what he was talking about. She looked around at all the firemen in her upper hallway, with their gear and blaring radios, and became even more confused.

"You rolled on me?" She was genuinely surprised.

"Code Three. You're damn right I did."

"But why did you do that? I... I'm fine."

"Do you remember what happened?"

"No," she said before he even finished his question. "I... I don't have any idea. Oh... wait a minute...."

She suddenly looked up at Rose and Sean, but she was mostly looking at Rose. Her eyes widened as her memory began to return. "I heard Rosie in her room and when I went to look, something...."

She froze, realizing there were about six guys standing around listening to her. She remembered very well what happened now but she didn't want to sound like a lunatic. Maybe she was mistaken. Maybe she had just dreamed the whole thing. In any case, she was suddenly very afraid and very confused. She looked at Cord.

"I'm okay," she said quietly. "I'm sorry you had to come all the way over here."

He was very gentle with her. "You've got a big bump on the back of your head," he said. "I would feel much better if you'd let us take you to get looked at."

She shook her head, nauseous with the motion. "I'm fine, really. I don't need to get looked at. I just need to go back to bed."

"Feel the back of your head."

Reluctantly, she did. There was a bump the size of a walnut on the back of her skull. Cord watched her face as she inspected the lump.

"Now," his voice was very soft. "If I had a lump like that, what would you tell me?"

Her lips twisted wryly. "To go to the hospital."

He just lifted his eyebrows at her and she dropped her hand, feeling a little more oriented but uncertain and rather ill. Moreover, the memories of what had happened were very strong now. She glanced at the firemen standing around, staring at her.

"Can... can you please tell them to go back to the truck?" she whispered. "I... I need to talk to you. Alone."

"Not unless you agree to go to the hospital and get looked at."

She frowned, pouting, but didn't fight him on it. She knew, deep down, he was right. So she nodded reluctantly and he sent the guys who manned the rig back down to the truck, but told the paramedics to meet him downstairs with a gurney because he would bring her downstairs himself. Everyone cleared out.

With only the sounds of the firemen downstairs and their crackling radios, Alix faced Cord, having no idea why she suddenly felt very scared. Perhaps it was because either option was scary – if she had only imagined the event or if it had really happened. Either way, she'd ended up with a big bump on her head. Her hand found its way to the lump again, fingering it.

"I'm not sure if I was dreaming or not," she said quietly. "I got up to go to the bathroom and heard those whispers again. Remember? The ones I heard a few weeks ago and you said it was probably someone's television up real loud?"

He nodded. "I remember."

She sighed faintly and dropped her hand from her head again because the bump really hurt. "I followed the sounds and heard them coming from Rosie's room," she whispered. "The door was cracked open so I peeked in but didn't see anything. Then the door slammed in my face and smashed my fingers. When I tried to get up again... I don't remember anything after that."

"That's because you slammed back into the wall," Sean said. The adults looked at him, noting his wide-eyed expression. "I saw it; she tried to get up but something slammed her back into the wall and knocked her out."

Cord's brow furrowed as he stood up, focused on the young man. "*What* slammed her back?"

Sean shook his head. "I didn't see anything," he said,

sounding rather apprehensive. "It was... was like wind or something. It just blew her down."

Cord looked both serious and confused as he returned his attention to Alix. "You got blown down?"

Alix didn't have any idea why she teared up. She was exhausted, her head hurt, and she just wanted to go back to bed. Her face crumpled and she looked at her lap, hiding her face from the kids so they wouldn't be frightened that she was crying. Cord put his hand on her arm, squeezing it, as Rose slithered down from her brother's embrace and climbed onto her mother's lap.

"Mommy," she said as she put her little hands on her mom. "Are you okay?"

Alix wiped at her face, trying to compose herself. "I'm fine, baby. I'm just tired."

"The sad girl is afraid she's going to get a spanking now."

Alix didn't know why she paid closer attention to Rose's imaginary friend, but she did. Things were odd enough that she was coming to think maybe there was something to this sad girl who seemed to follow Rose around, stealing stuffed animals and demanding ponies. It had never occurred to her that it might be something more than Rose's imagination.

"Why?" she asked reluctantly. "What... what did the sad girl do?"

"She pushed you."

"She did?"

"When you were at my door."

Apprehension began to creep over Alix. "Why did she push me?"

"Because she was afraid."

Alix paused, thinking of her next question because she felt rather foolish indulging in a four year old's fantasies. But given what just happened and the anxiety she was feeling, she was thinking she needed to.

"Rosie," she began carefully. "Who *is* this sad girl? Does she have a name?"

Rose nodded, without hesitation, but she was finding more interest toying with her mother's necklace. "Mer-*cy*," she enunciated each syllable. "Mommy, can I have some cookies?"

Alix ignored the cookie request. "What else did Mercy say about me? Why is she afraid of me?"

Rose still had one hand on the necklace as she pointed at Cord. "Him," she said without interest. "She says you do bad things with him and he's scary. She says you take your clothes off and roll around. I told her that he's my friend but she's afraid."

Shocked, Alix couldn't help the hand that flew up to cover her agape mouth. "Afraid of Cord?"

Rose was growing squirmy and goofy, too much stimulation in the middle of the night. She bounced around on her mother's lap as she spoke. "Wi-*ga*," she said as she bounced, being silly. *"Goody Good, Goody Good, 'ere snake and bird could.* She teached me that song. Mommy, I'm hungry. Can I have cookies?"

Alix looked into her daughter's big gray eyes before turning her astonished attention to Cord. She had no idea what to say as he met her gaze, steadily. Cord, however, could see the fear and apprehension in her eyes so he reached out and pulled Rose up from her lap, handing her back over to Sean.

"Come on, Dr. Hendry." He reached down and scooped Alix up from the floor, holding her against his big chest. "Let's go get you looked at."

Alix resisted. "But I can't...."

"You promised," he said sternly as he moved for the stairs,

looking back over his shoulder at the kids. "Sean, where's Hester?"

Sean was following with Rose in his arms. "She's not here."

"It's her night off," Alix put in, her arms around Cord's neck as he began to descend the stairs.

"Then get Rosie back to bed," Cord was speaking to Sean. "I'll bring your mom back in a little while."

Alix looked over Cord's shoulder at her children standing at the top of the stairs. "Go ahead," she told the boy. "I'll be back in a little while. Make sure the house is locked up."

Sean did as he was told. Alix, however, proved to be a rotten patient and did not do as she was told. She didn't want to sit on the gurney. Instead, she snuggled up to Cord and ignored the paramedics, so Cord climbed into the back of the ambulance with her in his arms and held her in his lap the entire way to the hospital.

The long night stretched into a long morning.

EIGHT

ALIX HAD a mild concussion and was sent home to rest. In addition to her four days off, she was given three more to recover, which Alix thought was great considering all of the renovations going on at the house. She felt as if she could really start getting some things done around the house that she hadn't been able to get to since she moved in. Cord, however, had other ideas.

Since she had been up all night, Cord sent the kids off to the mall, including Rose, so the house would be quiet enough for her to sleep. He had been up all night, too. So he got into bed with her once the kids had taken off for the pancake house, but they didn't do a whole lot of sleeping until it was nearly noon. Cord couldn't keep his hands to himself and Alix naturally succumbed, even with her headache. Exhausted, they finally fell asleep as clouds began to roll in from the east.

A nasty thunderclap jolted Alix awake. Wrapped up in Cord's big arms, she listened to the rain come down and the thunder roll over the steady rise and fall of his snoring. Glancing at the clock, she saw that it was a little past two in the afternoon and suspected the kids would be back at some point soon. Snuggling back against Cord, his arms tightened around her in his sleep and he stopped snoring briefly before resuming. Had Alix not been so exhausted, the snoring would have bothered her but, in a strange way, she found it comforting. She knew she could get used to it.

Her eyes were just starting to close when she heard something other than the rain or thunder. Her eyes popped open as she listened, carefully, for what she thought was a whispered word. It was more of a hiss, really, but she lifted her head, listening, as the rain poured down. She was just lowering her head back to the pillow when she heard it again. This time, she shook Cord awake gently.

He inhaled deeply, yawning, as he pulled her tightly against him and snuggled into her back. Alix patted his arm to get his attention.

"Cord," she hissed. "Wake up."

His face was pressed into her naked back. "I'm awake."

"I'm hearing those whispers again."

He didn't say anything for a moment, nor did he move. Then, his head came up, the blue eyes sleepy.

"Whispering?" he repeated.

Alix nodded and tossed off the covers, going in search of her clothing. Cord was afforded an unobstructed view of her delicious naked body as she went to her dresser and unloaded a pair of sweats and a tank top. He folded an enormous arm behind his head, watching her with pleasure, when he suddenly heard the whispering, too.

His smile vanished and he sat up like a shot. "What in the hell *was* that?"

Alix was already heading to the door. "I'm going to go see."

He leapt out of bed, finding his pants at the end of the mattress "Hold on," he told her. "I'm coming. Just hold on."

Alix stood at the door that led into the main hallway, listening, while Cord pulled on his briefs and his jeans. As his white t-shirt went over his head, he headed over to her.

"Okay," he whispered, opening her bedroom door. "Let's go."

Alix was more frightened than she cared to admit. The last time she heard whispering, she'd gotten knocked on her ass, so she held tight to Cord's hand as they carefully made their way down the hall. They could hear more whispering now, but it was more like a softly uttered cadence or song. It sounded so strange, as if the song were being sung underwater, for it had that echoing, gurgling effect. The closer they drew to Rose's room, where the sounds were coming from, the more frightened Alix became. When they came to the door, they paused to listen.

The whispering was steady now, but it was more than whispering. As they listened, they realized it was singing. Words became clear.

"*Goody Good, Goody Good, 'ere snake and bird could,*" went the small, childlike voice.

Alix's eyes were huge, shocked at what she was hearing, but Cord wasn't showing much of a reaction. He opened the door and pushed straight into the room.

Rose's room was empty. The bed was made and there were toys on the ground, including her beloved kitty, but it was completely empty. Still holding on to Alix, Cord made his way into the room, looking around to see if he could spy the source of the noise. When he turned to look at Alix, he could see how terrified she was and he put his hands on her arms, rubbing them comfortingly.

"I don't see anything," he said. "Does she have any radios or maybe a CD player that could have been playing?"

Alix shook her head, looking around fearfully. "She doesn't own a radio or CD player," she said. "Why is it so cold in here?"

Cord shook his head as the thunder rolled outside. "I have no idea," he said. "I'll check...."

The bedroom door slammed so hard that the entire house shook, causing Alix to throw her arms around Cord and practically jump on him. He held her tightly, startled.

"Holy Cow," he exclaimed. "This place has a hell of a draft. Is that what happened to you earlier? You said the door slammed on you."

Alix was holding him with a death grip. "That's exactly what happened," she replied. She was trembling. "Cord, there's no draft in this house that's going to slam a door like that."

"What do you mean?"

"I mean... oh, I don't know what I mean. I want out of here. I'm moving Rosie into another room."

He pulled her towards the door. When he put his hand on the knob, it was like ice. In fact, it was so cold that he jerked his hand away, peering closely at the old iron knob.

"What's wrong?" Alix demanded.

He shook his head and grasped the knob again. "Nothing."

He put his hand on the knob again but it wouldn't turn. In fact, the entire door was stuck solid and he let go of Alix as he tried to get a better grip on the door. For as big and as strong as he was, he couldn't get the door to budge. As Alix stood there and watched, increasingly apprehensive, something blew cold and hard into her left ear.

"Rose," it hissed.

Alix shrieked and bolted, her hand on her ear as she plowed in to Cord. Cord grabbed her just about the time the door flew open again, only this time, it opened inward and smacked Cord in the shoulder. He grabbed the door and Alix, with a frown on his face.

"What in the...?"

Alix ran past him, out of the room. He eyed the door that had been dead-stuck before following Alix out of the room.

"Alix?" he called as he tried to follow her path. "Honey, where are you?"

He could hear her shrieking. Following the sounds, her found her all huddled up on her bed. She was freaked out; he could see it. So he sat down on the bed next to her and pulled her into his big, comforting arms.

"It's okay," he said as he held her tightly, his mouth against her head. "It was just a big draft."

She shook her head, so hard that he had to pull his face away or get bumped. "Something whispered in my ear," she said. "It said 'Rose'."

He looked at her. "Honey, big old houses like this are very drafty, and probably this one more than most because of the state it's in. You've got the place all torn apart, so there are going to be drafts. That just the way they are."

She clung to him. "You heard the singing," she insisted. "That *wasn't* a draft."

He sighed. "Honey, there's got to be a logical explanation."

"There is." She lifted her head, looking at him with a wild-eyed expression. "This house is haunted!"

He resisted the urge to smile, suspecting it wouldn't be well met. "There are no such things as ghosts," he said patiently. "There's a reasonable explanation for everything."

"Ghosts are reasonable," she insisted. "How do you explain Rosie's little sad girl? She said that the girl saw us with our clothes off, rolling around. How would Rosie know that unless someone told her?"

He lifted his eyebrows. "Well," he said slowly, "there have been times when you and I have... you know, fooled around, and we thought Rose was taking a nap. Maybe she wasn't. Maybe she got up and saw us."

Because he was so calm, Alix was naturally starting to calm. Taking a deep breath, she simply shook her head. "Under normal circumstances, I would agree with you," she said. "But that door in Rose's room has slammed twice like that, and when it did it last night, it knocked me on my ass."

He grunted, wanting to disagree with her but not wanting to create an issue out of it. "Sean said you were blown down last night and that's how you hit your head," he said quietly. "Maybe a heavy draft caught you off guard, you slipped, and down you went."

Alix was shaking her head even as he said it. "That door slammed my hand," she said, lifting the slightly swollen fingers on her right hand. "I fell back because I was startled and ended up tripping over my own feet. I was trying to get back up again when something slammed me against the chest and... and then I woke up when you were sitting next to me."

He was serious as he listened to her. "What do you think slammed you back?"

She looked completely baffled, lifting her shoulders. "I don't know," she whispered, verging on tears. "There wasn't anything there. It was like...like a shove or something, or a blast of air. It just blew me off my feet and I hit my head."

He didn't say anything, mostly because she was about to cry. Cupping her face with his big hands, he kissed her to comfort her.

"Well," he said after a moment, "I'm sure whatever it is, we'll figure it out. I wouldn't worry so much. Whatever it is, I'll take care of it."

She wiped at her eyes. "What do you mean you'll take care of it? Are you a ghost hunter?"

He chuckled. "Not the last time I checked," he said, sobering. "I meant that I'll take care of you... protect you. If there's something going on, I'll help you get to the bottom of it, so I don't want you to worry."

She gazed at him, her tears gone as she thought on how chivalrous the man was. Feelings she'd had for him since nearly the beginning had only grown stronger and deeper. Reaching out, she put her hands on his neck, her fingers brushing against his cropped blond hair.

"I won't," she confirmed. "You've done a pretty good job of protecting me since the day I moved in and that chest fell onto me. Every time that Bat-Signal goes up, you're there. I don't think I've told you lately how much I appreciate it."

He smiled, a sucker for a woman running her fingers through his hair. More than that, he was a sucker for *her*.

"You're welcome."

"There's something else," she said. "You told me you loved me, twice, but you wouldn't let me get a word in when I tried to talk to you about it."

His smile faded. "What did you want to say about it?"

"Nothing. Except that I love you, too."

His smile was back, bigger than before. He couldn't even reply. All he could do was pull her into his arms and hug her tightly. As he rolled her over onto her back on the bed and loomed over her, she spoke.

"One more thing," she whispered.

He dipped his head low, kissing her nose. "What's that?"

"When people ask me if you're my boyfriend, what do I tell them? We've never really talked about our relationship in depth. I guess I just want to know what you're thinking and what your intentions are."

His face was an inch from hers as he hovered over her, his blue eyes intense. After a moment, he shrugged. "I'm just trying to take it a day at a time with you," he murmured. "I told you I wanted to show you how I felt about you, that actions spoke louder than words. I've just been trying to do that."

"And you've been doing a great job," she said. "But then what?"

He pondered the question. "That would depend on you."

"What do you mean?"

He sat back a little, so he wasn't right on top of her, and began stroking her arm. "I mean that you weren't exactly whole-heartedly receptive to a relationship with me from the onset," he said quietly. "I didn't want to chance chasing you away, so I've just tried to sit back and let you set the pace. So what I want out of this relationship really depends on you. What do *you* want?"

She lay there, looking up at him as she thought on her answer. "We really haven't talked about any of this."

"No, we haven't. But we've really only been seeing each other a month. We're still getting to know each other."

"Still, we probably should at least discuss this."

"I figured you would when you were ready."

She sighed. "I'm sorry if I've seemed closed off. I guess I've just learned to protect myself."

"I know."

She nodded. "I realize that, but what you don't know is that with you, I don't feel like I have to protect myself anymore. You're a man of your word and you do what you say you're going to do. You've shown me more love, loyalty, tenderness and compassion in one short month than anyone has ever shown me in my entire life. I can't help but love you, Cord. You're such a wonderful man and I feel so lucky. Really, really lucky."

He smiled at her words. "Me, too," he said. "But I will admit that I want more."

"What more do you want?"

He looked somewhat uncomfortable as he averted his gaze,

looking at her arm as he stroked it. "If someone asks me if I have a girlfriend, I want to say that I do," he admitted. "If someone asks me if I've found the woman of my dreams, I want to say that I have and that she feels the same way about me. If someone asks me when we're getting married, I want to tell them that we just haven't set the date yet. Do you get my meaning?"

She watched him as he toyed with the soft skin on her arm. Lifting a hand, she pinched his chin gently between her thumb and forefinger, and forced him to look at her.

"Spell it out, Trevor."

He gave her a lopsided grin. "I'm scared to. I'm scared I'm going to chase you off and I just couldn't live with that. Alix, I've been happier over the past month than I've ever been in my entire life. You are the woman of my dreams and to be able to call you my wife... it would be a dream come true. I'd have to wake up every morning to pinch myself. I love you so much, honey. I want to feel this way for the rest of my life."

She couldn't help but smile at him. It was such a sweet thing to say. She reached up and wrapped her arms around his neck, pulling him down to her level. He snuggled up to her, nuzzling her face.

"You can tell them you have a girlfriend," she whispered. "I'd love that."

"Really?"

"Really."

"What about the rest?"

She was quiet a moment. "Are you proposing to me? Because if you are, that was a pretty weak-ass attempt."

He stopped nuzzling her, lifting his head to see that she was grinning. Seeing that she was smiling brought around bravery he hadn't felt in years, and confidence in himself that he'd never had. He could see her happiness and love for him reflecting in her eyes. She was giving him an open invitation as far as he was concerned and he was going to take it.

"Alix Hendry," he whispered. "I love you more than I can express and the day I pulled that dresser off of you was the best day of my life. Will you please do me the honor of becoming my wife?"

She burst out giggling, squeezing his neck. He held her tightly and ended up stretching out on the bed next to her, cuddling with her as she hugged him. About a minute passed before either one of them said anything.

"I'm dying here," he said. "The longer you go without answering me, the more chance I'm going to die of embarrassment and a broken heart."

She giggled again, pulling her face out of his neck to look him in the eye. "Just tell people we haven't set a date yet," she whispered. "Tell them that your fiancée can't decide if she wants to get married in the summer or in the fall, so you're just going to have to wait until she makes up her mind."

He grinned before kissing her so forcefully that Alix had to pull away to catch her breath. He continued to kiss her neck, her cheek, feeling so much joy at the moment that he couldn't control it.

"We went from being boyfriend and girlfriend to being engaged pretty quickly," he finally murmured. "Are you sure you're okay with that?"

"Completely."

"Are you *sure*?" he pressed. "I don't want you to wake up tomorrow with a bad case of regret."

She shook her head. "I won't, I promise."

Before he could say anything more, they heard Chris' pickup truck pull into the driveway. Cord jumped up and went to the window just as the truck pulled close to the house to protect it somewhat from the rain.

"The kids are back," he said, moving for the door. "I'll go downstairs."

For discretion's sake, they often separated like that when the kids came around. It was becoming normal routine, being discreet about their relationship because they didn't want to make the children uncomfortable. But this time, Alix stopped him.

"Hold on," she climbed off the mattress. "That just reminded me... what about Cole? He's still not comfortable with you and me. What are you going to tell him about... well, about us?"

Cord stood in the open doorway, the one that faced the back stairs that led into the kitchen, watching her as she pulled on a pair of furry slipper-boots. He sighed thoughtfully.

"I'm not sure what to do about him," he said honestly. "I really haven't pressed him about it, just hoping he'd get used to the idea, but if you and I are getting married at some point, I supposed I'd better help him figure out what he's feeling. I won't lie when I tell you that I'm concerned about it."

Alix nodded seriously. "Me, too," she agreed. "I don't want him to be upset by the whole thing."

The kitchen door banged open downstairs and they could hear the kids coming in. Cord just stood in the door jamb, knowing it would be futile to try and get downstairs now. By the time the kids headed up the backstairs, led by Rose and Sean, he was leaning against the door jamb with his big arms folded in quiet conversation with Alix. Alix smiled brightly at her daughter, who was holding up an anime character lunch box.

"Mommy!" she said excitedly. "See what I got!"

"I see," Alix said. "I love it, baby."

Rose then showed it to Cord, who pretended to love it also. Then she ran down to her room and disappeared. Alix thanked her son, and Kyle and Chris who were standing on the stairs, for taking care of Rose. As the boys wandered back downstairs to the video game console, Alix turned to Cord.

"I don't want Rosie in that bedroom." She lowered her voice. "I'm going to move her across the hall. She'll be sharing a bathroom with Hester, but I think that's the best place for her."

Cord didn't argue with her. "If that's what you want," he said. "I'll move her bed over if you want me to."

"Do you mind?"

"Of course not. When do you want to do it?"

"Now would be good. I want to get her the hell out of that room."

He kissed her forehead as he pushed himself off the door jamb and followed her over to Rose's big bedroom that faced the front of the house. Just as they entered the room, Rose disappeared into her closet. As Cord went to the bed to begin breaking it down, Alix went over to the closet and stuck her head in.

"Rose – ?" she stopped, mid-sentence and stepped into the closed. "Rose Elizabeth, what in the world are you doing?"

Cord could hear them in the closet as he took the mattress off the bed, leaned it against the wall, and looked at the canopy part of the bed to determine what kind of tool he would need to dismantle it. But he heard the voices in the closet getting louder until Alix finally called him.

"Cord?" she said. "Baby, can you come here a minute?"

He loved hearing a pet name come out of her mouth, something that made him feel so whole and wanted and complete. He made his way over to the closet and stuck his head in, only to see Alix at the mouth of the narrow stairs that led up to the attic and Rose about four steps up. The little girl had her lunchbox in her hand and a stubborn expression on her face. Alix looked at Cord.

"I found the attic stairs," she said rather dryly. "Honestly, I didn't know they were here. There's an access trap door in the hallway outside and I thought that was it."

Cord stepped into the closet, eyeing the narrow staircase. "I saw this the other day," he said. "I wouldn't let her go up in there, honey."

"I know," she lowered her voice. "She said her sad friend told her to go up there."

He lifted his eyebrows at her, the corner of his mouth tugging. "I think *she* wants to go up there and she's playing you."

Alix tried not to grin as Cord held out a hand to Rose. "Come out of there, baby girl," he said to her. "Let's go move you into a better bedroom."

Rose had no idea what he was talking about but, liking Cord, she did as he asked. She came down off the stairs and took his hand as he led her out of the closet.

"Why do I have to go to another bedroom?" she asked.

Cord was very sweet with her. "Because your mama wants to paint this one and fix it up," he lied to her. "We're going to move you into another bedroom until this one is all fixed up."

"Can I bring my kitty?"

He smiled down at her. "You can bring everything," he said. "In fact, I'll...."

He was cut off when Cole stuck his head into the room, apparently on the hunt for his father. He looked at his dad and at Rose, but he didn't acknowledge Alix.

"Dad," he said. "I need to get some stuff for school but Chris can't take me. Can we go now?"

Cord lifted an eyebrow. "You were out for five hours and you couldn't have your brother stop off somewhere?"

"He didn't want to do it with everyone in the car."

"Why can't he take you now?"

"Because he says he has something to do."

Cord grunted, putting his hands on his hips as he looked at

Rose and then at Alix. Shrugging, he moved for the door. "Well, come on, then," he said, looking over his shoulder at Alix. "I'll be back later to help you move the bed."

Alix waved him off. "No worries," she said. "I'll see you later."

He winked at her when Cole wasn't looking and disappeared. Alix could hear everyone moving around downstairs, voices loud, the door slam, and then Chris' truck start up. Sean came barreling up the stairs and on into his room, and she heard the television go on. Thinking of her conversation with Cord earlier, and of the freaky events as of late, she began to move with a purpose in getting her daughter moved out of the bedroom.

The afternoon stretched into dinner and Cord called to let her know he was taking the boys to dinner, just the four of them, because that was what Cole wanted. Alix was completely fine with that and made dinner for her and the kids, a kind of chicken barbeque casserole with a cornbread bleu cheese crust on top. Sean loved it but Rose wanted peanut butter and jelly, so she made a sandwich for the little girl while she and Sean had the chicken. After dinner, when Sean and Rose were cleaning up the kitchen, she heard a knock on the front door.

The sun was almost down as she opened the door to find Cole standing there. Rather surprised, she smiled hesitantly at the young man with his father's blond hair and square jaw.

"Hi, Cole," she said. "Let me call Sean for you."

"No," the boy said before she could call her son. "I... I came to see you, Dr. Hendry. Uh... can we talk for a minute? In private?"

Intrigued, Alix stepped out onto the porch and closed the front door. She found that she was actually somewhat nervous, wondering if Cord had spoken to his son over dinner and now the kid was coming to her to hash it all out.

"Where's your dad?" she asked.

"Home," he replied. "He... he doesn't know I'm over here, so please don't call him, okay?"

Alix grew serious. "Of course," she sat down on one of her new patio chairs and faced him expectantly. "What's on your mind, Cole?"

Cole didn't say anything for a moment. He came over to the new patio furniture but didn't sit down. Instead, he leaned back against the new railing. Alix could see that he was flushed around the ears, nervous. She waited almost a full minute before he opened his mouth.

"My dad told me about you and him," he finally said. "I guess I want you to know that... Dr. Hendry, it's nothing against you at all, but I don't want you and my dad to be together. My dad... well, he's got enough in his life with his work and me and my brothers, and he doesn't need you. I don't hate you or anything, but I don't want you to be with him."

Alix felt sorry for the kid, trying to express himself in a grown-up world. "Okay, Cole," she said evenly. "But can you tell me why?"

"I just don't."

"There's got to be a reason," she said gently.

He started to fidget, pacing around and causing the floor boards on the porch to creak. "Yeah, well." He paced some more, growing increasingly agitated. "Maybe there is but maybe I don't want to talk about it because maybe it's my own reason. I just don't want you to date my dad anymore because he... I just don't want you to, okay?"

Alix was very calm. "Because he... *what*, Cole? What about your dad?"

Cole's agitation was joined by anger. "Why do you have to be so nosy? Can't you just do what I say?"

Alix shook her head. "Not without a good reason," she said

evenly. "Do you understand that you are asking me to change my entire life by not seeing your dad? Did you ever stop to think how I feel about him?"

Cole came to a halt, his eyes big on her. "How do you feel about him?"

Alix was quiet. "I love him," she said softly. "Just like you, I love him. I want to make him happy and, if you'll let me, I want to make you happy, too."

"I don't need a mother," Cole exploded. "I already got one but she's never around, so I don't need you taking my dad away, too, okay? He's all we have left and he already has a family. He doesn't need yours on top of that!"

So the reason was out in the open. Alix felt as bad as she possibly could but before she could reply, the front door opened and Sean emerged. His fair face was red with anger.

"Don't you ever talk to my mom that way," he snarled at Cole. "You can't come over here and tell her what to do."

Alix was up, putting herself between Sean and Cole. "Sean, baby, it's okay," she said gently, trying to turn him around for the house. "Cole's not telling me what to do. Please go inside and watch Rosie. I'll come inside in a minute."

Sean wouldn't be pushed around by his mother. He was furious and focused on Cole. "Do you hear me?" He jabbed a finger at the kid even as Alix tried to manhandle him back into the house. "Don't you ever come over here again and talk to my mom like that, because I swear to God, I'll kick you in the face. Your dad is the one who came on to her, so if you want to blame someone, blame your dad. He's been all over her and I haven't said anything about it, so you can blame him."

Alix was having a tough time getting Sean inside and she realized she needed to give her son all of her attention at the moment. Apparently, he had some issues, too, so she shoved him inside and forced a smile at Cole.

"I'm sorry, Cole," she said. "Please let me think about what you said and we'll talk another time, I promise. Thank you for taking the time to come over and talk to me."

She closed the door in the young man's face, focused on calming Sean down. But Sean didn't want to calm down and over the next hour and a half, Alix had to listen to Sean and his real feelings on the matter of her and Cord.

They weren't very good.

NINE

"WE'VE GOT A PROBLEM."

Those were Alix's words. Cord and Alix sat next to each other in the booth of a quiet little Italian restaurant over near the hospital. They were sitting as close as they possibly could without Alix sitting on his lap. He had his arm around her shoulders and was holding one of her hands.

They had talked four times on the phone since Cole's visit to Alix the previous evening and had decided it would be best to meet someplace where the kids wouldn't see them. Alix had been so glad to see him when he showed up at the restaurant that she had bolted out of her car and jumped on him, arms and legs all wrapped up around him. He held her tightly, kissing her within an inch of her life.

"I feel like we're sneaking around behind my parents' back," she giggled as they sat the table, her head on his shoulder. "I feel so clandestine."

He snickered. "Me, too," he admitted. "But considering what you told me about Cole and Sean, I think this is for the best right now until we can figure this all out."

She sighed as the waitress brought her a glass of red wine

and him a tall beer. "I agree," she said, taking her wine. "So what in the hell do we do about this? I don't even know where to start."

Cord collected his beer and, clinking it against her glass, took a long drink. "I don't know," he admitted. "So Cole really said that he was afraid you'd take me away from him?"

Alix nodded, sipping her wine. "It was so sad," she murmured. "He's so scared of losing you, Cord. He said you were the only parent he had left."

Cord sighed heavily. "Wow," he breathed. "I never knew he would even think something like that. It's not like I run off with women on a weekly basis or anything. The boys have always had me to themselves, since Cole was a baby. I have to say that I'm a little hurt that Cole wouldn't want me to be happy, though."

"I don't think it's that more than he's just afraid you'll do what his mother did," Alix said. "Did you say that you think she forgets she had kids from her first marriage?"

Cord nodded pensively. "She does. She hardly ever sees them."

"Cole is just feeling insecure. He's possessive of you and that's natural."

"What about Sean? How does he feel?"

Alix shrugged and sipped her wine again. "Like he's being encroached on. He's been the man of the house for four years and now you come along. He likes you a lot, but he feels threatened, probably just like Cole. Like he's going to lose a parent. But he'll come to terms with it."

Cord sighed heavily, toying with his beer. "I think," he said, "that this is all my fault. I'm the one who came on so strongly to you. I didn't give anyone time to adjust; I just bulldozed my way in because I was so attracted to you and so thrilled I'd found you that I didn't want to miss anything. I was afraid you'd slip through my fingers if I waited."

Alix put her hand on his chest, patting him soothingly. "It's nobody's fault," she insisted. "We were afraid that everything was happening so fast but I think we were only thinking of ourselves. We weren't really thinking about the kids, just assuming they'd go along with us."

He nodded, kissing the top of her head. "Chris and Kyle have been supportive, at least," he said. "Don't tell him I told you, but Chris thinks you're hot. He even fist-bumped me about it."

Alix giggled. Then, she sobered. "So what do we do? Do we have to sneak around like this for the rest of our lives?"

"No," Cord said flatly. "At some point, Cole is going to have to understand that I'm not leaving him and you're not taking me away. I love my son deeply, but I can't really let him control my life like this. I won't be held an emotional prisoner by a fourteen-year-old."

Alix shifted so she could look up at him. "But you can't let him feel insecure, like he's going to lose you."

Cord took another drink of his beer. "I'll talk to him about it. If I have to, I'll take him to a therapist. I've finally found the woman of my dreams and I'm not going to let my son ruin it. I'm sorry if that sounds selfish, but I'm just not."

Alix was subdued, thinking of Cole, of Sean, and feeling incredible sadness and disappointment. "Maybe you and I should talk to a child therapist and see how they would recommend we handle it."

"Maybe."

"I'll see if there's one at the hospital we can talk to."

"Sure," he wrapped both arms around her and pulled her tightly into the curve of his torso. "Meanwhile, I guess you and I need to take it a little easy in front of the kids."

She snuggled against him. "Agreed."

"It's really going to kill me to ease up with you."

"Me, too."

The waitress came and took their order. They ate their dinner over small talk and soft laughter as Cord told her some locker room stories of his days in the NFL. It was a Monday night and Cord had to work the next morning, but when the meal ended and they paid the check, he didn't want to leave her.

He took her over to the Salem Waterfront Hotel and Marina, checked into a room, and they spent the next two hours between the sheets. They both realized that time alone would be very precious and hard to come by, so they intended to take advantage of it. Close to eleven at night, Cord's cell phone went off at a most inopportune moment, so he let it ring until they were finished.

Exhausted, but in a good way, Cord lay on top of Alix for a several long and wonderful minutes before reluctantly rolling off of her and reaching for his phone on the nightstand.

Chris had left him a message. Two minutes after listening to it, they were both dressed and running out of the door.

———

"So, as you can see by the x-rays, he's got a concussion and a fractured left forearm," Alix was standing with Cord, Chris and Kyle in her office at the hospital and she delivered the news. "I want to keep him for twenty-four hours because of the concussion, but barring any complications, you should be able to take him home tomorrow."

Cord was pale and drawn as he listened to Alix's professional yet compassionate delivery of Cole's injuries. Seated in one of her leather guest chairs, he sighed heavily and wiped a hand over his face.

"Thank God," he breathed. "It could have been so much worse."

Chris and Kyle, too, were pale and drawn. Having found their baby brother at the bottom of the stairs in a heap had scared the hell out of them. All Cole could tell them was that Aram got in the way when he had gone downstairs to get something to eat, that the dog had somehow tripped him. The kid had fallen all the way down the narrow back stairs in his house as his father had cavorted in a hotel somewhere. At least, that's the thought that Cord couldn't get out of his mind.

"He's young, healthy and resilient," Alix tried to sound positive. She could only imagine the guilt and sadness the man was feeling. "He should be fine."

It was almost dawn, the sun starting to peek between the blinds in Alix's office. Cord just sat there, looking at her, wanting to say so much more than he had but refraining because of Chris and Kyle. Finally, he stood up, wearily.

"Well," he said, wiping his hand over his stubbled face again. "I'll go say goodbye to him and take Chris and Kyle home."

Alix, who had been seated behind her desk showing the Trevor boys a collection of Cole's x-rays, stood up as well.

"He's asleep now," she said as she herded them out of her office and into the corridor beyond. "He won't even know you're there. Go home, get some sleep, and I'll stay with Cole. I'll call you if anything comes up."

Cord dug into his jean's pocket and pulled out his car keys, tossing them to Chris. "Go wait out in the car for me," he told them. "I'll be out in a minute."

Chris and Kyle said goodbye to Alix, Chris even going so far as to hug her. She fought off a grin as they disappeared down the hallway, turning to Cord to see that he was watching her. She reached up and ran a soft hand across his cheek.

"He's going to be fine," she whispered. "Go home and get some sleep. I promise I won't leave him."

Cord stared at her a moment longer before exhaling sharply and drawing her into his enormous embrace. He just stood there and held her, tightly.

"God, I just feel sick about all of this," he whispered. "He could have broken his neck."

"But he didn't," she stressed, hugging him. "He didn't break anything other than his forearm and that's just a slight fracture. He'll be out of the cast in a month. Don't worry so much, okay? I promise I'll take very good care of him."

He kissed her cheek, her lips, before releasing her. "I know you will," he murmured. "Thank you for what you've done for him already. You took charge when I was having a hard time doing it and you never left him, not even for a second. You made sure he was all right the entire time and even if I wasn't madly in love with you already, that would have sealed the deal for me. I just can't tell you what that all meant to me."

He took her hand and kissed it sincerely. Alix smiled up at him. "You're welcome," she winked at him, glancing down the hall when a couple of nurses entered and started coming towards them. She let go of his hand. "For now, just go home. Call me when you wake up, okay?"

His blue eyes were soft on her. "You haven't slept all night, either."

"I'm fine. I'll probably try to sleep this afternoon."

"I wish it could be with me."

He said it so sweetly, so softly. "Me, too," she whispered. "But I will see you later for sure."

"You better believe it," he assured her, glancing at his watch. "Well, I guess I'd better get Chris and Kyle home. Do you want me to bring you some breakfast?"

She shook her head. "I'm fine, but thank you."

Cord couldn't help himself; he kissed her and hugged her tightly before releasing her. "I love you, honey. See you in a bit."

Alix waved at him as he started to move away. "Love you, too."

He winked at her and moved down the hallway, leaving Alix standing there, watching him, thinking he was just about the most beautiful thing she'd ever seen.

———

Cole slept well into the noon hour when the nurse woke him up to take his blood pressure and do a few other routine things. Alix had been down in the E.R. but the nurse had called her when he woke up. Alix finished up with the sutures she was placing in the shin of a man who hit himself with a garden hoe and headed up to Pediatrics.

As she approached the room, she could hear soft conversation inside. Entering the door, she saw a woman standing next to the bed, speaking with Cole. The woman was about Alix's height, with long blond hair and expensive clothes. When she heard Alix enter and turned towards her, Alix could immediately see the resemblance between Cole and the woman. Alix smiled when their eyes met.

"Hi," she said, extending her hand. "I'm Dr. Hendry."

The woman smiled in return. "Hello," she said. "I'm Dianne Norgren, Cole's mother."

Alix had suspected as much. She maintained her smile even though she was seriously looking the woman over, having heard so much about her. Mostly unflattering things, really, as far as the woman's competency as a mother went. She had always wondered what kind of woman could have just picked up and left Cord and the boys. She was about to find out.

"Well," she said as she crossed to the other side of the bed. "Has anyone talked to you about your son's injuries?"

Dianne shook her head. "I got a call from his father earlier today telling me what had happened," she said. "I came over as soon as I could. How is he?"

Alix smiled at Cole, who gazed back at her with a somewhat torn expression; he was still being very distant to her but there was something there that wanted to convey warmth. He was a very confused young man.

"He's going to be fine," Alix assured her. "The fracture is minimal and the concussion should go away in a day or so. I can show you the x-rays if you'd like...."

Dianne cut her off. "No need," she said, her gaze returning to Cole. "If you say he's going to be fine, that's good enough for me. He really gave his father a scare."

But he didn't give you a scare? Alix thought. She glanced at the computer screen next to the bed, looking over his stats. "These things happen sometimes," she said. "Dark stairs and dogs are a recipe for disaster."

Dianne grinned, still looking at her son. When she ran a hand over his blond head, the boy seemed to recoil.

"I suppose," she said. "It was stupid, really. Those dogs shouldn't even be in the house."

Cole tried to pull his head away from his mother. "I just didn't see them," he said, sounding angry. "I'm fine, Mom. You can go home now."

Dianne's grin faded as animosity from her son became evident. "I'll leave soon enough," she said, removing her hand. "I thought I'd bring your sisters over to visit."

Cole shook his head, hard. "No," he said flatly. "I don't want to see them."

Dianne eyed Alix, who pretended to busy herself with other things. "They miss you, Cole."

Cole just shrugged and looked away. Dianne pressed forward. "Don't you miss them?"

He just shook his head. He was obviously upset and Alix, coming to understand the relationship he had with his mother somewhat, was sympathetic.

"Cole should be getting lunch in a few minutes," she said to Dianne. "Would you like to stay for lunch?"

Dianne shook her head and looked at her watch. "I wish I could, but I can't," she said. "I need to be back at the office in an hour. I just came to see how Cole was doing."

"He's doing fine," Alix said. "He should be able to go home in a couple of days."

"Good," Dianne was back to smiling at her son. "I'll tell the family you're doing fine. Maybe we can have you over for a visit when you're out of the hospital."

Cole didn't even look at her; he just kept his head turned and his gaze averted. "Whatever Dad says."

Dianne's smile faded again. "It doesn't matter what your dad says," she said as she picked up her purse from the chair next to the bed. "It's whatever you say and I say. If I want you to come for a visit, you will."

Cole's head snapped in her direction, the pale eyes blazing. "Look," he said pointedly, "the last time I saw you was six months ago and if I hadn't broken my arm, I still wouldn't be seeing you, so don't act like you care about me or like you have any say in my life, okay? And don't go bossing me around."

Alix watched Dianne very carefully for her reaction, which wasn't long in coming. The woman's smile faded entirely and her jaw began to tick.

"Cole," she admonished sternly. "I'm sorry you're upset and I'm sorry you're hurt, but please don't speak to me like that. Of course I care about you; I'm your mom. I love you."

Cole turned away from her and closed his eyes tightly. "No,

you don't," he hissed. "Just... go away, okay? I don't want to see you anymore."

Dianne started to say something but Alix intervened; she had to. Cole had himself all worked up and she couldn't let it go on. She waved a hand at the woman.

"It's okay," she said, positioning herself over Cole protectively. "He's just tired. I'll take care of him."

Dianne had her purse on her arm, standing by the door. She looked at Alix, and Cole, and then back again before turning and leaving without a word. When the door closed, Alix looked at Cole.

"She's gone," Alix said reassuringly. "Are you okay? Do you want me to call your dad?"

He opened his eyes and looked at her with about as much animosity as he had looked at his mother. "No," he said. "I want you to go, too."

Alix's gentle expression faded. "I have to stay," she told him. "I'm your doctor. I have to check you out now that you're awake."

"No," he said, more loudly. "I don't want you to touch me."

"Why not?"

He was starting to become very agitated. "Because... because you're just doing it to score points with my dad!"

Alix frowned. "That's not true," she said. "I'm a physician. It's my job to take care of you and it has nothing to do with your dad."

Cole tried to move away from her across the small bed. "Leave me alone," he muttered.

Alix watched him, coolly evaluating his manner. She wasn't going to force herself on him but facts were facts; she was his doctor of record. She knew the kid didn't care about that, but it was important.

"Cole," she said evenly. "I need for you to listen to me. I

know you're upset and I can appreciate that, but it's important that you understand something – I am your doctor while you're here in the hospital. I know you don't like it, but that's the truth. I need to examine you and take care of you, and you're just going to have to deal with it. You can't always have what you want and in this case, you're not going to make me go away just because you tell me to, so let's try to get along so I can get you well and out of the hospital. Okay?"

Cole's head was turned away from her. He was staring at the wall. "Fine," he growled. "You do what you have to do. Then you can be a hero to my dad and you can both run off and get married and forget about the kids, because that's what happens when parents fall in love. I get it."

Alix sighed. "That's not what happens," she said. "We would never run off and leave you or your brothers, or my kids. You're our children and we love you more than anything."

Cole shook his head and looked at her. "That's not true," he said. "You don't love us more than you love each other. My dad would do whatever you said and forget about what I want."

"So you're supposed to be allowed to tell your dad how to run his life?"

"No," he said, tears forming in his eyes. "I told you before that he was all we have left; you've seen my mom and see how she is. We need my dad because my mom doesn't care about us at all. We need somebody to love us. If my dad loves you, who will love us the most? Not him, because he'll love *you* the most."

Alix's heart just about broke. She could see such a frightened, desperate young man underneath the animosity. "Oh... Cole," she breathed. "That's not true. He'll always love you and your brothers more than anything."

Cole broke down in sobs. "He's done it before," he wept. "He had a girlfriend once and she took all of his time. We never saw him. He'd be gone with her and Chris would have to make us hot dogs for dinner all of the time because we weren't allowed to use the stove. Chris walked me to school in the morning, too, and one time I had a school play and my dad didn't even come because his girlfriend made him go to something with her instead. If my dad gets with you, he'll forget about us completely. I love my dad. I don't want him to go away."

Tears streamed down Alix's cheeks and she wiped them away quickly.

"He's not going to go away," she assured him. "I promise, Cole, no one will be going away."

Cole snapped at her angrily. "Last night, I called him at the station because he said he was working," he said. "The guys told me he had taken the night off and I knew he was with you. He lied to us because he was with you, okay? So you know what I did? I didn't trip on the dog; I fell down the stairs on purpose because I knew if there was an emergency, he'd come back to me. I had to get him away from you and I knew he would come if something was wrong. So I fell down the stairs and he *did* come."

Alix was stunned. "Cole," she breathed, "you could have broken your neck. Do you realize how serious this is?"

Cole shrugged, wiping at his running nose. "I didn't mean to break my arm," he admitted. "I thought I could catch myself and just make a bunch of noise, but it didn't happen that way. I really did hit my head. I guess it was a stupid thing to do, but it got my dad back. That's all I wanted."

Oh, my God, Alix thought. The boy was resorting to hurting himself just to get his father's attention because he was so terrified of losing him to a new girlfriend. Distraught and heartbroken, Alix patted the young man's shoulder gently and left the room to make a phone call.

Cord was at the hospital in twenty minutes.

———

Alix was in the corridor when he arrived.

Cord burst out of the elevator and came charging down the hall into Pediatrics, spying Alix in the dim lighting near the door to Cole's room. He went right to her.

"What's wrong?" he demanded. "What happened with Cole?"

Alix was pale and drawn as she gazed up at him. She'd spent the last twenty minutes preparing what she was going to say to him and she wasn't looking forward to it. The truth was that it was tearing her up.

"Physically, he's on the mend," she said. "But his mother was here earlier. He didn't like that one bit."

Cord's tense features relaxed in understanding. Then, he took a long, deep breath, reaching out to take her arm as he slumped back against the cold, white wall of the corridor.

"Oh," he said simply. "Christ, you scared the hell out of me telling me I'd better get over here fast. I thought something was really wrong."

Alix looked at him seriously. "Something *is* really wrong," she said. "Cord, I'm not going to beat around the bush with this so I'll come out with it. We can't see each other anymore."

At first, her statement didn't register with him but when it did, his eyes widened and he came up off the wall. "What are you talking about?" he breathed.

Alix sighed sharply. "Look," she said, lowering her voice. "Last night, we met in secret because we've got two kids between us who aren't thrilled with the fact that we're dating. As a result, you weren't home when Cole fell down the stairs. Do you know what he just told me? He did it because you told him you were working last night so he called the station only to be told you had taken the night off. He knew you had lied to him about where you were so he staged that fall down the stairs because he knew you'd come home if it was an emergency. Trouble was, he actually ended up hurting himself even though he hadn't meant to."

Cord was pale. "He did that on purpose to get my attention?"

Alix was starting to choke up. "He did," she said. "Cord, we need to stop seeing each other for a while, at least until the boys can come to better terms with it. You can't have Cole pulling stunts to get your attention every time you're out with me and I can't have Sean bottling it up inside of him because he doesn't want to deal with it. We need to be unselfish about this and think about our kids."

Cord's expression was tight with grief. "I *am* thinking about my son," he said. "But I'm thinking about you, too. I can't let my fourteen-year-old son tell me how to run my life, Alix. I love you and he's just going to have to deal with it."

Alix's tears were breaking through. "You can't make me a priority over your son," she said, stifling sobs. "You would hate yourself for doing it and eventually, you might hate me, too, and I couldn't deal with it."

"I could never hate you," he breathed. "Please... Alix, there has to be another way."

She shook her head, wiping at her eyes and struggling not to openly weep. "There isn't," she whispered tightly. "It's not right to choose me over your boys and you know it."

Cord's chest was so tight with emotion that he could barely breathe. When he reached out to touch her, she pulled her hand away. He nearly shattered. "Alix," he murmured. "I love you. I will always love you. I want to be with you forever and you know that. Cole will come to terms with us. He'll see that...."

"And what if he doesn't?" she turned on him, wiping at her eyes. "What if the next time, he runs in front of a car or does something stupid like that? You will absolutely hate me for the fact that your son injured himself because of me."

"It wouldn't be because of you," he countered passionately. "I'm going to take Cole to a therapist or someone who can help him deal with these feelings. I can't let the fear of him doing something idiotic control me. I can't let him make a prisoner of me because he's afraid of losing me."

Alix just shook her head. "Just... settle things with him," she said, struggling to recover her composure. "I need to settle things with Sean. Until we do, please don't call me. Don't send me flowers, and don't come visit me at the hospital. I want you to stay away from me completely and deal with your son. Okay?"

Cord's eyes were filling with tears. "Please don't do this, Alix."

She couldn't say anything more. Hand over her mouth to fight off the sobs, she turned and walked away from him down the long hospital corridor. Cord stood there, tears in his eyes, until she turned the corner and disappeared from sight. His heart was in a million pieces, fragmented into shards so small he was sure he would never be able to put it back together again. His entire body hurt with emotion, from head to toe.

Slowly, his gaze moved to the door to Cole's room. *What he did was intentional.* Forcing himself to move, he headed into Cole's room. He had a few things to say to his son.

TEN

IT HAD BEEN A LONG SHIFT, longer still when the fire department brought in three car accident victims right before Alix got off shift. She found herself in Exam One with a guy whose chest had been crushed by the head-on collision. Even as she and her team lifted the guy onto the hospital gurney and she began her trauma assessment, she could hear more people being brought in as a result of the multi-car accident. She could hear the fire department radios going off in the corridor outside.

Although she was professional on the outside, on the inside, she was dying. She hadn't talked to Cord in five days and every one of those days was like living in hell. Especially at work; his fire station was assigned to North Shore so anytime there were medical calls, there was a huge likelihood he would show up. Every time she saw a fire engine or heard a radio, her stomach twisted in knots.

The injured man was going downhill fast so she ended up cracking the man's chest and doing an open heart massage as they cleared a surgery room. Alix jumped up on the side of the bed, bracing herself and doing the heart massage with her left hand as her team wheeled the gurney out and headed down the hall towards Surgery. She was so involved in watching the heart monitor propped on the bed that she didn't notice when the gurney wheeled right past Cord, who was standing at the nurse's station.

Bloodied up to her elbow, like she was doing battle surgery, Cord watched Alix jet by and disappear down the hall. His heart sank, the weight on his chest so heavy that he could scarcely breathe. Already, he was having difficulty functioning without her, but seeing her after five days of not laying eyes on the woman had him physically ill. It was too much of a blow to his battered heart. He'd never been so miserable in his entire life. Once the rig cleared the hospital, he went back to the station and went home sick for the rest of the night.

Only he didn't go home. He went back to the hospital and drove around in the parking lot looking for Alix's car. It was still there, parked in the staff lot, so he parked his truck over in a corner of the lot with a bird's-eye view of her car, and sat there, waiting, all night. He couldn't go home. Not until he saw her.

People came and went out of the hospital staff entrance and every time the door opened, he strained to see if it was Alix. But the night went on and she didn't appear. It was just before dawn when he caught glimpse of someone emerging from the staff entrance and, as luck would have it, it happened to be Alix.

Cord bailed out of the truck, making his way towards her car as the other vehicles in the lot camouflaged his approach. Heart racing, he reached her car just about the time she did.

Alix froze when she saw him standing by the trunk of her car, looking exhausted and pale. Having been awake almost twenty-four hours, and in a very brittle emotional state, one look at him was all it took for her to burst into tears.

"No," she sobbed miserably, moving to the other side of her car to get away from him. "Please, Cord... please, don't... please, just go."

Cord followed her, equally as emotional. Tears filled his eyes as he rounded the car to cut her off so she couldn't get away from him.

"Alix," he begged, his throat tight. "Please, honey, don't run from me. Please, I just... I just can't take this anymore. It's killing me."

She saw that he was blocking off the door so she backed away from him, slumping against her car. She sobbed into her hand, trying not to look at him.

"I know it is," she wept. "It's killing me, too, but we can't... Cole is your flesh and blood, and he's more important than our relationship. We discussed this; if you choose me over him, you'll never forgive yourself. He's your son, Cord."

He reached out and grabbed her. "I know he's my son." He tried not to hurt her as she struggled to pull away. "He's my son and I love him, but I love you, too. I love you more than anything, Alix. I've had five long days to think about this and I've decided that I'm a horrible, horrible father because I want to be happy. I want it more than I want Cole to be happy. He's afraid you're going to take me away from him and the only way we can prove him wrong is to show him. Alix, I swear, I can't live without you. I don't want to try. Please don't break up with me. I'll never recover, honey. *Please.*"

Alix looked at him, then, seeing tears streaming down his cheeks. She stopped fighting him but she didn't fall into his arms. She just stood there and trembled.

"I'm not sure if I can let you make that decision," she sobbed. "You'd hate yourself, Cord, you really would. And then you'd hate me. You can't choose a woman over your son. That's just not right."

His lower lip trembled as he looked at her. "It'll all work out if we just stay together and stay strong," he begged. "I can't let this go, honey. I just can't walk away from you. I've never loved anyone so much in my entire life."

"Neither have I," her sobbing had lessened but her entire body ached. He was still holding on to her arms and she crumpled, trying to pull away from him. "Cord, please let me go. It hurts... my entire body hurts when you touch me. You need to let me go."

His voice cracked. "I can't. I won't. I'll follow you forever, Alix. I can't ever let you go."

Her tears returned and she couldn't hold out against him any longer. With a big sob, she threw herself into his arms and together, they wept openly, holding one another, so very devastated by the circumstances. Cord began kissing her head, her cheeks, tasting her salty tears, drowning himself in the feel and taste of her. Their lips came together in a clash of flesh and passion and emotion before Alix ripped away from him, violently, and ended up stumbling. As he reached down to pick her up, she scrambled away from him and ran around to the other side of the car.

Cord followed, listening to her loud sobbing as she jumped into the car and slammed the door, locking it. He tried to open it, pleading with her, but she shook her head and turned the car on. He was still trying to open the door as she backed up and drove away, screeching out of the parking lot and tearing off down the boulevard.

Cord ran to his truck, tears all over his face, as he jumped in and followed.

———

Alix spent the rest of the day in her bedroom, unable to sleep, sobbing intermittently. She was so exhausted but her emotional turmoil prevented her from sleeping. After her run-in with

Cord in the parking lot, she'd come home and he'd followed, parking his truck outside her house and just sitting there. Once she realized he was parked outside, she couldn't bring herself to look out of the window but eventually, she did look later in the afternoon and the truck was gone. She collapsed in tears.

When Sean came home from school, he went to tell his mother hello but entering her room, he could see she was a wreck and he was distressed. He offered to make her something to eat, but she declined.

Increasingly upset, he simply left her alone, feeling guilty, as if he had contributed to this somehow. Maybe he hadn't accomplished her misery single-handedly, but he'd definitely been a part of it. So had Cole. They'd made their wants known to their parents and, like good parents, they had decided in favor of the kids. But that had been selfish. As Sean sat in his room and listened to his mother sniffle, he got on the phone to Kyle. Something had to be done about it. He just couldn't take her misery any more, no matter how hard she tried to keep it from him.

It was near sundown when there was a soft knock on Alix's door. Thinking it was Rose and Hester having returned from the playground, she sat up in bed as the door opened and Sean entered. But he wasn't alone; Chris and Kyle were behind him.

Shocked, Alix sat up in bed and tried not to look too shattered, but the truth was that seeing Cord's sons had tears on the surface again. As she grabbed for a sweat jacket to cover up with, one more person entered the room.

Alix found herself looking at Cole. The tall, blond kid remained by the door and wouldn't come any further into the room. Kyle, the biggest of the three brothers, stood next to him as Chris and Sean faced Alix.

"Mom," Sean began. He looked so very serious. "The guys and I have been talking and... well, we know you're sad without Mr. Trevor. I know how miserable you've been and it's just not right. You were so happy when you were with him and now... well...."

"My dad's miserable, too," Chris said. "All he does is sit in front of the television and watch the weather channel. He doesn't do anything else. He just sits there and stares. We've got all these football practices during the week and even though he's there, his mind isn't, if you know what I mean. Dad's just going through the motions these days. It's like... like something went out of him when you broke up with him. He's just lost."

He turned around and looked at Cole, who was standing rather defiantly back by the door. Kyle grabbed his brother and pushed him forward as Chris snatched him by the arm and pulled. Cole skidded across the newly stained wood floor.

"Cole has something to say to you," Chris said.

Sean and Chris stood back as Cole, his left arm in a cast that Alix had personally put on him, looked at her with a mixture of reluctance, defiance and remorse. As Kyle slipped from the room, Cole met Alix's red-rimmed gaze for a moment but then ended up hanging his head.

"I...," he started, paused, and started again. "I don't even want to talk about this."

"You said you would," Chris growled from behind him. "You promised."

Cole made a face, resistant to the end, but eventually seemed to give in. He stared at his feet as he spoke.

"I already told her all of this," he muttered, unhappy. "She knows... why."

"Tell her again," Kyle said warningly.

"Fine," he huffed. "I guess... well, my whole life, it's just been my dad. Other kids have two parents but I've always felt like I've only had one. My dad had had other girlfriends, but they didn't last very long and I was always happy about that because things could get back to normal. It was just us four guys, you know? We didn't need anyone else. Then you came along and my dad was so interested in you. We could all see it, the first time we met you even. My dad just had this look on his face like I've never seen before."

"And?" Chris prodded from behind.

Cole turned to glare at his brother before daring to lift his eyes to Alix. "And I was jealous. I was afraid he'd spend more time with you than with us and leave us like my mom did. But my dad said he's got room in his heart for all of us and that you're not going to take him away from us. I promised him I'd never do anything stupid again to get his attention and I won't. I'm sorry I did."

"My dad is really unhappy without you, Dr. Hendry," Chris said from his position over against the wall. He glanced at Sean before continuing. "We've all talked about it and we decided that it's good for you and my dad to be together because you make each other happy. What we feel... well, I'm all for it but I know Cole and Sean had some problems with it, but they just have to man up and accept the change. So I just have one question."

Alix was feeling lightheaded, so overwhelmed by what she was hearing that she was having difficulty standing. "What question?"

Chris opened his mouth but Kyle came back in the room and looked at his older brother. "Dad's on his way," he said quietly.

Chris nodded and returned his attention to Alix. "When you guys get married, are we all going to live here? I'm just saying that I get dibs on my own bedroom 'cuz I'm not sharing a room with any of these knuckleheads."

Sean took a good-natured swipe at him and even Cole snorted. Only Alix wasn't grinning; her legs were shaking so badly that she had to sit down on the end of the bed, trying to process what the boys had said to her. As the boys began to talk about who got what bedroom, she put up a hand.

"Wait a minute," she said, looking at Cole. "Are you telling me that you're okay with your dad and me? That you don't have a problem with us being together?"

Cole looked at her for a long moment before shaking his head. "My dad needs to be happy," he said simply. "You make him happy."

Alix exhaled heavily, as if the weight of the world just left her. Then she did it again and before she could draw another breath, she burst into tears. All of the snickering and chatter stopped in an instant as the boys, stricken, watched Alix have a meltdown. Sean and Chris went to her, Sean dropping to his knees beside her.

"Mom?" he put his hand on her arm. "What's wrong?"

Alix couldn't even answer him. She was absolutely overcome with emotion. Concerned, Chris bent down, trying to look her in the eye.

"Are you okay, Dr. Hendry?" he asked.

Alix bolted up from the bed, sobbing so hard that she was growing faint. She staggered into her bathroom and slammed the door, but the boys could hear her crying loudly. Startled, they looked at each other in various stages of shock when they heard a car pull up outside. Actually, it was more the roar of an engine and a screeching halt. They heard the car door slam, running feet, and the kitchen door thrown open so hard that it slammed into the wall.

Running feet were across the kitchen and up the back stairs. Then the second door in the bedroom that faced the kitchen stairs flew open and Cord was in the doorway, his handsome face taut with panic.

"What happened?" he demanded, then saw that all of the

boys were there, including Cole. His eyes widened on his youngest son. "Cole? What in the hell are you doing here?"

It was then that he heard the hysterical sobbing in the bathroom and after a few seconds of listening to the hysterics, his cheeks flushed red as he looked at the boys.

"Okay," he rumbled, struggling with his temper. "I'm going to try and stay calm, but why is Alix crying? What in the hell happened?"

Chris went over to his father. "It's not what you think, Dad." He could see the man was ready to blow his top. "We came to talk to Alix and...."

Cord cut him off. "Kyle called and said that I needed to get over here right away, that something had happened."

Chris tried to calm his old man down. "Dad, we came here to talk to Alix," he said, trying to finish explaining before his dad went on a rampage. "Sean called and said that Dr. Hendry was... well, it doesn't matter, but we all discussed the situation and we've decided that you and Alix are better off together. You love each other, and you make each other happy, and we want to see you all happy. That's what we told her."

Cord's pallor went from a reddish tone to somewhat ashen as Chris' explanation settled. "You... you told her that you wanted to see us together?" he repeated, stunned. Then he looked at Cole. "Son? Is... is that what you think?"

Chris, Kyle and Sean all turned to look at Cole, just to make sure he didn't go back on his word. Cole could feel their stares but he was looking at his dad. After a moment, he nodded. "Yes," he said, looking the least bit sheepish. "I'm sorry, Dad. I didn't mean to make you guys miserable. I was just... I was dumb, I guess. I know she won't take you away from us. I guess I just have to get used to her."

Shocked, Cord looked at his boys, at Sean, and felt much

the same way Alix felt; he was overwhelmed. After a moment, he just shook his head.

"Are you sure?" he hissed in disbelief. "Really?"

Chris nodded. "Really," he said. Then he pointed to the bathroom. "I'm going to take these boneheads out for something to eat, but you'd better calm her down. She's been crying like that for five straight minutes."

Cord moved for the bathroom door, somewhat haltingly, as Chris herded the boys out of the room. Struggling to recover his composure, Cord knocked softly on the bathroom door.

"Alix?" he said. "Honey, it's me. Can I come in?"

The door abruptly flew open and Alix was standing there, mascara all down her face and her cheeks pale. Cord took one look at her and his heart just about broke.

"Come here, honey," he whispered, opening his arms to her. "It's okay. Everything's okay."

Alix threw herself into his embrace, her arms going around his neck and her legs wrapping around his waist. She was back to sobbing hysterically and he carried her over to the bed, sitting down on the end and just cradling her. His tears were coming now, too.

"I'm so sorry." He held her head in his big hands and kissed her cheeks. "I'm so sorry you had to go through this."

Alix was struggling to pull it together; she was still reeling. "I didn't think I was ever going to see you again," she wept, fixing him in the eyes. "God, I look at you now and you're the most beautiful thing I've ever seen."

He laughed even as tears splattered on his cheeks. He just hugged her, so incredibly glad to have her in his arms again. He couldn't describe the euphoria, the surprise, the utter joy.

It was the best day of his life.

ELEVEN
LATE OCTOBER

IT WAS HALLOWEEN. The landscape had turned shades of yellow, orange and brown a few weeks back; all of the colors of fall popping forth that Alix had never seen on the west coast. It was really very beautiful and many a morning she would sit on her porch in the morning, sipping coffee and enjoying the day. If Cord wasn't working, he would show up when Chris came to pick Sean up for school. Dad would climb out of the truck, Sean would jump in, and all four boys would make the two mile trek to school as Cord settled next to Alix on the porch with coffee she had waiting for him.

After their brief break up, things had been extremely good between them. They didn't even speak of those five days they had been apart, mostly because they were still so emotional about it. They resumed a normal life but now they didn't hide their relationship from the children. They were still appropriate, and somewhat careful, but if Cord wanted to hold Alix's hand or put his arm around her in front of the boys, he damn well did it, which was pretty much all of the time. The kids had gotten used to the affection, even Cole and Sean. They didn't think anything of it anymore. Rose couldn't have cared less one way or the other, young and resilient as she was.

All Hallows Eve arrived with frost in the air and brilliantly colored leaves. As the sun began to go down, Cord fired up the jack-o-lanterns and put them on the front porch of Alix's house as she busied herself upstairs dressing Rose up like a princess. Once the pumpkins were strategically placed around the house and the candy was ready in the bowl, the boys lit fires in the dining room and living room fireplaces before begging Cord to be allowed to go out and scare up mischief.

Cord was in the kitchen as the sun set, with Hester at the sink, snorting, because the boys were ganging up on him. He wasn't sure what, exactly, they were going to do and he forbade them from throwing eggs or decorating front lawns with toilet paper. The boys assured him that they weren't going to do anything like that, but one of their friends was having a party and they wanted to go and hang out.

As Cord tried to find out what they were really up to, as he wasn't so sure about a party at a house where he didn't know the parents, Alix came downstairs with Rose all dressed up. She saw the four boys standing around Cord.

"All hail, foolish mortals," she said, helping Rose down the last step. "Princess Rose has arrived."

The men turned to see Rose in her pink gown, all dolled up. Cord grinned. "Wow," he said admiringly. "You look so beautiful, Rosie."

Rose had her magic wand in one hand and her bucket for candy in the other. She marched right up to Cord.

"Let's go," she told him.

Cord glanced at Alix as he spoke. "But someone has to stay here to give out candy," he told her. "You and your mom can go and I'll wait here."

Rose didn't like that idea and began to whine. "No," she said unhappily. "You come."

Cord wasn't sure what to say until Alix stepped in. She looked at the boys. "You guys stay here and pass out candy while we take her around the neighborhood. We won't be out long."

Kyle and Cole didn't like that idea and looked at Sean to disagree with his mother. Sean wasn't too keen on the suggestion, either.

"Mom," he was trying not to sound like he was whining, too. "We have a party to go to."

Alix fixed him in the eye. "When were you going to ask me if you could go? This is the first I've heard about it."

Sean didn't want to come across as if he were about to throw a tantrum. "I'm telling you now," he said. "You've been busy with Rosie all night."

"I saw you a half hour ago."

"So you're going to argue with me about it?" he thought he made a good attempt at turning it all around on her. "All of the kids are going to be there. Can we go just for a little while? Please?"

Alix twisted her lips wryly and looked at Cord. "Do you know these kids that are having the party?"

In response, Cord looked at his boys. "Whose house is it at?"

"Melody Longmyer's house," Chris said. "I promise we won't get into any trouble."

Chris was a responsible young man and Cord trusted him. So he reluctantly nodded, looking to Alix, who finally nodded as well. As the boys beamed, she held up a finger.

"With the provision that you guys give out candy for a half hour while we take Rosie around the neighborhood, okay?" she asked. "Please?"

Because Chris agreed, the rest of them nodded. Thrilled,

Rose led her mother and Cord out into the dusk to harvest her bounty of candy.

With the grown-ups gone and a big bowl full of candy in the house, Cole, Kyle and Sean tore into the candy bars as they spread out over the couch to watch television until Cord and Alix returned. Chris got a hold of the remote and began flipping channels, much to the other boys' frustration. As they began squabbling about it, the doorbell rang.

Kyle and Sean jumped up, giving out candy bars to about five or six little witches and ghosts trolling the neighborhood. When they closed the door on them, they ate more of the candy and realized the bowl was only about half full now so they stopped and pretended like they didn't notice how much candy they ate. As they made their way back into the living room, Sean came to a halt at the base of the stairs.

"Hey," he paused, looking up into the dark second floor. "Did anybody hear that?"

The only one who listened to him was Kyle. The big Trevor brother walked over to where Sean was standing at the base of the stairs.

"Hear what?" he asked.

Sean just stood there, ears attuned, his gaze on the darkened second floor. As Kyle looked at him curiously, Sean began taking the stairs two at a time.

"There it is again," he insisted.

Kyle followed. As the pair of them came up to the second floor landing, they both heard the faint, somewhat off-key singing.

"*Goody Good, Goody Good, 'ere snake and bird could*".

Kyle looked at Sean, stricken. "What the hell was *that*?"

Sean, spooked, shook his head. He was looking at Rose's old bedroom, now shut up with boxes in it. His mom had moved Rose out of it and never said why. After the night she was thrown against the wall, Sean had guessed. But he didn't like to think about that night because he thought he had imagined the whole thing.

Listening to the faint singing, he and Kyle crept towards the room. As they neared the door, the old panel unlatched. The boys froze. Then, the panel slowly creaked open.

The singing was louder now. Sean, driven by intense curiosity that was stronger than his fear, pushed forward with Kyle on his heels. Not only was there singing, but also an intensely strong smell of dirt. Like wet, moldering earth, it was a very distinct scent. As they came close to the cracked-open door, the panel yawned wider.

They could both see it in the room beyond. A little girl sat on the floor, apparently toying with something in front of her that neither boy could see. She was nebulous, like puff clouds, but defined enough to the point where they could see the entire body, a skinny little girl clad in a fine white dress. She had long dark hair and long fingers with oddly pointed nails. Whatever she was playing with twirled about in her ghostly hands as she busied herself with the activity.

Kyle was the first one to gasp, an ironically girlish sound coming from such a big boy. Sean went to slap a hand over his mouth but as he moved to do so, the little girl looked up from the floor.

Her face was misty and white, her eyes big black sockets and her mouth a jumble of blackened, sharp teeth. She looked right at the boys in the doorway, emitting a gurgling hiss that set Sean and Kyle's hair on end. The black, sharp teeth bared menacingly and the strangely long fingers lashed out their clawed nails. But as swiftly as that occurred, the girl abruptly vanished. In a split second, it was all over, leaving extreme cold and the smell of dirt in its wake.

Sean and Kyle were already on the run. They thundered down the stairs, hurling themselves into the living room.

"Come on!" Kyle shouted. "We have to get out of here!"

Cole was automatically following them, the youngest brother who usually went along with the rest, but Chris remained on the couch.

"Why?" Chris demanded.

"Dude!" Sean was heading for the front door. "There's a... a demon upstairs! We saw it! It's got crazy teeth and claws!"

That was all Cole needed to hear to confirm the reason he needed to run. He was at the door with Sean and the pair of them threw the panel open to find a group of kids on the front porch preparing to knock. They ran past the group as Kyle grabbed the candy bowl.

"Here!" he put the bowl in the hands of the first child he came to. "Happy Halloween!"

He continued off the porch, running after Cole and Sean, as Chris appeared in the doorway. The eldest Trevor brother was baffled by the behavior of the younger boys but as he looked at the puzzled parents and kids on the front porch of the house, an unearthly howling suddenly came from the upper floor.

Startled, Chris turned in the direction of the stairs and the second floor beyond, listening to groans and scratching noises. His heart began to race, just a little, as the sounds of dragging began to occur on the landing over his head. He just stood there, looking upwards, until his puzzled gaze came back to rest on the people who were now beginning to filter off the porch. One kid still had the candy bowl. Chris was about to take the bowl back when a massive bang sounded overhead.

It was enough to get him out of the house, too.

———

"I don't care what went on," Cord was upset with the boys. "You shouldn't have left the house with the lights blazing and candles in pumpkins on the porch."

Chris, Kyle, Sean and Cole were following behind Cord as they walked up the driveway towards Evenshade. They were torn between the man's anger and their sense of self-preservation.

"But I locked the door, Dad," Chris said.

Cord glanced at his son. "And that's another thing," he said with disapproval. "Since when do you believe in crap like that? You gave up believing in ghosts when you stopped believing in Santa Claus."

"You mean there's no Santa Claus?" Kyle looked crestfallen.

As Sean and Cole giggled, Cord shot his son a nasty look. "I'm really not sure how you thought I'd believe a story like that, but you need to cut it out. I know it's Halloween and all that, but don't turn your pranks on me."

"There were a whole group of people on the porch that heard the sounds, too," Chris insisted. "All of this groaning and banging. Honestly, Dad, I don't know what it was, but I wasn't going to stick around to find out."

They were at the porch of the house and Cord came to an abrupt halt, facing the group. "I'll tell you what it was," he began to point at Sean and Kyle. "You said those two went upstairs without you, right?"

Chris nodded hesitantly and Cord continued. "Somehow, some way, they set up a practical joke and you fell for it." He turned back for the house and pulled out his key. "I'm going to go upstairs and find the CD player they set up to scare the crap out of you and then I'm going to ground them both for a week."

Sean and Kyle frowned. "You can't ground me," Sean insisted weakly.

Cord cocked an eyebrow at him. "You want to lay money on that?"

Sean just made a face and looked away as Kyle jumped in to defend them. "Dad, I swear, I'm not making this up," he insisted. "Why would we? All I know is that we heard this weird singing so we went upstairs and there was this little girl up there only she wasn't a little girl; she had big holes where her eyes should have been and these scary sharp teeth. And the song she was singing...."

Sean piped up, cutting him off. "I've heard Rosie sing it before," he said as if suddenly remembering. "It went like... like ... 'Goody Good, Goody Good', or something that sounded like that."

Cord paused, looking at them as he inserted the key into the lock, before shaking his head and pushing the door open.

"Look," he said as the door swung wide. "I appreciate the fact that you're trying to scare all of us because it's Halloween, but you really shouldn't have left the house like this. Plus, you scared the crap out of Alix and Rose with your crazy story."

Alix and Rose were still down the street trick-or-treating as Cord had volunteered to go back to the house and see what was really going on. The boys had been positively frantic when they had found Alix and Cord a few houses down with the little princess, demanding candy from the neighbors, and had spooked Alix fairly good with their tales of a ghostly girl.

"I didn't mean to scare my mom, but it's the truth," Sean insisted. "We really *did* see a ghost and she really *did* sing that song that Rosie sings."

Cord stepped into the house, pretty much ignoring Sean's statement as he looked around. The fire was still blazing and the television was still on. He would have gotten extremely upset about it had it not been for one thing; it began to occur to him that Chris would never have run out of a house without turning off the television or dampening the fire. The kid had always been inordinately responsible. It wouldn't have been in his character to go off and leave everything blaring. For the first time, Cord began to feel a sense of unease.

"Chris?" he turned to his eldest. "Blow out the jack-o-lantern candles, okay? Let's start getting this place buttoned down for the night."

As Chris went out to the porch, Cole, Kyle and Sean stuck to Cord like glue. Where he went, they went. The house seem completely normal as Cord moved from the living room into the dining room, and on into the kitchen. His trio of shadows followed close behind.

"I'm not sleeping here tonight," Sean declared as they passed from the utility room and into a pair of small adjoined rooms opposite the living room. "No way I'm sleeping with ghosts."

"Yes, you are," Cord said steadily, inspecting the smaller built-in closets in one of the rooms. "In fact, we're all going to sleep here tonight because I have a feeling your mom might not want to sleep here, either, after she heard you guys. This house has her spooked as it is and she's going to need moral support."

"Dad!"

It was Chris, out in the main hall, and they all moved out there to see what he was shouting about. The moment they hit the entry, Chris pointed up the stairs.

"It's happening again," he whispered. "Hear it?"

Cord went to the base of the stairs, listening. He could, indeed, hear something, the same odd whispered singing he had heard once before when he had been alone in the house with Alix. It was the third time in as many months that this had been brought to his attention and he was starting to think that it wasn't a neighbor's television turned up too loud or the imagination of a young child. As much as he hated to admit it, there had to be another explanation, although he couldn't bring himself to believe that it was anything supernatural. Still....

He mounted the steps, listening to the softly uttered song that was emanating from the upper floor. He glanced back at the boys, huddled at the base of the steps, and by the time he turned his focus forward to see where he was going, something stopped him dead in his tracks.

Rose was standing at the top of the stairs, watching him. But something was off; Cord knew immediately that it wasn't Rose – the eyes were dark and sunken, looking blankly at him. The girl was dressed in a white knee-length dress with a high collar and long sleeves, looking like something from eras past when young girls would dress primly and prettily. He could hear the boys behind him gasping and hissing, but he kept his focus on the figure several feet in front of him and tried not to panic.

"Rosie?" he finally said, softly.

The figure twitched, shifted, and it was then that he realized he could see through her. He could see the light from hall bathroom shining through. Still, he couldn't believe what he was seeing, shocked into disbelief even though his eyes were telling him something completely different. The child-figure began to rock back and forth.

"*Goody Good, Goody Good, 'ere snake and bird could,*" it whispered. "*Mercy is revenge in Bebe's house.*"

The voice was oddly strained, with uneven tones that weren't of this earth. Shocked, Cord watched as the ghostly Rose opened her mouth to reveal sharp, blackened teeth. The mouth opened wider and wider still, and the head tilted back, the arms lifting as if to embrace the world. An otherworldly groan filled the air, seeming to come from the very walls, as the figure evaporated like a puff of smoke. Cord, in fact, watched the smoky mist drift up to the ceiling and vanish.

As quickly as she had appeared, the apparition disappeared.

Stunned, Cord stood on the stairs, midway up, trying to wrap his head around what he just saw. When he finally turned to look at the boys still standing at the bottom of the steps, he could see how terrified they all were, especially Sean. His eyes were bugged out as he pointed to the spot where the spirit had vanished.

"That was... that was *Rose*," he gasped.

Cord just stood there. He really didn't know what to say. Finally, he lumbered down the steps, slowly and laboriously, thinking many different things at that moment. But the most important thought he had was of Alix. He had no idea how he was going to break the news to her, but he had a feeling how she was going to react. It wasn't going to be a happy reaction.

"I think," he said slowly, "that you'd better let me tell your mother about this. No one else say a word, okay? Let her hear it from me. Also, I think we'll all be spending the night at *our* house tonight."

The boys looked at each other, nodding fearfully. "What *was* that, Dad?" Chris asked.

Cord just shook his head. "I have no idea," he said, looking to the apprehensive faces around him. "But I think I'd better find out."

TWELVE

"EVENSHADE IS a marvelous example of early Colonial architecture," the woman from the Historical Society was saying. "True saltbox architecture with sharp roof angles. And you say you're the new owner?"

Alix nodded her head as the woman came out from behind her desk to shake her hand. "Yes," she said. "We bought it a couple of months back and it's been going through some renovations. In fact, people from the Danvers Historical Society have been out to see it to make sure we're not altering the structure or destroying valuable historical material."

The woman nodded quickly. "Yes, I know," she replied. "I'm Mrs. Mowbray, by the way. My husband has been out to see the renovations a few times. He says the place is looking marvelous."

Alix shook the woman's hand. "Alix Hendry," she said, indicating Cord as he, too, shook the woman's hand. "This is Cord Trevor. He's my...."

"Trevor?" the woman cocked her head. "Not from *the* Trevor family? The descendants of John Trevor of the Mayflower?"

Cord nodded. "Yes, ma'am. That would be me."

Mrs. Mowbray was evidently thrilled. "I knew Cecily Trevor when I was a very young girl," she said. "Oh, it must have been in the nineteen thirties. Cecily had, I think, three brothers and a sister. The Trevors were one of the very first families to settle the area back in the day."

Cord nodded again. "Cecily is my great-aunt," he replied. "Her brother William was my great-grandfather. He passed away about twenty years ago, but she's still alive. She turned ninety-seven last month."

"Goodness," Mrs. Mowbray exclaimed. "Still living, did you say? Well, I was a very young girl when I knew Cecily. I was at least ten or twelve years younger than she was."

Alix couldn't help the grin on her face. "That makes you in your early eighties," she said. "I certainly hope I'm as active as you are when I get to be your age."

Mrs. Mowbray grinned. "That's very kind of you," she flashed her yellowed teeth. "Say... you're not from around here, are you?"

Alix shook her head. "California."

Mrs. Mowbray brightened. "I can tell," she said confidently. "You don't talk like one of us. Plus, you have that skinny California look to you. Pretty, like a movie star, you know?"

Cord chuckled. "Yes, she is very pretty," he said, returning the focus to the house. "Mrs. Mowbray, we came by to see what we could find out about the history of the house. Even though it's been in my family since it was built, other than general information, I don't know as much about it as I should. We were hoping you could help."

Mrs. Mowbray looked at him as if he had committed a sin. "You don't know about your own house?"

"No," he admitted. "The house was passed down through another branch of the family, so I've never been directly involved with it. All I could tell Alix is when it was built and by whom, but not much more than that."

Mrs. Mowbray understood, somewhat. "Well," she cocked her head thoughtfully. "When the new owner applied for the remodel permits, we looked into the history of the house and its significance, so I can tell you what we found out. What in particular did you have in mind?"

Alix and Cord looked at each other, shrugging. "Everything," Alix finally said. "We'd like to know whatever you can tell us."

Mrs. Mowbray indicated a table with some chairs around it. It was cluttered with neat stacks of books and historical periodicals, as every inch of the Historical Society seemed to be crammed with paper. The one-room office was full to bursting. As everyone took a seat, she began to speak.

"As I recall," Mrs. Mowbray began, "Evenshade was built in 1690 by Ezra Hyde Holcombe, who was thirty-eight years old when he married fourteen-year-old Abigail Williams after she fled the Salem witch trials. She was one of the chief accusers, you know."

Alix and Cord were listening intently. "I know," Cord nodded. "And the house was already built when Ezra married Abigail."

"Exactly."

"And then they had four children – Elizabeth, Mary, Matilda and John. There was another daughter that died in infancy, but those four were the survivors. My branch of the family descends from John."

Mrs. Mowbray nodded excitedly. "I remember hearing about that from Cecily back in the day. Anyway, because of Abigail's association with the witch trials, people were hesitant to come around, so the Holcombes lived a rather isolated existence in the house and, eventually, it was rumored that Abigail herself was a witch."

Cord lifted his eyebrows. "Interesting."

"It's true," Mrs. Mowbray suddenly jumped up and scooted over to the cluttered desk. "But given the notoriety of the trials, one shouldn't be surprised. Abigail, or Bebe as she was called by the family, was someone to be feared. She contributed to the death of a lot of people."

Bebe. Cord thought. *Wasn't that something the ghostly Rose had said?* But he didn't voice his thoughts, watching instead as Mrs. Mowbray rooted around her desk, looking for something.

"In fact," the woman finally pulled out a file folder and opened it up, reading the documentation as she headed back over to the table. "Sarah Good, one of the original accused, in particular, had it out for Abigail. There was bad blood between them ever since Goody Good caught Abigail stealing from them. Or, at least, that was what Sarah Good's child testified to. That seemed to be why Abigail accused Goody Good of witch-craft and contributed to her death."

Alix appeared both concerned and thoughtful. "I don't know that much about the Salem Witch trials," she admitted, "but it would make sense for the young girl to have it out for a woman who caught her stealing. But what does any of this have to do with the house?"

Mrs. Mowbray sat down, going through the papers in the file. "I'm getting to that," she said, inspecting what appeared to be the copy of a very old document. Alix and Cord could see the carefully-written long hand. "Again, this testimony comes from Sarah Good's daughter, Dorothy, but it appears that Sarah Good may have, indeed, had some hand in witchcraft. We have documentation that she cursed one of the judges at her trial, a man who died in the exact manner Goody Good had predicted. Additionally, Sarah Good was pregnant when she was imprisoned after the trial and gave birth to a daughter, Mercy, while in jail. Unfortunately, the baby didn't survive long, I'm sure due to poor conditions and malnutrition, among other things. But the odd part of this story comes in Dorothy Good's testimony after the death of her mother."

Alix was hanging on the story. "What's that?"

Mrs. Mowbray sighed faintly, reading the bottom of the document. "According to Dorothy, her mother told her husband, Dorothy's father, that she intended to inhabit the body of the baby after her death and bring curse and ruin to Abigail. She instructed the husband to bury the infant's body under Abigail's house. Dorothy states that the husband held on to the infant's corpse, storing it in the root cellar, until Sarah was hanged. Then, he kept track of Abigail as she fled Salem and when she married Ezra, the husband buried the baby's remains under Evenshade so Goody Good could forever haunt Abigail." She finally looked up from the photocopied document, smiling weakly at Alix and Cord. "Pretty morbid, I must say. But back then, the people were extremely superstitious so the suggestion of curses was taken very seriously."

Alix was just staring at the woman. Beside her, Cord put his hand on her knee and gently squeezed her comfortingly in spite of what he was thinking. *Mercy. Bebe.* Both words the little ghost girl had said. Things were starting to make some sense and he wasn't sure he was at all comfortable with what he was hearing, but for Alix's sake, he kept on an even keel.

"That's, uh, interesting," he said. "Is there anything else about the house that we should know, history-wise?"

Mrs. Mowbray looked back at her papers. "Let's see," she leafed through a few sheets. "The Holcombe family kept to themselves for a very long time. There's a letter from General Gates, the Revolutionary War general, which was written from Evenshade, and means he probably spent the night there once. We also have documentation that Fredrick Douglas attended a supper at the home given in his honor. Did you know that the Holcombes were part of the abolitionist movement?"

Cord nodded. "I knew. In fact, we've had a lot of civil rights activists and suffragists in the family."

Mrs. Mowbray returned to her papers. "The house has seen more than its share of history," she confirmed. "It's a significant part of the history of our nation."

Cord watched the woman ruffle through her documents. "It sure is," he agreed. "But beyond the history, are there any legends about it? You know – stories or hauntings – or anything?"

Mrs. Mowbray stopped going through the papers and looked at him, thoughtfully. "Nothing that's been documented other than the curse from Sarah Good," she said, "but I seem to recall hearing the place was haunted as a child. Just rumors, really. Everyone always called the place haunted but I imagine most of that was because it just *looks* like a haunted house. Why? Have you heard anything?"

Cord avoided the question. "What rumors about it have you heard?"

Mrs. Mowbray set the folder down completely as she pondered his question. "I seem to remember hearing the house was haunted by the ghost of a little girl," she said. "When I was a child, the kids used to say the place was haunted by a girl in white, only she wasn't really a little girl. She was Sarah Good returned to fulfill her curse. You haven't happened to have seen a little girl in white, have you?"

She said it with a smile, teasingly. But Alix, having sat largely silent throughout the meeting, didn't think it was a joke. She realized that she suddenly wasn't feeling too well. The stories of curses and witches had her stomach in knots, and when the woman asked the question, she simply shook her head and stood up from the table.

"You've been more than generous with your time, Mrs. Mowbray," she said as Cord stood up beside her. "Thank you for telling us what you know. It's definitely an interesting house."

Mrs. Mowbray stood up as well, looking rather confused at the abrupt end of their discussion. "Of course," she said. "We're always here to help, especially with a house of such significance to the community."

Alix was already moving for the door, feeling ill and flustered. "Thank you again. We appreciate it."

Mrs. Mowbray barely had time to bid farewell before Alix was out onto the sidewalk with Cord on her heels. Once outside, Cord put a big arm around her shoulders and pulled her against him.

"Hey, slow down," he murmured. "Why the rush? What's wrong?"

Alix broke down in quiet tears. "I don't know," she said. "All of that stuff about dead babies buried under the house and curses and witches... I just didn't want to hear anymore. I'm scared, Cord. The whole situation has me scared and sick."

He hugged her gently as they headed towards his truck. "I know," he said sympathetically. "But I thought getting some history on the house might help us understand what's going on."

Alix sniffed, wiping her eyes. "Me, too," she said. "But it's so awful. What do we do now?"

He was quiet a moment as he unlocked the truck and opened the door for her. As Alix climbed into the truck, he leaned against the seat, wedging himself in between her legs as she sat sideways on the seat. He wrapped his big arms around her as she caved in to his strength, her head resting on his chest.

"Let me think about this and come up with a plan," he said

thoughtfully. "I need to take a look at the basement and see if there are any areas where a body could have really been buried. The house has a full basement, though. I don't recall if there are any crawlspaces."

Alix snuggled against him. "Archaeologists have portable ground penetrating radar machines," she said. "Do you think we could contact a museum or a university and see if they'll come out and do a survey? If we tell them it's about the Salem witch trials, I'll bet we get some interest."

He kissed her on the top of the head. "That's not a bad idea," he said. "We could have archaeologists come out and dig around to see if they can come up with anything. The house is so historically significant that I'm sure we could get someone to come and do it. Maybe that'll help with the ghost problem."

Alix was feeling better, but only marginally. Cord gave her a big squeeze and made her put her legs back into the truck before he shut the door and went around to the other side. Climbing into the vehicle, he engaged the ignition and headed for home.

———

Quirt and Mary Trevor lived in a home built in 1790 along the banks of the Porter River in Danvers, not too far from where Cord lived. It was a beautiful Colonial-style home, painted the original shade of blue, and sat on a half-acre of land that included a tennis court and a swimming pool, and a very creepy cluster of ancient trees down by the river's edge. As a kid, Cord had always been afraid of them. The house had been passed down on his mother's side of the family, the Van Wycks, and a Van Wyck had lived at the property since the day it was built.

Cord was acting battalion chief on the day after visiting Mrs. Mowbray at the Historical Society and was driving the appropriate red SUV that declared his title. He pulled up his parents' driveway and climbed out, hearing the dogs inside the house go crazy. His parents had two Pekingese dogs or, more accurately, his mother had two Pekingese dogs that ruled the roost. His dad hated them. As Cord walked up the steps, he saw the dogs in the window, barking madly, and one of them pulled down the curtains. He laughed as he knocked on the door.

Cord could hear his mother approach the door, admonishing the dogs. The bolt was thrown and the panel opened.

"Cord!" his mother exclaimed, grabbing the dogs when they tried to charge the man in uniform. "Hi, honey. What brings you here?"

Cord came into the house, grinning as his mom wrestled with the dogs. "If they bite me, I'll punt them out into the river."

His mother made a face at him. "They're not going to bite you," she scoffed. "They're just excited."

She put the dogs down, who made a run at Cord until he stuck a big boot out and pushed them away. Then they ran the other direction, barking like crazy. He heard his dad coming up from the basement as he followed his mother out into the kitchen.

"I'm going to kill those damn dogs," his father said as he opened the basement door. He had something in his hands, fussing with it. "Shut the hell up!"

"Quirt!" Mary scolded. She didn't like anyone to yell at her dogs. "Look who's here."

Quirt glanced up at his enormous son. "Oh, hey, Cord," he said, still messing with whatever he had in his hands. "Long time, no see."

"I know; sorry. I've been busy."

"What brings you around?"

Cord leaned against the kitchen counter as his mother poured a cup of coffee. "Just driving between stations and thought I'd stop by," he said. "I haven't seen you two in a while."

Quirt sat down at the kitchen table. "You do better than your sister and brother," he said. "We go months without seeing those two."

"Kent's a busy guy," Cord said of his younger brother by two years.

"He's a chiropractor," Quirt said wryly. "How busy can he be? He goes to work at ten in the morning, leaves at four in the afternoon, and then golfs all the rest of the time."

"So go golf with him."

"I can't. He beats me and then makes me pay for everything."

Cord grinned. "You're a sucker if you let him do that to you," he said. Then he eyed the device his father was messing with. "What's that?"

Quirt glanced up at him. "A metal detector," he said. "I'm going to scan this entire property and see what treasures I can find. God only knows what the Van Wycks have buried around here."

"Bodies, more than likely," Cord said. "They were famous for deceiving the Native Americans and then killing them and calling it self-defense."

"Cord," his mother admonished. "Enough of that."

Quirt was grinning as he finished the adjustments on the electrical box in his hands. "Well, I intend to find all of the skeletons I can," he said. "Maybe I'll sell them to a museum."

"Or have the entire Iroquois nation down around this property trying to declare it a sacred burial ground."

"If that's the case, I'll sell it to them for five million bucks. Historical properties are worth a lot."

Mary, with two cups of coffee in her hand, put one down on the table in front of her husband and handed the second one off to Cord.

"You two are impossible," she sniffed. "Besides, this isn't 'just' historical property. It's family property."

"Speaking of family property," Cord said casually, "I told you that Evenshade was sold, didn't I?"

Quirt nodded, looking up at him. "You sure did," he said. "Didn't your new girlfriend buy it?"

Mary shushed her husband harshly but Cord grinned. "I know you think you're kidding, but you're not," he said. "I told you a doctor new to the area bought it."

"A woman," Mary said helpfully. "You said she has a couple of children. Are you... seeing her, son?"

Cord nodded. "I am," he said. Then, he sighed and ran a hand over his cropped blond hair. "I haven't seen you two in a while. A lot has happened. I don't even know where to start."

Quirt quit messing with the metal detector box and looked at him. "Are you really seeing her?" he asked. "I was just needling you. You only mentioned her once a long time ago, I think about the time she first moved in. But the way you spoke about her, I thought something might be up."

Cord grinned. "You could say that," he said, his voice softening. "I love her and we're going to get married."

Mary let out a squeal and ran at him, throwing her arms around his neck and giving him a big kiss on the cheek. "Cord, I'm so thrilled," she gushed. "When do we get to meet her?"

Cord was smiling at his mother. "Soon," he said. "It's just been a really busy time with her new job, the kids in school, my work... you know how it is."

Quirt was on his feet, extending a congratulatory hand to his son, who took it. "I'm sincerely happy for you," he said. "It's been a long time since... well, anyway, how do the boys like her?"

Cord shrugged. "Chris and Kyle think she's great," he said. "Cole has been a little slower to come around but he's okay with it now. In fact, Alix has a son a little older than Cole and the boys all get along great. She also has a four-year-old daughter who's just as cute as she can be."

"A girl?" Mary repeated. "Oh, happy day! You've got three boys, Kent has two boys, and Elizabeth has two boys, so I was thinking we'd never have a granddaughter."

"Rose is her name," Cord snickered at his mom's happiness over a step-granddaughter. "She's a doll."

"Rose," Mary repeated, rolling it off her tongue. "Can we invite ourselves to your house one day and meet everyone?"

Cord nodded. "Maybe this weekend," he said. "I need to check with Alix's work schedule, but I think she's off on Sunday."

Mary was thrilled as she turned to look at the calendar above the phone on the wall. "We're free," she declared. "Oh, Cord, this is such good news. When do you think the wedding will be?"

Cord shrugged and set his coffee cup down. "I'm not sure," he said. "I'm leaving that up to Alix. I think we'll probably move everyone into Evenshade since it's bigger than my house. In fact... that's actually what I came to talk to you about."

"What?" Quirt asked curiously.

"Evenshade," Cord replied hesitantly. "When Aunt Cecily owned the house, did she ever mention to you that it was haunted?"

Quirt's curious expression transformed into something thoughtful. "There has always been that rumor."

"I know, but did she say something about it?"

"Why do you ask?"

Cord lifted his eyebrows. "Because I've been spending a lot of time over there," he said. "I have to tell you that I've had some very weird experiences, including seeing a ghost."

"A ghost?" Quirt looked startled. "You've seen a ghost?"

Cord nodded. "Look, you know I'm not one to believe in that kind of stuff. In my world, everything has a logical explanation so I don't take lightly what I just told you and I hope you don't, either. I wouldn't make this stuff up."

Quirt was shaking his head before Cord even finished. "I know, son," he said, moving to reclaim his seat at the kitchen table. "You'd be the last one I'd expect to hear that kind of thing from. So it was really a ghost, eh? What did it look like?"

Cord took his coffee cup and went to sit at the table with his dad. "Like a little girl," he said frankly. "In fact, it looked like Alix's daughter, only there were big black holes where the eyes should have been and the teeth... big sharp fangs. It was the craziest thing you've ever seen."

"Was it the first time you've seen it?"

Cord nodded. "Seen it, yes," he said. "But I've heard it before. When Alix first moved in, she said she kept hearing a little girl singing and her daughter has this imaginary friend she calls the 'sad girl.' At first, the 'sad girl' did things like steal stuffed animals but then she grew more violent. She actually pushed Alix down and knocked her out. Then, on Halloween night, she sure made her presence known. We all saw her. It has made Alix understandably edgy so we went to see Mrs. Mowbray over at the Salem Historical Society. She told us a lot about the house, including the legend that Sarah Good had her dead baby, Mercy, buried under the house to curse Abigail Williams. Have you ever heard anything like that?"

Quirt was listening to him seriously. After a moment, he nodded his head slowly. "I have," he said. "From my grandfather. He was Aunt Cecily's brother, you know."

"I know. What did he say?"

Quirt cleared his throat softly, glancing at Mary as he spoke. "You're not going to like it."

"Why not?"

"Because he said they used to keep a ring of stones on the basement over what was presumed to be Mercy's grave," he said. "The stones were supposed to keep her evil suppressed. They've been there since the house was built. Have you looked in the basement at all?"

Cord's features twisted with confusion. "No," he said. "What the hell is this stone circle about?"

Quirt sipped his coffee as he thought on his answer. "You know," he said casually, "when you were young, you wanted to know all about our bloodlines and your legacy as a Caster, but when you got older, you didn't want to hear it anymore."

Cord stiffened up, sitting back in his chair. "Are you going to start that witch stuff again?"

"It's in your blood, Cord."

"It is *not* in my blood."

"As my son, my firstborn, it's in your blood. You have the casting gift."

Cord abruptly stood up. "I don't have anything," he snapped. "I came here to find answers but if you're going start up with that witch stuff again, then I'll just talk to you another time."

"Another time might be too late," Quirt said, his focus on the tabletop. "It sounds like the activity may be picking up. If the stone circle has been moved, then that could be a problem."

Cord stopped his agitated pacing and looked at his parents. It was clear that he was mulling over what his father said, and the truth was that he had come here for answers. Even answers he didn't like. Alix was involved and if she was in danger, then perhaps he really did need to listen to what his father told him. With a grunt of frustration, he reclaimed his seat.

"It's always witchcraft with you," he muttered. "So what's the deal? What's going on at that house?"

Quirt looked up at him. "I didn't ask for the gift any more

than my father did, or my grandfather," he said. "Abigail Williams was a witch of the greatest degree and she made sure that the males in her family line were given the gift of Casting because she was afraid if she passed her knowledge down to the women, they would be more easily persecuted. I'm sorry, but that's just the way it is. We have the power. But so did Sarah Good."

Cord sighed heavily. Then he put up his hands in a gesture of surrender. "Okay, so we have the power," he said. "And Sarah Good had the power. So it's really true that she had her baby buried under the house?"

"According to family legend, it is."

"Then why didn't Abigail just remove the body?"

"She couldn't get near it because Sarah had placed a spell on it," Quirt said. "Abigail countered the spell by putting a stone ring around the grave that was christened with a spell that would keep the evil in the grave from escaping. Trouble is, that house has always been cursed with a ghost of a small girl. My grandfather saw it and so did my father, so somehow, someway, something has managed to get out of that grave. Now it's haunting the house and I'm sure it will be particularly interested in you. It will know you as a Holcombe descendant. You may do more harm than good if you can't protect yourself and your girlfriend's family from it. Don't ignore it, son. That's the worst thing you can do."

Cord sat back in his chair, looking at his father in disbelief. "Are you serious?"

"You came here for answers, son. If you don't like what you hear, then I'm sorry, I really am. But that's what I've been told."

At this point, and given what he had seen, Cord was willing to go on a little faith. Still, he was confused and, if he were to admit it, a little frightened. He needed to mull all of the information over before he took the next step. With a heavy sigh, he stood up.

"Thanks anyway," he said. "I need to think about all of this. We'll talk again on Sunday."

Quirt and Mary stood up with him, following him out of the kitchen. "Do you want your mother to go over to the house?" Quirt asked helpfully. "She senses things, you know. Maybe she can help you make sense of this."

Cord looked at his parents, so seemingly normal; his father was a retired lawyer and city councilman for the city of Danvers and his mother had been a high school principal. Two nice, normal people who happened to be a warlock and a medium, respectively. Cord didn't know what to think anymore, but one thing was certain; he was starting to be just the least bit open-minded about it. After what he had seen, he had to be.

"Maybe on Sunday," he said. "Let's just play it by ear."

"Okay," Mary said, kissing her son on the cheek. "We'll see you then. We're looking forward to it."

Cord waved at his parents as he left the house and climbed back into the battalion chief's SUV. Backing down the driveway, his mind lingered on what his parents had told him. They'd known exactly what he was talking about, including the little ghost girl. That frightened him because it meant that whatever was happening at Evenshade had history. The evil had history.

He wasn't sure what he was going to tell Alix.

THIRTEEN

AFTER CORD'S visit with his parents, he had gone back to the station and done some of his own research on Evenshade and how it was linked to the Salem witch trials. He came across more information about a curse from Sarah Good against Abigail Williams, but nothing specific until he happened to be looking at images regarding the trial, woodcuts and the like. He also came across a seventeenth century woodcut commissioned by Sarah Good's daughter, Dorothy, that was the image of a house that looked strangely like Evenshade, with a devil-looking thing rising up out of a circle in the ground in front of it. After that, he had to stop looking because it was going to give him nightmares.

Later on that evening, Cord and his station had brought in a medical aid patient and he stood at the nurse's station, waiting for the paramedics to finish up so he could clear the rig. But he was mostly looking for Alix, as this was his third trip to the hospital during that shift and he'd already seen her twice. He looked forward to the medical aid calls these days just so he could see her lovely face. It always made his day.

As he stood at the nurse's station and chatted with an older

Black nurse he had known for years, he caught sight of Alix as she emerged from a corridor with a couple of men in suits. One man in particular was handsome and Cord felt territorial testosterone seizures coming on as he watched Alix interact with the two men. She was so fluid and lovely to watch. His eyes must have narrowed or he must have otherwise given a signal that he was mentally chest beating, because the nurse he was speaking with turned to see what had his attention. She grinned as she turned back to her computer monitor.

"There she is, Cord," the woman teased. "Go get her, honey. Don't let those men take her away from you."

Cord didn't take his eyes off the trio. "Hmmm," he grunted. "I'm bigger than they are. I can take them."

The nurse laughed. "I wouldn't worry about them too much," she said. "They're pharmaceutical reps. They come around here a lot."

Cord glanced at the woman, giving her a wry expression. "They better not come around *her* a lot, if you get my drift. Make sure they know that, okay?"

The nurse was still giggling, shaking her head. "She's only got eyes for you. Don't worry so much." Before he could respond, she glanced up at him. "How's she been feeling, by the way?"

Cord tore his eyes off the pair of men and looked at the nurse. "Fine, I guess. Why do you ask?"

The nurse shrugged. "She seems like she's been under the weather for the past few days," she said. "She was sick in the bathroom both yesterday and today."

"Sick how?"

"Vomiting. She actually had to leave a patient this morning because she was sick. I tried to get her to go home but she says she's fine."

His brow furrowed. "I didn't know anything about that," he

said. "But I've also been on a double shift. I haven't been home in a couple of days."

"It's probably just the flu."

He appeared upset as he began to move in Alix's direction. "Then what in the hell is she doing here?"

It was a rhetorical question. Cord made his way over to Alix as she was winding down her conversation with the suits. She saw him coming out of the corner of her eye, smiled at him, and then politely excused herself from the two sales reps.

"Hi, baby," she said, her eyes twinkling wearily at him. "Back again?"

He nodded, leaning down to kiss her and making sure the suits saw it. "What's this I hear you've been sick?"

Her smile faded. "I'm okay," she said quietly. "Don't worry about me."

He looked at her as if she had just made a ridiculous statement. "Of course I'm going to worry about you," he snapped without force. "What's the matter?"

Alix glanced around, looking rather hesitant. "Well...."

"Well *what*?"

She paused a moment, hesitantly, before grasping his arm. "Come back to my office for a second."

Cord had his radio with him so he let her pull him back to her office, tucked back in one of the multitude of corridors. She had a nice window view. As she closed the door, the radio chattered at Cord and he responded.

"I need to clear the rig, honey," he said. "What's up?"

"This will just take a minute," she said, gingerly rubbing her belly. "You haven't really been home so I haven't had a chance to talk to you about this."

"About what?"

She gazed up at him, his strong features and handsome face, and her stomach was all in knots. As he stood there looking at her expectantly, she suddenly ducked for the trash can, picked it up, and puked right into it. Startled, Cord put his hand on her back as she ended up dry heaving.

"Oh, honey," he said sympathetically. "You need to go home. How long has this been going on?"

Alix sat the trash can down, struggling to catch her breath. Her entire face was pasty-pale as she reached for the box of tissues to wipe her mouth off.

"A couple of days," she said. "It's going to get a lot worse before it gets better."

"Why would you say that?"

She looked at him, then. She sighed heavily. "Because it's not the flu," she said. "It's morning sickness. I'm pregnant."

His reaction was instantaneous. "You *are?*" His eyebrows flew up and the color drained from his face. "Oh... my God, you're *pregnant?*"

She couldn't tell if he was happy or angry. "Yes," she said, sounding weary and defeated. "I had the lab do a test this morning and it came back positive, so I'm seeing the OB/GYN later today."

Cord stood there and stared at her, shocked to the bone. But with his next breath, he was throwing his arms around her and lifting her off the ground, hugging her so tightly that she grunted.

"Oh, my God," he gasped again. "Are you serious? A *baby?*"

Alix was coming to figure out that he was happy about it. "Yes," she winced when he squeezed too hard. "Baby, put me down, please. My stomach can't take this."

He set her down immediately. "I'm so sorry," he said, concerned. "Did I hurt you?"

She grinned weakly, patting his cheek. "No," she said. "But you need to be mindful of my belly. Next time you do that, I might puke all over your shoulder."

He laughed, happily, his big hands on her arms. Then he just stared at her, slowly shaking his head. "I can't even tell you how happy I am right now," he said hoarsely. "I just feel like... like the luckiest man in the world. Really? A *baby*?"

She couldn't help but giggle at his enthusiasm. "Really," she confirmed. "A baby."

Cord pulled her into his arms again, only this time, much more gently. "Oh, honey," he murmured, kissing her head repeatedly. "I'm so thrilled about this, I just can't tell you."

Alix gave in to his hug, his comfort, taking satisfaction in it like nothing she had ever experienced before. It brought tears to her eyes and she snuggled against him, letting herself get swept up with his power and warmth.

"Good," she murmured. "I've suspected for a week or two but I guess I didn't want to admit it. When the nausea started coming on, I figured I'd better face facts."

He released her from the hug but his arms were still around her. "What time is your doctor's appointment this afternoon?"

"Four."

"I'll be here."

She smiled weakly at him. "You don't have to," she said. "It's not a big deal. He's just going to examine me and give me a due date."

"Like I said, I'll be here."

She chuckled, seeing there was no dissuading the man. Putting her hands on his cheeks, she stroked his face affectionately.

"We've already got five kids between us," she said. "Looks like we're going to have an even half-dozen."

He just grinned like a fool. "Maybe it'll be a girl."

"Is that what you want?"

"I just want a healthy baby, but I'd love to have a girl. I don't have one, in case you didn't realize that."

She laughed, patted his cheek, and kissed him. "I did, in fact, realize that," she said as she released him and opened her office door. "So now if you see me duck for the trash can, you'll know why. But keep it to yourself, okay? I just started this job and now I'm pregnant... I'm not sure how my new colleagues are going receive the news."

He grew serious. "I don't give a damn how they receive the news," he said. "This isn't their decision or their choice."

He was starting to get worked up and she shushed him, her gentle hands to his face, her fingers across his lips.

"It's okay," she assured him "Don't get upset about it. I'll all work out."

He was genuinely angry. "You'll tell me if someone gives you a bad time about this, right?"

She nodded patiently, holding his hand as she led him out of her office and into the corridor. "Of course I will."

"I mean it, Alix. If anyone hassles you about this, they're going to have to deal with me."

She continued to nod patiently and steadily, pausing to kiss him before they made the turn that led out into the emergency department.

"See you back here at four," she said, trying to get his mind off his frustration. "Go tell your buddies what I told you but tell them to keep it to themselves for a while, okay?"

He was successfully diverted. "Okay," he said, the lure of telling his fellow firemen the good news bringing the smile back to his face. He bent down and kissed her again. "I love you. See you in a bit."

Alix watched him walk out into the emergency room, his proud stride and powerful body. The man made her heart flutter just to look at him. But that warm and wonderful thought was cut short as she had to rush back into her office for the trash can again.

Cord didn't make it for her doctor's appointment but Alix suspected it was because he was on a call. The man would have come unless it had been utterly impossible for him to get away. So she had a consultation with Dr. Sutton, an OB/GYN who had come to her highly recommended, and Dr. Sutton did an ultrasound that revealed a viable pregnancy. Based on his calculations, Alix's due date was June 4, which meant she was about eight weeks along. When she got out of Dr. Sutton's office, she called Cord's cell phone but it went straight to voice mail, so she left a teasing message that would make him crazy until he called her back.

Grinning, she went back to work in the emergency department, reviewing the chart of a kid who had been in a car accident and consulting with the orthopedic surgeon. When she was finished with the consultation, she walked up to the nurse's station with some lab paperwork in her hand and noticed that both television sets were turned to a news channel. Glancing up, the first thing she saw was a building on fire. Upon closer inspection, it was a church with a very tall steeple. Curious, Alix tried to hear what the newscaster was saying.

"What's happening?" she asked the half-dozen nurses who were crowded around the nursing station.

The Black nurse who knew Cord was the first to speak. "The Tabernacle Church is on fire," she said. "Apparently, it's been burning for a while. Part of the roof has caved in and...."

The phone rang, interrupting her. The nurse answered the phone and after a few quick words, hung up the receiver. She turned to the group behind her, including Alix.

"That was city fire," she said. "They're sending over some injuries and want us to be prepared. Burns, trauma, that kind of thing."

"Did they say how many?" Alix asked.

The woman shook her head. "No," she replied. "But there must be quite a few if they're calling ahead."

Alix had been through that kind of drill before, especially in Los Angeles. She snapped her fingers because she was the only doctor in the emergency room at that point.

"Let's get rolling, folks," she said as the group started to move. "We'll set up triage right here in front of the nurse's station and tag accordingly. Has everyone been through something like this before?"

A couple of the younger nurses shook their heads, looking rather wide-eyed. Alix mainly focused on them.

"You've been trained in the S.T.A.R.T. system, right?" she asked. "Simple Triage and Rapid Treatment?"

When the women nodded, she continued. "We'll tag according to the severity of injury," she said. "Black for morgue, red for immediate, yellow for delayed, and green for minor. Do we have a stash of triage tags?"

The senior nurse was already pulling out the box of tags. Alix pointed at her. "Grace, you meet the ambulances as soon as they pull in and start tagging," she said, grabbing another nurse. "Deb, you coordinate them as they come in to the E.R. I have a feeling I'll be tied up, so it's up to you and Grace to coordinate, okay? Also, someone call Dr. Philby and Dr. Potts off their break. They must be in the cafeteria because that's where I saw them heading. And someone call the department head and tell him to get in here. We're going to be full."

Everyone started moving, including Alix. Confident everything would work like a well-oiled machine, she changed into fresh scrubs and washed her hands, preparing for the onslaught. She also took a couple of antacids because her stomach was starting to lurch again. She didn't want to have to make a break for a trash can at an inopportune time.

The first ambulances rolled in less than ten minutes later. Alix took the first case, a young man who had fairly serious burns and a crushed sternum. She was focused on her patient and not listening to much of what was going on, but at some point, she began to hear murmurs of injured firefighters. She tried to fight down her anxiety by focusing on her patient, but she was pulled away from the young man. Once she had him stabilized she focused on a firefighter who had his entire right side smashed when part of the roof of the church caved in.

He was badly injured and badly burned, but Alix remained calm and soothing with him, feeling increasingly apprehensive for Cord's safety. She had every reason to believe he had been fighting the church fire because of the proximity of his station to the blaze, but so far, he hadn't shown up in the emergency room and for that, she was extremely grateful. As she worked to stabilize the young firefighter whose greatest concern seemed to be if he would have any scars on his face, Dr. Potts, one of the other E.R. doctors, entered her exam.

"Dr. Hendry," he reached out and pulled her away from her patient. "I need you to come with me."

Alix left her patient in the hands of a competent nurse and followed Dr. Potts into the main area where the nurse's station was. All of the exam rooms were full, as was the big open area near the nurse's station. There was quite a triage going on, like M.A.S.H. surgery, and she faced Dr. Potts, who put his arm around her shoulders.

"I wanted to be the one to tell you that Captain Trevor is here," he said softly.

It didn't really register with Alix what he meant. She began to look around. "Where is he?"

"In Exam Two," Dr. Potts, an older man with a truly gentle manner, was trying to go easy on her. "Let me give you a rundown of his condition before you go in there; he's got a fractured pelvis, six broken ribs and a collapsed lung. I think he's also got some internal injuries so we're having the portable MRI brought down here. He may need surgery, Alix. I've already called your partner, Dr. Levenger, and he's on his way. I wouldn't expect you to do this."

Alix stared at the man as his words began to sink in. Her heart began to race and she could feel the tears springing to her eyes, but she fought it. Still, she couldn't help the abject grief that was tearing at her.

"Oh, my God," she breathed, turning towards Exam Two. "I have to see him."

"You'll have to do the surgical consult," Dr. Potts said. "The sooner we can diagnose, the sooner we can get him into surgery. Dr. Levenger is going straight to surgery to scrub up when he gets here, so you'll have to do the evaluation. Okay?"

Alix was already moving for the exam room, somewhat unsteadily, nodding her head to Dr. Potts' question.

"Okay," she whispered.

"Are you all right?" Dr. Potts was following her. "I'll help you out on this, but I wanted you to know what was going on, Alix. I'm so sorry."

Alix didn't acknowledge him. She walked straight into the exam room, ignoring the firefighters crowding around the door, only to see Cord lying on the gurney, covered in filth. He had his turn-out pants on, and his boots, but his clothing had been cut away from the waist up and IVs were running into both arms. His eyes were closed, his body prone, and he looked to Alix as if he were already dead. It was a horrifying sight.

A sob caught in her throat as she went to his bedside, struggling with every ounce of strength she possessed not to break down. Cord's chart was up on the monitor and she took a moment to examine his stats. His blood pressure was low but his electro-cardiogram was good, so she took some comfort with that. Then she noticed x-rays up on the view plate all along the wall. She paused, looking at an x-ray of Cord's pelvis, his lungs, his neck and his spine. She could feel Dr. Potts beside her.

"How long has he been here and nobody bothered to tell me?" she hissed.

Dr. Potts tried not to look too contrite. "About twenty minutes," he said. "You were busy with another patient and I wanted to get Cord stabilized before we told you."

Alix was furious, mixed in with her grief. She opened her mouth to blast Dr. Potts when Cord's soft voice interrupted her building tirade.

"Alix?" he murmured.

Her head snapped in his direction, noting his eyes were open and he was looking at her. When their eyes met, he smiled. "Hi, honey."

Alix went to his bedside but she couldn't speak. The tears were building up, spilling down her face as she grasped his hand and tried not to fall apart. Finally, she put a hand across her mouth so she wouldn't break out into gut-busting sobs.

Cord could see her breaking down and he tried to lift a hand to comfort her, but it was fairly impossible with the IV lines. He shushed her. "It's okay," he assured her, squeezing her hand. "I'll be okay. I've got the best doctor in Salem on my side, right?"

Alix could only nod her head, so very devastated. "What happened?" she whispered.

Cord sighed, squeezing her hand again as he closed his eyes. They'd given him something for the pain and it was making him very sleepy.

"The roof caved in," he muttered. "I was too dumb to get out of the way."

A sob escaped her lips then as she struggled not to openly weep. "Oh, my God," she whispered. "I... I can't believe this."

His eyes rolled open again and he focused on her. "Everything is going to be fine," he said, as if she were the one that needed reassuring. "Tell the boys I'll be home in a few days. I'll be fine, I promise."

He drifted off, the pull of the drugs too hard for his wounded body to resist. Dr. Potts put his hand on Alix's shoulder as she struggled.

"His vitals are stable for now," he assured her. "I've given him some Demerol, so he's not in any pain, but his blood pressure is flirting with the danger zone."

Alix wiped furiously at the tears coursing down her cheeks, focusing on what she was trained to do. Her breakdown had been brief but now she had to get down to business. Cord's life depended on it.

"Cord" she said quietly, putting her hands gently on his abdomen. "Baby, I need to examine you, okay? Can you please tell me if this hurts?"

He laid there, eyes closed, as she probed around his belly. His left side was pretty well battered, his magnificent chest bruised and cut. He was silent until she came to the left side of his stomach. A couple of gentle pushes just beneath his rib cage and he grunted. Alix paused and looked up at him.

"Does this hurt?" she pushed again, very gently.

He grunted again and his eyes rolled open. "A little bit, yes."

"Do you have any pain in your left shoulder?"

"My whole left side is killing me."

Alix poked around a few more times before checking the drainage tube stuck in his side, draining into a bag next to the bed.

"There's a lot of blood in his drainage bag," she muttered to Dr. Potts.

Potts nodded. "I know," he said quietly. "That makes me think he's ruptured something."

Alix concurred. "No doubt about it," she said. "In fact, I can't wait for Dr. Levenger. Let's get him up to surgery now."

"But, Alix...."

"*Now*, Dr. Potts," she snapped, louder. "I'm not waiting another minute. If he's bleeding out, I need to get in there. Please make sure I have a surgery room cleared because he's going right now."

Dr. Potts sighed heavily. "You know I can't let you...."

"Yes, you can," her tears were fading and she was becoming more businesslike, utterly stubborn and pushy. "I'm not his wife. I'm not a relative of any kind. I'm taking him in for surgery immediately. If you don't like it, file a grievance with the Board. I have work to do."

With that, she began issuing orders to the nurses in the room and, even though they all glanced at Dr. Potts, they began doing her bidding. Monitors were unplugged and Cord's bed was shifted into the wheeled position. Dr. Potts, knowing it would be of no use to try and stop her, made his way out to the nurse's station to make sure a surgery bay was cleared out. Dr. Hendry was on her way.

Alix was at Cord's head, softly but steadily issuing orders to the nurses who were wheeling him out, when they wheeled the bed past a collection of firefighters still standing outside of Cord's room. When the men saw Alix, Steve, the firefighter who had once tried to pick her up, reached out to gently touch her arm.

"Dr. Hendry?" He caught her attention. When she turned to look at him, impatient, he spoke quickly. "Cord... I just want you to know he saved a lot of guys today. Take good care of him, okay?"

Alix came to a halt even though Cord's bed kept going. "What do you mean?"

Steve was dirty, grimy and exhausted. He sighed heavily.

"He was inside the church with several other firefighters when part of the roof collapsed," he said. "Cord jumped right in and started pulling guys out, dragging them to safety. Because he was trying to pull the last guys free, he got caught in the second part of the roof collapse. It came down right on top of him. I swear to God, it's a miracle he survived. So you take good care of him, okay? He's our hero today."

Alix's tears returned. She was only able to keep herself in control if she was thinking about the surgery ahead, and not the fact that it was on Cord, but Steve's soft words had her breaking down a little bit. She touched the man's arm, smiling even as she wiped the tears away.

"He's always been my hero," she whispered. "He's the most important thing in the world to me. I promise I'll take excellent care of him."

With that, she scurried after Cord as he disappeared down a corridor. The firefighters from Station Four watched her go, each one of them saying a little prayer for Captain Trevor and his beautiful young surgeon.

FOURTEEN

CORD AWOKE to the faint sound of Alix's voice.

It was soft and gentle, and although he could hear her, he couldn't make out the words. He was in a haze, warm and liquid, but gradually the haze burned off and he found himself facing the soft fluorescent glow of a hospital room. There was pain and discomfort there. Opening an eye, he saw that Alix was standing right next to the bed.

"The drainage is becoming less," she was saying to someone. "We can probably remove the tube in a day or two, depending on how he's healing up."

"I'm going to heal up fine," he mumbled, his tongue thick and dry. "I'm fine already."

Alix gazed down at him, smiling. "That's what *you* think, big boy," she said. "I'm going to keep you here a couple of days longer if I have to sit on you."

"You might have to," he said. Then he opened both eyes, sleepy and drugged, and gazed up at her. "But I do know one thing."

"What?"

"I must be in heaven."

"Why?"

"Because there's an angel standing next to the bed," he muttered, watching her giggle. "How are you?"

"I'm good." Alix leaned down and kissed him on the forehead. "How do you feel?"

"I'm hungry."

She laughed. "We'll get you something to eat," she said. "Want some good news?"

"Sure."

"You didn't lose your spleen, although it was touch and go for a while," she said, stroking his head. "Everything is intact but you're very bruised internally. You got off lucky, my love."

He sighed, grunting because taking a deep breath hurt his cracked ribs. He lifted a hand, one that wasn't stuck with IV needles, and Alix held it tightly.

"So I'm going to make it?" he asked.

"You're going to make it."

He opened his eyes and looked at her. "Did you do the surgery?"

Her smile faded. "I did," she said. "I wasn't going to let anyone else touch you."

He smiled at her. "I've got the best doctor in Salem."

Alix leaned forward, kissing his lips sweetly. It was a painfully tender moment, one wrought with relief and joy. Tears sprang to Alix's eyes but she fought them. There was much cause for rejoicing.

"Hey," she said, kissing his cheek one last time before pulling away. "You've got about twenty people out in the waiting room to see you. The boys are here, your parents are here, your brother is here, and there are about ten firemen I don't know waiting to see you. I really think you should see the boys and your parents, but everybody else can wait."

He closed his eyes for a moment, still in the pull of the drugs. "So you met my parents, did you?

She chuckled. "I did, and I met your brother, too," she said. "They knew exactly who I was when I said my name, even before Chris did any introductions. Your mother even hugged me."

He grinned. "How are the boys?"

Alix stood up from the bed. "Chris is a rock, like always," she said. "Kyle is quiet and Cole looks like he's been crying. They're afraid. I'll bring them in, okay?"

He nodded weakly. "Okay."

Alix left him and headed out to the waiting area that was crowded with people. Some were sitting, some were standing, but nearly everyone seemed weary and concerned. When the group saw her coming, they perked up and turned their attention towards her. Alix smiled at the anxious faces to let them know everything was okay.

"He's awake," she said, mostly speaking to the boys and to his parents. "His vital signs are steady and he's lucid. He's going to be fine."

Everyone hissed their relief, happy encouragement going all around. Cord's mother wiped her nose with a handkerchief.

"How does he feel?" she asked. "Does he feel okay?"

Alix was gentle with her. "He feels as good as can be expected at this point," she said. "He says he's hungry and that's a good sign. Let me take the boys in there for a few minutes and then you can go in and see him."

Mary nodded and blew her nose as Chris, Kyle, and Cole gathered next to Alix in a group. She smiled at the boys and motioned for them to follow. Back down the sterile hallway they went, entering Cord's room where the nurse was adjusting his fluids. When he saw the boys come in, he extended a hand to them.

"Hey, guys," he said. "Come on in."

Timidly, the three boys stepped into the room, followed by Alix. Chris was the boldest, approaching his dad and taking the man's hand. He held it tightly.

"How are you?" Chris asked, deeply concerned.

Cord wriggled his eyebrows. "I've been better," he said. "But I'll be fine. I don't want you guys to worry, okay? God, I don't even know where to start. How long have I been out?"

"It's Friday," Chris said. "You got hurt on Tuesday."

Cord thought on that, trying to clear the cobwebs out of his weary mind. "Where have you been staying the past few days?"

"With me," Alix said quietly. "They've been staying at my house at night and Hester has been there to make sure they're taken care of. Your mom took them back to your house last night and stayed with them."

"Gramma cooked a huge breakfast this morning," Kyle said, grinning, trying to lighten the mood. "I tried to go back to bed afterwards but she made me go to school."

Cord grinned at his big-eating son. "You guys have probably been eating like kings between Alix and Gramma."

"It's hard to say who's a better cook," Chris agreed. "I'm leaning towards Alix. She makes this thing called a Dutch Baby. It's like a giant pancake-popover thing and... oh, wow, is it good. That, and some bacon and eggs, and I'm pretty happy."

"Are you going to get out of here soon, Dad?" Cole asked. He was standing back by the wall, looking forlorn and scared. "How long are you going to be here?"

Cord turned towards his son. Indeed, he looked as if he had been crying. "Not too much longer," he said. "I'm going to be fine, okay? I told you not to worry."

"I'm not," Cole insisted. "I just want to make sure... you know, that you're okay. That you're coming home soon."

"I'm coming home soon, I promise."

Cole looked embarrassed by his display of emotion and looked at his feet. Cord eyed his youngest son for a moment before looking to the older boys. "I'm feeling kind of tired," he said quietly. "Can you ask Gramma and Grampa to come in here for a minute? Cole can stay with me until they come."

Chris and Kyle bowed out, leaving Cole and Alix with their dad. Alix thought to leave, too, so Cole could have some alone time with Cord and slipped out with the excuse that she had something to do. When it was just Cord and Cole, Cord held out his hand to his youngest. Cole came forward and let his dad grab hold of him, pulling him closer.

"You okay?" Cord asked.

Cole nodded but the minute he did so, the tears started to come. "I'm okay."

Cord watched him struggled. "Were you scared?"

Cole nodded furiously. "Everybody was scared," he said. "And Alix... she never left you. Even when we came in to see you after you had surgery, you were still knocked out and she was with you the whole time. Sean said she didn't come home for two straight days."

Cord suspect as much. He knew Alix and knew she would have stayed with him constantly to make sure he was okay, but still, he was touched by such devotion. "She's a good doctor," he said quietly.

Cole was looking at his dad's big hand as it held his, dwarfing it. "She saved your life," he insisted. "I heard some of the firemen talking when you came out of surgery. They said she saved your life."

"She did."

Cole hung his head. "Dad, I know I was mean to her when you guys first got together," he said, struggling to find the right words. "But... well, she saved your life and I'm glad it was her. I mean, I'm glad she did it. She's okay."

Cord smiled faintly as he deciphered what his son was trying to say. "You mean that she's okay with you now."

"Yes."

"She's proven herself worthy."

"Kind of."

"I'm glad," he murmured. "Did you tell her that?"

Cole looked mortified. "No way!"

Cord laughed, squeezing his son's hand. "Maybe someday you'll tell her."

Cole turned bright red but was saved from saying anything more as his grandparents entered the room. Quirt and Mary went straight for the bed, all but ignoring Cole, but he was okay with that. He actually felt better than he had in days.

Cole turned for the door just as Alix was coming in and their eyes met. Normally, he would have tucked his head down and kept walking but this time, when she smiled, he returned it. For a moment, he just stood there and smiled at her, finally looking away in embarrassment and continuing out of the door. It was a warm, wordless gesture that was completely unexpected. But the acceptance, the silent thanks, was there. In fact, Alix was shocked. A good shock, but shocked nonetheless.

Everything was going to be okay.

———

"Carefully," Alix admonished the boys. "Be careful of his left side."

Chris was on his dad's left side while Kyle was on the right. Cord had his arms around his boys' shoulders as they helped him from the truck and, very slowly, walked him towards the kitchen door of Evenshade. The ground was even and there were very few steps, unlike his house which on a raised foundation with steps everywhere. Cole was behind his father, his hands carefully on the man's back to prevent him from falling backwards if he lost his balance.

"I'm okay," Cord assured the collection of concerned family members. "Just take it slow and I'll be fine."

Sean was at the kitchen door, holding it open, as the Trevor boys helped their father in through the opening. Five days after his run-in with a collapsed roof, Cord had been released from the hospital and was off duty for at least six weeks until he healed up. Alix stood back, holding Rose's hand, as the boys moved Cord inside.

Once inside the kitchen, Alix picked Rose up and moved to the back hall and the two smaller rooms that were back behind the living room.

"Bring him in here," she instructed, daughter slung on her hip. "I've got it all set up down here for him so he doesn't have to take any stairs."

The boys very carefully assisted their father across the back hall and into the first room, which Alix had set up with a fold out couch, a big television, and more pillows and blankets than the man would need in a lifetime. Rose slithered down from her mother's arms and ran to the fold out bed, jumping on it, as the boys eased Cord down onto the mattress.

"I'm good," he insisted, grunting as he gingerly tried to get comfortable. There were a lot of hands trying to help him. "I'll be fine, really."

Alix was putting pillows behind his back, trying to help him find a good position, as Rose slipped in under the radar and tried to climb on his lap. Cord grunted again as the little girl made contact with his bruised body.

"No, Rosie," Alix grabbed her daughter before she could do any damage. "Cord has boo-boos. You can't jump on him, okay?"

Cord put his arms up for the little girl, pulling her out of

Alix's arms. "She's okay," he insisted. "She can sit right next to me and we can watch television."

As Rose happily sat next to Cord, the boys were all over their dad. "Dad, are you hungry?" Chris asked, rather anxiously. "We can go get you something to eat."

"Nobody is going anywhere," Hester was in the doorway, watching everyone hover over Cord. "I've made lunch and there's plenty. Pulled pork barbeque."

Sean and Cole made a break for the kitchen to get some food while Chris and Kyle maintained vigilance over their father.

"Do you want something, Dad?" Kyle pressed. "A sandwich? Soda?"

What Cord really wanted at the moment was just to be left alone but he knew everyone was very concerned about him. He felt awful that he had upset everyone so badly, but he also felt incredibly blessed and grateful to be alive.

"Sure," he said after a moment, giving in to his boys' anxious faces. "A sandwich and a soda would be great."

He watched his boys run off, turning to Alix as she stood next to the bed. Their eyes met and he smiled, reaching out to take her hand.

"How are you doing today, honey?" he asked. "Feeling okay?"

Alix smiled, squeezing his big hand. "I'm fine," she began to choke up. "I'm more worried about you. How are you handling the Percocet?"

He could see she was starting to get weepy so he kissed her hand, squeezing it. "It makes me kind of tired, but the pain isn't nearly what it was," he assured her. "Besides, I have a great doctor. I'll be up and moving around in no time."

Alix wiped at her eyes before the tears could escape. "I'm

sorry," she whispered. "I'm not usually so emotional about things, but I'm a little hormonal."

He kissed her hand again, lifting Rose up so she was over on his right side. "Come sit down with me," he murmured. "I haven't had the chance to hug you yet today."

Alix sat down beside him, very carefully, and he put both arms around her, hugging her gingerly as Rose got a hold of the television remote and turned on the set. Cartoons began to dance across the screen as Cord buried his face on top of Alix's head, holding her against his chest.

"Thank you," he said. "For everything you've done for me, thank you. But I feel like I'm really putting you out by camping out in your study."

Alix lifted her head, kissing him sweetly. "I'm so happy to do it," she assured him. "In fact, they let me take a few weeks off with FMLA. Levenger was really generous about letting me take the time off to care for my 'significant other'."

He looked surprised. "Really?" he said. "You did that?"

She grinned. "Of course I did," she replied. "But I have to be careful about rationing it because I want to take time off when the baby is born, too."

His grin broadened. "So I get you all to myself for a while?"

"You sure do. At least, until the baby comes."

He snorted happily, pulling her into an embrace again, made slightly awkward because of his aching ribs. Next to them, Rose was laughing happily at the sponge and starfish cartoon as the boys came back into the room bearing plates of food. Cord glanced up at his boys as he released Alix.

"Speaking of babies," he muttered, accepting a big plate of barbeque from Chris. "Wow, thanks for this. Looks great."

Chris handed him napkins as Kyle put a soda on the table next to the fold-out. "What babies?" Kyle asked.

Cord looked at Alix, who shrugged at him with a smile

playing on her lips. Cord gazed up at the boys standing around, all four of them.

"I think we could all use some good news," he said, looking at the concerned and eager faces. "I know it's no big secret that Alix and I are going to get married. You guys are cool with that, right?"

The boys nodded. Even Cole and Sean, the original hold-outs, nodded without hesitation. It was evident that they had become completely comfortable with the relationship between their parents. Cord reached out and grasped Alix's hand as he continued.

"Well," he said after a moment, "this has been such a bad week for all of us and I want to change that. I'm going to heal, everything is going to be fine, and Alix and I are getting married very soon. Plus, there's something else we need to talk about and I hope you guys will be as happy as we are. Alix and I are going to have a baby next summer."

Kyle and Cole looked at their dad with their mouths hanging open while Chris just started laughing. "I'm going to be leaving for college," he said, pointing at the younger boys. "You dudes are going to have to change the diapers."

He was having a great time at his brothers' expense. Eventually, Kyle and Cole began to grin but Sean, standing next to Cole, was just staring at his mother. Without a word, he turned and left the room. Alix watched her son go.

"I'll be right back," she said, getting up off the bed and following Sean's trail.

She found him out in the driveway, heading for the big shed that still housed some of the old furniture. Alix caught up to him as he neared the old structure.

"Hey," she said, gently grasping his arm. "Where are you going? What's wrong?"

Sean pulled away from his mother, looking at his feet.

"Nothing," he said, although he was still walking. "I don't know. Just... leave me alone for a while, would you?"

Alix continued to follow him. "Please, Sean," she commanded softly. "*Stop*. Please tell me what you're feeling. Please tell me why you're upset."

He came to a stop but he wouldn't look at her. He just stared at the ground, kicking at little pebbles. "I don't know what I'm feeling," he muttered. "I guess... I guess I'm feeling weird."

"Why?"

"Because," he kicked a pebble away, growing agitated. "Because if you're... you're going to have a baby, that means... I just don't like thinking about that."

Alix could see what he was driving at, embarrassed and frustrated. "You don't like the thought of sex?"

He nodded sharply but kept his mouth shut. Alix could feel a great deal of sympathy for the confused young man and labored to keep the conversation sensitive yet comforting.

"Cord and I are adults," she said. "We can make decisions like that for ourselves. Most importantly, we love each other very much and when adults love each other, sex is a part of that demonstration. It's normal and natural."

He sighed sharply. "I just don't like to think about him... you know, *touching* you... it's just weird."

"Then don't think about it," she said frankly. "You shouldn't be, anyway. What Cord and I do is our business and you need to accept the fact that your mother isn't dead, Sean. She's in love with a very good man and this baby is a result of that love. We're very happy about it and I hope you can be, too. But I want you to know that you can always talk to me about this kind of thing, but if not me, there are lots of other people who would be happy to help you work through your feelings."

He just shrugged, still kicking at the ground, and Alix took a few steps in his direction. "I love you, Sean," she said gently. "You're my firstborn, my son, and I love you more than anything. You know that. This baby won't take away from that and getting married to Cord can't take away from it, either. Nothing will ever change that. Okay?"

Sean looked at her, then. "Why is it okay for you and Cord to have a baby and you're not married?" he wanted to know. "If I got some girl pregnant right now, I'd get in big trouble."

It was a legitimate question. "Because Cord and I are responsible adults, with jobs, and we're able to make decisions like that for our lives," she said honestly. "You're sixteen years old, Sean. Do you have any idea how having a child would affect your life? You'd grow up in an instant and end up having to be an adult before you were emotionally ready for it. Do you have a job? A place to live? A college degree? No, you don't. You don't have any of these things; therefore, you can't make a responsible decision like that about your life. You'd have two human beings dependent on you and no way to provide for them."

Sean fell silent, kicking at the ground. His mother, as always, made sense. But he still wasn't sure how he felt about anything. More than anything, he just wanted to be alone so he could sort it all out. He waved his mother off.

"I get it," he said. "I'll be okay. I just need to... think."

Alix sighed, watching her handsome son as he struggled with his feelings. "If you want to talk, I'm just inside." She pointed to the house as she began wandering back towards it. "Or if you want to talk to Chris or Kyle, you know they'll listen. Cord's pretty wise, too, you know."

Sean just nodded and waved her off again, so Alix headed back into the house. He wandered out to the old shed that was so picturesque amongst the trees and tall grass. There was still a ton of old furniture out in it and he leaned against the big dresser that had nearly squashed his mother that day so long ago when they had first moved in.

He sighed heavily, thinking on his mom's announcement and the way his life was changing. He wasn't the only one in for a change but he felt like it; for so long it had only been him and his mom because his dad really hadn't been around much and when he was, he never seemed to take a lot of interest in his only son. Therefore, Sean and his mother had been very close; this move to the East Coast had been okay with him because he didn't hold any real fondness for California and if he were to admit the truth, he kind of liked having three brothers. It made him feel part of something bigger, like he wasn't so alone anymore.

But then there was Cord, the man he was now sharing his mother with. He had resigned himself to that, but now with the baby, he was going to have to get used to that, too. Now, instead of just him and his mom and Rose, there were four other people in his family and soon a fifth. He knew how much his mother loved Cord and he'd stopped being jealous of that long ago. They were all melding into one big family, something he never thought he'd be a part of.

Sitting down on an old chair next to the dresser, he thought about the new baby and wondered if it would be another boy. There sure would be a lot of boys in the family, but he was okay with it. In fact, if he thought hard on what his mother said, he was okay with everything. He was loved, he was happy, and, in the end, that was all that mattered.

FIFTEEN
DECEMBER

MRS. MOWBRAY STOOD on the wide porch of Evenshade, gazing up at the structure with some awe and fear. The last time she'd seen Evenshade had been decades ago; she lived in another part of town these days and didn't get much opportunity to get over to the older section that used to be the outskirts of Salem Village. Evenshade had gone through a great deal of renovation and looked beautiful. She was duly impressed.

Knocking on the big, newly restored front door with its original knocker, she was in the process of inspecting the door itself when it suddenly opened. A young man stood there, gazing back at her.

"Hi," he said.

Mrs. Mowbray smiled nervously, displaying her yellowed teeth. "Hello," she said. "I'm from the Salem Historical Society. I'm looking for Mrs. Hendry."

"Dr. Hendry is my mom," the young man said. "She's in the kitchen; I'll get her."

Mrs. Mowbray waited patiently on the door stoop as Sean wandered down the wide central hall, calling for his mother. As she heard chatter towards the back of the house, Mrs. Mowbray peered inside the house, studying the newly renovated floors and spectacular staircase that led up to the second floor. Everything, from what she could see, was beautifully restored. As she squinted at an eighteenth century portrait of a woman in a white dress on the wall near the door, Alix emerged from the dining room.

"Mrs. Mowbray," she greeted her. "Please come in. I'm sorry my son didn't invite you inside to wait."

Mrs. Mowbray stepped inside, shaking Alix's extended hand. "Not to worry," she said. "He was very polite."

"Thank you," Alix said, but she could see the woman's attention was on the house. "Did you drop by to see the house? I'd be happy to show you around."

Mrs. Mowbray nodded. "I would love to see it," she said eagerly. "However, my purpose today was not to see the house. It was to give you a little more information about the legends surrounding it. After you left a few weeks ago, I did some research and found out a few things you might like to know."

Alix was eager to hear. "Of course I would," she said, indicating for the woman to follow her back to the kitchen. "Would you like a cup of coffee? I just made some fresh."

"Thank you," Mrs. Mowbray said as they entered the kitchen.

The kitchen was a masterpiece of stainless steel appliances, granite countertops, and black and white flooring that all blended seamlessly to create a restored kitchen space that looked chic yet appropriate for the age and architecture of the house. Alix indicated for the woman to sit at the stylish kitchen table and Mrs. Mowbray took a seat, setting her purse and a briefcase-like bag on the chair next to her. As Alix poured the coffee, Mrs. Mowbray looked around the spectacular kitchen.

"The house is beautiful," she said sincerely. "You have done a remarkable and tasteful job of restoring it."

Alix came over with the cups and set one of them down in front of Mrs. Mowbray. "Thank you," she said as she sat at the table. "We're still working on the bedrooms upstairs but it's almost finished."

"I'm sure this house never looked so good, even when it was new."

Alix grinned, pleased that the woman from the Historical Society thought so much of what she had done. But she noticed that Mrs. Mowbray had brought some things with her so she indicated the briefcase.

"So," she said, "what else have you found out about the house?"

The old woman immediately began opening up her bag. "You really whet my interest when you came a few weeks ago asking about this house," she said as she pulled out some papers. "I thought I'd look into it some more to see if I could find out anything else. Since it is so heavily associated with the Salem witch trials, I started there. I searched many different documents without any luck until I came to the journal kept by Dorothy Good. If you recall, that was Sarah Good's daughter."

Alix nodded, interested. "I do," she said. "What did she say?"

Mrs. Mowbray passed her some photocopies. As Alix peered at the copies made of faded, barely legible writing, Mrs. Mowbray began to speak. "Those are copies of a section of Dorothy's journal that I thought you would find interesting," she said. "Dorothy was only four or five when her mother was sent to jail and, subsequently, Dorothy was questioned by the inquisition and also put in jail. She was the youngest person to be accused of witchcraft during those trials."

Alix lifted her head and looked at Mrs. Mowbray. "Four or five years old?" she repeated. "She was my daughter's age. She was just a baby."

"Yes," Mrs. Mowbray agreed sadly. "But, as a child, she was interrogated and admitted to all sorts of things, including incriminating herself as a witch. She had a big imagination."

Alix refocused on the photocopies with very juvenile writing on them, shaking her head with disbelief. "Kids that age make up all kinds of things," she said, immediately thinking of Rose and the sad girl who followed her around. She found herself struggling to shake off the feelings of unease as she had come to discover that Rose hadn't been making up that particular friend. "Children that age hardly have a grasp of anything beyond their own growing worlds. I can't believe adults would have taken anything seriously from a five-year-old."

Mrs. Mowbray nodded. "Sad, but true," she said. "In any case, it was well known that Dorothy Good suffered from mental issues the rest of her life and it was attributed to her incarceration. It seems strange that a child that young, who was really only jailed for a few short months, should be so mentally troubled by so short an exposure, so I started reading her journal to see if there was something more to it, perhaps something more that happened during that time. I think I found it."

Alix perked up. "What did you find?"

Mrs. Mowbray sighed heavily and took the photocopies back from Alix. She shuffled them around before she came to the one she was looking for. She glanced at Alix, perhaps apologetically, before continuing.

"Dorothy wrote in her journal of her mother bearing a child in jail," she said. "This, too, is documented, but apparently Dorothy was the only one present when her mother gave birth to the baby. That, in and of itself, would probably scar a child, but there's more to it. According to Dorothy, she was released from jail a short time before her mother was hanged and when she was released, she says that her mother had her smuggle the baby out of prison. She said her mother told her to take the baby to Bebe's house."

Alix cocked her head thoughtfully. "Bebe's house?" she repeated. "I thought the husband brought the dead baby here to bury it under the house?"

Mrs. Mowbray shook her head. "According to Dorothy, she's the one that took the baby from the jail," she said. "Now, you must remember that Dorothy is barely older than a toddler herself at this time so her recollections may or may not be entirely accurate. But she states that she took the baby to Abigail's house but that her pet snake told her to throw it down the well because it was evil. So she did."

Alix's eyes widened. "She *threw* the baby down the well?"

Mrs. Mowbray pointed at the photocopy that apparently contained the fateful entry. "That's what she says."

"So the husband didn't bury it?"

"Not according to Dorothy."

"But there's no well on this property that I know of."

"To protect the water source and to make it convenient, wells were sometimes sunk and the houses were built up around them."

Alix looked stricken. "In the basement?"'

"Exactly."

Alix's mind began to race. So much of this weird tale was starting to make sense; most importantly, both tales she had heard referred to something being buried under the house. It was true that there hadn't been any more paranormal events since Halloween and there were days when the house seemed very charming and normal, but now she was starting to feel creeped out again. She didn't like it at all.

"That poor little girl," she said after a moment. "If this is true, what a burden she carried."

"Enough of a burden to mentally scar her for the rest of her life."

"That's for sure," Alix said, thinking on a five-year-old throwing a dead baby into the well. "I don't even know if there's a well in the basement. The laundry room is down there but I haven't really gone exploring."

Mrs. Mowbray returned her attention to the photocopies. "I suppose this all really doesn't matter in the long run," she said. "I just brought it to your attention because I thought it was interesting. Just more folklore."

Alix still wasn't happy about it. "I suppose," she said. "Thank you for sharing this. Can I keep these photocopies?"

Mrs. Mowbray nodded. "I brought them for you."

"Thank you," Alix said again, peering at the copies of the very old script. "This story of Sarah and Dorothy and Mercy just seems to get sadder and sadder. Whatever happened to Dorothy?"

Mrs. Mowbray shrugged. "She lived the rest of her life as an outcast, at least until her late teens," she said. "After that, no one seems to know. I can't find any record of her as an adult, or if she even married or had children of her own. I did find reference to her working as a servant girl, but that's really it. Being mentally unstable limited her in many ways."

"So she just disappeared?"

"It seems so."

Alix thought on that. "How strange," she muttered. "And how sad."

Before Mrs. Mowbray could reply, Rose came running into the kitchen. She ran straight to her mother, looking shyly at Mrs. Mowbray. Alix put her arms around her daughter and kissed her head.

"This is my daughter, Rose," she said. "Rosie, this is Mrs. Mowbray."

Mrs. Mowbray smiled at the little girl, her ugly teeth evident. "Hello, Rose," she said, glancing at Alix. "I see the resemblance between you two."

Alix smiled, hugging her daughter. "I've heard that more than once," she said, looking down at Rose. "My mother says it all of the time."

"She's right," Mrs. Mowbray said, focusing on Rose. "How old are you, young lady?"

Rose held up four fingers. "Four."

"Do you go to school?"

"Sometimes."

"Ah," Mrs. Mowbray said confidently. "You must be in nursery school."

Rose didn't say anything; she was too busy acting shy and shoving her fingers in her mouth. Alix gently removed them and turned to Mrs. Mowbray.

"Well," she said, standing up to signal that their conversation on the mysteries of the house was over, "it was really nice of you to come out today. Would you like to see the rest of the house before you go?"

Mrs. Mowbray nodded enthusiastically. "I would love it, thank you," she said. "As I told you before, I knew Cecily Trevor when she lived here and that was back in the nineteen thirties."

Alix listened with interest as she took Rose's hand and began walking from the kitchen. "When I moved in, I think there were still remnants of the house from that period, including the big cast iron sink in the kitchen, which we kept. We just had it refinished. Did you notice?"

Mrs. Mowbray looked at the sink, nodding her head in approval. "Beautiful," she said. "It looks like you kept most of the flooring intact."

Alix nodded. "I did," she said. "All of the flooring was saved. So was the banister on the front stairs."

As the women lost themselves in a discussion about the house, Rose began to hum. Holding her mother's hand, she hummed that strange little song that she seemed to have made up since they had moved into the house.

"*Goody Good, Goody Good, 'ere snake and bird could,*" she sang as she walked with her mother. She seemed to be looking off to her right, as if something was trailing behind her. Then she suddenly came to a stop and tugged at her mother. "Mommy?"

Alix was pointing out the details of the two hundred-year-old banister but she paused. "Yes, baby?"

"Mommy, the sad girl says we can't go upstairs," Rose said.

In days past, Alix wouldn't have given Rose's comment any credence. She would have ignored it. But these days, when Rose spoke of the sad girl, she was inclined to listen whether or not she wanted to. Call it a hunch, or instinct, of the need for self-preservation, but she would make herself listen. She could feel the hair on the back of her neck go up.

"Why not?" she asked softly, trying to keep the conversation between her and Rose as Mrs. Mowbray inspected the banister.

Rose looked up at her mother with her big gray eyes. "She doesn't like the lady."

Alix glanced at Mrs. Mowbray. She tilted her head in the woman's direction. "Her?"

Rose nodded solemnly. "She says she can't go upstairs."

Alix's jaw ticked as she thought on how to proceed. She was afraid of what would happen if she ignored the warning, having experienced a taste of the entity's power before.

"Rosie," she said carefully. "Where is the sad girl?"

Rose turned around, pointing down the hall. "There."

"Is she watching us?"

"Yes."

"Can you see her?"

"Yes."

Alix looked down the hall. Back there was the corridor to the study, the kitchen, and the rear of the house. She pondered the situation for a moment before turning to Mrs. Mowbray.

"If you want to step into the living room, you can see the hearth with the original stonework," she said. "There's even an iron arm in the mortar that they used to hold pots and kettles and things. You're welcome to take a look while I take care of something."

Mrs. Mowbray nodded eagerly. "Thank you, I'd be happy to."

Alix waited until the woman wandered into the living room before turning to her daughter. "Show me where the sad girl is."

Silently, Rose led her into the back hallway by the utility room. She pointed to the doorway leading into the utility room.

"Here," she said.

"Is she there now?"

"Yes."

Alix fixed on the open doorway, taking a deep breath as she composed her thoughts. "Rosie, you told me her name once," she said. "What was it?"

"Mer-*cy*."

"Mercy?"

Rose nodded. Alix felt rather sick to her stomach. "Oh, Christ," she whispered. "She told you her name was Mercy?"

"Uh-huh."

Alix looked at the doorway again, trying very hard not to feel frightened. *Mercy... wasn't that the name of Sarah Good's dead baby?* Alix seriously resisted the urge to run and take her daughter with her. Rosie had mentioned the name before, once when Alix had gotten knocked out by an unseen force, but she hadn't paid much attention to it. Now, she wished she had.

Pieces of a very sinister puzzle were coming together and she didn't like it one bit.

"Rosie?" she asked.

"What?"

"Is she still there?"

"Yes."

"What is she doing?"

"Looking at you."

Alix realized she was trembling. She focused on the empty doorway, summoning her courage. When she spoke, it was to the air.

"Mercy," she whispered. "I know you know me. I'm Rose's mom. I know you are sad and scared, but you are not allowed to tell me what I can do in my own home. This is my home now and I'm the master. Do you understand me? I want you to go back where you came from and stay there. You are not welcome here."

She was met with silence. After a moment, she turned to Rose. "Is she still there?"

Rose shook her head. "She went away."

It was then that they heard a massive thump overhead and the entire house shook. Alix raced to the front staircase just about the time she heard Sean yelling upstairs. Mrs. Mowbray bolted out of the living room and met Alix by the front door.

"What on earth was that?" the old woman asked, breathless.

Alix looked at her as she mounted the steps. "We... uh, we still have some renovation going on up there," she said quickly. "Would you mind letting yourself out? I need to see what's happened."

Mrs. Mowbray nodded, watching Alix fly up the stairs. She was concerned but she did as she had been asked and headed for the door. As she opened it, she realized that Rose was standing behind her, gazing up at her. Mrs. Mowbray forced a smile at the little girl.

"It was nice to meet you, young lady," she said. "I hope we meet again soon."

Rose simply nodded her head and closed the door on the woman, very nearly pushing her from the house. Mrs. Mowbray swore she caught a glimpse of another little girl standing on the staircase just before the door shut and blocked her view.

It was a little girl in a white dress that was the image of young Rose Hendry.

———

TWO WEEKS LATER

The wedding planner had done a spectacular job of decorating the house and grounds of Evenshade in fabulous winter colors, making the old house with the frightening reputation look like something out of a wedding magazine. It was a winter wonderland, a full-blown Christmas wedding complete with white trees and crystal lights everywhere. The theme was winter white with hints of silver and gold, and the wedding itself was set for the winter solstice, December twenty-first, at sunset. It was a magical time of the year.

Alix had taken the week off of work to prepare for the wedding although the wedding planner had it well in hand and Cord wouldn't let her do any work. He, too, had taken almost three weeks off of work and with a few of his buddies and his sons, took to re-landscaping the backyard where the wedding was to take place.

As the weather hovered in the teens and the brisk feel of winter kissed the landscape, Alix and Rose watched from the warm comfort of the house as Cord, Chris, Kyle, Sean, Cole, and about six firefighters ripped up the backyard and laid out an exquisite network of rocks and landscaping. A gazebo went up and a waterfall and pond went in. Sod was laid, one that was resistant to the extreme cold, and shrubbery was planted.

Since it was heading into the dead of winter and a snowstorm had been forecast for Christmas Eve, Cord didn't worry about flowers. He simply lay down what he could and hoped it would keep its green color until after the ceremony. After that, it could turn purple for all he cared. He just wanted it looking good for the wedding.

His work buddies worked for free food and beer, which Alix kept amply supplied. She made big pots of chili or chicken and dumplings, her favorite, and fed them hot food every couple of hours. She also checked fingers and noses periodically for frostbite. Chris and Kyle worked silently alongside their father but Cole, being younger and not so hearty, would sneak inside to warm up along with Sean, the California boy, who had never dealt with weather this cold. He had no idea how to cope with it.

The first day of the landscaping party had been brutally cold and Alix brought Sean indoors after just an hour because his lips were turning blue. He got angry with her about it because he didn't want his future stepbrothers thinking he was a wimp, but the truth was that she gave him a great excuse to warm up.

Once the landscaping was down, the wedding planner went to work with her exquisite white lighting and other marvelous effects. It was absolutely gorgeous and the night before the wedding, Alix and Cord had stood on the back porch, arms wrapped around each other, and just admired everything. The whirlwind courtship was culminating in a dreamlike wedding, and they were still both coming to terms with it. Deeply in love and deliriously happy, they were both savoring every minute of it. It was unbelievably right, all of it, and they were very thankful.

On the night before the wedding, the snowstorm hit. Alix awoke in her bed, alone, as Cord and his boys were down the road at his house, to Sean yelling excitedly about snow. Staggering out of bed, she had opened the shutters to be faced with a world blanketed in white, including her brand new landscaping. She had been standing there staring at it in wonderment when her cell phone rang. She didn't even have to look at the number; she knew who it was.

"Hi, babe," she said, sounding sleepy.

Cord's voice was warm and deep. "Hi yourself," he said. "How are you feeling this morning?"

"Surprisingly well," she said. "In fact, I've woken up every morning for the past couple of weeks and have felt fine. I think the worst of the morning sickness curse is over."

"Thank God," he breathed quietly. "But speaking of worst, have you looked out the window lately?"

Alix grinned. "I'm looking out of it now," she said. "I think I see your house buried under a bunch of snow."

Cord snorted. "You think you're kidding," he said. "I'm going to send Chris and Kyle up to the house to shovel the driveway and put down salt. I'll be up in a few minutes to take a look at the backyard and see what we need to do about cleaning the snow off the gazebo and such."

"Okay," she said. "I'll make some breakfast."

"Thanks," he said. "We'll be right up. I love you."

"Love you, too."

Alix hung up the phone and went to take a quick shower. It was hot and wonderful, steaming up the bathroom, as she finished up and dried off. She took care to rub oil over her growing belly so she wouldn't get stretch marks, inspecting her belly in the mirror and realizing it had grown quite a bit over the past few weeks. She was nearly four months along and suspected it was going to be a rather large baby.

Drying her long hair and putting on a bit of make-up, she dressed in stretchy leggings and a gorgeous oversized sweater that was warm and cozy. Pulling on her fuzzy boots, she headed downstairs to begin breakfast which, for Cord and his boys, was a rather large affair. They were big boys and they liked to eat, so the moment she got into the kitchen, she went straight to the refrigerator and pulled out the eggs. That was where she started.

By the time Cord and his boys rolled up several minute later, Alix already had a mass of scrambled eggs with ham, bacon, potatoes and juice on the table. As the door opened and they began piling in, she put the first big stack of pancakes on the table. Chris, Kyle and Cole threw themselves at the table with its cornucopia of breakfast delights while Cord went to Alix and took her in his arms.

"Hello, beautiful," he said, kissing her lips.

"Hi," she said, kissing him in return. "Correct me if I'm wrong, but I don't think the groom is supposed to see the bride before the ceremony."

He cocked an eyebrow at her as he headed for the table. "Correct *me* if *I'm* wrong, but I don't think the bride is supposed to cook for the groom and his sons before the ceremony."

Alix giggled and flipped a pancake. "It's the least I can do before I throw you all out into the snow."

Cord sat down as Chris handed him the plate with the eggs. "We're used to it," he said, scooping out a healthy portion of eggs. "Besides, I already called some of the guys. They're coming over in a while to help get this place cleaned up."

Alix finished up pancake round number two and put the plate on the table as Sean came down, lured by the noise. He sat between Kyle and Cole, already getting a ribbing for the fact that he was still in his pajamas. Alix grinned, pouring Cord and Chris some coffee, thinking she would be very happy to listen to the brotherly teasing for the rest of her life. When she should be on duty in the emergency room, she was making pancakes, pouring coffee, and loving every minute of it. Her entire life had been filled with ambition and medicine, but the past few months had seen that drastically change. Ironic how the right man could change everything.

Rose began to cry as she was pouring some orange juice for Sean so she raced up the back stairs and into her daughter's bedroom. Rose was still in one of the back bedrooms because Alix didn't want her returning to the front bedroom where the sad girl seemed to pay so much attention to her. However, when she entered Rose's pink and white princess bedroom, her daughter was nowhere to be found. But she could still hear the crying.

"Rose?" Alix called out. "Where are you?"

No answer but more crying. Alix went into both bathrooms and Sean's room but she still couldn't find her daughter. As she came back out into the corridor, she noticed the door to Rose's old bedroom slightly ajar. Feeling the least bit of trepidation, she pushed it open and stuck her head in.

"Rosie?" she called.

There was more crying but it was louder now. Alix stepped into the room, which had now become a storeroom for boxes and stuff that Cord was moving into the house, looking around to see where her daughter was and what had her so upset. But Rose didn't seem to be anywhere in the room. Puzzled and concerned, Alix was about to turn for the door to call down to Cord for help when she noticed that the closet door was cracked open. She immediately went to it and opened it.

"Rosie?" she called up the narrow attic stairs. "Are you up there?"

"Mommy!" Rose cried, sounding frightened. "Mommy, come get me! She won't let me leave!"

Alix started to take a step when an unseen hand suddenly shoved her back. She stumbled out of the closet, backwards, but when she tried to grab the door, it slammed in her face. It was a loud and violent sound. Rose started screaming and so did Alix.

"Cord!" she shrieked.

She could hear the cavalry coming up the back stairs. It sounded like a thundering herd. Cord burst into the room, followed by all four boys. Alix pointed at the closet door in a panic.

"She's up there and I can't get the door open!" she cried.

Cord raced to the door, listening to Rose's screaming in the attic. He pulled and pulled but no matter how hard he tried, he couldn't budge the door. Alix began crying, terrified for her daughter, as Cord ended up pulling the door knob right out of the door.

"What the hell?" he exclaimed, looking at the old iron latch in his hand. He tossed it aside and tried to get his fingers into the mechanism to open it. "What in the hell is wrong with this door?"

Alix was in tears. "It pushed me back and slammed the door in my face when I tried to get to Rose."

He looked at her. "What pushed you back?"

She was nearly hysteria. "That big draft you said didn't exist," she said angrily. "It pushed me out of the closet and slammed the door in my face. I need to get to my daughter!"

Cord had his hands full with a panicked fiancée and a jammed door. He turned to Chris. "Find me something," he said with urgency. "An axe, a hammer... any kind of tool I can use to bust this door down. *Go!*"

Chris was off. Cord grabbed his biggest son, Kyle. "Help me with this door," he said. "We're going to try to kick it down, okay?"

Kyle put his size fourteen feet to work. He and Cord began kicking at the door, anything to get it to move, but it seemed more stuck than ever. Even the old wood of the panel seemed like concrete; no cracks or chips. Alix was panicking, which in turn fueled Cord. They could all hear Rose screaming. But then, it abruptly stopped.

The sudden silence was electrifying. Alix stopped crying, her eyes wide with terror as she looked at Cord. He glanced at her but didn't take the time to stop and comfort her. He was desperate to get the old door open. Looking around the room, he could see a big brass lamp base, heavy and well made. He grabbed it and returned to the door, lifting it like a hammer and preparing to take a swing. But just as he brought it down, the door swung open.

Rose was standing there. Cord was already in full swing, bringing it right down on Rose's head before he could stop himself. He heard Alix scream and he even heard the boys yell, but he was already in motion. It all happened too fast. But just as soon as he delivered a blow that would have surely killed the child, she vanished into thin air. All that was left was an open door and a dark, empty stairwell.

Cord nearly had a heart attack. He dropped the lamp base and pitched forward, stumbling into the closet and onto the stairs. Alix was literally on his heels as he raced up the steps.

"Rosie?" he yelled. "Rose, where are you?"

They reached the top of the steps, into the dark and eerie attic with its shadows and crevices. There was a ton of old junk up here, left by previous tenants and owners, stuff that had accumulated over the years. Boxes littered the area, a dark and dusty expanse that stretched the entire length of the house.

Cord charged into the attic, looking around frantically for Rose. Kyle and Sean and Cole were right with him, looking behind boxes and moving things aside to see if she was hiding anywhere. They were all frantic with worry. Alix, however, had turned to the right while everyone else went to the left. She spied her daughter over near one of the small windows that faced the south side of the house.

"Rose!" she cried.

She ran to her daughter and dropped to her knees as Cord and the boys thundered up behind her. Rose had been sitting on the floor when Alix picked her up, clinging fearfully to her mother.

"Rosie!" Alix gasped. "Are you okay?"

Rose threw her arms around her mother's neck and refused to let go. Alix couldn't even pry her away to get a look at her and when Cord tried, she screamed, so he let her alone. Alix held her daughter tightly, sitting on the floor of the attic. At least her child was in her arms now, and safe, so Alix took a lot of comfort in that. But not for long; she was frantic to know what had happened.

"Rosie," she said gently. "Please tell me what happened. Did you accidentally get locked up in here?"

Rose shook her head. "No."

"Then what happened?"

She pulled her head out of the crook of Alix's neck, snot and tears all over her face. "The sad girl told me to come up here because we would play a game," she said. "When I wanted to leave, she wouldn't let me."

Alix swallowed hard, feeling a great deal of fear creep over her. "The... the sad girl kept you up here?"

"Yes."

Alix didn't ask anything more, at least not at the moment. The truth was that she wasn't quite sure what more to say. As she comforted her daughter, Cord was standing over the pair, protectively, feeling very frustrated and, if he were to admit it, a little frightened. He knew what he had seen in that darkened closet; it was the image of Rose, just as he had seen on Halloween night. When he'd brought the lamp base down, he swore he had killed Rose and to see the image disappear... well, he was having a difficult time reconciling it. He didn't believe in ghosts but he'd seen one – twice. He'd even talked to his parents about it. Maybe there was something more to this than he was willing to admit. Still, he was having a tough time accepting everything. He just couldn't seem to wrap his mind around it.

"Come on, honey," he said gently, putting his hands on Alix's arms to help her stand up. "Let's get her downstairs. It's cold and dusty up here."

Alix nodded, trying to stand up with Rose in her arms but she couldn't quite manage it. Sean had to come to her rescue and took Rose because she wouldn't go to anyone else, including Cord. When Sean took Rose and Cord helped Alix stand, they both noticed something on the floor beneath them. Alix had been sitting on it, blocking it. Curious, they peered at it.

"What in the hell is this?" Cord asked.

Alix shook her head, looking at the floor board partially pulled away. Cord got down on one knee and pulled at it. He ended up popping it out completely, as it wasn't secured in the least. A hidden compartment lay beneath and Cord pulled out what appeared to be a series of documents bound together. They were extremely old, brittle and yellowed, with a texture like dead fall leaves. Cord peered at them curiously before handing them over to Alix.

"More mysteries from this house," he muttered, watching Alix carefully inspect the brittle documents. "Can you make out anything?"

Alix squinted at whatever was written on the paper. "No,"

she said, shaking her head after a moment. "I can't see in this light."

Cord stood up. "Let's get out of here," he said, gently ushering everyone back towards the stairs. "We'll take this all downstairs and have a look."

The Trevor boys pounded down the attic stairs followed by Sean carrying Rose, and finally Alix and Cord. Cord shut the closet door leading up into the attic and pointed at the children.

"Nobody goes up there again," he said quietly, firmly. "All right? Agreed?"

The boys nodded and Cord looked specifically at Rose. "No more going up there," he told her with gently sternness. "It's dangerous, honey. I don't want you to get hurt. Okay?"

Rose nodded unsteadily and Cord rewarded her with a kiss on the cheek. "Good girl," he said. "Now, let's go back downstairs, finish breakfast, and start getting the driveway cleared. We've got a big day ahead of us."

Everyone started moving. Alix collected Rose from Sean and passed the old documents back to Cord. As the boys headed back downstairs, she went back to her bedroom with Cord on her heels. He set the old documents on his dresser as Alix set Rose down on the mattress and checked her arms and upper torso for injury. She checked the little girl's head, scalp, legs and feet before she finally eased up. Then, she stood back and put her hands on her hips.

"Now," she said to her daughter, "tell me everything that happened. You said the sad girl wanted to play. What did she want to play?"

Rose looked pale and tired. She shrugged her little shoulders restlessly and began to crawl off the bed.

"She said she wanted to call her mommy," she said. "She said I had to help her but I didn't want to play and then she wouldn't let me get out. Mommy, I'm hungry."

Alix watched her daughter climb off the bed, feeling apprehension at her statement. "She said she wanted you to help her call her mommy?" she repeated.

Rose was heading for the door. "Yes."

"But... who is her mommy?"

"I don't know."

"She didn't say?"

"She said her mommy was waiting for her to call her."

"Why?"

Rose didn't know. She just kept walking, heading out of the room and towards the back staircase. Alix let her go, calling down to Sean to let him know she was coming down the stairs. Then, she looked at Cord and expressions of confusion passed between them but in Alix's case, there was more to it. She was weary, emotional, and hormonal, and Cord watched as her eyes filled with tears.

"What in the hell is happening around here?" she hissed. "You saw that... that girl in the closet. I thought it was Rose and you almost... you...."

She couldn't finish her sentence and Cord took her in his arms, holding her tightly. He thought back to that moment when he thought he'd killed Rose and it shook him up. In fact, the more he thought on it, the more nauseous he became.

"I know," he said when she couldn't go on. "I saw it, too. I thought I'd killed her. I swear that little incident just took twenty years off my life. I'm *still* shaking."

"What are we doing to do? Why is this all happening?"

"I don't know but I intend to find out."

Alix wiped at her eyes and lifted her head to look at him. "How?"

He sighed heavily. "I'm not sure this is even the day to talk about this," he said. "We're getting married in about eight hours.

I want to focus on that and not this... this craziness that seems to invade every inch of this house."

Alix pulled away from him gently and went to the tissue box. "Then you really do think something is going on now."

"I can't deny what I've seen."

"You sure didn't believe me in the beginning."

"I've change my mind. I can't refute what I've seen. But like I said, I really don't want to focus on that today."

Alix put the tissue to her nose. "I don't want to focus on it, either, but we don't really have a choice." She blew her nose. "What are we going to do? I don't want people in the house and suddenly this... this ghost makes an appearance."

He shrugged. "She seems rather selective when she makes her appearances," he said quietly. "She doesn't seem to do it for anyone but us. I'll see if I can find a medium or a psychic or something to come in here and see what they can figure out. I'll get help for this, honey; I don't want you to worry about it."

Alix blew her nose again. "Of course I'm worried about it," she said. "This sad girl seems to be fixated on Rose and I'm scared for my daughter. She's downstairs with the boys eating breakfast now and I don't even want to let her out of my sight. What happens if the sad girl takes her out on the roof next time and tells her to jump? I'm scared to death."

Cord sighed again and went to her, kissing her on the forehead. "Let's just get through today and we'll worry about the rest of it later," he said quietly. "Okay? I don't want anything to spoil this day I've waited my whole life for."

Alix gazed up at him, his handsome face and hopeful expression, and began to soften. "Okay," she agreed. "While you guys are shoveling snow, I think I'm going to lie back down for a while. This whole incident has me kind of rattled."

He agreed. "Me, too," he said. "You and Rose take a nap and let us handle the house."

They turned for the door but as they did so, the old documents Cord had set on the dresser caught their attention. Cord reached out and collected the documents, thinking about making heads or tails of the situation, but reconsidered. He opened up his top dresser drawer and carefully put them inside with his watches and handkerchiefs.

"I'm going to call Mrs. Mowbray at some point and take those documents over to her," he said "She seems very interested in this house, so I'm sure this will be a real thrill. Maybe... maybe there's something in there that will help us figure all of this out."

"And solve it?"

"I hope so."

Alix sighed heavily and he kissed her head, giving her a gentle and encouraging squeeze. Together, they headed back downstairs to finish breakfast and move ahead with their day.

They had a wedding to participate in.

SIXTEEN

AT FOUR O'CLOCK, Dr. Alix Hendry became Dr. Alix Hendry-Trevor. Dressed in a Medieval-looking white brocade wedding gown with an empire waist that disguised her growing belly and a white faux fur cape, she married Cord in the gazebo in the backyard of Evenshade in front of thirty people. It was a very small wedding of mostly Cord's people because Alix's were all out in California. Alix's two cousins managed to make it, however, and two aunts, but her parents had passed away a few years earlier so she had no immediate family present. Being an only child, she was fairly alone in that department.

But no longer; she now had a husband, his three boys, his parents, two sisters-in-law and two brothers-in-law, and four nephews. It was a big and happy family that was thrilled to welcome her. She had never actually met Cord's brother and sister, Kent Trevor, a very handsome man with Cord's smile, and his sister, Elizabeth, who was very pretty and very sweet. They were both very gracious and very friendly to her, and Alix took to Elizabeth immediately.

About halfway through the wedding ceremony it began to snow, so they finished their vows with snowflakes on their eyelashes. Rose, who had been the flower girl, grew restless by the time Cord kissed his bride and he soon found himself carrying his new stepdaughter down the aisle. He held Alix's hand tightly, never more happy or proud of anything in his life, as they headed from the garden straight into the house. The guests, cold and being snowed upon, quickly followed.

The caterer had set up inside the house and a fire burned brightly in every fireplace so it was very warm and festive. The big dining room in the front of the house was set up like a buffet and as the guests began to serve themselves ham, turkey, prime rib and other succulent items, Cord and Alix and the immediately family went back outside to take a few pictures that were quickly hampered by both the weather and the setting sun. After taking several lovely shots, everyone hustled back inside and the reception was full-on.

Evenshade was perfectly laid out for entertaining because, back in the day, it had been the only house for miles around big enough to accommodate more than ten people. It had seen its share of events. Along with the big dining room, it had enormous double parlors that, at some point, someone had removed the pocket doors and turned it into one enormous room. There was a partial wall in the middle of it as a result, but it didn't impede the flow.

People ate in the big living room or wandered back to the library or den where Cord had recovered from his injuries, warmed by the inviting fires in the fireplaces in each room and enjoying the atmosphere. With the firelight and gentle lighting, one could almost see people in Colonial American attire moving from room to room, or envision how they spent their evenings. At Evenshade, it was easy to see.

As the wedding photographer took Cord and Alix into the library to shoot some portraits of just the two of them, the rest of the family were free to eat. As the Trevor boys and Sean tore into the ham and beef, Mary and Quirt worked around them and managed to fill their plates. While everyone else went to the living room to eat, Mary and Quirt ducked into the kitchen where the caterer was quietly working. Sitting at the lovely kitchen table, they tucked into their food.

"I haven't been inside this house since I was a boy," Quirt said, looking around the stylish kitchen. "It's changed a lot."

Mary had her fork in her hand and was picking at her food. Mostly, her attention seemed to be on the house. She looked around as her husband spoke.

"I've never been in here," she said. "Wasn't your Aunt Cecily the last family member to live here?"

Quirt nodded, his mouth full of prime rib. "Yes," he said. "Then she rented it out, oh, thirty years ago before she went to that retirement community."

"We haven't seen her in a few years."

"I know," Quirt said, looking guilty. "We really should. She's the last one of that generation left."

"We should have brought her to the wedding."

"She lives in Arizona, Mary, and she's ninety-seven years old. She's not going to travel well."

"Still," Mary said wistfully, setting her fork down and looking around the room. "Maybe we should have at least called her."

Quirt shook his head, shoveling in mashed potatoes. "Why?" he asked. "There's no point."

Mary let the subject drop. She could hear people in the other rooms, talking and laughing, but she wasn't in the mood to do either. She seemed very uneasy. Quirt finally noticed that she wasn't eating.

"What's wrong?" he asked, gesturing at her plate. "Why aren't you eating?"

Mary shook her head, her eyes moving up to the ceiling of the room. "I don't know," she said. "There's something...."

"Something *what*?"

Mary shook her head again. Then, she stood up. "I need to... walk around a bit," she said. "I need to see the rest of the house."

Quirt caught on to what she was saying. "Why?" he asked. "What's going on?"

"I'm not sure."

This time, Quirt set his fork down because he could tell she was uneasy. "Did you see something?"

"No," Mary said faintly. "But I feel something."

"Like what?"

She didn't reply. All she could do was shake her head because she really wasn't sure. All she knew was that she was very unsettled. Slowly, and with some trepidation, she began to walk towards the back stairs that led up to the second floor. She peered up the darkened stairwell.

"I don't think Cord wants you wandering around," Quirt told her.

Mary didn't take her eyes off the stairwell. "He's busy right now," she said. "Besides, he won't mind if I want to see the house."

Quirt looked around, noticing the door to the basement underneath the stairs that led up to the second floor. His gaze lingered on it. "If we go anywhere, it should be down in the basement to see if we can find remnants of that stone circle," he said quietly. "Knowing Cord, he hasn't done a thing. Maybe it's up to us to take a look."

Mary was still fixated on the second floor. "After I've seen what's up here, maybe we will," she said.

She started up the stairs and Quirt sighed heavily, setting his fork down. Dutifully, he followed.

The second floor was quiet and dimly lit as light and noise

from the first floor drifted up the stairwells. Mary went to the first door she came to which happened to be Alix's bedroom. She stuck her head in, looking around the exquisitely decorated room, visually inspecting everything. But she was doing more than that; she was reaching out with her senses, especially that sixth sense that sometimes saw or heard things that no one else could.

Mary had always had the gift, ever since she had been a child and old enough to understand that sometimes she saw people that no one else saw. It was something her daughter had also inherited. The entire Trevor family was gifted one way or another, but some family members didn't accept those gifts, Cord included. She'd long learned to accept his reluctance even though it still saddened her a bit to think on it.

Mary stood for several long minutes studying Alix's room before moving on. The next room was Rose's old room and she quietly opened the door only to be faced with stacks of boxes and a deserted room. The rest of the house was so lovely that this room, and a very big one at that, seemed oddly out of place. Curious, she stepped inside. Quirt was behind her, more interested in the boxes than in the room. As Mary wandered into the middle of the room, she suddenly came to a halt. Quirt was still peering at the boxes, being nosy and lifting lids to see what was inside, when he happened to glance over at his wife and saw her stagger.

"Hey," he called over to her. "What's the matter?"

Mary had her hand at her throat, her wide eyes staring up at the ceiling. "There's something...," she trailed off and then cocked her head as if listening to something. "Do you hear that?"

Quirt looked around the room. "Hear what? I don't hear anything."

Mary's movements were odd and jerky as she moved

around, listening. "Singing," she said. "I hear a child singing. Can't you hear it?"

Quirt shook his head. "Nothing, Mary."

Mary picked her way through the dusty, cluttered room, ending up near the closet. She looked at the door, noting the ripped-out latch. Puzzled, she stuck her fingers into the hole and opened the door. It was dark in the closet, a soft *whoosh* of stale attic air caressing her face. As her eyes adjusted to the darkness, she could see a set of narrow steps leading up. Her gaze trailed up the stairs and at the very top, she could see the outline of a small child silhouetted in the darkness. She froze.

"Quirt," she hissed. "Come quick!"

Quirt scooted over to the door to see what had his wife so excited. When he peered up the steps, there was nothing there. Simply darkness. He looked at his wife.

"What is it?" he asked softly. "What did you see?"

Mary was pointing up the steps. "I'm not sure," she said. "It looked like... like a child."

"A *child?*"

She nodded firmly. "It was there and then...."

As she spoke, the light in the stairwell seemed to change, like the flicker of a soft white light or perhaps the moon glow when clouds pass over it. It was very faint but noticeable, flickering almost like static. Dim, bright, dim, bright.... Suddenly, a small girl was standing on the flight of stairs midway down. Both Mary and Quirt jumped back as she was illuminated by the flicker. But when the flicker grew dim again, she was gone.

Quirt opened his mouth to say something to Mary but the flicker came back again, stronger than before, and like a strobe light flickers violently, the little girl was suddenly standing in front of them at the base of the stairs. She flickered in and out, in and out, and with each successive flicker, her dark eyes turned to boiling liquid dark, running down her face, and her dark mouth opened to reveal ugly, sharp fangs.

Quirt slammed the door and grabbed his wife, running for the door to the bedroom, but it slammed in their face. Startled and terrified, Quirt crashed into the panel, hitting his head, as Mary smashed into the back of him. They both turned around, facing the bedroom that was now flickering strangely, also, to see the ghostly girl standing a few feet behind them. All running face and fanged mouth, the child with the stringy dark hair and old-fashioned dress cocked her head in a curious gesture.

"Ent thou home?" she hissed. *"Whereas Rose?"*

Mary and Quirt gazed back in various stages of terror, but Quirt regained some of his composure. He had to; otherwise, he was going to climb right through the wall and probably kill himself. He forced himself to breathe. *Just breathe!*

"Who are you?" he asked, trying not to sound terrified.

The ghost girl simply stared in return. At least, that's what they thought she was doing; they really couldn't tell because she had no eyeballs, just big black holes in her face. She took a step or two closer, the fanged mouth flexing horrifically. Then, a skeletal hand lifted, the bony fingers pointing directly at them.

"Fetcheth my Rose," she garbled.

Above all of their fear, they recognized Rose's name. Mary, her curiosity overcoming her fear, endeavored to communicate. As a medium, and a very good one, she tried to be clinical about it, but it was an uphill battle. Whatever stood in front of them wasn't a little girl; she knew that. It was a spirit, or perhaps something even worse, manifesting itself as a child. It was a deceiver, something very wicked trying to make itself seem harmless. Every sense in her body was telling her that.

"Rose?" she repeated. "What about her? Is she your... your friend?"

The ghostly girl lowered her pointing finger. She took

another step towards Quirt and Mary but they realized she wasn't walking at all; her feet were mist and not even touching the floor. She seemed to be turning her head in Quirt's direction.

"*Thou Bebe stock?*" she asked in that oddly hissing tone.

Quirt had no idea what she said but he knew it wasn't good. He was a warlock, an artist in the magic arts, like his father and his father before him. The entire line back to Abigail Williams had the skill and knowledge, old practices that were kept private and secretive. It was in their blood, as he had told Cord. Like brown eyes or freckles, it was just something his family had. As he gazed at the fanged ghost, he drew upon that innate part of him that understood things of the paranormal nature. He accepted that there were things of this earth that could not be explained. But this thing in front of him... it was evil. He knew that in his gut, just like his wife did.

"*Tenet creatura, redire unde orta es. Non es hic susciperent,*" he said, lifting his hand to her. "*Recede et non revertitur.*"

The ghostly girl snarled at him, her mouth opening wide and an unworldly hiss bursting forth. Her bony hands turned to claws and lifted in their direction but Quirt didn't back down. He jabbed a finger at the ghost.

"*Et vade, te creaturam malam,*" he said louder, casting a spell of departure and banishment. "*Et revertatur in domum discedere inferni. Non habetis hic potentia.*"

The ghost girl began to dissipate, like steam, but the gaping mouth continued to hiss. The horrible teeth gnashed at him. Quirt lifted both hands, palms-out, as if shoving the ghost girl and her evil away from him.

"*In nomine Iesu Christi, ego præcipio tibi, et numquam ad locum istum omnia saecula saeculorum,*" he commanded. "*Et vade!*

A clawed hand swiped in his direction but turned to mist

when it made contact with Quirt's arm. Mary shrieked and yanked open the bedroom door, pulling Quirt with her. As they fled into the hallway, the hissing followed them until the bedroom door slammed shut again. They raced down the stairs and into the living space below.

Cord found his parents on the porch a half hour later, sitting huddled up on the patio furniture as the snow fell and the night deepened. They wouldn't go back in the house no matter how much he tried to coax them.

———

"Dad, it's really freezing out here," Cord said. It was nearing midnight and all of the wedding guests had departed, but Quirt and Mary remained on the porch. Cord had brought them blankets and hot coffee but they still refused to budge. "Can I at least convince you to come into the kitchen?"

Quirt shook his head, his arm around Mary, who was wrapped up in a quilt with a cup of coffee in her hand.

"Son, I'm not trying to be difficult, truly," he said, "but no amount of convincing is going to get me back into that house again, not ever. I told you that."

Cord sighed heavily. "Yes, but you won't tell me *why*," he said. "What in the hell happened that made you run out of the house and sit in freezing temperatures?"

Quirt eyed the front door as it opened and Alix appeared. She was out of her wedding dress and swathed from head to toe in a ski jacket, mittens, heavy pants, and boots. She was ready for the cold. She smiled timidly at Quirt and Mary as she made her way over to Cord, who put his arm around her.

"You two are going to get frostbite out here," she said. "Won't you please come inside?"

They both shook their heads as Mary spoke. "Where is your daughter?" she asked.

"Rose?" Alix said. "I put her to bed."

Mary shook her head, almost violently. "Please," she begged. "Don't leave her alone. Don't ever leave her alone in this house again."

"Why not?"

Mary looked at Quirt, guiltily, and Cord had enough. He pulled out a chair that was sitting back against the wall and put it right in front of his parents. He planted himself in it and faced them.

"Look," he said, his voice low but firm. "Something happened this afternoon and you need to tell me what it is. What has you two so spooked that you'd sit out here and freeze?"

Quirt cleared his throat and glanced at his wife. "Well," he said reluctantly. "We... we just didn't want to ruin your wedding day, that's all."

"The wedding is over and the guests have gone," Cord said, sounding rather irritated. "You can't ruin anything. Tell me what's going on."

Quirt sighed heavily, taking a sip from his coffee cup before he spoke. He was gathering his thoughts, not wanting to over-dramatize what he'd seen but not wanting to diminish it, either. He and Mary had spent the past few hours trying to figure out what, exactly, to tell their son. They opted for the truth.

"Your mom wanted to see the house earlier," he said, which really wasn't a lie. Mary *had* wanted to see the house. "We were upstairs and ended up in that front bedroom with all of the boxes. When we were there, Mary thought she heard singing coming from the attic so she opened the closet door – you know – the one that leads up to the attic. We got more than we bargained for."

Cord suspected what his father was going to say. "What did you see?"

"A little girl," Mary said, looking between Cord and Alix. "There was a little girl there and... well, she was a ghost. Her feet didn't reach all the way to the floor and she had big black holes where her eyes were supposed to be and sharp teeth. I think she asked for Rose."

Alix, standing behind Cord, began to feel weak in the knees. She suddenly bolted for the house and Cord jumped up, running after her. The two of them raced up the stairs and threw open the door of Rose's bedroom only to find the little girl sound asleep. Vastly relieved, Alix went into the room and touched her daughter's head, just to make sure everything was all right. She couldn't even describe the terror she was feeling now that Cord's parents had seen the ghost girl; things were getting worse. She could feel it.

By the time she turned around, she could see Quirt and Mary standing behind Cord in the hallway. Evidently, they decided to overcome their fear of coming into the house with the prospect of a child in danger. Quietly, Alix walked out of the room and carefully shut the door. She faced Mary and Quirt.

"What else did she say?" she whispered. "That little ghost girl has been hanging around Rose since we moved in and she's getting bolder. What else did she say about my daughter?"

Mary shook her head. "I don't know," she said. "I didn't understand what she was saying but I did understand your daughter's name. Alix, I don't know if Cord has told you, but I'm a medium. I have been all of my life. I sensed something dark and heavy when I entered the house today and those feelings made me want to look around. I'm sorry if I was being nosy; I wasn't trying to be, but the feelings I had were becoming overwhelming. When I entered that front bedroom, I felt such anger and sadness. It was like... like hysterical grief that had transformed into something very sinister and evil. When the girl appeared, I felt such darkness from her. I can't describe it any better than that. She is here and she means to do you harm, I feel. You mustn't leave Rose alone in this house. In fact, I want you to move. Move back to Cord's house. Just don't stay here."

Alix felt as if she had been hit in the gut. She actually sucked in her breath. She looked at Cord, her eyes wide with fear and grief. Then her eyes began to fill with tears as hard as she tried to stop it.

"I... I don't know," she whispered, averting her gaze. "This is my home and I've put a lot of money into it. I love it; my kids love it. Cord and I are going to make our home here and I don't want to abandon it, but if my daughter really is in danger, then I have to protect her."

She was starting to cry and Cord put his arms around her, holding her close. As Alix buried her face in his chest, he looked at his parents.

"Mom, I respect your gift," he said quietly. "You know I do. If you say there's something awful here, then I believe you. I've seen it, too. But Alix and I need to talk about this, okay? I appreciate your advice, though."

Mary was saddened by Alix's reaction and put her hand on the woman's back. "I'm sorry, Alix," she said. "I didn't mean to upset you so much. I just thought you needed to know."

Alix sniffled and took Mary's hand, holding it tightly. "I appreciate it," she whispered tightly. "I'm glad you did. There's been a lot of crazy stuff happening around here and hearing you talk about it... it just validated it for me. Something really terrible *is* going on."

Mary squeezed her hand. "Quirt cast a banishment spell but I don't know how well or how long it will work," she said. "It seemed to do some good. The entity seemed to lose some of its steam."

Alix looked at Quirt curiously. "Banishment spell?" she repeated. "How would you know that?"

Quirt looked embarrassed and hesitant. He glanced at his son as he spoke. "Oh, that," he said, clearing his throat nervously. "Cord can tell you more about that. It's just a little... something I do."

"Did you really?" Cord interrupted, seriously questioning his father. "What did you do?"

Quirt shrugged, not wanting to make a big deal out of it. But he gazed at his son with equal seriousness. "Told it to leave and never come back," he muttered. "Threw a few licks at it. Spun a fairly powerful web of protection, I hope. Cord, did you ever go down to the basement to see if there were remains of a stone circle?"

Cord shook his head. "I've been down there a few times, especially since the Historical Society told us about the legend of Mercy Good's grave, but I haven't checked for a stone circle since you and I discussed it."

"Maybe you should give it some thought."

"Maybe."

Before Alix could question them further about spell casting and stone circles, Mary squeezed her hand again. "Can I please make a suggestion? Can I take all of the children back with me to our house?" she asked. "It would give you two a chance to have a honeymoon night without five children in the house and you wouldn't have to worry... well, you know, worry about Rose."

Alix wiped at her eyes, looking up at Cord for his response. He shrugged faintly, as if inclined to agree. She returned her attention to Mary.

"Are you sure?" she asked. "That's a lot of kids invading your home."

"We would love it. We don't often get our grandkids and I look forward to getting to know our new ones." She squeezed the woman's hand one last time. "Please, Alix?"

After a moment's hesitation, Alix agreed. "Okay," she agreed. "The boys are still awake so you can go tell them to pack up. I'll get Rose ready."

Vastly relieved, Mary and Quirt went to get the boys organized as Alix and Cord took care of Rose. Within a half hour, all five kids were strapped into Quirt and Mary's big SUV and heading back to their house. As Alix and Cord stood in the living room and watched them drive away down the dark and snowy street, Alix turned to her husband.

"Now," she said, "what's this about stone circles in the basement and your father casting spells?"

He faced her in the soft light of the fireplace. "Are you sure you want to hear this tonight?"

"You'd better tell me everything."

Cord drew in a long, deep breath as he collected his thoughts. He pulled Alix into his arms, kissing her forehead before speaking. He found he was very nervous about it, terrified it would change her mind about him. But he knew, at this point, he had no choice. He had to come clean.

"Well, Your Honor, it's like this," he said, watching her grin. "Last month, after the incident on Halloween when the ghostly girl scared the boy's right out of the house and then made an appearance to me, I went to see my parents. I thought they might shed more light on the history of the house than what Mrs. Mowbray told us since my dad's aunt lived here for so long. My dad elaborated on the legend of Mercy Good being buried under the house. He told me that Abigail knew that the baby had been buried underneath the house to bring a curse upon her and that she cast a spell over a circle of stones around the grave to keep the curse at bay."

Alix was listening intently. "Is that the circle of stones he referred to?"

"Yes."

"He asked you if you had gone down in the basement to look for them."

"Yes, he did, but I haven't done it. With everything that's gone on since he told me, I just haven't had the time."

"So when were you going to tell me what he said?"

He sighed. "I just didn't want to freak you out more than you already were," he said. "Honey, there's been so much going on and you were stressed out enough as it is. If I didn't tell you, it was just to help keep you sane. I hope you understand that."

Alix nodded, her eyes glittering at him in the firelight. "I do," she said evenly. "But from now on, don't hold anything back like that, especially when it's a situation where my children are involved. I need to have all of the facts, okay? I'm not a weakling. I can take it."

He was properly contrite. "I know you're not a weakling," he whispered. "I wasn't trying to pull a fast one on you or hide anything from you."

"I know you weren't," she said. "But what's this about spell casting? What the hell is up with your dad?"

There was another big confession on the horizon. Cord scratched his forehead in thought as he pondered the right way to deliver the news that Alix had just married into a family of witches. He found himself praying that she would be understanding or, at the very least, accepting.

"I told you that my family descends from Abigail Williams," he began, "who, in fact, was a very skilled witch. It was something in her blood, something she had within her like a gene or a curse, something that she passed down through the male line in my family through her son, John. All of the firstborn males carry this trait. My father has the gift of Casting, as did my grandfather and his father before him. In my family, it's as natural as breathing. What you heard was my father talking about casting a spell of banishment on the ghostly girl."

Alix looked at him with astonishment. "Are you serious?" she asked. "He thinks he's a witch?"

Cord shook his head. "He doesn't think he is," he said. "He *is* a witch. Well, a warlock, really. I've seen him...well, it doesn't matter, but believe me when I tell you that he is effective. He's very good."

Her mouth popped open. "Really?"

"Really."

She was truly astounded. "But... but you've never talked about this before," she said. "You've never made any mention of this, and... and if it's passed down to the firstborn males in your family, then that means you do it, too?"

He shrugged, averting his gaze. "I've spent most of my life ignoring what's in my blood," he admitted. "When I was young, I thought it was really cool. I wanted to learn all about it, but the older I got, I realized that I was the only one of my friends who could cast spells so in my mind, it became uncool. I didn't want to be different. I wouldn't speak to my father about it for years even though he tried. When I was young and learning about my heritage, my father and grandfather said I had the greatest gift of Casting they had ever seen. It came really easy for me. But when I grew older, I didn't want to do it anymore. The last time I used it, years ago, was in self-defense and I didn't have a choice or some friends would have maybe died, but... I just don't like to talk about it."

Alix was dumbfounded. After a moment, she simply shook her head. "Cord," she said, "you can't be serious. Are you telling me that you're a witch?"

"Warlock, but yes."

"God's honest truth?"

"God's honest truth."

Alix was torn between disbelief and fear. She simply didn't know what to say. Seeing her reaction, Cord sighed faintly.

"Honey, do you remember when the roof collapsed on me a couple of months ago?" he asked.

"Of course I do."

"Do you remember the guys telling you that it should have killed me?"

"Yes."

He looked her in the eye. "It didn't kill me because I had half a chance to cast a protection spell, something that held that roof long enough so that the full weight didn't crush me. Sure, it came down, but it could have been so much worse. I saw it coming and was able to remember things that my father had taught me, spells of protection, enough so that I was able to deflect that roof somewhat. It saved my life and I suppose, ever since then, I've been a little more willing to discuss something I haven't discussed in thirty years. I'm willing to discuss who and what I really am."

Alix's eyebrows lifted. "A witch?"

"My dad likes to call us Casters, as in spell casting."

She stared at him. True, she was wallowing in disbelief but there was another part of her that was very intrigued. She knew he wouldn't lie to her but, much like ghosts, she had to see it to believe it. It was the scientist part of her brain and not the part that went on faith. She should have thought the man was crazy but she couldn't bring herself to do it. After what she'd seen in Evenshade, she had more acceptance for things out of the norm. Perhaps anything was possible, even a new husband who thought he was a witch. After a few seconds of indecision, she finally shrugged.

"Okay," she said. "If you say so, I'll accept it. I can't say that I really believe it, but I'll accept it. But you should have told me all of this sooner."

"It just never came up," he said. "Does it change your mind about me?"

She laughed. "If it did, it's too late now," she said, but his expression was still tense and she could see he was serious. She softened. "No, it doesn't change my mind about you. I still love you madly and it doesn't change a damn thing."

He visibly relaxed. "Thank you," he said. "I have to admit I was a little worried. This isn't a normal confession like I'm secretly a crossdresser or I was born with a third leg that I keep hidden."

She giggled. "It's weird, but I suppose after seeing ghost girls, I'm open to anything now. Who's to say things like witches and warlocks don't exist after all?"

He went to her, putting his arms around her and giving her a sweet hug. "Thank you for being so understanding," he murmured. "It's a load off my mind. But now that it's over with, I say let's get the honeymoon started."

"You don't waste any time, do you?"

"Not when you're involved, I don't."

Alix laughed at him but they were both distracted when, in the bedroom directly overhead, they began to hear soft singing. The singing grew louder and soon a massive thump shook the house. Cord went to investigate but he naturally came up with nothing.

They spent their honeymoon night in a motel.

SEVENTEEN
JUNE

THE EVENING WAS UNUSUALLY cool for early June as Cord finished up with the dishes because it was Hester's night off. The boys had done the cooking so he was doing the cleaning. Now, all four boys were in the den playing a war game on the giant, flat screen television. Cord had already gone in three times to tell them to hold it down, but the noise was starting to get loud again. It was hard to play war video games and not get loud about it.

Turning on the dishwasher, he dried his hands off as he went back into the study for the fourth time in the past twenty minutes. The boys caught him out of the corner of their eye, abruptly shutting down the volume and the noise when he walked into the room.

"Sorry, Dad," Chris said. "We're trying to keep it down."

Rather than become irritated with them, Cord smiled weakly. "I know you are," he said. "Do the best you can. I'm going upstairs for a while."

Rose, tucked in behind her brother on the other side of the couch, slithered down and went to Cord, taking his hand. Cord looked down at her, shaking his head.

"I thought you were upstairs," he said. "What are you doing down here?"

Rose gazed up at him with her big gray eyes. "I wanted to play, too."

Cord's eyebrows lifted. "War games?"

Rose just nodded. "They promised to play bunnies and duckies when they were done."

She was referring to her favorite video game and Cord looked at the group of boys, cocking a fatherly eyebrow. "They promised, did they?"

"Yes," she said solemnly. "They told me if I was quiet that they would play with me later."

"And they will, too. Starting right now."

Kyle and Cole groaned but Chris dutifully shut off the war game and went on the hunt for the bunny game. Delighted, Rose ran back into the den as Cord, with a smirk on his face, headed for the back stairs.

Mounting the steps, he emerged into the hall and headed for the master bedroom door, very carefully opening it so he wouldn't disturb Alix. He flipped on the hall light because it was so dark, glancing down the long hallway purely out of habit. It had been a long time since he had last seen a surprise in the dark. In fact, since their wedding on that cold December day, they hadn't seen a trace of the ghost girl. She had virtually disappeared.

Whatever his father had done, whatever spell he cast, must have worked because the house had been utterly quiet for six months. In fact, Chris now occupied that giant front bedroom where all of the occurrences happened and there hadn't been a peep. But they kept the closet door and the stairs to the attic bolted. No one was willing to take any chances or rock the boat. Better to let sleeping ghosts lie.

Cord was thankful, too. Without the paranormal element,

Evenshade was a wonderful family home and he loved it here. Even the dogs, who had initially been very fearful to come into the house back in the fall when he had moved in, now freely roamed the house and slept on beds they weren't supposed to sleep on. But Cord was incredibly happy, more than he had ever been in his life. As he quietly opened the door to the bedroom he shared with his wife and poked his head in, he was surprised to see that Alix was awake, lying on her side as she watched television. Cord smiled when she looked over at him.

"Hi, honey," he greeted, moving to sit beside her on the bed. "How are you feeling?"

Alix rolled onto her back. At nine months pregnant and two days over her due date, she was in a miserable state. It was exhausting to stand and uncomfortable to lie down. Alix rubbed at her enormous belly and made a pouting face.

"I'm sore," she said. "I'm sore, stiff, tired, and exhausted. The baby's lying on my diaphragm and I can't sleep."

He grinned as he sat next to her. "Did you try to move him?"

She began pushing at the top of her belly. "He won't budge," she said miserably. "He's too big. There's no room for him to roll around anymore, but as long as he's head down, I don't give a damn. He's pointed in the right direction."

Cord laughed, putting his hand on her colossal belly. "It'll all be over soon."

"Maybe sooner than you think."

"Why do you say that?"

She shifted on the bed, grunting as she tried to find a comfortable position. "Because I think I'm in the early stages of labor," she said. "My lower back and thighs are very achy. I can't tell if they're contractions yet, but I'm definitely achy."

Cord's grin faded and he grew serious. "Do we need to call Dr. Sutton?"

Alix shook her head. "I don't think so," she replied. "Not yet, anyway. Let's see how the next few hours go."

"If you say so."

She squirmed again and held up a hand. "Help me up, please."

He stood up and carefully pulled her into a sitting position. Then he pulled her off the bed and made sure she was steady on her feet before letting her go. Alix waddled into the bathroom and shut the door as Cord lay back down on the mattress and began surfing the channels. He found a baseball recap and was watching the scrolling scores when Alix emerged from the bathroom.

"Anything exciting going on in there?" he asked.

She shook her head, frustrated. "No," she said flatly. "No mucus, no blood, no nothing."

"Sealed up tight."

She made a face as she walked, rubbing at her back as she headed back to the bed. "Can we take the dogs and go for a walk?"

Cord rolled off the bed. "If you want to," he stood up. "Are you sure you feel up to it?"

She nodded as she hunted around for her shoes. "I can't lie down anymore," she found her shoes and handed them to him so he could put them on her. "My whole body hurts from laying down all of the time."

He held her steady as she lowered herself on the edge of the bed, lifting a foot so he could slip on a little white tennis shoe. "I don't want you wearing yourself out walking, though." He tried to be gentle with her because her emotions were volatile these days. "Dr. Sutton wanted you to take it easy."

He apparently wasn't gentle enough because her nose scrunched up in a frown. "I gotta do something to get this labor going," she said, unhappy. "I need this baby to be born. Do you realize I haven't seen my feet in over a month?"

Cord laughed; he couldn't help it. "That's why you have me around," he told her. "I can see your feet and they look great."

She grunted, making faces. "If the walking doesn't work, then we're going to try sex next."

"Dr. Sutton said we probably shouldn't with the baby so low in your pelvis."

"I don't care what he says. The stimulation should trigger something."

Cord didn't argue with her; he just finished putting her shoes on. Collecting her jacket, he went down the stairs in front of her, making sure she was steady as she labored down the steps. He tried to help her on with her jacket but she shooed him away, too hot for the jacket. Tossing the jacket on to the kitchen chair, he went to the study and stuck his head inside.

"Alix and I are going for a walk," he told the kids, now crowded around the television playing bunnies and duckies. "We'll be back in a little while."

They boys waved him off, as did Rose, who was front and center with the video controller. As Cord moved into the back hall as he headed back to the kitchen, he whistled softly and Manitou and Aram, sleeping where they weren't supposed to be on the living room couches, bolted up and trotted into the kitchen. Cord intercepted them before they could happily knock Alix around, putting on their leashes.

Alix was already opening the kitchen door, heading out into the summer dusk as the fireflies were just starting to get busy. It was a lovely evening and she sighed, feeling more cramping in her back and hips as she observed the pink and blue sunset. With the dogs taking the lead, Cord and Alix headed down the driveway.

"I've been thinking something," Alix said.

Cord was trying to hold both dogs' leashes in one hand and Alix in the other. "What's that?"

"Well," she said thoughtfully, "now that we've moved Hester downstairs because we turned her room into a nursery, we really should build her a bathroom. Right now, she's sharing two bathrooms with five kids and four of them are boys."

Cord considered her suggestion. "Her bedroom isn't big enough to install a bathroom in," he said. "But we could probably enlarge the half bath in the utility room and put in a shower. That's a fairly large room so there's enough room to do it."

That made Alix happy. "Good," she said cheerfully. "Will you talk to your friend at work that does construction on the side and see if he'll give us an estimate?"

"Of course."

They were down the street, heading towards Cord's house down in the glen. Cord finally took the dogs off their leashes and they ran around happily, jumping around in the grass but avoiding the street. Alix's gaze was on the blue house down the road, now with a different car in the driveway and lights on in the kitchen.

"Do you miss your house?" she asked.

Cord was shaking his head even before the question left her mouth. "No," he said. "My sister and her kids love it and I love where I'm at right now. There's no place else I'd rather be."

She smiled up at him. "A house with five kids, a housekeeper, two big dogs and a massively pregnant wife?"

He laughed. "I love my life. You have no idea how much."

She giggled because he was, carefully noting the increase in cramping in her back and hips, now joined by cramping in her thighs. She paused, hunching over slightly and rubbing at her belly. Cord paused beside her, watching her with some concern.

"Are you okay?" he asked.

Alix nodded but didn't stop rubbing at her stomach. "I'm really hoping I'm in the early stages of labor," she said. "I've got fairly significant cramping in my back and legs, plus noticeable pressure in my pelvis."

"Any pain?"

She shook her head. "Nothing unusual or unbearable."

"Maybe we should head back to the house."

Alix shook her head and resumed walking. "I'm fine," she insisted. "In fact, I was thinking... oops... uh oh...."

She came to an abrupt stop. Cord stopped right next to her. "What's wrong?"

She didn't look particularly distressed but he noticed she was standing oddly. "Uh...," she turned rather stiffly in his direction. "My water just broke."

Cord could see a big wet stain in the crotch area of her black yoga pants. He immediately grasped her by both arms and turned her in the direction of the house.

"Here we go," he said calmly, although his heart was starting to race with excitement. "Let's head on back to the house."

Alix let him turn her around and they slowly began to make their way back to the house. He tried to pick her up at one point but she squawked at him so he stopped trying and just held her tightly as he assisted her up the hill towards the house. By the time they hit the driveway, she grunted and stopped.

"What's wrong?" Cord asked.

She was breathing heavily and steadily, sucking in air through her nose and blowing it out her mouth. "Contraction," she said, then straightened up after a moment. "Wow, that was a strong one, like all of a sudden. Weird."

Cord glanced at his watch so he could start timing the contractions, feeling excitement and joy like he'd never felt in his life. He had one arm around Alix's waist while his other hand held her left elbow, gently escorting her up the driveway.

He was supporting her, surrounding her, protecting her with his body as well as his mind. He was giddy thinking about what they were preparing to go through.

"You know," he ventured, "I was really excited when the boys were born, and happy, but I didn't feel the thrill with them that I feel with this baby."

Alix looked up at him. "Why?"

He shrugged, his gaze on the house in front of them, the very reason they had met in the first place. "I'm not sure," he said. "It just all centers around you, and this house, and the warm feelings I have for it because it's where I met you. Having a baby with someone I love so much is something I never really thought I'd experience. It's such a beautiful and emotional thing because every time I look at this baby, I'll see you. It's like a culmination of a love I never thought I'd experience. I'm not sure if I can explain it better than that."

He heard sniffling and looked down at Alix, who had tears in her eyes. "That's so sweet," she whispered. "I feel the same way. I really do. I'm so proud to be your wife and to be having your baby. My whole life has revolved around my career and my ambitions, but over the past year it seems to be all centered around you and the kids, and I'm not unhappy about that at all. In fact, I've never been happier. I love the way my life turned out and it's all because of you."

He smiled, giving her a squeeze as they made their way slowly up the driveway. Cord whistled for the dogs as they approached the kitchen door, opening the door and calling for the boys as he helped Alix inside. Just as she crossed the threshold, she grabbed Cord's hand hard enough to break bones and nearly doubled over.

Cord had her in his grip as she suffered through another very strong contraction. Chris and Kyle came into the kitchen in time to witness Alix grunting through the pain and Cord counting it out and telling her to breathe. Their eyes widened.

"The baby's coming?" Chris looked seriously concerned. "What can we do, Dad?"

Cord was calm on the outside but on the inside, he was apprehensive like any father. "Get the dogs in," he told them evenly. "I'm going to take Alix over to the hospital."

Alix started shaking her head. "I don't think that's a good idea," she was panting. "I've got a huge amount of pressure in my pelvis right now and that pain was really strong. I don't know if we'll make it. You'd better call the ambulance and tell them to bring an incubator."

Cord's composure took a hit. "Seriously?"

She was breathing easier now that the pain had passed and turned to look at Cord. "Seriously," she said, her voice softer. "Did I mention that I had Rose in forty-four minutes from start to finish?"

Cord's eyebrows lifted. "You did not."

She nodded wearily and turned for the stairs. "Help me upstairs," she said, turning for the boys that were still standing in the kitchen. "I want you guys to find all the clean towels you can and bring them up to our bedroom. Then I want you to pull out a bunch of those baby receiving blankets from the nursery; they're in the bottom drawer of the dresser and they've already been washed. Bring those in as well, along with a couple of diapers."

She said it so calmly that the boys moved to do her bidding without much reaction, but the more they thought on the fact that Alix was about to have the baby right there at home, the more terrified they became.

As Cord helped Alix up the back stairs, he was feeling the terror as well. Well, shock was more like it. He'd delivered his share of babies, but never his own child. He tried not to think about what could go wrong and the fact that they weren't in a hospital. He just tried to focus on Alix and take his direction from her.

"I'm sorry, baby," she said as she reached the top of the stairs, breathing heavily. "I'd do this myself, but I don't think I'm going to be able to deliver my own baby."

He smiled at her, trying to be calm and confident in order to keep her calm. "Not to worry," he said. "I've done this a few times. Everything will be fine."

Alix was holding on to both of his hands as she waddled stiffly into their bedroom. Then she stopped, looking at the bed.

"That's a new mattress," she sighed. "I really don't want to get it all messy."

Cord lifted an eyebrow at her, prying his hands away from hers so he could start getting everything ready. He went straight to the bed and yanked off the covers.

"I don't think we have a choice unless you want to give birth in the bathtub," he said, pushing the covers up against the wall to get them out of the way. "Besides, there's a waterproof mattress pad. It won't get messed up."

He went over to the phone on the night stand and dialed 911 as Alix shuffled into the dressing area by the bathroom. As Cord explained to the 911 dispatcher the situation, he could see her struggling to get her pants off so he made his way over to her, phone cradled between his ear and shoulder, and helped her peel her pants off. Just as he was hanging up with the operator, another hard contraction seized her and she doubled over, falling forward onto her knees as Cord dropped to his knees beside her. He held her tightly as she grunted through the contraction, encouraging her to breathe, breathing with her so she'd get into the rhythm. He felt her go limp in his arms as the pain subsided.

"Ouch," she finally gasped, her head resting against his bicep. "That one really hurt."

He kissed her forehead, her cheek, as she slumped exhaustedly against him. "Come on." He stood up and carefully put her on her feet. "Let's get you changed and onto the bed."

Alix simply nodded as he held her with one arm and began digging through drawers with the other. He came across a summer nightgown, a light garment he'd seen her wear a few times, and set it aside as he stripped her of the rest of her clothing. He could hear the boys running around downstairs, and dogs barking, as he pulled the nightgown over her head. Then, holding on to her hands, he walked her over to their bed and gently sat her down.

Alix lay back on the bed, sighing heavily. "Do you want to check me?"

Cord nodded. "I probably should. Let me wash my hands."

As he went into the bathroom to wash his hands, Chris and Kyle appeared at the bedroom door with the towels and blankets Alix had asked for. Due to the angle of the room, all they could see was Alix lying on the bed, but they could hear their dad in the bathroom with the water running.

"Alix?" Chris said timidly. "We have the stuff. Where do you want it?"

Weary, in pain, Alix motioned the boys to come in. "Bring them over here," she said, pointing to the end of the bed. "Just set them down."

They did as they were told, lingering apprehensively at the edge of the bed. "Do you need anything else?" Chris asked. "Shouldn't we be boiling water or something?"

Alix laughed softly. "Only in the movies," she said. "But you can stay if you want. I don't mind if you watch the birth."

Cord picked that moment to come out of the bathroom,

drying his hands. "I'm not sure that's a good idea," he said, looking at his boys. "It might be a little much at their age."

"Why?" Alix wanted to know. "It's all part of life. Think of the bond they'll feel with this baby after having watched the birth."

Cord looked at his two oldest sons, who were gazing back at their father with some fear. He chuckled weakly and shook his head.

"Although I agree it is a natural part of life, the truth is that the experience will probably scare the crap out of them." He motioned to the door. "Go downstairs and wait for the ambulance."

The boys were gratefully fleeing the room when Alix suffered through another contraction. She grunted loudly, bringing her knees up as Cord went to the bed and reminded her to breathe. Hand on her hard belly, he waited until the contraction subsided before grasping her ankles and parting her legs. He sat there for a moment as if indecisive. When he spoke, it was hesitantly.

"I'm trying to be clinical about this, I swear I am," he said, meeting her gaze. "But I have to tell you that this is really strange for me."

"Why?" she asked.

He shrugged, running a hand up her soft calf. "Because the only time I'm down on this end of you is when we're, you know, doing sexual things, and sticking my fingers up you to check and see how much you're dilated...."

"... turns you on?" she finished for him.

He nodded. "Honestly, yes," he made a face. "That's kind of sick, isn't it?"

She laughed. "Absolutely not," she said. "I'd worry if it didn't turn you on. You're my husband – putting your fingers there is *supposed* to turn you on."

He fought off a grin. "Are you sure I can't get a little something out of this before the baby stretches you all out and I have to wait six weeks before I can resume my husbandly duties?"

Alix started laughing. "Are you saying you'd rather check me with your penis instead of your fingers?"

He laughed in return. "Would you have a problem with that?"

Alix was really laughing now. "What do we tell the paramedics when the baby is born with a big wad of semen on his head? That you're turned on by a woman in labor?"

Cord was giggling like a fool, running a hand over his face at the mere thought. "God, that's so pathetic," he snorted. "I feel like a depraved maniac."

Alix just laughed and laughed. The humor was good, loosening her up, but another contraction slammed her and the laughter vanished as she grunted again and closed her eyes, breathing through it until it passed. Cord gently rubbed her thighs, waiting for the pain to pass, before slipping his fingers into her to see if he could determine just how dilated she was. Within a few seconds, his eyes widened and he withdrew his fingers.

"Honey," he said, rather frankly, "the baby's head is right there. How long were you having that cramping?"

Alix was quickly entering the realm of misery. The last contraction hadn't subsided completely and she could feel another one coming on.

"A while," she admitted. "But it wasn't particularly painful. Just dull aching, like I told you. Why? What's wrong?"

Cord shook his head, bracing her legs further apart and laying towels down around her pelvis. "Nothing that I can tell," he said. "Except the baby is going to be crowning with the next few contractions."

Another strong contraction rolled over Alix and she grunted

loudly, grabbing her legs behind the knees and drawing them up. "Oh, God," she groaned. "I really need to push."

Cord kept focused. "Go ahead," he told her calmly. "Push with the next contraction and let's see where we're at."

Panting, struggling to control her breathing, Alix could feel the contraction subside. She lay on the mattress, staring up at the ceiling, feeling her body start to tighten again and a huge amount of pressure in her pelvis. This contraction was a stabbing pain all throughout her pelvis, back and thighs, and she labored not to cry out as it gripped her.

"Oh ...God," she grunted, bearing down with all her might. "Is he crowning yet?"

"Not yet."

She pushed harder. "Now?"

Cord could just see the top of the little head making its way into the world. "Almost," he told her steadily. Then he noticed something unusual but kept his calm. "Honey, he's sunny-side up. I'm going to have to turn him a little."

The baby was coming face-up instead of face-down. This made things more difficult for Alix, to be sure. She was in extreme pain but she didn't do anything more than scrunch up her face; no screaming, no crying. She just kept blowing out her cheeks, puffing.

"I can tell," she gasped. "It hurts like hell."

Cord tried to slip his fingers in to turn the baby slightly so the shoulders could pass through, but he had a very big head and movement was tight. Another contraction came and Alix bore down, grunting as she pushed, and Cord was able to turn the baby slightly as most of the head slipped forward. But he could already tell that the baby was very big and he tried not to panic; the child was wedged in tightly. Face-up babies had a tendency to get stuck.

They could both hear sirens coming down the street, telling them that the ambulance and paramedics had arrived, but Cord kept focused, trying to keep Alix calm as the infant seemed to be somewhat stuck. With every contraction, Alix bore down as hard as she could and Cord was able to turn the baby a little more, trying to get those big shoulders through, but they weren't making much progress. By the time the paramedics thundered up the stairs and charged into the room, Cord had just managed to get the shoulders turned enough so that the baby's entire head popped through.

There were four paramedics in all and two ambulance attendants. The paramedics, seeing the state of the birth, gently but firmly rolled Cord out of the way. They all knew Cord to varying degrees and an older paramedic, who had worked with Cord years ago, just grinned at the somewhat pale-faced father and had him sit at Alix's head.

"We got it from here, Dad," he said. "You sit there with the wife until it's over."

Bloodied hands and all, Cord did as he was told and got in behind Alix to help support her back as she tried to push the massive baby out. With their equipment and tools, two of the senior paramedics settled in between Alix's legs to do the rest of the dirty work.

Alix winced at the gentle tugging and twisting going on, struggling to push forth the child. At this point, however, most of the battle was over and with another few good pushes, the baby slid out into waiting hands. Immediately, lusty screams filled the air.

"Is he okay?" Cord demanded. "How does he look?"

The paramedics were suctioning out the nose and mouth, but they were grinning. One of them wrapped the baby up in a green, sterile, scrub-like wrapping and put the squealing infant on Alix's chest.

"That's one big baby, Cap'n," the man said. "Congratulations on your daughter. She's got to be nine pounds easy."

Alix let out a triumphant, if not exhausted, crow. "A girl!" she gasped, trying to get a good look at the squirming child. "Baby, it's a girl!"

Cord had tears in his eyes as he wrapped his arms around Alix and the baby, trying to get a good look at the red little face.

"I heard." He kissed Alix repeatedly on the cheek, the lips. "Thank you, honey. Thank you so much. She's gorgeous."

Alix accepted his kisses, returning a few, wallowing in the love and adoration filling the air between them. It was sweet and warm, making her very emotional. She began to unwrap the baby, inspecting her fingers and toes, running her hand over the shoulders and collarbone to make sure nothing was broken or out of place after the lightning-fast, but tough, delivery. Cord had his hand on the baby as well, gently touching her round little belly.

"Hello, Katharine," he said, then looked at Alix. "Is that still what you want to name her? After my mother and grandmother?"

Alix nodded, all warm and cozy as she gazed at her blond-haired daughter. "Katharine Mary Hendry-Trevor," she said. "I love that she'll go by Kitty like your grandmother did. That's such a sweet little name."

Cord grinned. "Rosie is going to be disappointed that we didn't name her Princess Luna."

Alix laughed. "She'll get over it," she said, pulling her eyes off the baby long enough to look at Cord. "Speaking of Rosie, you'd better go tell the kids everything is all right. Tell them they have a new baby sister."

Cord kissed her, kissed the baby, and then wearily rose to his feet and made his way to the bedroom door. Just as he went to the back stairs, he could see men from his fire station lingering on the stairwell and down in the kitchen, and he descended the stairs with a big grin on his face. They must have heard the call go out, the address, and decided to roll on it. In fact, there was a whole herd of firefighters in his kitchen. His men caught sight of him and gravitated in his direction.

"Well?" Steve Cokes demanded. "What do we have?"

Cord laughed, holding up a hand as he stuck his head out into the hall. He could see the kids huddled up near the couch in the living room, with Rose on Sean's lap. He called out to them.

"Hey," he motioned to them. "Come here."

The boys bolted off the couch and went to him, eager to hear the news. Cord tried not to touch them with his still-bloody hands, but he couldn't help putting an arm around Chris' shoulders. He just grinned like a fool.

"It's a girl," he said to a chorus of happy exclamations. "Katharine Mary. She's big and gorgeous."

Sean was holding Rose, his gaze looking up the stairs. "How's my mom?"

Cord looked at the young man, seeing how worried he was. He softened. "She's fine," he said. "Do you want to go upstairs and see for yourself?"

Sean nodded and Cord let him go upstairs to see his mom. He held his boys back a moment to let Sean and Rose see their mother first. He could hear their soft voices upstairs and Alix's voice as she introduced them to Baby Kitty. Cord was conversing with his men, talking about going out and celebrating that night with a few beers, when Sean and Rose came back downstairs. Cord looked rather surprised to see them.

"So that's it?" he asked. "You don't want to see her any more than a couple of seconds?"

Sean shrugged and set Rose to her feet. "The paramedics told us to come down and get you."

Cord's smile vanished and he took the stairs two at a time. By the time he got there, one of the paramedics was holding the baby while two of them were doing something he couldn't see. They looked very busy.

"What's going on?" Cord demanded as he walked up to the bed.

The older paramedic turned to answer him but Alix, flat on her back and staring up at the ceiling, answered instead.

"Hemorrhaging," she said softly. "The placenta tore."

Cord knew he went pale and it was a struggle not to panic. He drew on his training, every ounce of it, to calm himself down and think clearly.

"How bad?" he asked.

The older paramedic gave him a long look. "Bad enough," he said. "We need to move."

Cord had to let the shift captain take charge of moving Alix into the ambulance because he was quickly becoming a wreck. She was pale, eyes closed but conscious, as they labored to stop the bleeding before carrying her downstairs to the waiting gurney. It was his worst fear come to life and he stayed with Alix, holding her hand, stroking her forehead or her face, as she piped up now and again to give them direction, but she was fading. They had to get her to the hospital.

Two of the paramedics had the baby and were setting her up in the incubator in the kitchen as six firefighters, including Cord, brought Alix down the back stairs and lay her on the gurney. Cord could see the kids standing in the doorway of the utility room, watching with big eyes, so he quietly directed Chris and Kyle to take the kids back into the study to get them away from the scary activity going on. Rose, however, started to cry when Sean picked her up to take her back to the study, which brought Alix around.

"Rosie?" she turned her head weakly, looking for her daughter. "It's okay, baby. Mommy's going to the hospital for a little while but I'll be back."

Rose wouldn't be soothed. She was frightened by the strange men and bustle going on in the kitchen and reached her arms out in her mother's direction even as Sean tried to carry her away. Cord was distracted by the crying little girl and turned to say something to her. It was then that he noticed tears on Sean's face and he left Alix in the care of the paramedics to go and comfort her children.

"Hey," he put his big hands on Sean's shoulders. "She's going to be okay. Sometimes when women have babies, they have some ... issues. We're taking your mom to the hospital to make sure she's okay and the doctor needs to check the baby out, too. Okay? I don't want you to worry about her."

Sean was struggling. Seeing his mom looking so awful on the gurney, with a half-dozen guys hovering around her, scared him. He wiped at his eyes while trying not to be too obvious about it. In his arms, Rose howled.

"I know," he said bravely. "I guess... well, it's just kind of a lot going on, that's all."

He was trying to be courageous and Cord patted him comfortingly on the shoulder before holding out his hands to Rose to see if she wanted to come to him. She slithered into his big arms because she thought he was going to take her to her mother. Cord carried her outside with him, following the gurney to the ambulance, as Sean brought up the rear.

"Did you see the baby, Rosie?" Cord asked.

Rose looked over at the incubator they were rolling towards the ambulance. She nodded, sniffling, before looking back at her mother. "I wanna go with Mommy."

Cord kissed her cheek. "I know," he said, watching them load Alix up in the rear of the ambulance. "But Mommy has to see the doctor right now. We'll come right back."

With that, he handed Rose back over to Sean and leapt into the back of the ambulance with Alix. A pair of firefighters slammed the doors closed, bolted them, and then banged on the doors to let the driver know they were closed. The ambulance took off.

Chris, Kyle, Cole, Sean and Rose watched it drive away, followed by two rigs and a battalion chief car. As quickly as the firefighters had arrived, they were gone, following Cord and Alix to the hospital. Chris and Kyle looked at Sean, standing there holding his weeping sister.

"Let's go," Chris said. "We'll take my truck over to the hospital."

Sean nodded, somewhat numbly, as Chris and Kyle took charge. Kyle ran to get Rose's car seat out of Alix's car while everyone else went into the house, turning off televisions, lights, and making sure the dogs were corralled. By the time they locked the house and ran back outside, Kyle had the car seat in the back of Chris's truck and they coaxed Rose into it. Once she was secured, everyone else climbed in and Chris took off for North Shore.

As they pulled out of the driveway, no one noticed the small girl watching them from the master bedroom window. It was Rose's face, looking through the glass with big black eyes. They were sad eyes. But then the mouth opened, the great fanged teeth were bared, and the image faded away as the sound of child's voice filled the air.

"Goody Good, Goody Good,
'ere bird and snake could;
Mother dies with blood in mouth,
Mercy is revenge in Bebe's house"

There was a new baby in the house. The evil had returned.

EIGHTEEN

BY THE TIME they got to the hospital with Alix, she was fading in and out of unconsciousness with weak vital signs. The trip over had seen her deteriorate considerably, leaving Cord struggling not to lose his composure completely. As they rushed Alix into an examination room and whisked the baby up to Pediatrics, Dr. Potts and Debra made Cord stay out.

"I need to be in there," Cord was angry as well as panicked.

Debra kept her hands on his big chest, preventing him from pushing past her as Dr. Potts raced into the exam room after Alix.

"Cord, go up with the baby to Pediatrics," she said calmly, steadily. "We'll take care of Alix, I promise. She's in good hands."

Cord wasn't convinced. "Please," he begged softly. "Just let me go in there. I swear I won't get in the way."

Debra felt for the man. She was pretty emotional herself. She had heard the call go out for Alix and she had prepped the exam room for her arrival. Alix had become a good friend and to see her friend in distress deeply upset her. But she had to stay calm if there was any hope of keeping Cord calm. She shook her head, keeping her hands on his chest as if the gesture would hold back a man twice her size.

"You know and I know that it's much better that you stay out here," she said firmly. "Cord, I want you to listen to me; you know she's in good hands. They'll do everything they can. If you want to stay, you're going to have to stand here with me because you know I'm not going to let you go in there. Okay?"

His gaze was on the exam room door where Alix had disappeared. He could see people moving around, quickly, and a call went out to Gynecology. He could also see the paramedics milling around in the room, now assisting the doctors. So many people assisting his wife as he stood there helplessly. A hand suddenly went to his mouth but he caught sight of the dried blood all over it, realizing it was Alix's blood, and tears sprang to his eyes.

"Oh... God," he breathed. "It can't be that serious, right?"

Debra could see that the man was verging on a breakdown and she quickly ushered him over to the wall where a bank of seats sat beneath a bright window. It was a private spot and she pushed him onto a chair.

"Cord, sit," she directed firmly. "I want you to sit here and I'll go find out how she is. Okay? Stay here."

He nodded, staring at his hands. Then he put them over his face and hung his head. Debra, gazing at him with great concern, had another nurse come over and sit with him while she went to Alix's exam room. She had no sooner entered the room than they were lowering the bed and wheeling her out.

"We're off to surgery," Dr. Potts was pushing at Alix's head. "We need to get in there and clean her out."

Debra stood back out of the way, watching them push Alix past her. She turned around to tell Cord, but she bumped into the man because he was standing right behind her. As they wheeled Alix past, Cord clamped on to her hand and was pulled along as they went.

Alix had regained some level of consciousness. She felt Cord's hand in hers and she opened her eyes, gazing up at him as they moved her bed into the elevator.

"Hi," she whispered, smiling weakly.

Cord didn't trust himself to speak. He held her hand tightly, gazing down at her with a lump in his throat. But he couldn't stop the tears and by the time they got on the elevator and the door closed, he was struggling not to sob.

"Hi," he said in a strangled whisper.

Alix, as dazed as she was, could see how torn up he was. She squeezed his hand as tightly as she could.

"I'm going to be fine," she whispered, trying to sound confident. "They're going to do a D & C on me to clear out any remaining tissue. I'm going to heal up just fine, okay? I don't want you to worry."

He nodded, but his face started to crumple and he hung his head, tears coursing down his cheeks. Alix, seeing him so distraught, was starting to tear up herself.

"Please, baby," she murmured. "Please, don't cry. Everything will be okay. Please? I love you."

He let out a choked sob. "I love you, too," he wept, wiping furiously at his cheeks with his free hand. He took in a deep breath, struggling to recover. "I'm sorry. I'm usually better at holding myself together."

She squeezed his hand, a faint smile on her face. "Remember when you were injured in the roof collapse?" she whispered. "I was a mess, remember? I know how you feel."

The elevator doors opened and they wheeled the bed out. The doctors and nurses were trying to ignore the conversation going on between Alix and Cord but it was difficult. It was sad, in so many ways. Dr. Potts even got a little misty-eyed though he pretended otherwise. When they reached the big doors that led into Surgery, Dr. Potts stopped Cord.

"She goes in alone from this point," he said. "Dr. Sutton is already waiting for her inside, so have a seat out here and we'll let you know when she's done."

Cord still had Alix's hand even though they were trying to wheel her into surgery. "Okay," he said reluctantly, looking down at his wife. He held her hand up to his lips, kissing it tenderly, before bending over and kissing her on the lips very sweetly. His big hand was on her head as he gazed steadily at her. "I'll be right here. I swear, I won't leave."

Alix put up a hand, one with needles in it, and stroked his cheek. "I'm going to be fine," she murmured. "I want you to go over to Pediatrics and see how Kitty is, okay? That would make me happy."

Cord took another deep breath, nodding reluctantly, and kissed her hand once more before letting it go. The last he saw, they were wheeling his wife into surgery and he struggled not to come apart again. She had asked him to check up on their daughter and he would oblige, although it was difficult for him to leave the area. He very much wanted to be near Alix, but he had promised her he'd go see the baby. Hesitantly, wearily, he made his way to Pediatrics.

———

Katharine Mary Hendry-Trevor was nine pounds and eleven ounces, and twenty-one inches long. As Cord stood over her incubator, watching her scream, he could see that her pale blond hair was drying in the warmth and her fat, little hands were waving furiously. He had to grin at his daughter, a big, healthy girl that had wreaked havoc on her mother. When the pediatrician declared the baby healthy, Cord sat in a rocking chair and gave the baby her first feeding.

Kitty was an angry and hungry girl, but the moment Cord put the nipple in her mouth, she settled right down and fed eagerly. He held her close, watching her eat, seeing Alix in that little face. The nurses in Pediatrics were aware that Alix was in surgery and they called up to Surgery every few minutes to get updates. So far, Alix was still in surgery, so an hour after she was wheeled in, Cord sat feeding the baby, praying that his wife was going to be all right. He just couldn't stomach the alternative.

He was in the process of burping the baby when he glanced up and saw five familiar faces looking at him through the nursery glass. Chris, Kyle, Cole, Sean and Rose were watching him burp the baby and he grinned when he saw the kids, taking the baby over to the glass so they could see her better. Chris and Kyle thumped on the glass to get the baby's attention while Cole just kind of stood there and looked at her. He wasn't much into babies. Sean and Rose, however, seemed the most distant and Cord could see that they were very worried for their mother. Cord gave the baby back over to a nurse and went out into the hall.

"Dad, how's Alix?" Chris asked him before he could speak.

Rose wanted to go to Cord so he held out his arms for the little girl, who snuggled up to him. "Where's Mommy?" she wanted to know.

Cord kissed her cheek. "Mommy is still with the doctors," he told her. "You can go see her soon, I promise."

"Is she okay?" Sean asked, his expression sad and apprehensive.

Cord felt bad for the young man who was very close to his mother. "She's going to be fine," he said. "I told you that sometimes women have issues when they have babies. It's a big event for a body. The doctors are taking care of her right now."

"Where is she?"

"In surgery."

Sean took a deep and rather startled breath, as if that thought hadn't occurred to him. He averted his gaze and hung his head, staring at his feet. Cord watched him a moment, knowing he had to stay strong for Sean. His boys were concerned, of course, but Sean was the most affected. If for no other reason, Cord had to remain strong and confident for the young man.

"She's going to be fine," he said again, putting a hand on his shoulder. "They just needed to fix her up. She should be out soon and you can see her then. Okay?"

Sean drew in a deep breath before nodding his head. "Okay."

Cord patted his shoulder. "Meanwhile, your new baby sister is doing great," he said. "It looks like she's going to have blond hair like you."

Sean smiled weakly. Cord was about to suggest they go down to the cafeteria and get something to eat when his parents came around the corner from the elevator. Cord lifted his hand in greeting as Mary practically ran to him.

"Chris called us," she said, urgency in her voice. "How's Alix? How's the baby?"

Cord hastened to reassure his mother. "Alix is in surgery but she's going to be fine," he said steadily. "They just had to clean her up a bit. And your new granddaughter is doing great. Nine pounds, eleven ounces. She's big and healthy."

Mary shrieked with glee. "Chris said it was a girl!" she said, clapping her hands happily. The nursery window was right there and she went straight to it, like a moth to flame. "Where is she?"

Cord, with Rose still in his arms, pointed to the bassinet at the end of the very first row behind the glass. "There she is," he said with pride. "Katharine Mary. We're going to call her Kitty, after Grandma."

Mary was all over the situation. She sighed with delight at her first granddaughter, desperate to hold the baby. All she could talk about was how she wanted to kiss her cheeks and eat her up, which concerned Rose a bit until they explained the figure of speech to her. As they all stood there and admired the pink and rosy infant, a nurse emerged from the nursery.

"Cord," she said quietly. "Your wife is out of surgery. She's in recovery."

Cord immediately handed Rose over to Sean and assured the young man he'd send word to let him know how his mother was doing. Racing down to the second floor, he very nearly ran the entire way to the surgical recovery area. When he gave the attending nurse his name, she let him into the dim, quiet room.

There were two other patients being tended to other than his wife. The nursing presence was heavy as women in scrubs moved about, silently checking monitors and drips. Dr. Potts was standing over Alix along with the OB/GYN who had been on-call. There was also another doctor in scrubs that Cord didn't recognize. When they saw Cord approach, they moved their conversation in his direction.

"Cord," Dr. Potts greeted. He indicated the unfamiliar physician. "This is Dr. Ranj. He's a cardiologist."

Cord wasn't particularly comforted by that knowledge but shook the man's hand. "Nice to meet you," he said. "Uh... why does my wife need a cardiologist?"

Dr. Potts put a hand on Cord's shoulder. "We lost her pulse when she was on the table," he said as gently as he could. "We were able to get a rhythm again, but I wanted her checked out by the cardiologist. That's what took so long. Dr. Ranj is one of the best."

"She'll be fine, Mr. Trevor," Dr. Ranj, an older Indian-American man, spoke softly. "Her cardiac enzymes are fine and all of the tests are coming back acceptable. I'm just going to watch her for the next couple of days to make sure everything is okay."

Cord felt sick. He swallowed hard. "Oh, God," he finally breathed. "She went into cardiac arrest?"

Dr. Potts nodded. "She had lost a significant amount of blood," he said. "Her body was reacting to the stress. But she's doing much better now. She should be able to go home in a few days if she continues to improve."

Cord merely nodded his head, feeling overwhelmed and anguished. "But...," he said, his throat tight with emotion. "She's okay? Her uterus – everything – is okay?"

The OB/GYN nodded. "She'll be fine," he said. "We cleaned her out and she should recover fully."

Cord breathed a heavy sigh of relief. A lump welled up in his throat and he could hardly speak. "Thank you," he whispered. Then he gestured at Alix, lying pale and sedated on the gurney. "I'd really just like to sit with my wife now."

The doctors let him go. Cord made his way over to Alix, gazing down at her sleeping face, and he couldn't help the tears. God, he was all shook up. Taking the chair next to her, he sat down and wiped away the tears. Then he took her hand and held it tightly. He didn't know what else to do but give thanks.

He thanked God she was going to be okay.

NINETEEN

"ALIX?" Cord called up to his wife. "Honey, do you want something to eat? I'm making the boys sandwiches."

Eleven days after the birth of baby Kitty, the situation in the Hendry-Trevor home was back to normal. The dogs were sleeping where they weren't supposed to be, the boys were taking over the television in the den with their war games, and Cord had let Hester go because he had taken four months off to tend Alix and the baby after the harrowing delivery. They didn't need a live-in any longer, although it had been a good parting. Hester wanted to go home to Louisiana, anyway. Truth was, Cord was thrilled and content to be a house-husband now, in charge of everything. He was exactly where he wanted to be.

Alix had been home for seven days and had recovered rapidly. In fact, Cord was having a tough time keeping her down. She was supposed to be on bed rest for a couple of weeks but that wasn't panning out because she wouldn't stay down. Physicians made rotten patients and Alix was no exception. The more Cord tried to keep her down, the more she resisted him. Even now, he could hear her moving around upstairs. He finally put Chris on finishing the sandwiches and went upstairs to see what she was doing.

Cord found Alix sitting on the floor of Rose's pink princess room with the baby in her arms as she and Rose were picking up the clutter. Alix would pick a book off the floor and hand it to Rose, who would then put it on her bookshelf. As Cord stood in the doorway, he watched Rose put away two books and a doll. When Alix finally looked up and saw him, she smiled.

"Hi, babe," she said.

He smiled in return, coming in to the room. "Hi," he said. "What are you doing?"

Alix picked up another toy and handed it to her daughter. "Cleaning up," she said. "What are you doing?"

He bent over and scooped the baby out of her arms, cradling his precious little daughter, who was swaddled tightly and sucking furiously on her pacifier. "I was making the boys some lunch," he said, gently rocking the baby. "Do you want a sandwich?"

Alix rolled onto her knees, stiffly, and crawled over to collect another toy for Rose to put away. "I guess so," she said. "I'll come help you."

He shook his head. "You don't need to help me," he said. "In fact, you probably shouldn't be crawling around on the floor like that."

She eyed him as she sat back on her heels. "I'm fine," she said. "I feel a lot better when I'm moving around and not lying like a slug on the bed."

He grinned. "Doctor's orders," he pointed out. "You're supposed to be taking it easy for the next two weeks."

Alix made a face as she struggled to get to her feet, grabbing hold of Rose's dresser to pull herself up. "Screw the doctors," she said. "They're a bunch of quacks."

Cord laughed. Holding the baby in one big arm, he reached out and took Alix's hand, walking out into the hall with her.

"Put the baby in her bassinet," she told him as he headed for the back stairs. "She needs to take a nap."

His face fell. "Can't I hold her a little longer?"

Alix smirked. "You can feed her when she wakes up," she said. "Seriously, Cord, you can't keep walking around with her all of the time. She has to learn to be by herself once in a while. She needs to learn to sleep somewhere other than in her father's arms."

He made a face at her, not particularly pleased by that answer, but dutifully took the baby into their bedroom and put her gently in her plush bassinet. The bassinet itself tended to move around; Alix would put it on her side but somehow it always ended up on Cord's side. He fussed over the baby to make sure she was comfortable and settled before quietly leaving the bedroom.

Out in the hall, he wrapped his arms around Alix, kissing her head and cheek as she tried to walk down the hall. She giggled, unable to really fight him off because she was still rather stiff from the difficult birth. He finally let her go as they descended the stairs into a kitchen where the boys were consuming most of the lunch meat. Alix fought off Kyle as he tried to take some of her sandwich meat as she made lunch for her and Rose to share. He grinned when she pushed him.

Cutting the sandwich into four sections and carefully peeling away the crust, as Rose wouldn't eat a sandwich with the crust on it, she put it on a plate and grabbed a few napkins. As Cord sat down with the boys, listening to them talk about the football practice that was coming up in a few weeks for the start of the fall semester at school, Alix headed back up the stairs with the sandwich.

Rose was no longer picking up her room but rather playing

on the floor. The room was still messy. Alix sighed as she stood in the doorway, knowing it would be a long process for her daughter to clean her bedroom. Setting the plate down on the floor next to Rose, she headed back over to the master bedroom to check on Kitty because it was habit with her; she tended to check on the infant about every ten minutes or so, sometimes more, which made for a disruptive sleep pattern. Still, she couldn't help it; it was just the way she was and she had done the same thing with Rose and Sean when they had been babies.

Quietly, she pushed the door to the bedroom open. It was quiet and dim inside. The bassinet was pushed up against her side of the bed and she crept over to it, peering over the side. The bassinet was empty. Startled, she tossed back the little blanket that was there, the one Kitty had been swaddled in. The baby was missing.

"Cord!" she screamed.

Alix came flying out of the bedroom, hearing Cord as he charged up the stairs. They nearly collided at the head of the staircase.

"Kitty's gone!" Alix shrieked. "I went to go check on her and she's gone!"

Cord looked at her, horrified, before pushing past her and running into the master bedroom. Alix ran in behind him with the boys bringing up the rear. They had heard the scream, too, and had come running.

Cord was tearing apart the bedroom. "Where in the hell is she?" he boomed. "What in the...?"

He ran at the windows, seeing if somehow, someway, someone had crawled into a second floor window and kidnapped the baby. But the windows were secure, locked from the inside. He dropped to his knees and looked under one side of the bed while Alix did the same thing and looked in from the other. The underside of the bed was dark but clear. Cord's head popped up and he looked at the boys, clustered around the door.

"Search every inch of this house," he snapped. "*Go!*"

They boys scattered. Alix, hearing the thunder of their feet as they raced around on the hunt for their baby sister, began to panic. Her hands went over her mouth and sobs bubbled up, like gasping pants. Cord, seeing that she was breaking down, vaulted over the bed and ended up on the floor beside her. He threw his arms around her and held on tight.

"It's okay," he assured her urgently although he was verging on panic, too. "We'll find her. Don't worry, honey; she'll be fine."

Alix was hysterical. "Call the police!" she cried. "Oh, my God, where could she go? Someone took her!"

Cord was up, grabbing for the phone but a yell from Chris stopped him. "Dad!" he bellowed. "In here!"

Alix and Cord scrambled up from the floor, crashing into each other in their haste to move. Cord ended up picking Alix up off of the floor, practically carrying her down the hall in the direction of Chris' voice. They realized the commotion was coming from Chris' bedroom and they blew in the door about the time Sean, Cole, and Kyle got there. All of them were cramming in, jockeying to get a look at what the excitement was about. Chris was pointing to his bed frantically.

"Look!" he said. "She's here!"

Alix and Cord rushed to the bed where Kitty was laying. She was awake, with the pacifier in her mouth, squirming around as she stared at the ceiling. Alix yelped when she saw her daughter, lying on the mattress without a scratch. She slapped her hand over her mouth to keep from sobbing out loud. Still, the tears of joy and relief came. She dropped down on the bed beside the baby as Cord hovered over her.

"Oh, God," she breathed, struggling not to openly weep.

She ran her hands over Kitty's skull, her neck and shoulders. "She... she seems fine. Not a mark on her. How in the world did she get here?"

No one could tell her. Cord's big hands were on the baby as well as if to see for himself that she was in one piece. He was shaken to the bone. When Alix finally picked the baby up and held her tightly, Cord's hands never left her. His grip was on the baby, on his wife, as if holding the two together. His pale face turned to his sons.

"Chris," he said. "How did she... she was just laying here on the bed?"

Chris nodded firmly. "I came in here to look for her and there she was. She wasn't even crying."

He sounded frightened. In fact, they were all frightened. Cord looked around the room at his sons, seeing that all of them were apprehensive. He struggled to calm down and think clearly. He was so rattled he could barely form a thought.

"Okay," he said, taking a deep breath for control. "If this was some kind of joke, then now's the time to tell us. But just so you know, I don't think it's very funny."

"How could it be a joke, Dad?" Kyle said. "We were all downstairs eating. You saw us the entire time and we never came upstairs."

Cord conceded the point. But then, he cocked his head as if a thought just occurred to him and he looked at his wife, who was struggling to calm down herself.

"Rose was up here," he said quietly. "Do you think...?"

"Rosie!" Alix called before he even finished his sentence. "Rosie, please come here."

They could hear little footsteps pelting the wooden floors as Rose emerged from her bedroom. After a few moments, she appeared in the doorway. She had a plastic plate in her hand, looking at her mother and stepfather with her big gray eyes. Alix tried to keep her voice calm as she spoke.

"Rosie," she said. "Do you know how Kitty got into Chris' bedroom?"

Rose nodded solemnly. "Yes."

Alix's heart skipped a beat. "How?"

"The sad girl."

Alix's terror returned full bore. "What do you mean? Did she bring the baby in here?"

Rose shook her head. "She told me to take her."

Alix's eyebrows lifted. "*You* carried Kitty in here?"

Rose nodded. "The sad girl said that her mommy wants her."

Alix looked at Cord, her eyes as big as saucers. They were all thinking the same thing, sickened that evidently the sad girl was making some kind of resurgence. So many months of peace and now this. Alix wasn't quite sure how to process it but she knew one thing; she couldn't put her family in harm's way. If the activity was kicking up again, she wasn't going to stick around.

"I can't have the babies exposed to this," she whispered, panic in her voice. "I need to take them out of here. We're not staying here."

Cord nodded soothingly, his arms around Alix and the baby. "It's okay," he murmured, kissing her head. "We won't stay here."

"I'm getting out," she said, increased urgency in her voice. "I'm going to pack right now."

Cord could see how terrified she was. "Okay, honey, okay," he said calmingly. "Go get packed. I'll figure out where we'll go."

"Us, too, Dad?" Chris wanted to know. "Do we have to leave, too?"

Cord let Alix go with the little girls, off to pack their things. He stood in the doorway of Chris' room, genuinely distressed. Brow creased with worry and thought, he put his hands on his hips.

"I suppose that depends," he said. "This ghost girl has never bothered you guys. Do you feel safe staying here?"

The four boys looked at each other, trying to decide if they were scared enough to leave, but none of them wanted to be the first one to admit it. Chris, unable to get a real response from his brothers or from Sean, looked at his father.

"I don't feel threatened," he said. "I'll stay."

"Me, too," Kyle said. "If Chris stays, I stay."

Cole and Sean looked at each other a moment before Sean finally spoke. "I want to go with my mom," he said quietly, "but if the guys are staying, I'll stay."

Cole looked around at his brothers, his father, before sighing heavily. "I'll stay," he muttered.

Cord scratched his head wearily, letting his hand slap back down against his thigh. "Okay," he said. "If that's what you want to do, that's fine, but for tonight I'm taking Alix and the girls to a hotel somewhere."

"Are you going to stay with her?" Chris asked.

Cord pondered the question. "Maybe not," he said. "If the activity kicks up tonight, I want to be here. In fact, I may call Grampa and have him come stay here, too."

They could hear Alix slamming drawers in her haste to pack the girls' clothes. She was telling Rose to gather her things, encouraging the little girl to move quickly. There was a great deal of panic in her voice even though it was controlled. They could all hear the fear, feeling it in the very air they breathed. Cord finally gave a heavy sigh.

"You boys stay here," he said. "I'm going to run over to

Grampa's house to let him know what's going on and bring him back. I think we need some help. Hang around here for Alix's sake, okay?"

"Sure, Dad," Chris said.

It took Cord almost a half hour to convince Alix to let him leave the house without her. She didn't want him to go. He had to explain his reason over and over because she refused to accept it. Finally, she relented and when he moved quickly to retrieve his car keys, he happened to notice the very old documents that they had found in the attic still tucked into the drawer. He'd never taken them to Mrs. Mowbray. His gaze lingered on them a moment, wondering what secrets they contained and if, in fact, there was something in those fragile yellow pages that could help them. After a few seconds of indecision, he grabbed the documents along with his keys.

"I promise I'll be back within the hour," he told Alix, who was moving around behind him throwing baby things into a suitcase propped up on the bed. "The boys will be here so you won't be alone. If things get bad or start picking up again, just get out. Go somewhere and call me. Okay?"

Alix had Kitty in one arm, stuffing the suitcase with the other. "Okay."

He bent over and kissed her swiftly. "I love you," he murmured, kissing her again and then kissing the baby's head. "I'll be back."

As Cord headed out to his truck, he noticed that the sky was starting to cloud over and a summer storm threatened. Once he got on the road, he used his smartphone to find a hotel for the night as he headed over to his father's house. His mind focused ahead on his father and what they needed to do in order to clear Evenshade once and for all of the ghostly spirits. He was determined to rid them from the house once and for all because they certainly couldn't go through the rest of their lives afraid of their own home.

With his mind occupied on what he had to do, he was unaware that back at the house, a storm of epic proportions was brewing. Tonight would decide who remained at Evenshade – the flesh and blood occupants, or the dead ones.

TWENTY

"YOU FOUND these under a floor board in the attic?" Quirt repeated what he'd just been told, moving from the living room into his study to get his magnifying glass. "These have got to be a couple of hundred years old. This is actually hide and not paper."

Cord had just walked in the door with the horror story of the moving baby and, in the course of the conversation, handed his father the documents. Quirt took one look at them and headed for his study. He knew they were something special and he was eager to take a look. Mary followed the pair, wringing her hands with apprehension.

"I told you to move out of that house," she said to her son. "There is something very evil there."

Cord held up a hand to quiet his mother, his patience thin. "I know what you told us, Mom," he said, "but the activity has been gone over the past several months. After Dad cast the banishment spell, we though the spirit was gone so there really wasn't any reason to pick up the entire family and move."

Quirt bent over his desk and picked up his magnifying glass. Cord inhaled the must and pipe-tobacco smell of the room; as a kid, he'd always loved that smell. It brought him comfort. As Cord inhaled and tried to calm down, Quirt flipped on the green banker's light on his desk and put on his reading glasses.

"Dad, I need you to come back to the house with me," Cord said as his father peered at the old documents. "Something is brewing and I want to stop it before it gets going. Alix isn't going to stay there tonight; she's terrified for the girls and I don't blame her. The boys are there, though. The spirit doesn't seem to be interested in them."

Quirt grunted in response as he examined the documents. Carefully, he laid them out on his desk; there were five sheets of very old vellum. Under the bright white light of his desk lamp, he fixated on them. The edges were damaged, curling up, but it didn't diminish the historical significance. He was fascinated.

"You need to get everybody out," he said, eyes glued to the pages. "Tell the boys to come over here. They can stay with us."

Cord didn't say anything for a moment; he was watching his dad as the man read over the old vellum in search of whatever answers or information they might provide.

"What about Chris?" he asked softly. "We may need him."

Quirt glanced at him over the top of his glasses. "What do you mean?"

Cord crossed his enormous arms, his gaze fixed on his father over the top of the desk lamp. "You don't have to lie about it anymore," he said quietly. "I know you have been working with Chris on casting. I know you've been doing it since he was small. He must be pretty good by now."

Quirt just stared at him. Then, he lowered his gaze back to the documents. "He's better than I am," he said, rather contritely. "Who told you?"

"No one. I've just seen the clues now and again. I'm not an idiot."

"I never said you were. But knowing how you felt, we didn't want to upset you. Chris takes it all very seriously."

Cord simply nodded his head and looked at his mother, who was standing in the doorway looking rather guilty. "You're not mad, are you?" she asked.

The corners of Cord's mouth twitched. "No, I'm not mad," he said. Then he sighed heavily. "It's in his blood. I suppose I can't deny him his legacy."

Mary smiled timidly and went to stand next to her husband as he inspected the documents. Cord leaned against the big, heavy desk, watching his parents as they examined the antique papers.

"Dad, I really need to get back to the house," he said. "You need to come with me."

Quirt nodded. "I will," he said. "I want your mother to come, too. I can't sense things like she can."

Cord looked dubious. "It might be dangerous," he said. "That entity has been known to get violent. It knocked Alix out once. I'm not sure I want Mom to...."

"Holy Smokes!" Quirt suddenly exclaimed, interrupting his son. "Do you know what these are?"

"What?" Cord demanded.

Quirt picked up the third sheet of vellum and scrutinized the faded brown writing. He seemed quite excited and quite entranced. When he spoke, it was with awe.

"They're curses," he said. "By damn, these are curses on other people, among them Sarah Good and William Good, her husband. I see several names here, all listed with curses. I think there's even a curse here written for Dorothy Good; I can clearly see the name."

"Curses?" Cord bent over so he could see what his father was referring to. "Can you read them? Are they in English?"

Quirt nodded. "It's English," he said, squinting at the writing. "Back in Colonial America, they spoke and wrote English although it differs from the language we use today. Still, it's generally the same. I can read it pretty clearly."

He suddenly began shuffling through the papers, rapidly, as if he was looking for something. Cord alternately looked at the documents and his father's expression. He could feel an odd sense of urgency emitting from his father, something electric in the air. It made his heart beat faster.

"What's wrong?" he asked. "What are you looking for?"

Quirt didn't answer for a moment; he was still shuffling the pages around, reading the front and back of them, holding up a hand for patience when Cord asked him again. After several long moments of inspecting the papers, he sat back in his chair and pulled off his glasses.

"You said you found these under the floor boards in the attic?" he asked.

Cord nodded. "On the day Alix and I got married, Rose got trapped up in the attic," he said. "When we finally found her, she was sitting near a floor board that was partially pulled away. This is what was underneath it."

Quirt stroked his chin, eyeing the documents on the desk. "*How* did Rosie get trapped up in the attic?"

"She said the sad girl took her up there," Cord replied. "She said the sad girl needed to call her mother. She probably meant that the sad girl needed to talk to her mother, or maybe even summon her mother, but she used the word 'call'."

Quirt inhaled slowly, thoughtfully. His gaze was still fixed on the desktop. "And the floor boards were pulled up right next to her?"

"Yes. Why?"

Quirt cocked an eyebrow. "Because," he said, swinging the chair around so he was facing Cord, "I'll tell you what I think. These curses were written in blood, because that's how you write an effective curse, and I'm going to theorize that it was Abigail Williams who did it. Who else could it be? It has Sarah Good, William Good, and Dorothy Good's names on it. Plus, I swear I see the name of Rebecca Nurse, who was another woman accused of witchcraft during the Salem witch trials. Here; let me read you the one that has Sarah's name attached to it as 'Goody Goode'."

Cord held his breath as Quirt picked up the second parchment and held it under the light. "*A breath of wind, a mark of sin, evil doer drink of blood. Beneath the earth, feel my curse, with my hand to 'ever crush you,*" he said. "*Malum infans, putrescet Satanae ut canis. Te et matrem tuam aeternum ardebit.*"

Cord thought hard on the Latin translation; he had learned the language as a child, the language of the Casters, and it took very little for him to recall what he knew. He had a strong gift of recall and a nearly photographic memory. Puzzled, he looked at his father.

"Evil Infant," he muttered, "rot as Satan's dog? Burn with your mother for eternity in hell?"

Quirt nodded. "Very good," he said. "That about sums it up."

Cord began to feel a heavy sense of foreboding. It was nearly oppressive and he actually put his hand to his chest, feeling fear as he had never felt in his life.

"Christ," he hissed. "She's talking about being beneath the earth and crushing with her hand, like... like someone was buried and she was sitting on top of them, keeping them down."

"Like the stone circle over the grave that was supposed to keep the infant rising up."

Cord thought on that, hard. Then, he started to shake his head as pieces of the malevolent puzzle began to come together. Suddenly, things were becoming clearer and he couldn't help the flood of emotions that washed over him as a result. But there were some aspects that were still foggy. It was going to drive him crazy if he didn't figure them out.

"Wait a minute," he said, voicing the thoughts that were filling his head. "This doesn't make any sense. You said that Abigail laid down that stone circle to keep the infant, Mercy, from coming out of the grave and thereby fulfilling Sarah Good's curse that she would inhabit the dead body of her infant after her own death and haunt Abigail. But, clearly, there is a ghost girl in our house. What if... what if it's *not* Mercy at all? What if it's the other little girl in this scenario, the one who took the infant to Abigail's house at her mother's request? What if our ghost girl is actually Dorothy Good?"

Quirt pondered that revelation. "But how? She's not buried on the property."

Cord's mind was moving swiftly. "That we know of," he said. "In fact, Alix told me that Mrs. Mowbray told her that there's no record of what happened to Dorothy Good. For all we know, she's hanging around Evenshade because of the terrible things done to her mother and sister. Maybe it's been her all along pretending to be Mercy."

Quirt lifted his eyebrows. "It makes sense," he said. "The infant, and consequently Sarah Good, are suppressed under that stone circle and presumably can't get out, yet there's a ghost of a girl running around. Didn't you say that when Rose was trapped in the attic, the sad girl told Rose that she had to call her mother?"

Cord was electrified by the thought. "Yes!" he exclaimed, as if it had all suddenly come clear. "That's what she said; that the ghost girl wanted to call her mother. Dorothy Good is trying to release the curse on her mother, which is why she took Rose to the attic to retrieve the curse that was buried under the floor board. Don't you destroy a curse by burning it or otherwise destroying whatever it's written on?"

Quirt nodded firmly. "Throw it in the fire, dissolve it in water," he said. "She could have had Rose do any of those things. She's using Alix's daughter to free her mother and unleash her on the house and the descendants of Abigail Williams."

Cord's mouth popped open in shock. "Oh, God," he breathed. "If that's the case, then what can we do?"

Quirt stood up, setting his glasses on the desk as he began to collect the antique papers. Something told him to bring them along.

"We need to get over to the house," he said. "Call Alix and tell her to go to a hotel with the girls. Get them out of there. That ghostly girl is trying to unleash hell over there."

Cord was already on the move.

———

The storm that had been brewing since Cord's departure let loose about twenty minutes after he left. There was thunder and lightning, filling the sky with turbulence.

Alix ignored the downpour as she continued packing for the little ones and for herself. The boys had gravitated into the master bedroom where Chris now sat on an overstuffed chair, holding Kitty, while Sean and Kyle entertained Rose. When she wanted to go back into her bedroom, they followed. Cole remained with Chris, watching little Kitty as Alix finished packing.

A massive roll of thunder shook the house, followed by great flashes of lightning. Alix finished up with her bag, gazing out of the window and watching the rain pound. Then she looked at her watch, noticing that Cord had been gone almost an hour.

"Your dad should be back soon," she said, turning to the boys. "Are you sure you don't want to come with us?"

Chris shook his head. "We'll be fine here," he said. "That little ghost girl isn't going to start anything with me."

Alix grinned, moving over to the chair and gazing down at her contented daughter as she suckled her pacifier furiously, staring off into space. She put her hand on Chris' shoulder.

"You're a good big brother," she said. "You can have babysitting duty any time."

He grinned, looking at the blond-haired infant. "I'm okay unless I have to change diapers," he said, seeing Cole standing next to him out of the corner of his eye. "Cole can do it. He gets the dirty work."

Cole wrinkled up his nose and moved swiftly for the door. "No way, dude," he said. "I'm not doing any of that."

Alix laughed, watching Cole bolt down the stairs, undoubtedly heading for the den and the video games. He took any chance he could to play when Chris and Kyle weren't around because they tended to take everything over, including him. Alix bent over and gently took her daughter from Chris.

"Okay," she said. "You're free to go now."

Chris stood up from the chair, watching Alix as she headed over to the bassinet. "I don't mind," he said. "Like I said, as long as she doesn't stink, I'm good."

Alix snorted as she lay the baby down and rolled her onto her side. "I've got news for you," she said. "They all stink at one time or another. You can't get away from it."

"That's why I have three little brothers to take care of that," he said. He watched Alix as she doted over the baby. "Uh... will you be okay up here if I go downstairs?"

Alix waved him off. "Of course," she said. "I'll yell if I need you."

"Okay."

He left the room, heading downstairs to commandeer the video controller from his weaker, younger brother. Alix turned to watch him go, thinking he was a pretty good kid. In fact, she had lucked out where her stepsons were concerned; they were all very good boys and she loved them. She was a very fortunate woman.

Kitty wasn't happy in her bassinet and started to fuss, so Alix bent over to pat the baby on the back, trying to calm her down. She could hear Rose and the boys across the hall in Rose's room, messing around. Somebody dropped something because she could hear the thump, followed by a muttered apology. The commotion was comforting. It made the frightening events that happened earlier seem a million miles away. Peace was once again settling.

Alix sighed, still patting the baby as the infant seemed to calm. Maybe she was overreacting about the whole thing; they'd gone the past six months without a single paranormal experience, so maybe this was just a flare up, quick to rise and quick to leave. She truly hoped so because she didn't want to leave her house. This was her home and something worth fighting for. When Cord got back, she would talk to him about it. She was starting to think she'd blown the entire thing out of proportion.

"Mom?" Sean was standing in the second doorway that faced the kitchen stairs. "We're going to go downstairs and play video games."

Alix looked over her shoulder at him. "Okay," she said. "Where's Rose?"

"She's going with us."

"Good. Don't let her out of your sight."

"I won't."

The kids headed down the back stairs about the time baby Kitty seemed to fall asleep. Alix carefully stopped patting and removed her hand, being very quiet as she moved. Kitty seemed to be a light sleeper. Closing both bedroom doors, she remained in the bedroom but went into the bathroom to take a quick shower and change. She knew Cord would be back any minute and she wanted to be ready.

As the door to the bathroom closed and the sounds of the shower could be heard, the thunder and rain pounded the old house. The upper floor was relatively quiet except for the shower while downstairs, the comforting sounds of zombie screams and gunfire could be heard. Evenshade was settling back to normal and even the dogs, in their permanent places on the living room couches, were snoring away. Until Aram's eyes opened and his head came up.

Dark doggy eyes stared at the front staircase, dog senses reaching out to hear or see or feel. Sounds from the video games were loud in the living room, but that's not what had Aram's ears up and his nose twitching. There was something else, something only he could sense.

Quietly, he got off the couch and wandered over to the stairwell, looking up to the second floor. He could hear the shower going up there. Sniffing at the air, he trotted up the stairs and came to a halt at the top of the landing. His attention was on Chris' bedroom door.

Down below, Manitou was up. Whatever had Aram up had him up as well. He moved swiftly, racing up the stairs to the top of the landing where Aram was. Both dogs moved towards Chris' bedroom door but came to an abrupt halt when the door slowly creaked open.

Aram bared his teeth menacingly, growling at what he could only see as a black, writhing mass. To the human eye, it was invisible, but to his dog senses, it was something black and frightening. Manitou saw it, too, and he began to snarl.

The mass retreated into Chris' bedroom but didn't close the door. The dogs, their hackles up and still snarling, followed. They entered the room, seeing the black mass near the closet door that led up to the attic. The mass moved away from the door and skirted the wall, moving up to the ceiling and hovering over them. Aram barked savagely, followed by Manitou. Manitou even lunged at it. But quickly, the black mass darted towards the bedroom door and shot through it, out into the corridor. The bedroom door slammed behind it, trapping the confused and frightened dogs inside Chris' room. Manitou went to the door and scratched at it, whining. But nobody heard him.

In the den below, Rose was sitting on the couch as all four of her brothers played a gory zombie apocalypse game. It was too scary and gory for her, so she didn't want to watch it and quickly became bored. She got a hold of a pen on the end table and scribbled on a magazine that was there, drawing doodles over a woman's face. Over her shoulder, her brothers were on a killing spree, congratulating each other on messy kills. Rose continued to scribble.

"Rose!"

She heard her name, like a soft breath of wind. It had come from the den door and she looked up but didn't see anyone. Returning to her doodles, she heard her name again.

"Rose, hitherto!"

Looking up, she saw the sad girl standing just outside the doorway. Dressed in her usual white dress with a smock-like apron over it, the sad girl's long, dark hair hung to her waist while her pale face with dark, shiny eyes gazed steadily at Rose. When she smiled, it wasn't with sharp teeth but with a sweet little grin. She motioned to Rose, who promptly set the pen down and climbed off the couch. The brothers, completely focused on their zombie game, never noticed when she left the room because their backs were to the door. Rose left and they were never the wiser.

Out in the dim corridor that ran between the living room and the den and library, Rose walked up to the sad girl.

"Good day, Rose," the sad girl whispered.

Rose didn't say anything at first. Then, she cocked her head. "I don't want to play with you anymore," she said.

The sad girl's smile faded. "*My truest Rose,*" she murmured. "*My mother is very sad. She needs help.*"

Rose could hear her brothers yelling behind her. "I don't want to help," she said.

"*But my mother is sad. Doest thee not know concern? Only thou may help her.*"

"I don't wanna."

The sad girl was clever. "*But thou must,*" she insisted. "*If thou does not, terrible things will happen to thee's mother. Is that what thee wishes?*"

Rose's brow furrowed with concern, with anger. "No!"

"*Help me now or terrible things will occur!*"

"No, don't!"

The sad girl could see Rose's agitation. It was as she had desired; the reaction of raw fear. She knew the feeling well. She fed off it, drawing strength from it.

"*The infant,*" she whispered. "*You must bring her to my mother. She wishes to see her.*"

Rose was frightened and confused. "I can't. My mommy won't let me."

"*But you must. The infant will make my mother well again. You must help her.*"

Rose looked at the sad girl dubiously. "Where is your mommy?"

"*We shall see her.*"

The sad girl moved away from Rose, with legs that were mist and didn't touch the ground. Rose followed her into the kitchen, dimly lit as the storm pounded outside. The sad girl pointed a bony finger at the basement door.

"*Bring the infant,*" she whispered.

Rose shook her head again, fearfully, but the sad girl seemed to shape-shift into something more frightening and ominous.

"*Bring the infant,*" she said, her voice otherworldly and deep. "*If thou does not, terrible things will happen to thee's mother.*"

Rose was tearing up. "I'm going to tell my brother what you said!"

The sad girl had no sympathy. "*If thou does, I will kill them and make them go away forever. Is this what thee wishes?*"

Rose wiped furiously at her eyes as the tears started to fall. She could only shake her head. Terrified, she reluctantly headed up the back stairs.

TWENTY-ONE

ALIX GOT out of the shower and quickly dried off, pulling the clip out of her hair and brushing it back into a quick ponytail. Changing into skinny jeans and a big sweater, she came out of the bathroom and headed over to the bassinet to check on Kitty. She was halfway across the room when the doorbell went off. Diverted from the bassinet, she opened the door that faced out onto the landing that contained the back steps. Over to her right were the main upstairs hall and the front stairs. As the rain pounded, she scooted down the stairs and opened the front door.

Mrs. Mowbray stood on the porch, her half-closed umbrella in her hand. The woman was positively soaked. Alix quickly ushered her in, closing the door behind her and shutting out the wind and the rain.

"Good heavens," Alix exclaimed. "What on earth brings you out on a day like today?"

Mrs. Mowbray smiled weakly, showing off those great yellowed teeth. "I'm so sorry to barge in like this."

Alix shook her head as she took the woman's dripping umbrella and put it in the umbrella receptacle. "No bother at all," she said. "How have you been? It's been a long time since we last saw you."

Mrs. Mowbray nodded, her movements sharp and bird-like. "Back in December," she said. "I heard you and Mr. Trevor got married."

Alix smiled. "We did," she said. "I just had a baby a couple of weeks ago."

Mrs. Mowbray threw up her hands. "Heavens!" she said. "Congratulations. You must be extremely busy. I'll only take a moment of your time, I promise."

Alix led her into the living room with its lush furnishings. "No problem," she said. "My husband should be home any minute and we have plans after that, but until then, I'm all yours."

Mrs. Mowbray had a leather briefcase with her. She perched on the edge of Alix's couch and began opening the case. "Well," she said, "I'll get right to the point. As you have figured out, I am quite fascinated with the history of this house. The last time I was here it was because I'd discovered new information on the house and that's why I'm here today. A colleague of mine at the Historical Society reminded me that today is the day that, three hundred and twenty-one years ago, Sarah Good was hung for witchcraft. Did you realize that?"

Alix's smile faded and somewhere in the pit of her stomach, a seed of fear sprouted. "No, I didn't," she said evenly. "How... interesting."

"I thought you might like to know that," Mrs. Mowbray said, not catching on to the apprehensive inflection in Alix's tone. She seemed quite jovial as she pulled a leather pouch out of her briefcase. "As you saw at the Historical Society, we have lots of boxes and files containing priceless pieces of Salem's history. While I was working through a box that had been long stored away, I came across this leather pouch with a note on it. It seems that this pouch contains the actual amulet worn by Abigail Williams to ward off Goody Good's curse. Oh, it was a well-known curse back then because nearly everyone who was hung for witchcraft spun some sort of threats or curse before they went to the gallows. Our boxes are full of charms and amulets to ward off curses and evil. Since you own the house now where the curse is said to reside, I thought you might like to have it."

She pulled forth a small pouch made of yellowed material, strung on a strip of leather like a necklace, and carefully handed it over to Alix. Awed, Alix held the amulet in front of her to inspect it.

"Oh, my," she said softly. "This is... well, thank you so much for this. It's really fascinating."

"Isn't it?"

"What's in it?"

Mrs. Mowbray shrugged. "Who knows?" she said. "Often-times, it was things like crow's feet, or a chicken tongue, or something like that. But here's the interesting part – it was in a box with other items someone had donated from Evenshade back around the turn of the last century. One of your husband's ancestors must have donated it. There are all kinds of things in the box but mostly paper and records. Would you like to see them someday?"

Alix nodded eagerly. "I'd love to," she said, eyeing the woman as she lowered the amulet. "Is there anything more about this place being cursed in those records?"

As Mrs. Mowbray laughed and started to reply, the house phone rang. Alix jumped up, thinking it might be Cord. She held up a hand to Mrs. Mowbray.

"Hold that thought," she said quickly, setting the amulet on the coffee table. "I'll be right back."

As Mrs. Mowbray remained in the living room, Alix scur-ried to the back hall that linked with the den and library. She happened to scoot past the den, glancing at the bodies there and counting four. She took another few steps towards the ringing phone in the kitchen when she sudden came to a halt and retraced her steps. The boys were so involved in their game that only Chris noticed Alix when she stood in the doorway.

"Hey," Alix said loudly over the sounds of rifle fire and ringing phones. "Where's Rose?"

The boys immediately came to a halt and looked around the room and at each other. There was a phone extension in the den, still ringing, and Alix went to pick it up before the boys could answer her. It was Cord on the other end.

"Alix?" he said.

"Hi, babe," she said. "Hold on a second."

She put her hand over the receiver and spoke to the boys. "Where's Rose, guys?"

Sean was already on his feet, dropping the video game controller. "She was just here," he said. "Maybe she went to the bathroom."

"Go check," Alix insisted urgently. "You were supposed to be watching her, Sean Patrick. Find her!"

As Sean ran off towards the downstairs bathroom, Alix uncovered the receiver and spoke to her husband.

"Sorry about that," she said, apprehension in her voice. "Where are you?"

Cord was in his car on the other end of the line, trapped behind a tree that had fallen in the storm. He was going to have to backtrack about a half mile out of his way to get around it.

"I'm on my way home," he said. "Honey, I want you to listen to me very carefully."

Alix felt a twinge of fear. "Of course," she replied. "What's going on?"

Cord spun his truck around in the rain and floored it in the opposite direction. "I've got my dad and mom with me and we're heading back to Evenshade," he said. "I reserved two two-bedroom suites at the Marriott in downtown Danvers. I want you to pack everyone up right now, get in the car, and head over there. Don't delay; get everyone moving and get in the car. Okay?"

"Cord, you're scaring me," she said. "What's wrong?"

The weather was vicious as Cord tried to navigate through the wind and rain. "Honey, I can't talk about it now because it would take too long," he said. "Just get everyone into the car and go. Get out of there."

Alix was quickly growing terrified. "Okay," she agreed. "We'll go right now. Will you meet me there?"

Cord blew right through a stop sign. "No," he said. "We're coming to the house. Put Chris on the phone, please."

Alix turned to Cord's sons, who had stopped playing their video game and were now watching her with varied degrees of concern. She held the phone out to Chris.

"Your dad wants to talk to you," she said.

Chris stood up and took the phone from her. Just as he did, Sean burst back into the room.

"Mom," he said, sounding scared and breathless. "I can't find Rose. She's not in the bathroom."

Alix fought down the panic that surged through her veins. "Did you check all the rooms downstairs?"

Sean nodded. "All of them," he said. Then he looked at Kyle and Cole. "Come on; help me find her!"

The three of them thundered out of the room and charged up the stairs. Alix turned to Chris to have him inform Cord of what was happening when a massive burst of thunder ripped across the sky and lightning lit up the clouds as if it were broad daylight outside. Lightning was striking in all directions, hitting trees and power lines. The entire house shook violently as the lights abruptly went out.

On the other end of the phone, Cord found himself listening to a dead line. "Chris?" he shouted. "Alix?"

There was no one there to answer him.

———

"The phone is dead," Chris said, hanging the receiver back up. He looked around the back room. "Whatever knocked out the power knocked out the phones."

After the conversation Alix had just had with Cord, she was struggling not to break out into full-blown hysterics. She took a deep breath, laboring to keep a calm head.

"Let's find some flashlights, then," she said evenly. "There's one in the kitchen drawer and one upstairs in our bedroom. Your dad told us to get out of here but we need to find Rose first. Go get the flashlight in the kitchen and find Sean."

Chris was on the move, heading out into the dark hall on his way to the kitchen. As he hit the kitchen door, he began to hear something, like chanting. It was very strange. Alix was already heading up the back stairs but Chris followed the sound, ending up in the dark living room to a strange woman bent over on the couch. She was chanting steadily.

"Hey," he said, entering the room. "Who in the hell are you?"

Mrs. Mowbray abruptly sat up, her eyes wide at the young man. It was so dark in the room that it was difficult to make out any features, but Chris could see the dim reflection of big, yellow teeth.

"*Thou Bebe stock?*" she hissed.

Chris just stared at her, having no idea who the woman was or what in the hell was happening. He could hear running and shouting over his head on the second floor but down here in the darkness of the living room, he felt very much alone. He reached out and grabbed her by the wrist, yanking her so hard that she fell to her knees.

"I don't know who you are or why you're here, but you get the hell out of here or I'm calling the cops," he said, dragging her across the floor. "Get out!"

Mrs. Mowbray raked her nails across his hand, drawing blood and causing him to release her. She recoiled back from him, hissing and crawling like some kind of bizarre creature, finally ending up over by the fireplace. As the lightning flashed and the thunder rolled, she draped herself bizarrely over the back of the couch and pointed a finger at him.

"*Vade fili diaboli, de quo egressus es ad terram,*" she hissed. "*Discedite a me maledicti in utero!*"

Chris knew casting when he heard it. The woman was trying to banish him somehow, curse him, and his training took over. Everything his grandfather had taught him, the history and usage and spells, now came front and center as he faced off against something beyond the normal and sane world. He was teetering on the edge of darkness, this house and all those in it, and he called upon his ancestors, his gift, and his training to help him through it. Now, he was being tested. He must not fail. Lifting a hand, palm out, he countered the wicked words cast at him.

"*Animalis diabolica, et vade hinc redire,*" he said slowly and deliberately. "*Non habetis hic potentia. Et hic habet potestatem a Deo potestas ritum suum protecti sumus. Nunc eamus!*"

Mrs. Mowbray hissed viciously at him and fell off the back of the couch. Chris could hear Alix screaming about the baby but he couldn't answer; he had his hands full. Whatever was facing him was something purely evil and wicked. He couldn't even feel fear at the moment; all he could feel was the will to survive.

"*Portae inferi te expectant!*" Mrs. Mowbray shouted.

The woman brought up a hand in a sweeping motion as if throwing a ball. What burst forth was a pocket of energy, slamming into Chris and knocking him backwards. It was strong, but not strong enough to take him down. He brought both hands up, palms out and fingers splayed for maximum conductivity. He was going to return the volley.

"*Et infirmus Fatuæ creatura non superesse!*" he boomed.

An unseen wave of energy hit Mrs. Mowbray and sent the woman careening back into the wall. She hit it so hard that a vase on the mantel toppled over and hit her on the shoulder, sending her down to the floor. But Chris wasn't done; he flicked a hand at the heavy picture frame hanging above Mrs. Mowbray's head and the thing flew off the wall and straight down onto the woman's skull. Mrs. Mowbray collapsed in a heap.

Chris waited for the woman to get back up but when she didn't, he hesitantly made his way over to her, peering down at the unconscious body. He kicked her but she didn't move. Terrified she might rise up again, he grabbed the nearest lamp and used the cord to tie her hands behind her back. Shaken, he became more aware of the panic going on around him, enough so that it spurred him into action.

Just as Chris came running out of the living room, Alix was flying down the front stairs. "Chris!" she cried. "Rose and the baby are missing again! Check the library!"

"I will," he assured her breathlessly. "But there's a woman in the living room... honest, Alix, she tried to kill me. She was casting spells."

Alix's eyes widened with shocked. "She *what*?" she gasped. She peered into the living room and was only able to see a pair of feet near the hearth; the rest of the body was blocked by the couch. "Oh, God, that's Mrs. Mowbray from the Historical

Society but I can't worry about her now. We have to find Rose and Kitty!"

Chris went on the run. Fighting off hysterical tears, Alix ran into the kitchen to search the utility room when she happened to run by the rear staircase and the basement door. Her flashlight fell across the basement door and she saw that it was partially ajar. Horror swept her; what was it Cord had said? A circle of stones over the grave of Mercy Good, forever keeping her from rising up to fulfill her mother's curse? Alix's entire body went weak with utter and complete fear but she forced herself to remain strong; she had to. Her daughters were missing and she had to save them.

"Chris!" she screamed. "Sean! The kitchen!"

She could hear the boys running from all parts of the house. Someone had found the dogs in Chris' room and she could hear them barking, running down the stairs as their nails clicked against the hardwood floors. Chris was the first one to reach her.

"What is it, Alix?" he asked, frantic. "Did you find them?"

Alix pointed at the cracked basement door. "They must be in the basement," she said, throwing open the door and feeling fear as she had never felt in her life. She called out into the pitch-black darkness. "Rosie? Can you hear me? It's Mommy! I'm coming, honey!"

The narrow stairs leading down to the basement were blacker than black. Alix took the lead, shining a light down the steps, wondering how in the hell Rose managed to lug a newborn infant down them. But she couldn't think about that now. She had to get to her girls and not let her panic overwhelm her. As she neared the bottom of the steps, she called out again.

"Rose?" she cried. "Where are you? Answer me!"

It was quiet and she took the last step, ending up in the laundry area. Chris was behind her, as was Kyle, Sean, and finally Cole.

They were all behind her, two of the boys with flashlights and the other two with flashlight apps on their smartphones that were blindingly bright. The entire laundry area was lit up. Alix was looking around frantically when she suddenly spied Rose standing near a break in the wall that led to an area that she had never really explored. Cord said it was a storage area, a large and foreboding space beneath the house, but she had never personally seen it.

Rose had Kitty clutched under the arms, the newborn's body trailing down her sister's torso. She had her pacifier in her mouth and was wide awake as she suckled madly. Even from where Alix stood, she could see the baby sucking and she seemed quite calm. From the way Rose was holding her, her head and neck were braced against Rose's shoulder and surprisingly stable. But Alix felt more panic than she ever had as she moved towards her daughters.

"Rose!" she cried softly. "Baby, what are you doing? Let me have Kitty."

Rose turned around and disappeared into the storage area. Alix and the boys ran after her, their flashlights falling on a vast area under the house that was directly beneath the living room. There were a few boxes, an old chair, a pile of dirt against the eastern wall, and a large dirt area off near the southeast corner. Rose was heading for the big dirt area.

"Rose!" Alix ran after her. "Give me Kitty!"

As soon as she got near her daughter, it was as if an unseen hand slapped her back. Alix felt the force of the blow and flew backwards, into Kyle, who mostly broke her fall as they both went tumbling. Chris came to an abrupt halt, lifting his hands in preparation for both a defensive and offensive stance. There was something down here, something evil that didn't want them to gain control of the little girls, and he was ready to fight.

"Sean!" he yelled. "Get the girls!"

Sean charged forward, reaching for Rose, but he was

knocked back by the same thing that had hit his mother. He fell over in the dirt, grunting with the impact.

"Rose!" he hollered. "Come back! Don't go over there!"

Alix rolled to her knees, feeling a good deal of pain considering she was still sore from giving birth. Her entire body hurt but it wasn't going to stop her. She started to crawl towards Rose, who had now come to a halt. The little girl was standing on the dirt with her baby sister clutched against her. As Alix tried to stand up and make her way towards her, it was then that she began to see a pile of stones.

Cold fear flushed through her. "Oh, God," she hissed, shining her flashlight on the stones. "There's something over there. See it?"

Chris was still frozen in place, his hands up in front of him in what was seemingly a defensive gesture. He turned his flashlight in the direction Alix was indicating. Their flashlight beams crossed, illuminating the area. Cole, creeping up behind Chris to take a closer looked, gasped.

"It's a hole in the ground," he said, sounding frightened. "There are stones all over the place, but I see a big hole in the ground."

Alix panicked; she couldn't help it. "Rosie!" she wept. "Come back, baby, please! Don't go over there! It's dangerous!"

Rose was just standing there, holding her baby sister. She hadn't moved but she could hear her mother weeping behind her. She turned to look at her.

"Mommy," she said, sounding frightened. "The sad girl says her mommy wants Kitty. If I don't give her Kitty, she said she's going to hurt you and I won't see you anymore."

Alix let out a scream of anguish. "That's not true!" she cried, staggering to her feet. "Rosie, she's not going to hurt me. You can't give her Kitty, do you hear? Kitty is your sister and she's my baby. She's *mine!*"

Rose was torn and terrified. She began to sniffle, breaking down as the stress of the situation crushed her. "Mommy, help me!" she cried.

Alix took off at a dead run, only to be brutally knocked down again as she drew close to Rose. Lying on her back in the dirt, groaning in pain, she wept loudly.

"Let my daughters go, you bitch!" she cried. "They're just babies, for Christ's sake! Sarah Good, I know you had your own daughters taken from you but I didn't do it, do you hear? *I didn't do anything!* Let my daughters go!"

She was sobbing, rolling over onto her side and struggling to crawl in Rose's direction. Slowly, painfully, she pulled herself across the dirt, striving for her daughters with every fiber in her body, reaching out for them and begging God to help her. She was able to get within a few feet of them when something abruptly caught her eye. Something was moving around the edge of the hole.

Like something out of a horror movie, a hand came out of the darkness of the hole, ghostly and skeletal, and grabbed hold of one of the stones on the edge of the depression. Alix came to a halt, startled and disbelieving, as another hand came out and held fast to the stone. A head popped up, with hair made from cobwebs and a face that was purely skeletal and bony. The eyes were dark and sunken holes and when it seemed to focus on Alix, it hissed an unearthly howl. The entire basement lit up with sounds of the netherworld as voices from beyond filled the air.

With terrifying groans and gasps, half of the skeletal body emerged, covered with dirt and shreds of some kind of shroud. It was positively horrendous; a ghoul from the grave so terrible that not even Hollywood could have imagined it. The stench from the corpse filled their nostrils, something between rot and sin. A thin finger, pure bone, extended to Rose.

"*Hitherto, Rose,*" it rasped.

Rose started crying. Because she was crying, the baby became restless and the pacifier popped out. The baby let out a loud wail and Chris, still standing several feet away with his hands raised, belted out a loud and terrible chant.

"*In nomine sancte et qui te audiunt mea decedere terra hac,*" he yelled. "Go back where you came from, you freakish son of a bitch!"

With that, he extended his fingers and threw a ball of energy at the creature that sent it staggering back. It was enough of a distraction for Alix to lunge at her girls, grabbing them and falling over backwards with them both clutched against her. With panicked grunts, she rose to her knees and began to scramble away, trying to get her girls out of the line of fire, but she didn't get very far before something grabbed hold of her ankle. She didn't even look to see what it was; she screamed at Sean.

"Sean!" she cried. "Take the girls! Get them out of here!"

Sean, Cole, and Kyle came running. Chris extended his hands again, casting another force of energy at the creature to distract it. It was enough to cause the creature to falter as Sean grabbed Kitty and Cole grabbed Rose. Kyle grabbed hold of Alix, pulling her away from whatever had her, but it was a losing battle. Something was dragging her back towards that dark hole in the ground where the creature was lurking. Chris tried to hit it again with another spell but he was quickly growing exhausted. As Cole and Sean raced up the basement steps, a figure suddenly appeared at the top.

Cord stood there, flabbergasted by the sight of his sons running up the steps with the girls in their arms. Before he could say a word, Sean burst forth.

"Mom's in trouble!" he yelled. "You have to help her!"

Cord barreled down the steps with Quirt on his heels. Mary

was standing at the top of the stairs, urging the boys to come to her. They made it to the top and she took the infant, practically shoving the boys out into the kitchen. As Mary took the little girls out of the house and ran them out to the car, Cole and Sean raced back inside and headed back to the basement. This was their fight, too, and they were going to see it through.

Meanwhile, Cord hit the basement floor running. He could see Chris with his hands up in front of him and Kyle with a hold on Alix, who was being dragged by her feet across the basement floor. The problem was that there wasn't anything visible holding her. Something wicked and transparent had hold of his wife and as his eyes adjusted to the darkness, a flashlight beam from Chris' flashlight fell against the dark hole on the southeast side of the house.

It was then that he saw the ghoul from the hole, clinging to the disarray of stones around it as if trying to pull itself out. Shocked, and terrified for Alix, he ran to his wife and grabbed her by the arms to stop her momentum.

"Cord," Alix gasped, holding on to him. "The girls...."

"They're safe," he said, grunting as he yanked on her. "My mom has them. They're safe."

Alix groaned as Cord pulled and the force that held her pulled even harder. Kyle was still pulling on her but he was getting dragged, like some macabre tug-of-war. Cord could see that they were fighting a losing battle and his panic took over; lifting a hand to the ghastly creature in the well, he threw out the most potent spell he could think of.

"*Auctoritate patrum nostrorum ab hac pelle duco in terra virtutem eorum*," he said, holding out a big fist in the direction of the creature. "*Omnia in nomine sancti huius et ad te absolvo te ab inferno. Et revertetur ad terram hanc vultis abire gravem!*"

Quirt was slightly more composed than his son, but he could see a life or death battle in front of him. Whatever that horrific thing was emerging from the hole, he was going to deal with it. He couldn't even think of the fact that it was something not of this world; all he could think of was saving his grandsons and son and daughter-in-law. He, too, extended a fist at the gruesome creature and began to cast.

"*Vade malignis*," he said. "*Et vade in nomine Christ!*"

With all of the casting being thrown at it, the creature began to weaken. It hissed and writhed, trying to climb out of the well but being thrown back by Cord and Quirt. The drag on Alix had lessened and with one big yank, Cord was able to pull her free of whatever force was holding her. She fell back behind him, crawling away across the dirt floor, as Cord rose to his feet and jabbed a finger at the ghoul.

"You can't have my family," he boomed. "I'm sorry your life was ended unfairly and I'm sorry you lost everything, but you can't have my family to replace yours. Abigail placed a curse on you but what you really want is peace. It's what we all want. For whatever curse is keeping you and your daughters here, I will lift it. Do you hear me? I'll lift it. I don't want to live this way any longer. The time for vengeance is over. *In nomine Christi, ait finitur. Vade in pace.* Dad, do you have the vellum?"

Quirt pulled out the yellowed piece of vellum that had the curse written with Sarah Good's name on it. He had brought it with him, although at the time he hadn't a particular purpose with it. All he knew was that something told him to bring it and he had. Now, he knew why. Pulling out his Bic lighter from his pocket, the one he used to light his pipe, he lit the vellum on fire, holding the end of it as it burned.

"*Vade in pace,*" Quirt repeated softly. "*In nomine Christi, ait finitur. Vade in pace.*"

As the vellum burned and Quirt dropped it into the dirt, watching it turn to ash, the creature shrank back and the horrible hissing noise it had been making faded away. In the beam of Chris' flashlight, the ghoulish monster suddenly diminished, eased, and changed colors from a sickly gray to a pure white. As Alix, Cord, Quirt, Chris, Kyle, Cole, and Sean watched, the creature, in all of its horrific glory, simply faded away.

The sudden silence was uneasy. Cord took Chris' flashlight and timidly made his way over to the hole with the scattered stones around it. He shined the flashlight down the shaft.

"It's a well," he said after a moment. "There's a lot of rubble down there, but it looks like the original well."

"That's where Dorothy cast the baby," Alix said, sitting on her bum with her hair in her face. She was breathless and weak. "She was trying to force Rose to cast Kitty in there."

Cord looked down the shaft filled with rocks and debris. "Maybe she figured an eye for an eye," he muttered. "Who knows? Maybe she figured since she had lost her baby, she wanted one that had descended from Abigail."

"The woman who ruined her life in the first place," Alix murmured. She ran a shaking hand over her forehead in a weary gesture. "Do you really think it's over? What about Dorothy? Where is she? If that was Sarah Good in the well, *where* is Dorothy?"

Cord shook his head as he picked up one of the scattered stones. "I have no idea," he muttered. "Maybe we'll never know."

With that, he tossed the stone aside and it crashed into the brick foundation wall a few feet from the well. It shifted one of the old bricks and broke the mortar seal, causing part of the wall to give way. Cord jumped back so he wouldn't get caught in the tumbled of bricks, waving his hands in front of his face to dissipate the big cloud of brick dust that billowed up.

As the dust began to settle, he shined the flashlight into the broken part of the wall, seeing that there was a gap behind the wall that had been bricked over. Beyond the dust that was still floating in his flashlight beam, he could see something tucked back in the darkness of the gap. Moving closer, he could see a moldered-over skeleton was gazing back at him, chained up to the wall.

Dorothy Good had finally been found.

TWENTY-TWO

"SHE HAD all sorts of stuff in her car," the police sergeant was saying. "All kinds of things from the Salem witch trials and stuff about curses and witchcraft. Turns out that woman, Mrs. Mowbray, is a descendent of Sarah Good. Maybe she thinks she's a witch, too. In any case, she's in the back of the police unit spilling her guts right now. She wanted to drive your family out of the house so she's been laying curses down now for a while. Did you two go and see her at the Historical Society some time back?"

Alix, wrapped up in a heavy coat, was standing with Cord in the driveway of Evenshade. She nodded to the sergeant's question. "We did about eight months ago. I had just purchased the house and wanted more information about it."

The sergeant glanced over at the woman in the police car. "She said that," he replied. "That's how she found out that your husband was a descendent of Abigail Williams. Did you know that today, three hundred and twenty-one years ago, Sarah Good was hanged?"

"We did."

He pointed at the police car with his pen. "That's why she had come over here today," he said. "To exact some kind of curse on the anniversary of Sarah's death, so she says."

It was the early evening and the storm that had rocked the area all afternoon had passed, leaving wet land and a cloudy sky in its wake. There were four police cars in various positions around the driveway and a supervisor's unit. Mrs. Mowbray sat in the back of one of the cars, weeping loudly and confessing her sins. Alix couldn't even look at the woman; after what had happened that afternoon, she was shaken to the bone.

"That's why she seemed so interested in Evenshade," she said. "That woman has been around here for her entire life. She knew everything about it. She even knew my husband's great-aunt who used to live here."

The police sergeant wriggled his eyebrows as he continued to jot notes in his binder. "Is your aunt still alive?"

Unlike his wife, Cord had been staring at the police car. "She is, in fact. She's ninety-seven years old and in great health."

The sergeant looked up from his notes. "I'll bet if you ask her, Christina Mowbray might have even tried to bring her down as well."

Cord nodded his head, pulling Alix closer. He hadn't let her out of his sight since the incident in the basement an hour earlier. He wasn't entirely sure he would ever let her, or his children, out of his sight ever again.

"Maybe I will," he said. "So what happens to Mrs. Mowbray now?"

The cop shrugged. "She tried to kill you and your family," he said. "I'd say she's in a lot of trouble, even at her age. Our detectives will be contacting you tomorrow to get the full story. At least you can all sleep peacefully tonight knowing that woman is in jail where she can't get to you."

Alix looked up at Cord, who gazed down at her. Silent words passed between them. They hadn't told the police the full story for obvious reasons. Nothing about ghouls from the grave or witchcraft; after Chris had told them what happened in the living room with Mrs. Mowbray, they had called the police and told them that the woman had tried to harm their children, which wasn't far from the truth.

Whatever curse had been going on at Evenshade, Mrs. Mowbray had clearly exacerbated it with the continued cursing she had evidently been doing. Moreover, the amulet she had given Alix was evidently full of cyanide which, when it seeped through the amulet and rubbed off on the fingers, could have been slowly ingested. At least, that's what Mrs. Mowbray had confessed to the arresting officer. In any case, the woman was going away for the rest of her natural life. It was a bizarre end to an even more bizarre story.

"Well," Cord said, giving his wife a squeeze as he faced the sergeant. "Thank you for coming. It's been a busy afternoon."

"It sounds like it," the sergeant said. "And as for the skeleton in the wall down in the basement, I've put in a call the Massachusetts Department of Archaeology. I'm sure they'll be all over you in the morning; with the historical significances of this house, that's something they're going to love to investigate. Those people are kind of strange."

He was grinning as he said it and Cord smiled weakly. "I'm curious to see what they can find out," he said. "It might be nice to have an identity."

The sergeant glanced at him. "On a two hundred-year-old corpse? Good luck with that."

"It's probably even older than that given the age of the house."

"That's certainly possible."

The sergeant closed up his binder and said his goodbyes, heading back to his unit. Alix and Cord stood there, watching the Danvers police units pull out of the driveway one by one, heading back to the station through the dark and wet night. When the last unit pulled out, Cord turned to Alix.

"Are you sure you're okay?" he asked. "Maybe we should take a trip over to North Shore and have you checked out."

Alix shook her head emphatically. "I'm fine," she said as they turned and headed back to the house. "My girls are safe, the boys are safe, and I'm totally fine."

"Are you sure?"

She nodded as they entered the kitchen from the driveway and shut the door. Alix removed her coat and laid it over the chair.

"Are you sure it's safe to stay here tonight?" she asked.

Cord went to the coffee pot where a fresh pot await. He grabbed a cup. "If I didn't think so, we'd be over at the Marriott," he said, pouring. "But the girls are sleeping with us tonight... just in case."

Alix sat down as he brought over two cups of steaming coffee. "You know," she said softly as she took the cup from him, "every time I think about everything that happened today, it just seems like a dream. I swear I saw all of this in a movie once."

He smiled as he reached out, taking her hand as he sipped his coffee. "I don't think you could make this stuff up," he said. "Even in a movie, who would believe it?"

Alix laughed. "Me," she said, giggling. "It happened to me! A ghost tried to kill me! My husband is a witch! Oh, my God!"

She was rather dramatic about it and he laughed, glad she had at least retained her humor in spite of the dark situation. "I'll bet you never banked on this when you moved here," he said. "I wanted to add a little excitement to your life, but not like this."

She leaned against him, wrapping her arms around his neck and rubbing noses with him. "You've done more than add excitement to my life," she murmured. "You've given me the most wonderful life possible. The best thing that ever happened to me was when that dresser fell on me out there in the driveway."

He snuggled with her, feeling her warmth and life and love. "And Batman came to the rescue."

"My own personal hero."

He grinned, kissing her sweetly. "You better believe it."

She looked him in the eye, a knowing twinkle in her gaze. "After what I've seen today, I'm inclined to believe anything about you."

The State of Massachusetts Department of Archaeology invaded the next day and spent the next six months excavating the skeleton behind the wall and the basement in general, including the well. Indeed, they found the bones of two infants buried deep in the rubble, lending truth to the legend of Mercy Good but they had no idea who the second child was. Perhaps they would never know. When the excavations were complete, Cord petitioned to have the bones of all three corpses buried near Sarah Good and the State complied. Dorothy and Mercy were buried together with the unknown infant in sight of their mother's grave.

After that, Evenshade became a nice, normal home without ghosts or curses or terror. The Hendry and Trevor children grew up there, happy and healthy, and Cord and Alix went on with their lives and careers, more in love than they ever were. Life was never better, and when Carolina Alexandria Hendry-Trevor was born eighteen months after her older sister, Kitty, Alix and Cord considered their lives, and their family, complete.

Still, the bassinet would end up on Cord's side of the bed

even when Alix rolled it on to her side. Given the history of the house, Dad was very protective of his little girls.

It was in his blood.

THE END

AUTHOR'S NOTE

The tale of Sarah Good and Abigail Williams is a true one for the most part. Abigail really did accuse Sarah Good of witchcraft during the Salem witch trials, and Sarah really did have a daughter named Dorothy who led a rather sad and pathetic life. But beyond that, the rest of the story is purely fiction and should be taken as such. Evenshade, the house, does not exist except in the mind of the author, although it makes for a great creepy setting!

AFTERWORD

The tale of Sarah Good and Abigail Williams is a true one for the most part. Abigail really did accuse Sarah Good of witchcraft during the Salem witch trials, and Sarah really did have a daughter named Dorothy who led a rather sad and pathetic life. But beyond that, the rest of the story is purely fiction and should be taken as such. Evenshade, the house, does not exist except in the mind of the author, although it makes for a great creepy setting!

ABOUT THE AUTHOR

ABOUT KAT LE VEQUE

KATHRYN LE VEQUE is a critically acclaimed, USA TODAY Bestselling author (having hit the list over 30 times), an Indie Reader bestseller, a charter Amazon All-Star author, and a #1 bestselling, award-winning, multi-published author in Medieval Historical Romance with over 150 published novels. Kathryn also writes Romantic Suspense as Kat Le Veque.

Kathryn has received praise for her writing and has won several awards for her work, including two nominations for the Holt Medallion. Her books have topped bestseller lists, and she has gained a loyal fan base that eagerly anticipates each new release.

Kathryn is a talented author who has made a significant impact on the world of historical romance fiction. Through her captivating storytelling and meticulous research, she has enchanted readers with her tales of love, adventure, and the enduring power of the human spirit.

Kathryn loves to hear from her readers. Please find Kathryn on Facebook at Kathryn Le Veque, Author, or join her on Twitter @kathrynleveque, and don't forget to visit her website at www.kathrynleveque.com.

ALSO BY KAT LE VEQUE

The Unholy Angels
Hour of Surrender

Trent Chronicles
Valley of Shadow

The Eden Factor

Canyon of the Sphinx

The Eagle Brotherhood
The Sunset Hour

The Killing Hour

The Secret Hour

The Unholy Hour

The Burning Hour

The Ancient Hour

The Devils Hour